PARALLEL WORLDS

BOOK ONE

PARAWORLD ZERO

Matthew Peterson

~ Matthew Peterson ~

Blue Works
The Young Adult Division of Windstorm Creative
Port Orchard • Washington

Paraworld Zero: Parallel Worlds Book One

published by Blue Works

ISBN 978-1-59092-491-4
9 8 7 6 5 4 3 2
First edition January 2008

Cover and interior images by Matthew Peterson.
Cover background image by Estella Del Sol of Blue Artisans Design.
Design by Buster Blue of Blue Artisans Design.

For information on hardback, film or other subsidiary rights, contact us at
360-769-7174 or legal@windstormcreative.com

Blue Works is the young adult division of Windstorm Creative, a multiple-division, international organization involved in publishing books in all genres, including electronic publications; producing games, toys, videos and audio cassettes as well as producing theatre, film and visual arts events. The wind with the gear center is a trademark of Windstorm Creative.

Blue Works
c/o Windstorm Creative
7419 Ebbert Dr SE
Port Orchard WA 98367
www.windstormcreative.com
360-769-7174 ph

Blue Works is a member of the Orchard Creative Group, Ltd.

Library of Congress Cataloging in Publication data available.

Dedication

To my loving wife and to our five wonderful boys,
who prayed and prayed for my dream to come true.

Acknowledgments

Many people have played a role in the creation of my book, but none more than my family. For over a year, my little children prayed in earnest for Windstorm Creative to publish *Paraworld Zero*. Their sweet prayers have finally been answered. I would like to thank them for their faithfulness.

My wife deserves more gratitude than I can give. She has been the pillar of strength that has kept me going all this time. Her inspiration has made my book what it is today. Thank you, my dearest friend.

Other family members–especially my parents, my wife's family, and my "almost" twin brother, Paul–have also lent me their support and encouragement. Thank you, guys. I love you!

Many thanks go to the writers at critiquecircle.com and critique.org. I wish you all success. Lastly, I'd like to acknowledge the works of J.R.R. Tolkien, Lloyd Alexander, and Douglas Hill. Without their inspiring books I never would have started this project. They gave a young boy the power to dream. And now I can share that dream with everyone.

PARALLEL WORLDS

BOOK ONE

PARAWORLD ZERO

Matthew Peterson

PROLOGUE
THE STORM

The woman was dying, and no one on Earth would mourn for her when she was gone. Not a soul would know of the secrets she possessed or of the ultimate power that emanated from within her limp body. The hope of the universe was about to be lost–that is, unless she arrived at the hospital in time.

A torrent of watery darts hit the windshield as the ambulance squealed around another corner. The hospital was not much farther. A spark of lightning erupted in the night sky, as if to point the way the ambulance should go. Rumbling sounds resonated from the darkness above, accompanied by a faint groan of atmospheric indigestion echoing in the distance. The storm, like the mighty hand of a demon, buffeted the vehicle with its cold fist, but the driver remained steadfast.

"We're losing her," a paramedic cried.

"Come on, lady. You can make it," another said.

The vehicle skidded to a complete stop, and the back doors flung open. Interns rushed to help with the gurney, but in the process, one of them slipped on the wet concrete and lost his grip, causing the stretcher to jolt. The poor woman, her skin infested with blistered lesions, lifted her head and moaned. One of the students gasped.

A paramedic took hold of the gurney and entered the emergency room. He tried to keep his eyes away from the grotesque figure in his care, tried not to even breathe the same air that spewed from her deformed lips and nostrils. Visions of horrible diseases filled his mind, but he dispelled them with the thought of a quick dispatch to labor and delivery.

A consternated expression etched itself across the gynecologist's face. Word of the woman's arrival had spread quickly. The doctor peered at the sores on her face and arms. "What happened to her?"

"I dunno," the paramedic said. "She's all tripped out and won't say noth'n."

"I see."

"Someone found her in a park and called it in," he added. "She's not contagious, is she?"

The gynecologist winced but remained silent. He looked closer at the gruesome sores on her body, then pulled up her sleeve and discovered more pustules on her arm. He checked her legs and found that they too were infected.

"I have no idea what this is. Almost looks like she's been exposed to something." He turned to a young nurse. "Do an ultrasound and get blood and tissue samples. Keep me posted."

"Aren't ya gonna set up a quarantine or something?" the paramedic asked.

"I want to know what we're dealing with before we put the whole city in a panic. It could just be an allergic reaction."

The woman on the gurney jerked upright, as if waking up from a nightmare. "My son!"

"Calm down, ma'am. We're here to help."

"My son . . . Simon . . . His name is Simon," she mumbled. "And his . . . And . . ." Her eyes glazed over.

Just then, the doctor noticed the blood and discharge on the sheets. "Nurse, delay that order. We're not going to have time for tests." The patient arched her back and screamed. "Her baby wants to come right now. Let's get ready."

The paramedic left, and the nurses took charge. They moved the pregnant woman directly to a birthing room. The windows streamed with rushing water, and the howling wind fought against the thick glass. Ferocious thunder hammered the building, making the surgical instruments vibrate. One nurse held up a sterile gown for the doctor to put his arms through while another nurse doused the woman's belly with clear gel.

The doctor held her hand gently. "What's your name?"

The monitor picked up a huge contraction, which surged throughout the woman's body like a tidal wave. She clenched his fingers in a vice-like grip.

"Forget the ultrasound," the doctor said, releasing his hand and stumbling past the nurse. "I can already see the head. That was fast. Ma'am, I need you to push."

The woman held her breath and pushed. Her face turned red. She let out a deep sigh and pushed again. Beads of sweat collected on her forehead.

"Almost there . . ." the doctor said mechanically. "Almost there . . ." A twinge of nervousness crept into his voice as three pustules on the woman's skin burst. He adjusted his hands, avoiding the thick liquid that oozed from the open sores. "Just one more push."

Within moments, a baby's cry filled the room. The doctor picked up a plastic syringe and suctioned the amniotic fluid out of the newborn's small mouth. A nurse handed him a pair of surgical scissors.

"Congratulations! You have a boy." He snipped the umbilical cord.

Suddenly, an explosion of bright blue light sprang from the baby and shattered the glass in the doors and windows. The medical personnel dropped to the floor. A whirlwind of pastel light filled the once-bland room, and a strange mist arose from somewhere below. The wisps of sparkling color danced upon the plumes of thick smoke and vapor, making it hard for anyone to focus his or her eyes. The doctor looked up, squinting to see through the chaos, and gasped as he witnessed the infant emerge from the translucent smoke.

Simon was floating in the air.

"Oh, my . . ." cried a nurse from beneath a table. Breathing hard, almost to the point of hyperventilation, she made the motions of a cross on her chest.

Simon looked in her general direction, his brown eyes wide open and his arms flailing about. He drifted towards the bed, the smoke parting on both sides of his frail body as he moved, and came to rest in the arms of his mother.

Smiling, she brought out a necklace she'd been wearing beneath her blouse. Attached to the gold chain was a medallion–about the size of a silver dollar, ebony in color, and beautiful in workmanship. The colorful lights reflected off the metallic pendant as she placed it on her son's bare chest.

She looked at the doctor and whispered, "Give him this." Then she closed her eyes and died.

The smoke and colorful lights soon dissipated, leaving the small room cold and lifeless as before. Everyone remained silent. Not even the wind outside dared to make a sound. The storm had finally ended.

CHAPTER 1
SIMON'S BAD DAY

Two knives, protruding from the knuckles of a leather glove, vibrated above Simon's sweaty forehead. The boy, small for his age, desperately held on to the man's wrists.

"I have you now," his assailant snickered as the tips of the blades scraped against Simon's glasses. An evil grin spread across the villain's scarred face.

"*Never!*" Simon shouted.

With a sudden eruption of energy, he threw the dark man off and leapt to his feet. Demonstrating perfect form, Simon kicked the menacing glove and shattered the twin blades. The second his foot landed on the ground, he spun in the air and sent a crescent kick hard into his opponent's face.

Simon walked up to his fallen enemy, who by this time was cowering on the floor, and proclaimed, "As long as there's good in the world, evil will never prevail!"

A tumult of cheers and clapping came from the ecstatic crowd nearby. Confetti filled the air, and young girls swooned around the scrawny boy, asking for autographs.

A TV reporter with a microphone ran up to Simon and announced, "I'm here with Simon Kent, who just saved the city of New York from certain doom. Simon, I have just one question I think everyone here would like to know the answer to: Why are you in your underwear?"

"*Wh-Wh-What?*" he stuttered.

"Why are you in your underwear?"

Simon looked down and realized he wasn't wearing anything but his glow-in-the-dark Batman boxers. Looking up, he saw the crowd of pre-teenage girls and boys laughing at him.

"Do they give you special powers?" the reporter asked with a smirk. She burst into laughter.

"*Simon—Simon!*"

Simon opened his eyes and found himself sitting at a desk in Mr.

Bartholomew's seventh-grade English class.

"Nice of you to join the class, Mr. Kent," the teacher said. "I think we have time for one more book report. Why don't we have Simon go next?"

Simon's heart sank. He took a puff from his inhaler and fumbled around in his fanny pack. A handheld video game machine, erasers, old candy corn from Halloween, a couple of extra batteries, some chewed-up pencils, and a few quarters, but no book report.

"I–I can't seem to find it."

"Mr. Maloy." The teacher turned to a neighboring classmate. "What happens to students who forget their homework?"

The boy, caught off guard, thought for a moment. "Um . . . they get detention?"

"No, no, no! Well, yes, in some cases–but that's beside the point." Mr. Bartholomew turned to his favorite student. "Jenny, can you help us out?"

"Certainly," she said in a superior voice. "They fail."

"That's correct. They fail. Anyone who thinks he or she can just sleep through life–or my class, for that matter–has another think coming. You can't expect to succeed in life if you–"

Just then, a wonderful ringing noise flooded Simon's ears. It wasn't a pretty tone by any means, but to Simon, it sounded like a chorus of angels swooping in to carry him away from the horrible situation. It was the school bell.

All of the kids jumped up to leave, but Mr. Bartholomew stood his ground. "You can't expect to succeed in life . . ." he said loudly to get their attention. The students paused, and the teacher finished his lecture with, ". . . if you don't *apply* yourself." He directed his last comment specifically towards Simon.

■ ■ ■

Children from seventh to twelfth grade stampeded through the hallways to get to their classes. Simon felt like a dwarf among giants, not just because of his low status on the totem pole but because of his unusually short height. He was a sickly boy with plastic-framed glasses, thick chestnut hair, and a slightly crooked nose. His legs were birdlike, and his ears seemed to stick out too far from his head.

His only love in life was playing video games; it was the only thing he was good at. He could outplay just about anyone, and he knew it.

"Simon Kent," a slow, cold voice sounded from behind. Simon cringed. He stuck his face in his open locker, hoping the person would go away.

"I heard about what happened in English class. Mrs. Trimble will be so disappointed in you . . . She may even take away your video games."

Simon turned around to face the sophomore behind him. "Y-Y-You're not going to t-t-tell her, are you?" Simon stuttered only when he was really nervous, and the thought of having his most prized possessions taken away simply terrified him.

"Oh," the older boy said melodramatically, "I'm sure she'll find out sooner or later." He chuckled as Simon squirmed.

"Hey, Butch," came the sultry voice of Sara Parker, the most beautiful girl in school. Two large boys followed her: Buz Atkins, the biggest kid in school, and Spike Peters, the oldest kid in school. No one knew how old Spike really was, but rumor had it that he'd been held back three years in a row. "Are you coming over tonight?" Sara asked, her lips pouting.

"Yeah," said Butch, "I'll be there." He smacked Simon on the back. "See ya later, punk." At that, he walked away with Sara, leaving Buz and Spike behind to torment Simon. Both seniors laughed maliciously, but Simon didn't know why.

Tall, handsome, and full of muscles, Butch was the envy of all the students in school. He always knew what to say to make people like him or do what he wanted. Sara, his girlfriend, was just crazy about him–and everyone else was crazy about her.

Even as a sophomore, Butch was the star quarterback and held awards for just about every sport Simon could think of. He wore his letterman jacket every day to display his many achievements. On top of all that, a flock of students consistently hovered around him, basking in his glory.

But Butch had a dark side that only a few knew about. Simon had lived with him in the foster home–often referred facetiously as "the orphanage" by many of the children–for almost three years now, and he was keenly aware of the horrible things Butch would do during his sadistic mood swings. For example, one time Butch poured toilet cleanser into Simon's ant farm in retaliation to a simple quarrel; the poor insects never stood a chance.

Unlike Simon, Butch entered the orphanage at age twelve. His parents had been abusive. Simon remembered one day overhearing Butch tell the younger kids a story about how he had been locked in the basement for two weeks without food and how he had to drink from the toilet to survive. Simon doubted the validity of his story, but then again, there might have been some truth to it.

"*Ouch!*" Simon yelped. Someone had just kicked him. "Ouch! Stop it!"

Everyone–especially Buz and Spike–seemed to be attacking him. The kicks weren't dreadfully hard, but for a small person like Simon, they were earth-shattering.

Simon dropped his books by accident, and when he bent over to pick them up, he received two more swift kicks from behind. The teenagers broke into laughter as Simon's face smashed into the hard tile floor. His glasses broke and a trickle of blood appeared from a tiny cut above his eye.

Tripping on his books, the young boy fumbled for cover while the bullies followed in pursuit. Desperate, he rushed to the emergency exit and flung open the doors. A loud warning bell echoed through the hallways, but Simon didn't hear it, for he was already maneuvering his way through the parking lot.

He found himself running down a busy street. Normally, his first instinct would have been to head towards the orphanage, but another building drew his attention instead–the video arcade. A sign at the door read: NO STUDENTS ALLOWED BEFORE 2:00 P.M.

His watch showed 1:23 p.m., so he sat down at the edge of the curb and counted the reasons why nobody liked him. He even surprised himself by the extensive list he created. How could someone be so unloved?

As the minutes passed by, he noticed a bunch of large black ants attempting to carry a green leaf with a nest of caterpillar eggs attached to it–a food source that would sustain the insects for some time–but the leaf hardly budged. Simon gazed in amusement as a family of smaller ants kept walking onto the leaf, weighing it down. Perturbed by this, the larger ants would let go of the leaf to chase off the smaller ants, but as the big ants were lured away, the remaining small ants monopolized the leaf until they too were forced away by their larger cousins. The two types of ants fought in this manner, over and over. And after several minutes, the leaf hadn't moved even one centimeter.

Suddenly, a screeching tire rolled over both groups of ants. Mrs. Trimble had just pulled up. She rolled down her window. "Simon, let's go home."

"How did you know I was here?"

"This is where I'd go if I just had a bad day," she said with a warm smile. Simon got into the station wagon, and they drove off.

■ ■ ■

The orphanage, which was really just an old two-story home, belonged to Mrs. Trimble, a kind, elderly woman who loved her job very much and loved her foster children even more. But since her husband's recent passing, she had been forced to reevaluate her position as overseer of the foster home. She wasn't as young as she used to be, and she found herself relying more and more on the aid of her niece, Maggie.

Although she took care of a handful of adolescents, most of her affection centered on Simon. She even enrolled him in karate lessons to help raise his self-esteem. Some of the other children in the foster home thought she showed favoritism, but Simon knew the real reason she paid so much attention to him: He reminded Mrs. Trimble of her son.

After attending to some menial tasks and thanking her niece for babysitting once again, Mrs. Trimble walked into the children's bedroom on the second floor, holding a bottle of alcohol and a clean rag. Simon was sitting on the edge of a well-used bed, playing a video game on his handheld device. A tiny six-year-old named Dimitri sat next to him and watched in awe.

"Dimitri, what have I told you about getting too close to the other kids?" Mrs. Trimble scolded. "The whole reason you stayed home from school today was so you wouldn't make anyone sick."

"Sorry." The little boy sneezed. Dimitri was a cute blond-haired boy with a good heart, deep blue eyes, and a stuffy nose.

The boy exited the room, but Simon didn't seem to notice; he sat in his own little world, covered by shadows. Mrs. Trimble turned on the light, but the room didn't brighten very much because three of the four light bulbs had already burned out. She noticed the sheet of paper taped to Simon's back. It read: KICK ME!

"Oh, my goodness!" Mrs. Trimble exclaimed, pulling the paper off his back. She turned the sheet over and read the first sentence of Simon's book report. "Who would do such a thing?" Simon didn't even look up.

She dipped the rag into the alcohol. "This may hurt a bit."

She wasn't kidding! Simon thought. His cut stung as she patted the dried blood on his forehead. He flinched to remind her of the pain but not enough to stop himself from playing his video game.

Mrs. Trimble removed his broken glasses. A spider web design ran down one of the lenses, while the warped frame pushed the other lens out of place.

"Simon, why do you insist on wearing these things? You know you don't really need glasses."

"You wouldn't hit someone with glasses, would you?" he asked dryly, not moving his eyes from the video display.

"Of course not." She pulled open a drawer that contained a slew of eyeglasses, most of which were damaged, and tossed the broken pair in with the others. The old woman fumbled around the drawer until she found a good pair. She put them onto Simon's face. "So you think the kids at school will stop hurting you if you wear glasses?"

"Not just the kids at school. Butch has it in for me."

"Butch?" she said, surprised. "Butch is as gentle as a lamb."

"No he's not!" Simon shot back. "He's the meanest person I've ever met."

"Look, Simon, Butch has had it pretty bad. His parents were murdered a few years ago . . ." She paused, then continued, ". . . on his birthday, of all days."

"What happened?" Simon remained intent on his game.

"I'm only telling you this so you'll understand where he's coming from. What I tell you stays in this room, okay?"

Simon nodded.

"His mother and father were stabbed to death, and the killer was never found. You remember when he first came here? He was the most troubled boy I'd ever seen. It took days before he could talk to the police."

"I didn't know," Simon whispered.

"Not many people do." Mrs. Trimble stood up to put the alcohol back into the bathroom cupboard. She started to walk away.

"Where's my mom and dad?"

Mrs. Trimble turned around. The young boy had switched off his video game and was looking up at her, longingly. Although she had been the only mother he had known, it wasn't enough; he had to know the truth.

"Where's my mom and dad?" he asked again, more firmly. He wasn't about to let her dodge the question–not this time.

She looked solemnly at the carpet. "You don't know, do you?" she whispered. "I never did tell you . . . I suppose it's about time I did." She sat next to him, and Simon's stomach churned in anticipation.

"I wasn't there when it happened, but I was told that when you were born, you really gave the doctors a show. Your mother was–how should I say this?–not *well-to-do*."

"What do you mean?"

"She was homeless–a vagrant, I suppose. She came into the hospital with no money, no ID, and just the clothes on her back. Well, she did have something. Come with me."

The two of them walked out of the room and into the hall.

What in the world could it be? His stomach did somersaults, and his weak lungs forced him to take a deep puff from his inhaler to compensate for his excitement.

In all the years Simon had been at the orphanage, he had never been inside Mrs. Trimble's bedroom–not many of the children had–but that was exactly where the old lady was leading him. She pulled out a key and unlocked the door.

Nearly everything in the room looked older than Simon: a battered coffee table and lamp, a few Oriental rugs, pictures of relatives, an aging record player, and so on.

Simon noticed a black and white photograph of a young man dressed in a pilot's jumpsuit, standing in front of an airplane. This must have been Mrs. Trimble's son, David, before he was shot down in the Vietnam War. Simon frowned at the old photograph. How could he, a scrawny boy, remind her of the big, strong man in the picture?

"This way," she said.

Mrs. Trimble urged Simon to the back of the room. She detached part of the molding from the wall, revealing a secret compartment. Several shiny objects glistened from the rays of sun that crept in through the wooden blinds. From within the tiny hole, Mrs. Trimble brought out a jet-black medallion attached to a thin golden chain.

"This was your mother's," she said, handing it to him. Simon stared at the strange engravings embedded in the medallion. The metal was cold to the touch, but it seemed to warm his heart.

"Simon," she continued slowly, "your mother isn't coming back. She died in the hospital when you were born. She said she wanted you to have this."

Simon felt as if his heart had just been ripped in two. "And where's my dad?" he asked behind a sniffle, dreading the answer.

"I don't know. Your father was never found. In fact, we don't even know what your mother's name was . . . but I think you should know that she loved you very much. No one can describe the love a mother has for her son."

Tears welled up in her eyes, and the two of them hugged. As they embraced, Simon gazed at the old photograph sitting on the mantel. Mrs. Trimble's large and handsome son was just so different from what the boy had expected . . . so different from Simon.

■ ■ ■

That night, Simon lay sobbing in his bed. Everyone in the house was asleep–or at least, he thought they were–but then Dimitri's small, familiar voice broke the silence. "What's wrong?"

Simon wiped his eyes. "Shouldn't you be in bed?"

"I couldn't sleep," Dimitri said innocently. "Why are you crying?"

Tears trickled down Simon's face. "Because I killed my mother." He wept bitterly.

Dimitri put his tiny arm around his friend and comforted him in the dark.

CHAPTER 2
BUTCH

"Francis Eugene Oswald, you get back here!"

"Yeah, Francis, you get back here," Dimitri said, imitating Mrs. Trimble.

Everyone laughed but stopped when the teenager snapped his head around in disapproval. "My name is *Butch,*" he growled, slamming the door behind him as he left.

"I don't know what's happening to that boy," Mrs. Trimble said to no one in particular. Butch had missed curfew last night and had come home with a black eye.

The children ate their breakfast merrily while Mrs. Trimble beat the life out of a bowl of eggs. "Simon," she yelled, "come and eat, or you'll be late for the bus!"

"I'll get 'im," squealed Dimitri. He leapt from the table and ran up the stairs. Simon lay motionless in his bed. "Simon! Simon! Wake up . . . wake up . . . wake up, Simon . . . wake up, Simon." Dimitri prodded relentlessly until Simon responded.

"Go away," the twelve-year-old mumbled incoherently into his pillow.

"But you'll be late for school."

Simon looked up at the little boy. No, not the puppy-dog eyes! He was powerless to resist Dimitri's long face. "Okay–squirt. I'm getting up."

Simon lumbered to the bathroom and opened the medicine cabinet. Several large bottles spilled out into the sink. Mrs. Trimble had been informed previously that she should keep the medications behind lock and key, but over the years she had become lax with the rules. Besides, Simon was the most obedient child she had ever known.

A large array of pill bottles, consisting of different sizes, colors, and labels, rested on the shelves. They all had one thing in common: Simon's name printed on them.

As early as the boy could remember, he had always been sick. If it wasn't one thing, it was another. He could have sworn he'd had the chicken pox three times now, and he was the only kid he knew who received medical supplies as Christmas gifts instead of toys. Someone even had the audacity to give him a thermometer–with his name imprinted on it, no less!–for his ninth birthday.

Simon swallowed half a dozen colorful pills. He slapped some cold water on his brown hair and wrestled with the perpetual rooster's tail on the top of his head.

Back in the bedroom, he filled his fanny pack with his video game machine, a couple of extra games to play during lunch, and some spare batteries. He glanced at his watch and panicked. He *was* going to be late for the bus!

Simon started to run when a glint of light caught the corner of his eye. He looked over at his bed and discovered the source of the light. The medallion seemed to be looking up at him, beckoning him.

He walked over to his bed and picked up the cold piece of metal. A feeling of caution–or was it foreboding?–came over him. He rubbed the medallion between his fingers methodically. What was this, and why had his mother wanted him to have it?

Simon raised the necklace above his head. Holding onto the gold chain, he let the medallion drop. Mesmerized, he watched–for what seemed like an eternity–as the medallion spun in front of his face, untangling itself from the chain. The round pendant appeared as though it was suspended in midair, and Simon felt like life itself had gone into slow motion. With each rotation of the hypnotic charm, a ray of light threw itself against his pale face. Faster and faster . . . the medallion spun out of control. Suddenly, it stopped moving, as if some invisible hand had intervened.

Closing his eyes and taking a deep breath, Simon put the medallion on for the first time.

"*SIMON!*" yelled Mrs. Trimble from downstairs.

Startled, he opened his eyes, tucked the necklace under his button-down shirt, and rushed down the stairs to catch the school bus.

"You forgot your lunch!" Mrs. Trimble yelled after him, a bit too late.

He ran along the sidewalk, waving his hands up and down like a wild bird. The yellow bus finally stopped, and Simon boarded.

"Sorry," he mumbled as he passed the bus driver. The burly man sitting in the driver's seat shook his head disapprovingly but said nothing. The bus lurched forward.

Simon swayed back and forth as he stumbled down the narrow pathway, frantically searching for an empty seat. An outsider might have thought the driver was driving recklessly on purpose to make the young boy fall down, but a seasoned passenger like Simon knew that this was standard driving protocol for a bus driver. During a particularly sharp turn, his body was propelled into an open seat.

"Hey, Simon," came the familiar yet troubled voice of an older girl.

Simon stared with his mouth agape at Sara Parker. "Oh, s-s-sorry, S-S-Sara."

He moved to stand, but she grabbed his arm to stop him. “Simon, it’s okay. Please stay.”

A look of confusion spread over his face. Although it was strange that the prettiest girl in school wanted him to sit next to her, it was even more strange that she was sitting alone in the first place. After a minute of awkward silence, the only thing the boy could think to say was: “Where’s Butch?”

“I don’t know,” she answered slowly. “I haven’t seen him since last night.” She paused for a few seconds. “Simon, you know Francis pretty well, don’t you?”

“Yeah.” Simon’s eyes widened at hearing her call Butch by his real name. The last time he uttered the word *Francis,* he found himself dangling upside-down with his head stuck in a stinky toilet.

“He wouldn’t do anything *crazy,* would he?” she asked with hesitation in her voice.

“Crazy? Crazy in what way?”

“He wouldn’t . . .” she started. “He wouldn’t . . . *hurt* anyone, would he?”

“Well,” Simon said thoughtfully, “Mrs. Trimble says he’s gentle as a lamb.”

Sara smiled. “Yeah, I think so, too.” But then a wrinkle appeared on her forehead. “It’s just . . . sometimes he seems to be one way, and then the next minute, he’s a totally different person. Last night he got beat up, and to tell you the truth, I just don’t know how he’s going to react.”

Simon nodded his head. He had a few ideas of what Butch would do to the unfortunate soul who had injured him, but he thought it best not to share them with Sara.

Several students dropped their bags as the bus came to a screeching halt. The kids began to push their way down the aisle.

Standing up, Simon said, “Well, I hope everything goes all right for you . . . If you n-n-need someone to t-t-talk to . . .”

“Oh, you’re so sweet,” she said, leaning towards him. For a split second, Simon thought she was going to kiss him–but he’d never know for sure because, at that moment, the impatient kids forced him down the aisle. What was he thinking? Of course she wasn’t going to kiss him–maybe a pat on the head, but not a kiss. She was several years older than Simon, leagues apart in social standings, and just so beautiful. But, still . . . she had leaned over.

Sara, the prettiest girl in school, stood up and called out over the empty seats, “Thank you, Simon.”

Beaming from head to toe, the boy floated the rest of the way down the aisle. Actually, he was carried and pushed by the students, but he hardly noticed.

■ ■ ■

The first two class periods flew by without a problem, but Simon dreaded his next class: math. He wondered why the school forced him to take math in the first place. Why couldn't he just buy a calculator instead and skip the class altogether?

The school hallways were a beehive of activity. Simon's locker stood at the end of the building, which meant he had to brave his way through a sea of upper-class students every day to get there–never a fun journey for the small boy. He hated being enrolled in one of the few schools in New York that insisted on keeping grades seven through twelve in the same building.

Simon stopped to get a drink and noticed Butch standing next to an open locker nearby. The teenager was trying to be inconspicuous but failed miserably. He wore a long, black overcoat, steel-tipped boots, and a pair of dark sunglasses–attire that was very out of character for the sophomore, especially since few people had ever seen him in the halls without his letterman jacket.

A moment later, Buz and Spike–along with three other seniors–congregated at the locker. Buz and Spike looked like a couple of henchmen as they crowded around Butch in a tight circle. Simon couldn't see what they were doing because of their bulky overcoats.

He took a big gulp of the cold, stale water and wondered if the liquid ever circulated in the drinking fountain or if it just lay there stagnating day after day. While musing on this singular thought, Simon turned his head just in time to catch a glimpse of something he wished he hadn't seen.

Spike was handing Butch a gun.

At that moment, Butch glanced over at Simon, and their eyes made contact. Simon quickly turned his full attention to the drinking fountain, hoping Butch wouldn't realize he had seen the exchange.

Panicked thoughts raced through his head. *Oh, wonderful water! Just drink'n water here. Nothing but cool crisp water. Didn't see anything at all. No need to come over here and kill me . . .*

One more gulp and Simon knew he'd be sick. He turned his head ever so slowly towards the lockers, but Butch and his minions had left.

A loud ringing sound boomed throughout the hallways, causing the boy to jump in fright. This time it wasn't the sweet sound of angels he heard but the bitter sound of doom; he was late for Mrs. Cunningham's math class.

Simon sprinted down the hallway as the last remnants of life disappeared into the safety of the classrooms. The halls now appeared empty.

Not bothering to stop at his locker, he dashed around a corner. Just one more hallway to go and then–Simon didn't see it coming. One moment he was running, and the next, his frail body was thrown against a locker like a rag doll. He couldn't feel the ground under his feet anymore, and the back of his head pulsated with pain.

A faint whisper sounded in his ear. "If I so much as hear you peep a word about this, I'm going to make you wish you were never born."

Simon's vision became blurry, but he still recognized the outline of Butch pinning him against the steel wall. He grunted as the sophomore ground his shoulder blades into the locker. Then he gasped when the bully pressed a cold knife against his throat.

"Do you understand me?" the menacing figure threatened. Simon nodded.

"*What's going on here?*" roared Principal Harmon from behind.

"Not one word," the young man whispered as the knife vanished into the dark recesses of his black overcoat. Butch gritted his teeth and gently placed Simon back on the ground. "Nothing, sir," he said coolly. "We were just playing."

"That's not what it looked like to me," the principal snorted. "You!" He pointed a stubby finger at Simon. "Go to class." He looked at Butch and growled, "And you. Come with me."

"Why? I didn't do anything." The teenager folded his arms in defiance.

Principal Harmon waved at Butch's long overcoat and said, "Don't be coy with me. You know that's against dress code."

Simon felt his heart start to beat again as he walked to his classroom. He tried to forget what had just happened, but he couldn't purge the memory of the knife from his mind–how the sharp blade touched his skin and how deftly Butch handled the weapon. Butch had used that knife before; Simon knew it. He searched his neck for blood but found none. Relief came for a moment but fear returned when he reached Mrs. Cunningham's classroom.

He climbed up on his tippy-toes to look through the window in the door, but his short height prevented him from seeing anything. The boy jumped up and down, but the dumb window remained out of reach. He huffed. Why did God have to give him a body from the reject pile?

Feeling extremely nervous, he opened the large door and slipped into the classroom. Luck was on his side! Mrs. Cunningham was facing the chalkboard. Simon glided down the row towards his desk just as the old woman started to speak.

"Mr. Kent," she said, her smoke-stained lungs crackling, "since you're already up, please come to the chalkboard and solve this problem for us." At that, she added a couple more digits to the end of the equation.

Simon moved towards the chalkboard slowly, as if he'd been asked to place his head in a guillotine. He wondered which was worse.

"Well? Come on, Simon. We don't have all day," coughed the teacher. Mrs. Cunningham was the ideal model for an antismoking commercial. One view of her on TV would be enough to scare anyone out of taking a puff.

It's just a simple long-division problem, Simon thought. *I can do this.*

All the arithmetic he had learned from seven long years of school lay before him, taunting him. He picked up the yellow chalk and tackled the problem head-on, beginning with simple division.

Screeeeech! The chalk shrieked against the board, and everyone in the classroom cringed in their seats. A few girls brushed the goose bumps from their arms, and Mrs. Cunningham closed her eyes.

"Sorry."

He finished the division part of the problem. Now for multiplication. It seemed awfully hot in the room, all of a sudden, and Simon felt extremely uncomfortable. Next came addition. The students started to chuckle. *Wait! Next comes subtraction, not addition!* Simon undid the top button of his shirt and continued.

A woman's voice came from the intercom in the ceiling. "Sorry for the interruption, but is Simon Kent in the room?"

"Yes, he's here," the teacher hacked.

"Please have him go to Principal Harmon's office immediately."

"*Oooooh,*" the kids in the room teased.

"He's on his way," Mrs. Cunningham replied. "Well, Mr. Kent, you got a good start on this problem. We'll save it for you, so you can finish it when you come back."

Simon hunched his shoulders and sighed. Mrs. Cunningham stretched out her hand to take the chalk and eraser, but before Simon could give them to her, he sneezed and sent a mushroom cloud of dust into her face. He handed the chalk and eraser to Mrs. Cunningham–who looked at them distastefully–and started his long trek to Principal Harmon's office. The boy was in no hurry to get back to the math problem, especially after the chalk incident, so he took his sweet time.

Along the way, he noticed a police officer carefully withdrawing a handgun from a locker. The officer moved the gun with a pencil, so as to not put his fingerprints on the weapon.

"Oh, yeah. Come to Daddy," the officer said, dropping the gun into a plastic bag. He looked up at Simon. "You Simon?"

"What?"

"Are you Simon Kent?"

"Oh. Yes," Simon said sheepishly. He looked at the officer's uniform and read the name tag: MCKENZIE.

"We got some questions for ya, kid. Follow me."

As Simon neared the principal's office, he could hear an argument taking place on the other side of the door. "You can't hold me here," Butch yelled. "That knife was just a birthday present."

"Was this gun a birthday present, too?" Officer McKenzie asked as he walked into the room bearing the weapon. The office overflowed with people–including Buz, Spike, Butch, Principal Harmon, another officer named Petri, and a few more students whom Simon didn't recognize. Butch sat with handcuffs on his wrists, and a knife with a curved ivory handle in the shape of a cobra lay on the hardwood table.

Scowling at Simon, Butch sprang forward, attempting to head-butt the boy, but Principal Harmon held him back. Simon hugged the doorframe.

"You told him where it was, you little twerp!" Butch said.

During the excitement, Spike jumped in front of the policemen to distract them while two of the other seniors snuck behind the men and knelt on all fours. Most officers, even ones stationed at high schools, wouldn't have been so naive, but these two might as well have gotten their badges from crackerjack boxes.

"You know what, guys?" Spike said as he tapped the officers' badges with his fingertips. The men were slow to react. "You two are so oblivious, I bet you'd *fall* for anything."

"Huh?" both officers said in unison.

"Exactly."

With his hands already on their chests, Spike applied a little pressure, and the two men both toppled over the kneeling students.

Butch exploded with energy, releasing himself from Principal Harmon's grasp. Still in handcuffs, he grabbed the knife off the table and lunged at Simon. Simon's eyes widened as adrenaline shot through his veins. He slammed the door and ran for his life.

"We're gonna get you, punk!" Butch yelled, kicking the door.

Butch, Spike, and Buz exited Principal Harmon's office unhindered and pursued Simon down the empty hallway.

Two seconds later, Principal Harmon rushed out the door, threatening, "You'll all be expelled for this!"

■ ■ ■

"Here ya go, Butch," Buz said, tossing the handcuff keys to his friend; he had stolen them from Officer Petri during the commotion. While in full stride, Butch spun around and caught the keys from behind. However, not wanting to slow himself down, he didn't bother to use them.

Simon burst through the front doors of the school and headed towards the crowded parking lot. Panting heavily, he made his way through the first few rows of cars before he heard the three bullies yelling his name.

From a bird's-eye view, the parking lot looked like a garden with many colorful vegetables, big and small: red ones, blue ones, yellow ones, even neon-green ones; cars with low-riding bodies, others with jacked-up axles, and still others with mammoth tires. The lot contained minivans, trucks, convertibles, old station wagons, and many other varieties. With such a large selection of vehicles, Simon thought he could easily find a suitable hiding place, but to his dismay, he found none.

"There he is!" Buz shouted.

Butch slid over the hood of a new Corvette. As he did so, the knife and keys in his hands scraped the shiny red paint. Simon rolled under a large black truck just before Buz could grab him.

As if he'd done it a hundred times, Butch slid his hands down his body and pulled the handcuffs to the front. He jumped onto the bed of the truck so he could pounce on the seventh-grader when he came out the other side. Simon scurried like a centipede to the head of the truck and inched his way to the next vehicle.

"Come on out, Simon," Spike called, looking under the black truck to get a better view. "We just wanna talk."

"Yeah, *right!*" Simon blurted. "You want to cut me open and talk to my insides."

"He went under another car!" Buz exclaimed.

Simon crawled out from under a jeep and raced towards the fence. Fortunately, the large teenagers had trouble maneuvering through the tight maze of cars, thus giving the slender boy a chance to flee.

Simon made it to the outer fence and slipped through the bars just as Buz grabbed his shirt. The fabric tore, and Simon catapulted down the busy street.

"You guys go on without me," Butch ordered. He fumbled with Officer Petri's keys while his friends struggled to climb over the tall fence.

Simon stopped at the intersection and waited a few seconds for the light to turn red so he could cross. Buz and Spike bolted towards him like crazed football players in a sudden blitz.

"Come on! Come on!" Simon shouted at the light. The cars zoomed by so fast that he didn't dare to cross early; besides, it was against his nature to break the law. Soon, the light turned red, and Simon sprinted through the intersection.

The streetlight turned green when Buz and Spike started to cross. A small car swerved to miss the teenagers and ran into a fire hydrant. Water flew up into the sky and splattered against the windshield of a bus, forcing the driver to veer into oncoming traffic and smash into another car. None of the vehicles were going fast enough for anyone to get seriously hurt, but the whole intersection became a big watery mess. The two seniors didn't even look back to admire the wreck they had caused. Simon was escaping, and they needed to catch up with him.

The young boy felt as though his lungs were about to burst. While still running, he unzipped his fanny pack, pulled out his inhaler, and took a deep puff. He then collided with an old lady who had just exited a corner store with her bags.

Simon frantically gathered up her groceries, apologized, and ran off–but then he stopped, suddenly realizing that he had dropped his inhaler. Looking back, he saw the plastic dispenser resting in the gutter. His assailants were getting closer, so with bitter anguish, he turned around and continued running.

The old lady had taken only one step before she was knocked down again–this time by Buz and Spike as they rushed by. She watched sadly as several cans of cat food rolled down the sidewalk.

While maneuvering though the sea of pedestrians, Buz and Spike came upon a tall, slender woman wearing a red tank top and white Daisy Duke shorts. A little poodle stood by her side on a leash.

"Hey–" said Buz, suddenly stopping. "Nice dog."

The two boys stood there for a moment, leering at the curvaceous woman, trying to say something intelligent, until they heard the screech of a car and someone yell, “Hey, kid, get out of the road!”

The seniors turned around to see Simon running across a narrow street up ahead. Reluctantly, they pulled themselves away from the attractive woman and followed after the boy.

Simon darted down a side street between two large buildings and realized, to his horror, that his luck had finally ended; he had just run into a dead end.

CHAPTER 3
THE VISITOR

Buz snickered. "Oh, look at the little mouse caught in a corner."

Spike picked up a cracked two-by-four and tapped the side of an old, beat-up car. Buz found a red brick and followed suit.

Terrified, Simon ran to the far wall as the two older boys closed in on their prey. His heart pounded in his chest, and his eyes darted about, looking for an escape route. Dirty newspapers littered the dark alleyway, and streams of filthy water gathered in small pools about their feet.

"Look, guys," Simon pleaded, "I didn't say anything."

"Sure ya didn't." Spike laughed in a patronizing manner. "But just to be safe, we're gonna make sure you *don't* say anything."

At that, both teenagers ran towards Simon with weapons in hand, but just as they reached the petrified boy, a light blue mass of electricity appeared in the air behind them. The electrical cloud expanded to three feet in diameter and formed into the shape of a sphere. A flash of green shot out of the strange ball and smashed into Buz and Spike, forcing them to fall at Simon's feet. The ball of lightning disappeared as fast as it had come, leaving no trace of even being there.

Simon's mouth hung open in bewilderment. A young, beautiful girl sat on top of Buz and Spike. She wore a sleeveless green tunic that extended to her mid-thigh. The plastic fabric stretched across her chest like spandex, lay flat against her stomach, and hugged her hips. She also wore green boots that held onto her slender legs with several straps of leather. But despite her clothing, her most unique feature was her bright green hair; the long ringlets reached down to her thin waist and sparkled in the dim light.

"*Ahm-Chi Kuta,*" the girl said, looking down at the boys. "*Masta Baloo andga eichi?*"

"What on Earth are you saying, girl?" Buz answered back.

The strange girl jumped up, waved a small wand, and chanted, "*Aiyee, Aiyee, Aiyee bookata!*" The wand released a stream of light that engulfed her body for a second and then vanished. She opened her mouth to speak once more.

"*Guten morgen . . .*"

Spike scratched his chin.

"*Ohayo gozaimasu . . . Buenos días . . . Bonjour?*"

"Are you making fun of us?" Buz asked, raising his brick. He sat up and rubbed his head.

The girl smiled. "Good morning." Her clear voice was as soft as an autumn breeze.

"Good morning," Simon stammered. He could hardly believe what he had just witnessed. The strange girl had appeared out of nowhere.

She turned and said, "My name's Tonya. I'm from Paraworld 4329." Her yellowish green eyes sparkled as she spoke. "Wow, this looks *really* different from what I was expecting."

Tonya bent over and picked up a curious device she had dropped during her collision with Buz and Spike. It was about the size of a textbook but had two handles, several buttons and knobs, and a digital readout that looked almost like an odometer from a car. She banged the device against her wand as if she were trying to erase an Etch A Sketch.

"Ah, this thing's broken."

Simon looked over at the readout on the device. It appeared to have eight place markers for digits, but they were all spinning wildly, resembling a slot machine. The first marker became blank, and then the second, and then the third, and so on, until it reached the last place marker. The final marker spun for a second more and then went blank like the others.

"Oh, yeah, really funny!" Tonya smirked. "Someone's trying to play a joke on me."

"Excuse me, little girl," Spike interrupted. He grabbed his two-by-four and stood up. "We were in the middle of something here. Run along and play somewhere else."

She turned to Simon and asked, "Are these your servants? Because if they were mine, I wouldn't let them talk to strangers like that."

"You *are* making fun of us," Buz chimed in as he scurried to his feet, still clutching his brick.

"They're not very smart, are they?" She chuckled. "Professor Gwyn told me all about this paraworld. Is it true the younger you look, the older you really are?" She didn't wait for an answer. "I mean, that's simply amazing. I heard this is the only charted parallel world where everyone grows down instead of up. To think of it, I'd be considered an old woman here!"

She laughed heartily, but Buz and Spike were not amused.

"I can't quite put my finger on what paraworld your servants are from," she continued. "Oh, I hope this isn't on the test. I know they're not native to this paraworld–their bodies are too big and clumsy. I bet they're worker drones from Paraworld 5467. Am I correct?"

Simon just stood there with his mouth open in confusion. What a strange girl.

"Oh, fiddlesticks!" she exclaimed. "Let me see . . . Oh, I know! I should have seen it earlier. By the way they're holding their sticks and stones, they're from one of the prehistoric worlds, aren't they? So are their brains really the size of a walnut?"

"Okay, that's it," Buz grunted. "You're gonna pay for that!"

He picked up the girl as easily as he would a feather pillow and walked towards a large puddle of dirty water.

"Oh, dear," Tonya said, looking back at Simon. "Do you think he understood me?"

Simon couldn't answer because he too was being removed from the ground; he tried to free himself, but Spike had an iron grasp.

"We're going to teach you and your girlfriend a lesson," Spike said. "On three." He signaled to Buz. "One . . . two . . ."

"Oh, I see you can count," Tonya said with genuine surprise in her voice.

"*Three!*"

Buz and Spike launched the two kids towards the murky water. Simon hit the shallow pool with a hard thud, splashing water everywhere. He closed his eyes and moaned. After a brief moment, though, it occurred to him that he was the only one in the water. He rolled over and, to his astonishment, saw the young girl suspended above him in midair.

"What are you?" Spike shouted in disbelief. "You little freak!" He raised the two-by-four and lunged at the girl.

"*PROTECTION!*" Tonya exclaimed, raising her wand.

A sphere of golden light engulfed her body. She clutched her stomach in pain as yellow lightning bolts shot out of the sphere and wrapped themselves around Spike. He screamed in a high-pitched voice as the electrical ropes raised his body into the air.

Tonya went into convulsions, throwing her head back and forth in agony. She waved her wand uncontrollably. Suddenly, a bolt of red lightning ran down the alley and struck the long row of parked cars like a thread being sewn into fabric. The windshields, side windows, taillights, and mirrors exploded from the impact.

Resembling tentacles, the yellow bolts of electricity wiggled around as if they had a mind of their own. Mercilessly, they threw Spike's body from one building to the next. Two more giant arms–both emerald green–shot from the golden globe and grabbed two parked cars near the entrance of the alleyway. Crunching sounds echoed horribly in everyone's ears as the thick arms of electricity squeezed the cars tightly, making the hinges buckle. The awful crunching stopped for one second, and then the two vehicles rose fifteen feet into the air and smashed together with such tremendous force that when the two hunks of metal fell, neither of them even resembled cars.

Simon stood up and surveyed the destruction with eerie trepidation, but then he jumped as a lightning-entangled body descended just inches from his face.

Spike, hovering in the air before Simon, brought his head up slowly and whispered, "Help me."

Face to face, Simon stared into the hopeless eyes of the teenager who, just a moment ago, had threatened to shut him up permanently. Simon had always been intimidated by Spike–the way he pushed people around, the way his large biceps bulged under his shirt sleeves–but now the senior didn't seem so big anymore. Spike was just a bully–scared and pathetic. Quick as a whip, the tentacles jerked the teenager's body back and flailed him about the alley once more.

Simon glanced at the sphere of translucent light and saw the silhouette of Tonya lying in the bubble. She might have been unconscious or even dead, but he couldn't tell. He eased his way closer and tried to peer into the ball. Tonya's head twitched as though she were having a small seizure.

Mustering all of his strength and courage, Simon pierced the sphere with his hand. The hot, gooey sensation made him feel like he had just stuck his fist into a bowl of warm Jell-O. He extended his arm a little farther and grasped Tonya's hand to wake her up.

Tonya opened her eyes, and the sphere of light exploded all around them. The shock wave rippled up both sides of the two buildings and shattered every single window at the same time. A shower of broken glass plummeted to the ground, tearing through the hoods of the parked cars below. Simon shielded his face and collapsed as shards of glass whizzed by.

Dazed and in pain, he felt his vision slowly come into focus. Simon realized he was staring into Tonya's yellow-green eyes; she had fallen on top of him.

"Wow, that was great," she said, giggling.

Simon's mouth fell open in amazement. Her beautiful green hair had turned pitch black from the ordeal, but she didn't seem to notice yet.

The two children stood up and looked down the alleyway. Spike lay nearby, moaning to himself. All the cars had been destroyed, and glass was strewn everywhere. In the midst of everything stood a lone figure: Buz.

Simon limped over to the young man and saw tiny bits of glass stuck in his plump cheeks. Buz's face and body remained motionless, but his eyes followed Tonya's every movement. He trembled as she drew near.

"Buz?" Simon inquired.

The large boy fainted.

It was then that Simon noticed the onslaught of camera flashes coming from the entrance of the alleyway. Japanese tourists were videotaping them and taking pictures.

"How odd," Tonya said, looking at the group of frenzied tourists.

"Come on. Let's get out of here!"

Simon grabbed her hand and led her out of the alley and into the main street. The crowd backed up as the kids emerged onto the sidewalk.

"Wait, I need to meet up with my . . ." Tonya looked up at the multistoried buildings in surprise and quietly finished her sentence, ". . . class."

Simon pushed her along the street, away from the cameras and tourists.

■ ■ ■

Back at the disaster site, a dark figure entered the alleyway. Slivers of broken glass crunched under his steel-tipped boots as he walked over to Buz. The dark figure tossed some handcuffs onto the large boy's chest. Bending down, he reached into Buz's black overcoat and pulled out a small phone.

"You know that favor you owe me?" Butch's charismatic voice penetrated to the other end of the phoneline. "Forget about it. After what I'm about to tell you, you're going to owe me much more than you can imagine . . . Yeah, I'd say it's of national security."

■ ■ ■

Simon and Tonya made their way up the street about as fast as fish swimming up a waterfall. Everyone in the area flocked to the demolished alley to get a peek at what had happened. An old Japanese man showed a police officer the footage he had captured of the two children running from the scene.

Farther up the street, Simon sprinted past a policeman listening to his radio. *". . . thirteen or fourteen years old, Caucasian, green outfit, long black hair . . ."*

"Hold on. I see them," the officer responded to the broadcast. He chased after the two kids, but the wall of people hindered his progress.

"I can't believe this is happening," Simon yelled as the cop blew his whistle. "We have to hide!"

"I don't understand," Tonya said, gawking at the tall buildings. "Professor Gwyn said this civilization lived mostly underground. This is Marsupia, isn't it?"

"What?" Simon asked, looking for cover.

"Marsupia? Paraworld 1423?"

"I don't know what you're talking about."

He dragged her to the entrance of a narrow alley between two small buildings. Abandoned shopping carts, large beat-up dumpsters, and homeless people filled the sidewalks. At the end of the street, a never-ending parade of cars zoomed by, traveling perpendicular to the alley.

"*Freeze!*" shouted the policeman.

Tonya continued her babbling. "So if this isn't Paraworld 1423, then that means I'm gonna miss my test! I can't believe I got lost on my very first field trip–Professor Gwyn will be so upset with me. I won't even be able to see the twin moons of Marsupia. Oh, and I heard they're so lovely this time of year."

"You're going to see the inside of a prison cell in a moment unless you do something quick."

"Oh, my goodness," she gasped, finally realizing the situation they were in. The girl waved her wand in a quick circle, and everything went black.

"Well, this isn't what I meant," she scolded her wand. From the smell of old fish and rotten eggs, Simon knew exactly where they had been transported to: the inside of a dumpster.

"Quiet," he whispered.

For about a good minute, Tonya held her tongue, but then, as if receiving an epiphany, she blurted, "Wait a second! You're not an old man. You're just a little runt!"

"I'm twelve years old," Simon said. "You can't be much older than me."

"I'm almost fourteen years old–thank you very much. What's your name, anyway?"

"Simon Kent."

"Wow, you have two names?"

"Actually, I have three: Simon Theo–"

"Huh, you must be important. In my paraworld we only have one name. Well, unless you're a duke, or a lord, or a cleric–nobility sometimes have three names, unless, of course, you're a–"

"What do you mean by *paraworld?*"

"Parallel worlds," she said bluntly, as if that was all the explanation needed.

"What do you mean by *parallel worlds?*" he asked.

"You know! *Paa-raaa-llel wor-lds,*" she said, breaking the words up slowly. "Maybe my translation spell is wearing off. It's supposed to be permanent."

Simon sighed. The reality of what had just happened was starting to sink in.

"Let me get some light in here," she said. Just then, radiant beams of light shot out of her fingertips and flooded the inside of the smelly dumpster.

"Turn it off! Turn it off!"

"Sorry," Tonya said, clenching her fist. She opened her hand, and a faint luminescent glow emitted from the tip of her forefinger. "I'm not very good at magic yet."

"That was some pretty amazing stuff you did back there."

"Well, I don't know how that happened. All I meant to do was flash that boy in the eyes with some light, and the next thing I knew, I was casting spells like I was a super–" She paused. "No–an *ultramage*. You know, after three weeks of school, about the most I've ever been able to do was turn on my nightlight . . . Strange . . . I've never felt such power before."

"How did you get here?" Simon asked.

"With a paratransmitter, silly!" She laughed. "You're a funny little boy. You act as if you've never seen one before." She patted the book-shaped device in her hand. "This isn't one of those retarded paraworlds, is it? Where everyone has the IQ of a slug."

"This is Earth," Simon answered, exasperated.

"Earth? Earth? Never heard of it. Book, show me the coordinates of Earth." The paratransmitter groaned as if it had just busted a sprocket. Rows of lights flickered on and off, and then the whole thing went dead. "This thing's defective! I really . . . I real . . . I . . . *ACHOO!*" As Tonya let out a huge sneeze, she blew a large hole in the side of the dumpster. Trash flew into the air like feathers blowing in a windstorm. "Ah, *nuts,*" she cried.

"We better get out of here!" Simon shouted.

■ ■ ■

After seeing the explosion, a homeless man took a long swig from his bottle and watched the two children crawl out of the gaping hole. The old man took another gulp of whisky while Simon and Tonya ran down the alley.

A black shadow emerged from behind the dumpster and gazed at the torn metal in awe. The exit wound looked like some ferocious creature had ripped itself from the confines of the dumpster. The young man caressed his ivory-handled knife as he admired the damage. He turned and followed after Simon and Tonya.

■ ■ ■

Simon spotted a yellow taxicab parked at the side of the road. He opened the car door, and they both jumped in.

"Take us anywhere!" he said.

"Hold your horses, little boy. Let me see your money first," the taxi driver said in an Indian accent. No glass or metal partition separated the driver side from the passenger side; instead, the vehicle was equipped with a digital security camera.

Simon looked at the cab driver's name badge and said, "Come on, Abu. Help us out."

Peering out the window, Tonya saw two policemen run by. The officers both headed down the alley where the deformed dumpster lay.

"No can do. I have seven children, three cats, two goldfish, and a fat wife to feed. Now run along before I get nasty."

Simon opened his fanny pack and took out two crumpled dollar bills. "How far will this take us?"

"*Ohhh, my golly-golly!*" Abu squealed, looking at the small video game that had fallen out of Simon's pouch. "My kids just love those things! Tell me, do you have Space Goobers?"

"Well, uh . . ." Simon fumbled in his fanny pack. "No, but I do have Alien Combat."

"*Oooooh,* I tell you what. I'm going to Central Park to have lunch with my wife. For your Alien Combat, I take you with me. Deal?"

Simon struggled in his seat. He didn't want to give up his game.

Still looking out the window, Tonya saw the two policemen emerge from the alley and start to walk in their direction. A homeless man trailed behind them, gesturing wildly with his hands. Suddenly, the old man stopped and pointed towards the cab.

Without hesitation, Tonya snatched the video game out of Simon's hand and threw it to Abu, yelling, "Deal! Now drive!"

"Okey-dokey," the cabdriver said, pressing his foot on the gas.

Both kids fell back into their seats as Abu swerved into the onslaught of traffic like a madman. Within a second, the vehicle was swallowed up by a river of yellow taxicabs.

CHAPTER 4
SECRETS OF THE PARAVERSE

Tonya looked out the cab window in amazement. "This is fantastic!" she exclaimed. "I've never seen anything like it before. What do you call this?"

"Danger," Simon said, snapping on his seat belt.

"I think some of the paraworlds with limited E.M. waves have motorized contraptions like this, but why–"

"Excuse me for listening to your conversation," Abu interrupted, "but what are E.M. waves?"

"Electro-magical waves of energy. You know–the power source for magic."

"Oh, how interesting. Please continue."

Simon shot him a dirty look for interrupting their conversation.

"Are you telling me you've never heard of electro-magical waves?" Tonya said with obvious disbelief in her voice.

"Yes," Simon and Abu both replied.

"Abu, keep your eyes on the road," Simon warned as the cab veered sharply into the next lane.

Tonya looked dumbfounded. "This world is *full* of E.M. waves, and you're not even aware of magic?"

"I've never heard of these 'E.M. waves,' and I doubt anyone else has either."

At that moment, Tonya's book gave five sharp beeps. A row of lights on the top of the device lit up. "Impossible," she said. "There's no way this could be charged already."

"What do you mean?" Simon asked.

"Well, normally my paratransmitter takes all day to recharge itself, but it looks like it's already fully charged." A bewildered expression formed on Simon's face. Tonya gasped. "Oh, come on! You know what a paratransmitter is, don't you?"

Simon shrugged. He wasn't sure about anything anymore.

"When transporting to an alternate dimension, you can't just snap your fingers and find your way to the correct parallel world. And even if you could, you'd probably end up in an ocean somewhere, or even worse . . . you could emerge right in the middle of a solid object. That's where a mobile paratransmitter comes in handy. They've been around for a couple years now. I'm surprised you haven't heard of them."

"What do they do?"

"This little magical device stores up a ton of E.M. energy so it can transport you to the correct coordinates in the paraverse. The downside is that you then have to wait for it to collect enough E.M. energy to transport you back. But, hey, it's much faster than the old way of paratravel."

"Oh," Simon said, furling his eyebrows. "So what exactly are these 'parallel worlds' you're talking about?"

"'Parallel worlds?' You're not pulling my leg, are you?"

"There will be no leg pulling in this car, thank you," Abu informed her, misunderstanding the idiomatic expression.

Simon ignored the driver and said, "Tonya, listen to me. We don't have magic on Earth, and we don't travel to other worlds. Most people would think you're nuts for even suggesting such a thing."

Frustrated, Tonya spoke to her paratransmitter. "Book, give me the definition of parallel worlds."

The book moaned for a brief second, and then strange words appeared on the little screen. A voice sounded from the book.

> *"Parallel Worlds: Unique, alternate worlds that share the same location in space and time. Each parallel world is linked to the other worlds by an electro-magical force that acts like a conduit from one dimension to the next. Consequently, this electro-magical energy can also be tapped into for the use of magical spells and for transportation between other parallel worlds. See also paraverse."*

Simon rubbed his eyes. "Wow, now I'm really confused."

Tonya retorted, "Look, Simon, think of it as the road we're on right now. We have a lane to our left and a lane to our right. Each lane is like a parallel universe. We're all driving on the same road and going in the same direction, so each lane is parallel with the other. Now imagine that our car represents Earth. Let's just say that the car to our right is my paraworld, Chamel. For you to go from Earth to Chamel, you'd have to jump from this lane to the next lane. And like I said earlier, without the help from a paratransmitter, there's no way you could make the jump."

"Okay, I think I understand," Simon said. "It's almost like a video game."

"It would also be a good idea for a book," Abu added thoughtfully.

"Abu, we're trying to have a private conversation here," Simon scolded.

"Alrighty, I will not be listening anymore," the cabdriver said. "No listening from me. Nope! Not at all. My ears are shut."

Simon turned to Tonya. "How did all of this happen?"

"Well, after creating the original world, God got bored and thought to himself: 'I wonder what would have happened if I had done this?' So he started experimenting and then boom, boom, boom–tons of parallel worlds were born."

"Really?"

"No, I'm just pulling your leg," she teased.

Abu reacted. "I thought I said there will be no leg pulling in my–"

"Sorry!" she interrupted with a smile. "To tell you the truth, Simon, I don't know how it happened. It's the same thing with magic: Nobody knows where the E.M. waves come from."

Simon sighed deeply. This was a lot to take in. If he hadn't seen her magic firsthand, he would have dropped her off at the nearest looney bin. He looked over at the girl and noticed that her hair was slowly fading to a dark brown color. "Tonya, what's happening to your hair?"

"Oh, I think I'm feeling a little sick," she said nonchalantly. "My hair always turns brown when I'm feeling yucky."

"That's so weird."

"Yeah, the color of my hair changes all the time; it just depends on what I'm doing or how I'm feeling."

"Like a chameleon," Simon said.

"Or a mood ring," Abu chimed in.

"*Abu!*" Simon cried.

"*Ooooh,* very much sorry!"

Tonya continued. "Well, anyway, I don't feel like myself today. Maybe I'm just hungry." She called out to the driver, "Abu, can you drop us off someplace where we can eat?"

Pretending to be startled, the man responded, "What? Oh, I'm sorry. I was not listening–but to answer your question: Yes. There is a café one block from here. Shall I drop you off there?"

"Yeah, that would be great." Tonya closed her eyes and massaged her temples.

The yellow cab screeched to the side of the curb. Simon quickly got out and stretched his legs. He questioned whether he should report Abu's atrocious driving to the authorities but ruled against it. The last thing he needed right now was to get involved with the police.

"Thanks, Abu," Tonya said kindly.

"Well, I do not think the café will accept video games instead of money, but you can try." At that, the turbaned man disappeared recklessly into the rush of traffic.

The two children walked towards the café with their heads tilted upwards.

"Have you been here before?" Tonya asked.

"Not at this one. They used to be located near the park. Mrs. Trimble took me there once when I was younger. I remember seeing the tail end of a car stuck in the wall of the building. It was pretty cool."

Tonya's eyes widened but she said nothing. As they opened the front door, loud music spilled out into the air. A big smile formed on Tonya's face, and streaks of orange appeared in her curly hair.

"So what do you call this?" she asked, bouncing her head up and down with the beat.

"Trouble," Simon answered with a deep sigh.

A server met them at the door as they walked into the Hard Rock Café.

"Aren't you two supposed to be in school right now?" the bubbly young lady chided.

Simon wondered how the woman could have such a cheery disposition with that loud noise blaring everywhere.

"Actually, I'm on a field trip," Tonya answered.

"Oh. Where's the rest of your class?"

"I don't know. I got separated from them, but now that my mobile paratransmitter is fully charged with electro-magical energy, I'm sure I'll be able to transport myself back to my homeworld without any problems. I just need to get some sustenance before I leave."

"Okay then–well, I hope you find your class." The clueless girl laughed as though everything Tonya had just told her had gone through one ear and out the other. "Just follow me, and I'll take you to your booth."

Simon thought the young lady had either put her head next to the loud speakers too long or dipped her onion rings one time too many in the Heavy Metal Bar-B-Que sauce.

As their server led them through the restaurant, Tonya got excited at seeing the guitars, clothing, and other memorabilia hanging on the walls. The items on one wall in particular especially interested her.

"What's all this?" she asked, stopping their server.

"Oh, this is the *god wall.*"

Tonya turned her head sideways in astonishment. A canvas of polytheistic religious images covered the wall. "May we sit here?"

"Yeah, sure," the lady said, smiling. "Oh, I almost forgot. My name's Mandy, and I'll be your server today. To start you off, what would you like to drink?"

"Do you have Saparellia?"

"No, I don't think so." Mandy frowned.

Tonya persisted. "How about Mando Gwaki?"

"Sorry," said the young woman.

"Well, do you have–"

"We'll just have water," Simon said, cutting in.

Mandy looked like she had just lost her favorite teddy bear. People who ordered water rarely gave big tips. "All right, here's your menus. I'll be back in a moment with your . . . *water.*" Mandy spun around and walked off, discouraged.

Tonya looked at the god wall again. "Wow, so you worship many gods?"

"No," Simon replied. "Everyone just kinda picks the one they like."

"Interesting. You know, I've seen some of these gods before."

"Really?" Simon perked up. "Which ones?"

"Well, this is the main one I've seen," she said, pointing to some foreign money on the wall. "I think there are people in every paraworld who worship money above all else."

"Huh? I never thought of it that way. I guess you're right. The thing most people do all day is try to earn money. I guess it makes them happy."

"*Nah,* money doesn't make people happy. People earn money because they have to. You can't survive in the paraverse without it. It's the people who love money more than their family–more than their friends, more than anything else–who scare me. They tend to use that money to gain power and to influence people to do what they want. I should know . . . my father's one of them."

"I'm sorry to hear that," Simon said. "My father left before I was born, and I never got to meet him. My mother didn't have any money. I guess that's one reason why she died . . . At least you have a family." Simon turned his head and brushed a small tear from his eye. Why was he opening up to this strange girl?

"Oh, Simon, that's so sad," Tonya said softly. "I didn't know."

She put her hand on his and then leaned over the table and gave him a small kiss on the cheek. It was a very impromptu gesture–not something she was accustomed to doing–but, somehow, during that brief moment, it seemed acceptable–almost natural–as if they had been friends for an eternity. Tonya rubbed his shoulder with her other hand and sat down.

Wide-eyed and open-mouthed, Simon stared at her in shock; he had never been kissed before. Tonya slowly withdrew her hand from his and blushed. The orange in her hair morphed into a light pink color.

"Here's your waters," Mandy said, interrupting the awkward silence. "Miss, you have some way-cool hair. I'm always trying to color mine, but I can't ever get it to take."

"Thanks," Tonya muttered, taking a sip of water.

"So what'll it be today?" Mandy asked cheerfully.

"Don't worry, Simon," Tonya said, jingling a small green pouch in her hand. "Get whatever you want. I'm paying."

Simon looked at the skintight tunic his companion was wearing and wondered where she had been concealing that pouch this whole time.

"I'll have one of those over there," she said, pointing to the booth next to them.

Mandy wrote on a pad of paper and said, "Jumbo Combo."

Tonya flipped the menu over. "And give me a couple of these."

Mandy continued writing. "Two root beer floats."

A waiter walked by with some hamburgers and fries. "Oh! Oh! Those look good! I'll take two of those."

Mandy turned to Simon. "And for you, sir?"

"I'll just have some fries."

The server looked like she had just lost her teddy bear again.

"Come on, Simon," Tonya pushed. "You've got to be hungry." She pointed to the menu and said, "He'll have two of these."

Within a short while, hamburgers and fries covered their whole table. Tonya went berserk, inhaling her food. She acted like a five-year-old who had never been out of the house before.

"What's this?"

"Ketchup."

"What's this?"

"A pickle."

"What's this?"

"A toothpick–don't eat it!"

Tonya continued to drive Simon crazy with all of her mindless questions until their server showed up. "Wow," Mandy observed. "I can't believe you ate all this food."

Tonya took one more sip from her drink. "What do you call this, again?"

"Root beer float."

"It's very good. I think I'll have two more."

Mandy's mouth dropped. "All right, two more root beer floats coming up."

"And can you bring us the check?" Simon called out to the server as she walked away. He turned to his companion. "Tonya, how can you eat so much food and still be so skinny?"

"Well, actually, I don't usually eat this much," the girl confessed. "It's just, I've never had anything like this before. On my world we mostly eat grass and seeds."

"Grass!" Simon repeated incredulously.

"Yeah, the Elders of Chamel discourage us from eating meat because they're afraid people will revert to being savage reptiles." She snorted. "Scientists in my dimension think we evolved from lizards, but I think that's just a bunch of garbage."

"That's funny. A lot of people here on Earth think we evolved from monkeys or apes."

"Well, if I evolved from a lizard and you evolved from a monkey, then why do we look so much alike?" She ate the last fry on her plate and chuckled. "I suppose science is always the alternative to religion. There's a growing faction in the paraverse that claims that science is supreme over all–even over magic–and I've been told that these zealots can get pretty violent with their anti-magic views."

"So do you think of magic as a religion?" Simon asked.

"No, not a religion. I guess you could look at magic in the same way people look at money. It's more of a means to an end than anything. My teachers are always saying that–" She began to speak dramatically as though she were imitating a scholarly old man. "*Magic can be used for good or for evil; it can fuel the flames of war or it can soothe the anguish of pain.*" Her voice returned to normal. "But most people aren't inclined to perform magic in the first place because it takes training and skill. That's why I'm in school–to become the greatest magician ever! Well, at least that's what my parents expect of me."

"Here ya go!" Mandy appeared with two root beer floats. "Alrighty then, here's your bill. I assume you're going to pay for this with cash?"

Tonya opened her green pouch and spilled out a bunch of strangely shaped coins onto the table. "There ya go," she said.

Mandy picked up one of the square coins and tried to read the inscription on it. "Um," she started, "this all ya got?"

"Is it not enough?" Tonya asked in surprise.

"I'll tell you what," the young lady said with a forced smile. "You just stay right here, and I'll go get someone to help us."

Mandy walked away briskly.

"I don't feel so good, all of a sudden," Tonya said.

"I'm not surprised, after all you just ate."

"No, I've felt kinda weird ever since I arrived on your paraworld," she said, massaging her forehead.

Seconds later, Simon spotted Mandy and a husky man with a short beard walking towards them. "I think we're in trouble," he moaned.

"Hello, kids," the manager said in a not-too-pleasant sort of way. "I've been told that you don't want to pay for your meal."

"No, it's not that," Simon said. "My friend here is from out of town, and she didn't realize you wouldn't accept her money."

"Where are you from, young lady?"

Tonya huffed. "Paraworld 4329."

"Para what?" the man asked angrily.

"Maybe we could wash some dishes or something," Simon suggested.

"No, we have a way of dealing with customers who don't pay their bills," the manager said, wringing his hands.

Just then, the sound of a news reporter replaced all of the loud music in the building. The televisions hooked to the walls no longer displayed images of music videos but, instead, showed scenes of a demolished alley.

". . . *And the search goes on for the two children who, among other things, single-handedly destroyed more than a dozen cars and attacked two high school students. What you are about to see is exclusive footage of the attack.*"

The TV screens showed Spike being jerked around in the air by the yellow strings of electricity that Tonya had created during their encounter. Some people in the Hard Rock Café gasped, while others smiled uncertainly. The scene finally ended with exploding cars and shattering windows.

The news reporter continued, "I have here with me one of the victims of this brutal attack."

Buz's cut-up face appeared on the television screen. "We were just minding our own business when, all of a sudden, this alien girl came out of nowhere and tried to kill us."

"Alien girl?" the reporter asked.

"Yeah, she said she was from another planet and that she wanted to turn us into her slaves!"

The reporter faced the camera. "Well, there you have it. Is this really an alien invasion, or just an elaborate hoax perpetuated by a host of tourists and school kids? I can tell you this much: the government isn't taking any chances. Even as we speak, the streets of New York are being combed by armed troops. If anyone knows the whereabouts of these two children, you are encouraged to contact your local authorities immediately."

The TV then showed a closeup image of Simon and Tonya running away from the disaster site.

"So what world did you say you were from?" the manager asked Tonya as she squirmed in her seat.

CHAPTER 5
THE CHASE

Tonya grabbed her paratransmitter and dove under the table. Simon started to apologize, "I'm so sorry about–" but he was jerked to the floor. "*This!*" he yelped.

They sprinted towards the exit, but halfway there, a tall server holding a tray of food walked into their pathway. Tonya collided with the man, and they both fell in a heap. French fries flew in every direction. Tonya picked up a sandwich from the floor and took a bite.

"Oh, I should've ordered one of these," she said, taking another bite.

"Come on!" Simon yelled. He pulled the girl to her feet.

The loud music in the café blared wildly as Simon and Tonya made their way to the front door.

"Hold it right there," growled the manager. His large fingers clamped down onto Tonya's shoulder from behind. Instinctively, the teenager flung her arm to get loose, and the manager sailed across the room as though a great, invisible giant had just smacked him. He landed on a table, splitting it in half, and sent food into the air.

"Sorry!" Simon shouted before exiting the building.

A dozen men dressed in green fatigues marched in their direction. "We are in so much trouble," Simon moaned.

"This way," Tonya said. In the bright sunlight, Simon noticed her hair color had changed into a fiery red.

They ran down the street and took a sharp right. The road ahead seemed clear of danger, so they sprinted for two more blocks. Just as they reached the end of the third block, however, another group of army men spotted them.

Simon looked behind and saw the other party of soldiers approaching fast. Frantic and scared, he scanned the area for cover. In less than a minute, they would be surrounded. *Maybe it's for the best,* he thought. Then realization dawned on him: If he was sent back to the foster home, Butch would be there, waiting for him. With renewed vigor, Simon prepared to run. Suddenly, Tonya grasped her stomach and fell to her knees.

"What's wrong?" cried Simon.

"I feel nauseous."

"We have to go now!" Simon snapped. "If they catch us, who knows what they'll do to us?"

He pulled Tonya to her feet and forced her to run across the busy road. A barricade formed behind them as cars and trucks from every lane crashed into each other. Tonya turned around and uttered a spell. A layer of slick ice crept over the street and sidewalk, causing the soldiers and pedestrians to fall. Some of the people tried to clamber on all fours, but to no avail. The ice continued up the buildings and even made the birds slip from their perches.

"Wow," Simon whispered.

The two children continued running until they found a row of parked cars. Tonya hobbled from car to car, trying to find one that wasn't locked.

"What are you doing?" Simon yelled.

"We need to borrow one of these motorized contraptions," she cried. "I can't run any longer–something's wrong with me. My whole body hurts."

"Are you crazy? We can't just borrow a car."

Tonya approached an expensive-looking sports car, and a digital voice warned, "*Please step away from the vehicle.*"

"What is this?" she asked in shock.

The voice spoke again while Tonya jiggled the door handle. "*You have ten seconds to leave the vicinity before an alarm goes off.*"

"I think we'd better go," Simon said, eyeing the black exterior.

"Let me see here," Tonya said. She pulled up her tunic a little and revealed a small wand attached to her bare leg with a white garter belt.

So that's where she's been keeping it, Simon thought.

The car counted down: "*Five . . . Four . . . Three . . .*"

Tonya took her wand, tapped the keyhole in the door, and said loudly, "*OPEN!*"

To the surprise of both, the roof of the car peeled away like a banana and flung itself to the ground with a loud clank.

"Oops," Tonya said, looking at the convertible she had just made. "I didn't mean to do that. I was just trying to pick the lock."

She climbed over the door and hopped into the driver's seat. The inside of the car was decked out with speakers, a DVD-equipped television, voice-activated controls, and a top-of-the-line global positioning system.

"Get in."

"We shouldn't be doing this," Simon whined.

Ignoring him, Tonya placed her paratransmitter onto the leather seat next to her and tapped the steering wheel with her wand. The car jumped ferociously as if it were alive.

"*Please fasten your seat belts,*" the computer system prompted.

"Thank you," Tonya said. She put on her seat belt and turned to look at Simon. A group of soldiers had found them. "Get in, Simon!"

With little time remaining, Simon leapt headfirst into the back seat of the car. Tonya slammed the gas pedal to the floor. The sports car lurched forward and sped off down the street like a rabbit in heat.

"Don't worry, Simon," she called back to the boy being tossed around. "I watched real closely when Abu was driving us."

"*AAAH!*" Simon yelled as she veered to the side and bumped into a parked car. "That's just what we need: driving lessons from a cab driver!" He fumbled with the seat belt, but it wouldn't fasten.

"Wow, this isn't as easy as it looks," she said, stopping the vehicle three times in quick succession."No wonder a car smashed into the rock café."

Simon rolled his eyes. He pictured in his mind the ornamental car that used to protrude from the previous Hard Rock Café building.

Tonya moved slowly into the flow of traffic. "You know, I must admit, I didn't see any rocks in the café, soft or hard."

Suddenly, a person dressed in a dark overcoat hopped into the back seat of the convertible.

"How's it going, punk?" Butch asked menacingly.

Tonya gasped at seeing the young man in the rearview mirror. By this time, she had merged fully into the stream of traffic and was too scared to slow down or take her hands off the wheel. Haphazardly, she wove in and out of her lane, nearly hitting an 18-wheel diesel truck.

"Butch, what are you doing here?" shouted Simon over the roar of the engine.

"I just happened to be in the neighborhood, and I thought I'd drop in."

The sound of police sirens filled their ears as the wheels of the car squealed through a red light. The digital voice warned, "*You are approaching a street light.*"

"You're a little slow, car," Tonya teased.

"*Caution, you are driving twenty-seven miles per hour over the speed limit,*" the car retorted.

"Keep driving," Butch said.

"What do you want from us?" Tonya cried. She brushed several long strands of red hair out of her face.

Butch grabbed a handful of curly hair and pulled the frightened girl to the back of her seat. "I want that transmitter thing you've got," he said coldly in her ear. Tonya strained to reach the gas pedal, but Butch held her back. The sports car began to slow down.

"I don't know what you're talking about," she screamed.

"Don't lie to me," Butch spat. "I heard you talking about it when you were hiding in the dumpster."

With her back pressed against the seat, Tonya could barely hold onto the steering wheel. The car swerved into the opposing lane.

Tonya struggled to free herself from Butch's grasp. "Let–go–of–me!" She released the steering wheel entirely and pointed her wand behind her. A sparkling stream of light shot out of the wand and missed Butch's head by inches. He let go of her hair.

She forced the car back into the right lane. With one hand on the wheel and another clutching her wand, the young girl sprayed out a barrage of spells, but none of them made contact with Butch.

The two boys ducked in their seats as Tonya flailed her arm around wildly. She hit a fire hydrant with one beam of light, then a dumpster, and then some metal trash cans at the edge of the curb.

The sports car ran over a pothole in the road, causing everyone to fall back into their seats. Tonya inadvertently sent a stream of magical light into the sky, which scattered a flock of pigeons that had been nestling on a window ledge above.

A large semi-truck started to cross the intersection in front of them. Gasping in horror, Tonya dropped her wand in her lap, reeled the car to the left, and whizzed past the truck. The police followed suit, forcing the semi to jackknife onto the sidewalk. Pedestrians scattered for their lives.

■ ■ ■

A Cocker Spaniel barked ferociously at the fire hydrant that had been previously hit by one of Tonya's out-of-control spells. The red fire hydrant vibrated with harsh grinding sounds. Suddenly, the cylinder of metal stretched itself ten feet into the air. The top part of the fire hydrant split open and formed a gaping mouth full of sharp, metallic teeth. It thrashed around like a snake for a few seconds and then, without warning, came crashing down onto the poor dog below–swallowing it whole.

While this was happening, a short, stubby man eating a hot dog walked up to his immaculately clean car and pulled off a parking ticket that a police officer had placed under his wiper blade.

"Oh, *crap,*" he mumbled to himself as he crumpled up the piece of paper.

Just then, a small bird-dropping splattered on his clean windshield. Extremely perturbed, the man began to wipe off the mess with his ticket.

An ominous, dark shadow loomed overhead and made a loud warbling sound as it passed by. The unsuspecting man looked up to see what it was, and, at that very moment, a shower of white bird turd completely drenched him and his beautiful car. Revolted by the pungent smell and feeling absolutely disgusted, he wiped his face and attempted to open his eyes.

The horrible noise of crunching metal sounded from behind. When the man turned around, he saw a humongous pigeon perched on the top of his car, sagging the roof with its weight. Before he could scream, the bird snatched the hot dog out of his trembling hand and swallowed it in one bite.

Nauseated with fear, the short man stumbled backwards, away from the enormous bird. The pigeon twitched its head back and forth and hopped to the ground, but before it had even landed, the man's tiny car was propelled forward by the impact of something large. A massive dumpster had crashed into the vehicle. It chomped down on the hood like a dog consuming a bone. Two hefty legs of metal lifted the dumpster off the ground and allowed it to move about with incredible agility. Presumably, the dumpster had intended to gobble up the oversized bird but, instead, ripped the car apart with its powerful jaws.

After pulverizing the vehicle, the dumpster sprang into the air and landed on a minivan nearby. The windshield and side windows burst from the excessive weight.

Silver trash cans with legs of their own ran through the street like chickens with their heads cut off. One by one, the dumpster squashed the little cans under its doglike claws. Just after crushing the last trash can, it spotted the gigantic pigeon hopping away.

The dumpster knocked over a newspaper stand and bumped into parked cars while chasing the bird down the street. People fled in hysteria. Suddenly, the pigeon turned around, opened its beak wide, and sprayed a hot flame from its mouth towards the spastic dumpster. Badly scorched and starting to melt, the dumpster took one last leap towards the large bird, but the pigeon jumped into the air and flew off.

The animated fire hydrant, now extending thirty feet from the concrete, squirted water at the cars as they passed by. Seeing the singed dumpster not too far away, the metallic snake coiled and struck, piercing right through the dumpster's thick walls.

The dumpster rolled on the ground to get away, but this only hindered its escape; the movement simply allowed the fire hydrant to wrap itself around its prey more efficiently. Lying on its side, the dumpster's metallic feet kicked violently as the fire hydrant squeezed the life out of the metal box. The walls began to warp from the pressure, and the hinges began to buckle. In a desperate fit of rage, the dumpster seized the head of the fire hydrant with its huge jaws and clamped down tightly until, a moment later, both entities lay motionless on the ground.

■ ■ ■

Still driving frantically, Tonya had no idea of the chaos she'd caused with her misguided spells; she was more interested in keeping the car in one piece.

"*Warning! It appears that you may be driving recklessly,*" announced the car. "*In the event that you are pulled over by a police officer, you could face possible suspension of your driver's license.*"

"I don't think it's my driver's license these cops are after," Tonya yelled. "Besides, I don't have a license!"

Not bothering to slow down, Tonya took a sharp turn into a narrow alleyway. Butch and Simon flew to one side of the car. Several police vehicles and two army jeeps stood at the end of the road–leaving nowhere for Tonya to go. She stopped the car and looked back to see her pursuers blocking the pathway behind her. She was trapped.

"*If you have been drinking, it is advisable that you stop driving immediately,"* the car stated. "*Would you like me to call one of your listed designated drivers for you?*"

"Not now," Tonya said as she revved up the engine.

"What are you doing?" Simon cried.

Tonya didn't respond. Instead, she slammed her foot on the gas pedal and raced down the street towards the soldiers and officers sitting in their cars.

"You're going to kill us!" shouted Butch.

He reached over the seat to take hold of the steering wheel, but Tonya held on firmly. The policemen prepared to jump out of their vehicles. Butch grabbed Tonya's wand from her lap and waved it around chaotically.

"*Stop!*" he commanded, flicking the wand at the car. "*Stop! Freeze! Halt! Stop-Stop-Stop!* This stupid thing doesn't work!"

"Here, let me try," Simon yelled. He took the wand from Butch's hand. "*Alakazam! Hocus Pocus!* Pretty please?"

"Give me that," Tonya said in a disgusted voice. She snatched the tiny wand from Simon. The two boys closed their eyes and screamed. Within a few feet of ramming into a police car, Tonya yelled, "*FLY!*"

The black convertible leapt from the ground as if it were driving up some invisible ramp. Its rubber tires brushed the top of the first police car and knocked off one of the flashing red and blue lights.

The sports car jumped over the rest of the vehicles and landed upright onto the wall of a high-rise apartment building. Not losing any momentum, Tonya continued to drive. The wheels whirled against the side of the structure. Falling backwards into their seats, Simon and Butch opened their eyes in dismay.

"*Sensors indicate that the alignment of the wheels is no longer properly balanced,*" the car droned. "*Please have the vehicle checked by a mechanic at your earliest convenience.*"

"Oh, shut up!" yelled Butch.

"*Voice prompts deactivated. Have a nice day,*" the computer system said before going into standby mode.

Tonya zoomed over a little boy's bedroom window, which shocked the child so much that he closed his curtains and ran down the hallway to get his parents, screaming the whole way, "There's a car driving up our building! There's a car driving up our building!"

The flying car shot twenty feet above the apartment and came to a slow halt in midair–like a roller coaster reaching the summit before a great fall. Time seemed to stand still as Simon, Tonya, and Butch gazed dreamily at the Apache helicopters hovering on both sides of them.

Feeling woozy, Tonya turned her head sideways to look at the helicopter to her left. She imagined the aircraft's blades twirling in slow motion. "I feel dizzy," she whispered.

Tonya put her hand to her mouth and coughed. When she withdrew her hand, her palm was wet with blood. Her eyes rolled into the back of her head. She didn't know if the sickness came about by the food she'd eaten, the bumpy ride she'd just had, or by the simple fact that she was afraid of heights, but whatever the reason, it was enough to make her faint.

The lethargic dream ended abruptly, and the car began to drop from the pale blue sky. Plummeting downward with tremendous speed, it appeared as though someone had just pressed fast forward on time itself.

Simon felt his small body float away from his seat. He reached out and grabbed Tonya's paratransmitter, which was also levitating. Butch seized the other end of the device and dragged it and Simon towards him.

Back in the apartment, the little child's mother ran to the bedroom window and impatiently ripped open the curtains. "How many times have I told you not to make up stories, young man?" At that moment, the car rushed by and created a huge gust of wind that blew the woman backwards onto her son's bed.

"See, Mommy, I told you there was a car driving on our building," said the innocent boy with a proud smile.

Outside, Simon turned his head towards the driver's seat and yelled over the loud whistling of the car, "Wake up, Tonya. *WAKE UP!*"

"*Good afternoon,*" chimed the car as it awoke from its sleep mode. *"Welcome to the RX1000 voice-activated guidance system. Would you like your daily horoscope?"*

Tonya opened her eyes and responded sleepily, "No, thank you, car."

"*Tonya!*" cried Simon.

Realizing where she was, Tonya grabbed the steering wheel and forced the car to glide upwards from its descent. Just before taking flight, the rubber tires brushed the same cop car on the ground as before and knocked out the remaining red and blue flashing light.

The Apache helicopters chased after them as they flew above the streets of New York City. Tonya wove throughout the town, darting around buildings and flying under billboards to lose her pursuers, but the convertible was no match for an Air Force helicopter. Although the Apaches were armed with air-to-air Sidewinder, Stinger, Mistral, and Sidearm missiles, the pilots hesitated to fire within the confines of the city. Instead, they tried to flush the car into the open where they could shoot it down without hurting innocent people.

All the while, Butch and Simon fought for possession of the paratransmitter. If it were not for the car's sudden drops, dives, and jumps, Butch would have easily been able to rip the book from Simon's arms.

"Give me that thing," Butch said. He shook the young boy against the leather seat.

A row of flashing lights came to life on the paratransmitter. Strange characters filled the digital place markers, and a three-dimensional image of a white planet appeared on the display.

"Tonya, something's happening!" Simon yelled.

Totally engrossed in her driving, the teenager rotated around the Empire State Building as if she were following a trail up a tall mountain peak. Unfortunately, both helicopters were hugging the car so closely that

Tonya could hardly maneuver.

Butch reached into his black overcoat and pulled out his ivory-handled knife. He plunged the blade deep into the leather seat–just inches away from Simon's face. In horror, the boy gazed at the sharp fangs protruding from the gaping mouth of the white cobra in the handle. He noticed the menacing snake was staring back at him with just one green emerald eye; its other eye must have fallen out on some previous venture.

The row of lights at the top of the paratransmitter started to go out–one by one. Tonya screamed, and both boys turned around quickly to see what was wrong. A blazing stream of fire blew over their heads, and a giant pigeon came into view. Tonya let go of the wheel and covered her eyes as she collided with the massive bird in midair.

At that exact moment, the last light on the paratransmitter went out, and an explosion of blue electricity erupted all around them. The car disappeared immediately, leaving the charred remains of a fried pigeon and hundreds of scorched feathers to fall to the ground.

Down below, the stubby man drenched in bird turd was trying to convince a disbelieving police officer of his predicament when the cooked pigeon fell onto the officer's car, pulverizing the vehicle to the ground. The officer got to her feet and gazed in utter disbelief at the burning carcass. The short man smiled, his story suddenly gaining a new level of plausibility. "Now do you believe me?"

■ ■ ■

Rivers of what looked like thick, red blood mixed with orange oil saturated the colossal walls of the parastream. The two liquids rippled as waves of energy pulsated through the cavern in a heartbeat rhythm. A labyrinth of large tunnels jutted in every direction–each pathway leading to infinite possibilities. The glow of electrical blue light flickered on their faces as the momentum of the wormhole pushed the car along with tremendous force.

"What have you done?" yelled Tonya. "The mobile paratransmitter wasn't designed to transport this much weight!"

While being propelled through the vast maze of tunnels, the black convertible vibrated as though it were about to fall apart. Simon wondered if the journey would ever end as they passed though dozens of conduits at breakneck speeds.

Tonya experienced a feeling she had never felt before: car sickness. Butch and Simon, on the other hand, continued to fight over the magical book. Neither of the boys paid much attention to the countless passageways that zipped past them.

"Let go," Butch growled, raising his knife above his head.

With his black overcoat outstretched, the sophomore looked like some sort of demon, especially while standing on the seat and hovering over the boy. Simon's eyes widened, not because of the sharp knife but because of the sudden drop he saw that the car was about to make as it followed the pathway of the slipstream.

Simon let go of the paratransmitter. "Okay, it's yours."

An evil grin of triumph appeared on Butch's face as he clutched the magical book.

"See ya later, *Francis*," Simon said, grabbing his seat belt with both hands.

Confused, Butch turned around just in time to see the car take a nosedive. The young man soared out of the convertible–along with the paratransmitter–and was swept into another tunnel.

Simon dangled in the wind, desperately holding on to the seat belt with all the strength he could muster.

"Hold on, Simon!" screamed Tonya.

She hit the brakes, but nothing happened.

"*Passengers should always wear their seat belts,*" informed the digital voice of the car.

Tonya spun the wheel around and forced the vehicle to become level again, but in the process, she threw Simon's small body to the hood. By this time, the car was trembling so badly that the screws and bolts were starting to come undone. The front windshield ripped away, and Simon yelled as he slipped down the shiny, black hood.

Tonya didn't know what to do. She realized that, without the guidance of the paratransmitter, she was on her own to steer them to safety, but she didn't trust herself; she'd just started school, for heavens sake, and wasn't experienced with this sort of thing. No one was, really. After a brief moment of inner struggle, she came to the bitter conclusion that she had no choice but to manually enter one of the paraworlds–a decision every paratraveler hoped they'd never have to face. The probability of success was dismal at best, but she had to try.

"Hold on just one more second," Tonya shouted.

She slammed her foot on the gas pedal. The vehicle sprang forward, fueled by the last remnants of magical power from Tonya's spell, and miraculously entered one of the gateways. An explosion of blue light engulfed the car and sent them hurtling into a new world.

For a split second, Simon felt immense pain consume his whole body, but then everything became calm with a blanket of cold darkness that seemed to absorb every ounce of light around him. Succumbing to unconsciousness, Simon closed his eyes and acknowledged to himself that his universe was gone.

CHAPTER 6
THE POWER OF GEE

Somewhere high above Paraworld Bantu, a spy named Tabatha Burke hid within the metallic walls of a Raider space carrier.

"I think she went this way," yelled an officer, leading a group of soldiers down a dimly lit corridor.

Tabatha waited for the tapping of their boots to fade away before she emerged from the shadows. Her fair skin and big yellow eyes complimented her extremely thin figure. A black pseudo-skin material covered her entire body from head to foot and showed off her lean muscles as she pranced. She tightened the hood over her face and rounded a corner with catlike agility. The hall was empty.

Like a black panther, she glided through the hallway without making a sound, but then she halted suddenly at the *swoosh* of an automatic door. Tabatha clenched her fists and quickly opened her hands to reveal sharp, curved nails jutting from the tips of her gloved fingers.

With incredible speed, she ran up the wall, jumped to the ceiling, and sank her claws into the flat metallic surface. She pressed her body tight against the dark ceiling as a gangly man walked through the open door.

He spoke into a bracelet on his arm. "No, General, we haven't found her yet, but I assure you–"

"I don't want excuses!" boomed a loud voice from the bracelet. "If the information she stole finds its way to the Guardians of the Crown, our whole operation could be in jeopardy. I don't want her captured–I don't want her questioned–*I WANT HER DEAD!* Do you understand me?"

"*Yes, sir*." The response didn't come from the officer but from Tabatha.

She bent over and pulled the bracelet off the wrist of the unconscious man she had just fallen upon and spoke to the unseen general.

"General, could you tell me exactly what this is I stole from you?"

She held up a shiny datachip, about the size of a quarter, between her fingers as if she were inspecting a diamond.

"Tabatha!" yelled the general. "How could you betray me like this?"

"It's very simple, General," she said coyly. "You don't pay me as much as the Guardians do."

"But think about the cause!"

"Yes, the cause," she said, flipping the datachip into the air like a coin. "Your precious little crusade to rid the paraverse of all who perform magic." She closed her hand on the chip. "Well, General, if you haven't noticed yet, I'm somewhat partial to magic." She opened her hand, but the datachip had disappeared.

The red homing beacon on the bracelet started to blink.

"Gotta go!" she said, sliding the bracelet down the hallway.

Tabatha turned around just as a laser blast seared past her face. She said a word under her breath that sounded like *Balamee* and then raised her hands. Two faint discs of energy hovered about her palms.

Another laser came at her, but this time, with lightning-fast reflexes, Tabatha caught the blast in her hand, causing the laser to dissipate on contact. She absorbed two more blasts into her hands before she lashed out with glowing stars, which sailed through the air and hit several guards. The stars exploded with green and red light, paralyzing the victims upon impact and disabling some of the laser rifles.

Tabatha jumped backwards in a series of flips and then danced around the hall to avoid further contact with the laser fire. Because the ship was hovering in space above the planet, the electro-magical waves were scarce. She knew she couldn't defend herself with magic for long, so she decided to fall back on her hand-to-hand fighting skills.

Her decision was an unfortunate one . . . for the soldiers, that is; for Tabatha was of the Order of Gee–a group of trained fighters who intermingled the ancient art of karate with the awesome power of magic. Her muscular leg shot upward and kicked a guard square in the chest, leaving a faint trace of red florescent light in the air as the man flew backwards into three other soldiers.

Tabatha dodged as a large soldier clumsily took a swing at her with his rifle. She responded to his feeble attempt to hit her with a flurry of jabs to the solar plexus. Sensing movement nearby, she immediately fell into the splits as two armed soldiers–one on each side of her–fired their guns at the same time. Both men toppled to the ground.

She spun in a circle on the floor and knocked down two more attackers. Rolling forward onto her hands, she thrust her legs into the air and wrapped them around the neck of another soldier standing in front of her.

She paused for a moment and looked up at the young man's handsome face between her calves. "Hey, you're kinda cute," she said, squeezing tighter. She pulled her legs back with unnatural strength and sent the man crashing into a wall.

Tabatha glanced around and realized she was hopelessly surrounded, but a renewed sense of hope filled her soul as a sudden pocket of electro-magical energy surged past her. Not wanting to lose the opportunity, she drew upon the power of the E.M. waves by quickly raising her hands above her head and yelling, "*Splindore!*" A whirlwind of light lifted the remaining soldiers into the air and slammed them hard against the ceiling.

The strong wind blew off Tabatha's hood and played in her long white hair, making her pointy ears twitch in discomfort. When she lowered her arms, the wind ceased and the soldiers fell.

Drained, Tabatha bowed her head for a moment to catch her breath. She then sprinted down a narrow passageway and made a sharp turn. As she rounded the corner, she saw something thrust towards her face. Caught off guard, Tabatha turned her head to minimize the blow, but the rifle butt struck hard and sent her sprawling.

"That's for using me," came the cold voice of the tall gangly man she had incapacitated earlier.

Tabatha got to her knees and clutched her bloody forehead.

The officer kicked her in the ribs and said viciously, "That's for the general."

She rolled onto her back in pain and looked up at the man as he raised his gun towards her chest. Her vision went in and out of focus.

He smiled and said, "And this is for the cause."

Tabatha closed her eyes and heard the firing of a gun . . . and then a *thump* next to her. She opened her eyes to discover that she was face-to-face with the dead officer.

A tall, shadowy figure loomed overhead, pointing a gun in her direction. Tabatha squinted, but no matter how hard she looked, she couldn't see the man's face behind his black hood. Many of the lights in the area flickered out as he moved towards her.

"Thank you," she said, sitting up. Her ribs swelled with pain.

Too far away to assist her, the stranger extended the palm of his hand, as if he were requesting some sort of alm.

"What?" Tabatha said tersely, annoyed by the gesture.

Remaining silent, the cloaked figure snapped his fingers. Suddenly, Tabatha's body rose into the air. She whirled around as if she were strapped to some invisible gyroscope. From out of the blur, the stolen datachip dropped to the floor and rolled down the hallway.

The dark stranger magically summoned the chip to his hand and then turned around and walked towards an open door. He raised his fist nonchalantly and snapped his fingers to release Tabatha from his invisible grip, fully expecting her to fall unconscious to the ground–but before he reached the exit, the mechanical door shut itself. He spun around and saw that Tabatha hadn't crashed to the floor but was standing upright, reaffirming the notion that cats *do* always land on their feet.

"*ReGaurdae!*" she yelled, slapping her hands together.

She slowly pulled her hands apart, and a yellow rod with a glowing, inner flame extended from one palm to the other. When she could spread her hands no farther, she caught the rod in the middle and stretched it again until it formed into a full-sized staff.

The mysterious man dropped his rifle and pulled out a straight wand from within his cloak. He formed the shape of an oval in the air and bowed deeply, almost in jest. Angry, Tabatha charged and swung her magical staff towards his head with terrific force. Exhibiting little effort, the stranger blocked the attack with his wand and practically forced the staff out of Tabatha's hands.

She frowned, then reared back and took another swing, but with the flick of his wrist, the stranger blocked the staff just like he had before. Tabatha screamed in frustration and attacked with a series of impressive moves, but the dark man stood immovable, his tiny wand blocking each and every blow as if she wielded a dandelion instead of a weapon of war. Sparks showered the floor every time her yellow rod crashed against her enemy's wand, but he remained unaffected.

Tabatha wondered how the man could demonstrate his awesome powers with such little E.M. energy about them. Just then, the cloaked figure thrust out his free hand. Tabatha flew across the room and smacked into the far wall. Disoriented, she shook off the pain and hissed.

Steaming with rage, Tabatha picked up her yellow staff and broke it across her knee. She summoned all of the E.M. energy she possibly could to keep the inner flame from escaping. Then she raised both shafts into the air and spoke loudly: "*Spliteasto!*" This particular spell had always been difficult for her to perform, but after watching the sticks morph into what looked like a pair of glowing nunchucks, Tabatha smiled in approval, realizing that she had pulled it off flawlessly.

Methodically rotating the nunchucks across her toned body, she started towards her opponent again, but to her dismay, the dark figure reached into his cloak and pulled out another wand. The two magicians clashed in a melee of frenzied blows, but no matter how hard Tabatha tried to hit the man, he seemed to always block her attack.

Sparks exploded everywhere, as if they had just walked into a room full of lit fireworks. Horrified, Tabatha realized her foe must be an ultramage; how else could he summon every ounce of E.M. energy in the room to do his bidding?

The man partially disarmed her, sending one of her nunchucks flying behind him. His youthful speed surprised her. She lashed out with her remaining nunchucks, but they too were ripped out of her hand and thrown to the side. At that moment, the man crossed his wands and rasped the word, "*Valamure.*"

Tabatha's eyes widened in terror at the sound of that horrible word. *No, it can't be!*

With remarkable flexibility, she immediately arched backwards, hovering so close to the ground that her radiant white hair swept the floor. Thick, gray fumes sprayed out of the two wands and blew right over Tabatha's body, forming a semitransparent cloud above her.

After the cloaked man finished his spell, he threw something at his feet, which caused an explosion of smoke to engulf him. When the smoke cleared, he was gone.

Tabatha stood up and stared at the mass of gray moving against the ceiling. It was a wraith–a ghostly entity whose very touch sucked out the life of its victim. Magic of this sort was rarely performed because, even if the magician possessed the power to cast the spell, incantations of this magnitude took an immense amount of electro-magical energy to execute. And more importantly, the conjurer was usually the first to die. Nevertheless, the cloaked man *had* summoned the demon, and it was now Tabatha's problem.

Not waiting a second more, she rolled sideways and sprinted down the hallway with all her might. She opened a door and rushed past a small group of soldiers. Astonished at her sudden appearance, the men raised their laser rifles and started to fire. Tabatha threw herself down and lay prostrate against the floor as the large wraith glided through the wall behind her. Like apples falling from a tree, she heard the terrible thuds of bodies collapsing.

The deadly phantom hissed coldly in the air as it fed on the helpless soldiers. Its long, ragged robes brushed the ground just inches from Tabatha's face.

Tabatha wiggled her way across the room and fled out the side exit. She ran down a long corridor and finally found the transportation room–but just before she opened the door, she glanced back to see the hideous wraith enter the hallway.

Two technicians sat lazily at their desks.

"Get out of here!" Tabatha screamed.

Falling over each other, they stumbled out of their chairs and fled into an adjacent room. Tabatha's fingers ran wildly over the control panel as she punched in her coordinates. She jumped over the computerized console and stood inside a cramped cylindrical tube.

"Stop where you are," barked a soldier from behind the console. He pointed a weapon at her.

Tabatha gasped in horror as the monstrous wraith flew right through the man and continued towards her. Its wide mouth expanded to ten times its normal size as it prepared to swallow her whole.

With heightened reflexes, Tabatha flicked her wrist at the console and magically pulled a tiny lever. The glass tube erupted in blue lightening. Frantic, she attempted to shield her face with her arms but then disappeared into a cloud of electricity as the malicious wraith passed through the empty tube.

CHAPTER 7
PUDO

Pillars of white steam, wrapped around thick plumes of smoke, sputtered from somewhere below. A soft hum sounded in Simon's ears as he gazed sleepily at the vast funnels of vapor, embedded in clouds of ebony. The boy felt his body rise higher and higher above the unearthly ground. Then, suddenly, there was no darkness, no shadows, no evil nor despair–just an overwhelming harmony and a whiteness that swelled–so lovingly, so delicately–throughout his whole being. He was in a universe of immaculate light that sent his senses into a blissful state of euphoria.

Is this Heaven? he thought.

As if in answer to his query, a beautiful young woman, sitting atop a majestic beast, emerged from the mist above. The creature she rode resembled a lion but was considerably larger and broader. Its long, white beard grew down to its muscular paws, and its nostrils flared every time a puff of steam escaped its mouth. Simon felt pure love encompass his soul as the animal descended a narrow flight of steps.

The angelic lady wore a white satin robe that swept the marble floor as she moved. Her fair skin glowed with a radiance that Simon had never imagined possible, and her flowing hair seemed to be caught up in a peculiar breeze that followed only her.

As she drew near, her mouth widened into a pleasant smile that filled Simon's heart with warmth. She spoke in a musical tone that was pleasant to the ear yet sounded surreal and unnatural.

'Tis a musical prayer.
Words unsaid, unbinding, unknown.
'Tis the foundation of life, truth,
and thy inner-self entwined.
Within your destiny, it lies.
Inside your heart, it confides.

"What–" Simon stammered. "What is?"

She smiled and answered, "Magic." As the word left her tender lips, it seemed to echo over and over in Simon's ears. "*Magic–Magic–Magic.*"

The mysterious woman rode back up the marble steps and then turned around to say, "Your first gift, I leave unto you."

She blew the boy a kiss and then vanished into the thick clouds. Ever so slowly, the dreamlike environment faded away until only cold darkness remained.

Simon opened his eyes, and the flood of reality came rushing in. He squinted to see the outline of dwarf-sized men and women walking around the room.

"Where am I?" he asked, still a bit dazed.

"Simon!" exclaimed a familiar voice. "Simon, you're awake! Doctor . . . doctor, he's awake!"

The face of a small man, perhaps less than four feet tall, appeared above him. The man shined a tiny light into each one of the boy's eyes and announced in a high, squeaky voice, "Yep, he's awake." The doctor turned off the flashlight and stuck his meaty fingers into Simon's mouth and started to feel around. "Now tell me, boy, if this hurts."

Simon tried to talk, but the thick fingers in his mouth prevented him from saying anything comprehendible. He glanced over at Tonya. She looked different somehow. Her green hair was no longer curly, but something else seemed out of place. Had she gotten taller?

"Dr. Troodle, he doesn't understand you," Tonya informed the man. "He can't speak your language."

Gagging on the stranger's fingers, Simon jerked his head away and yelled, "Stop it!"

"Well, I understood that," Dr. Troodle said, stepping back.

Still confused, Simon sat up and shouted, "Where am I? Who are you?" He looked down at the sheets covering his nakedness and cried, "Where's my clothes!"

"I'm Dr. Troodle," the man said. "You had a pretty bad accident. For a few weeks we didn't think you'd live, but as the months went by you made remarkable progress. Your scars are healing just splendidly."

"*Months?*" Simon repeated, falling back into bed. He noticed his mother's black medallion intermingled with the cords and monitors attached to his chest.

"Yes, you've been in a coma for some time now. I don't think–"

Tonya cut in, "This is impossible! Dr. Troodle, do you understand what he's saying?"

"Yes, of course. Your friend speaks Pudo quite nicely–no accent at all."

She shook her head and said again, "This is impossible."

"What's impossible?" Simon said. He tried to recall the circumstances that had led him to his current predicament, but his memories were disjointed.

"*You can't speak Pudo,*" she yelled, her hair turning red. "Do you think that every paraworld speaks the same language? *No!* That's why we cast the language spell when we arrive at a new parallel world."

"Calm down." Her hysterical behavior took him by surprise. "Maybe I cast the language spell by accident when I had your wand."

"Believe me, runt, you have no magical abilities. Remember on Earth when you tried to stop the car before we started flying? Well, you were holding my wand backwards!"

Dr. Troodle intervened. "Konya is just jealous that you are such a quick learner." He laughed. "It took her two months to learn how to say, 'Where's the bathroom?'"

"My name is *Tonya*, not *Konya*," the girl fumed.

"Konya," Dr. Troodle said, adding more inflection in his voice.

"*TONYA! TONYA! TONYA!*" she roared.

The man tried again. "Konya."

"*AAAH!*" she yelled. "If I have to live in this parallel one more day, I'll go bonkers!"

Simon smirked. "Why don't you just cast that dumb language spell you were talking about?"

"Because there aren't any electro-magical waves on this planet," she barked. "Impossible, you say? *Noooo*–not for *Konya*! The one paraworld out there without magic and I happen to find it."

This didn't seem too unnatural for the boy, especially since he had just recently discovered that magical waves covered his own planet, but then the realization hit him that without E.M. waves he couldn't get back home.

"So are you saying we're stuck here?"

"Bingo! Give that boy a prize."

The doctor removed the monitors from Simon's bare chest. "It's obvious from your physiology," he noted, "that you're not from our world, but all this talk about parallel worlds and magic makes my head hurt. What's important now is that we find out how you're feeling, young man."

Simon took a deep breath of clean air and noticed the unfamiliar sensations throughout his body. The aches and pains he normally felt were gone, and for the first time in his life, he didn't feel the nagging urge to take a puff from his inhaler.

"I feel good," he said with a smile. "I feel really, really good."

"Fantastic," said Dr. Troodle. "When you first came to our world–"

"So I *am* in a different world," he said. "What do you call it?"

"Oh, I'm sorry. Pudo is what we call it. When you first came to Pudo, your motorized contraption was totaled, and you lost both of your legs, and you broke some bones in your face, and–"

"*What?*" Simon cried, grasping for his legs.

"Don't worry, Simon," Tonya reassured him. Her hair had already turned back to its natural green color. "They put your legs back on. I guess that's one thing I have to admit about this world–these people are geniuses. They have the best medical skills I've ever seen, and their knowledge of math and science is just phenomenal. Even their language is complex–" She turned her head away in shame. "Well, you wouldn't know about that."

"Hello, everyone!" a small boy entering the room called out in a high-pitched voice. He held a computer tablet in his hand and flaunted an enormous smile that stretched from one side of his face to the other. Dr. Troodle nodded to the boy and stepped away to talk to a nurse.

"I take it back–not everyone in this world is intelligent. Here's one right now who took a belly flop in the gene pool." She smiled at the boy as he approached. "Hi, *Thorny.*"

"How are you doing, Butblacruze?" he responded joyfully.

Simon laughed, but Tonya got upset because she couldn't understand the word the boy had just used. She begged, "Okay, Simon, tell me what he said."

The pint-sized boy looked at the bed in shock. "Oh, he's awake! Does he understand what we're saying?"

"Yes." Tonya frowned. "Somehow or another, he can speak Pudo." She turned to Simon and asked even more earnestly than before, "So, Simon, what was that word he just called me? I looked it up once, but the definition didn't make any sense. I'm still learning this stupid language."

"Don't tell her!" the boy said quickly. "That would ruin our fun." He extended his hand to Simon. "Hi, I'm Thornapple Troodle. I've been reading to you every day so we could be friends when you woke up. I've been dying to ask you something for months now."

"What is it?" Simon asked, shaking the boy's tiny hand.

"How do you kill the end boss on level ten? For the life of me, I can't seem to get past that part!"

Simon knew exactly what he was talking about. "You've been playing my video games? You're going to use up all my batteries."

"Batteries? So that's what you call them. I drained your *batteries* months ago. I want to make some new ones, but Father won't let me."

Dr. Troodle returned and spoke up. "I told you, son, to forget about it. That machine is a waste of time. It doesn't teach you anything of value. How are you ever going to get accepted to the university if your head is in the clouds?"

"But, Father, I don't want to go to the university. I want to be a painter."

The doctor cringed. "We've discussed this before, Thornapple. Our society has little need for art. You will go to the university, and you will like it."

"I will *not* go to the university!" The boy pouted. "And I would *not* like it! You just don't understand me." Thornapple ran out of the room and slammed the door.

Dr. Troodle turned to Simon and explained, "He's just going through puberty right now. All those hormones are impairing his judgement. Let's get you dressed, shall we?"

Simon tucked the sheets around himself. He had almost forgotten he was naked. The doctor tossed him a bundle of clothing and pushed a button on the bed stand. Immediately, an orange barrier rose from all four sides of the bed, blocking Simon from everyone's view.

Simon proceeded to get dressed in the Pudo clothing. "So what do you call yourselves?" he asked, trying to talk through the barrier.

"Puds," Dr. Troodle answered.

"So is everyone . . . is everyone . . . um . . ."

"Small?"

"Yeah."

"I'm actually quite tall for my species. In fact, Thornapple is the tallest one in his class at school. I suspect that someday he'll become a giant Pud if he keeps eating the way he does. How big are the people on your planet?"

"Well, I'm the smallest one in my class at school."

"That's amazing! Your people truly are giants. I wish my colleagues could be here to see you. To be quite frank, after taking a biological scan of your body, most of the scientists have had little reason to study you further. They're not really concerned with your behavior patterns, but your knack for the Pudo language might perk their interest. I must say the excitement of having alien visitors has died down considerably over the past few months."

"Ha! That doesn't stop your people from probing me whenever they can," Tonya said with a scowl.

"Your body is much more interesting than Simon's," the doctor said.

Tonya adjusted her tight shirt. "Yeah, I bet."

"Okay, I'm finished," Simon announced.

Dr. Troodle pressed the button on the bed stand, and the orange shield lowered. "You look funny," Tonya said between giggles. Simon wore a bright green shirt with yellow pants and white suspenders.

"You're not so hot yourself," he retorted.

Tonya looked like a baby doll that had been dressed in the wrong-sized clothing. Simon couldn't tell if she was wearing pants or just really long shorts, and he debated whether or not to mention that the seams on her thin shirt were coming undone.

"Hey, in some parallels this is pretty fashionable! Come on, Simon, let me show you around."

Simon leapt out of the bed, but the second his feet touched the floor, his legs wobbled around as if they were made of gelatin. He collapsed.

"Oh, dear," said Dr. Troodle. "I was afraid something like this would happen. We've never done surgery on a person like you before. We didn't put your legs on backwards, did we?"

"No, they're okay. I just don't seem to have very much strength in them anymore." He tried to stand but couldn't. "I can move my legs all right, but I can't put any weight on them."

"How peculiar. I assume you'll need some strenuous therapy before you'll be able to walk properly."

"I volunteer to help," Tonya said. "It's my fault he's in this mess in the first place."

"Thank you, Konya. I'll write up a program immediately. Nurse Salfree, fetch me a hover chair."

Soon, the nurse presented what Simon assumed was a hover chair, but it didn't have a back or any legs to it. Dr. Troodle and Tonya lifted Simon onto the seat. The doctor pressed a button, and two armrests–as well as a backrest–popped up. Simon felt the chair rise off the ground and hover in midair.

"Use this little stick to steer and these buttons to go up and down," the doctor instructed.

"This is awesome," Simon said, laughing. "It's just like my video games."

"Well," the doctor admitted, "I suppose your games do have some value to them after all."

■ ■ ■

Throughout the day, Tonya tried to help Simon walk, but to no avail; his legs just wouldn't cooperate. Simon stood between two bars and tried to pull himself forward. His shoulders hurt from holding his weight off the ground, and he became frustrated.

"Just a few more minutes, and then we'll start you on some leg exercises," said Nurse Salfree. She walked off to help another patient.

"Hello, everyone!" Thornapple announced as he made his loud entrance into the room. "Father wanted me to invite you two to dinner tonight." He looked at Simon dangling his feet above the ground. "How's it going?"

"Things would be going better if we didn't have any interruptions," Tonya said.

"Oh, come on, Butblacruze. I just want to help," he responded tenaciously.

"Don't call me that."

"Why? What's wrong with calling you Butblacruze?"

"Thornapple, if she doesn't want you to call her that, then don't," Simon said in a protective tone of voice. Regardless of the chivalrous gesture towards his friend, he still had to force himself not to smile at Thornapple's brave use of the word.

"Sorry," the boy said, hanging his head down. He shuffled his feet a little, then perked up and said, "You can call me Thorn if you want. All my friends do. What do your friends call you?"

"Simon."

"Oh," he said, discouraged. "Is it all right if I call you Simon?"

"Yeah, sure."

The boy smiled so widely that it looked like the top of his head was going to slip off. He jumped between the bars and lifted himself up so that he was almost level with Simon.

"I'm going to be a painter someday," he said, veering the conversation towards himself.

"What do you want to paint?" Simon asked, trying to be friendly; he wasn't accustomed to all this attention.

"Everything!" Thorn swung back and forth on the bars. "I want to paint the stars and the moon and the trees and the flowers and the–"

"And the stones and the pebbles and the rocks and the sand and the–we get the point, Thornapple," Tonya interrupted. "You wanna know what I want to be someday, Simon?"

"Not really," Thorn answered bluntly on Simon's behalf.

She gave Thorn a dirty look. "I'm going to be an E.M. Enforcer."

"What's that?" both Simon and Thorn asked at the same time.

"You've never heard of an E.M. Enforcer?"

"I never heard of E.M. *anything* until I met you, remember?" Simon answered.

"Well, an E.M. Enforcer is an elite magician–best of the best–who travels the paraverse and maintains the magical law. I guess you've never heard of the king and queen either?"

"Nope."

"Every paraworld has their own government and leaders, but they all answer to the High King for the basic universal laws. King Vaylen is the greatest sorcerer in the paraverse, and he sends the E.M. Enforcers out to enforce the law and to run his secret errands."

"What kind of laws are we talking about?" Thorn asked.

"You know–the basic stuff: misuse of magic, summoning demons, destroying cities–"

"Well, I'm glad to hear that destroying cities is against the law," Thorn joked.

Simon laughed.

"It's not that funny," Tonya chided, "if you happen to live in the city that's being destroyed."

"What do you want to be when you grow up?" Thorn asked Simon.

"I don't really know." Simon thought for a moment. "I think it would be fun to program video games."

"You wanna program–*video games?*" Tonya said as though she were saying a dirty word.

"Well, I guess I could be the supreme ruler of the universe instead," Simon said with a chuckle. "That is, unless the position is already filled."

Thorn beamed ecstatically. "Tell you what. I'll paint the worlds and the characters, and you can program them into a video game." He jumped down from the metal bars. "That reminds me. I brought your stuff." He opened a large bag and took out Simon's fanny pack. "Here's your video game machine–you still need to tell me how to get past level ten–and here's your glasses–you broke them in your crash, but I fixed them for you. My father says you don't need glasses, but I think they look cool."

Simon put his glasses on, and they instantly suctioned to his face.

"I improved them," Thorn said. "They won't come off unless you press this button to release them."

"Wow," Tonya said facetiously. "You must have a lot of time on your hands."

"Okay, kids," said Nurse Salfree. "Simon needs to get back to work."

Simon could barely hold onto the bars another second, so he was relieved when the nurse, a husky woman with bushy hair, suggested that he do some leg exercises on the floor.

"So, I'll see you at dinner?" Thorn asked, getting ready to leave.

"We'll be there," Simon responded as the nurse helped him to the floor.

"Great! Be there at six sharp. See ya later, everyone!" he shouted to the occupants of the room so they'd notice his grand exit.

"And good riddance," Tonya said after Thorn had shut the door.

"What do you have against him?" Simon asked. He raised his leg off the ground for a moment and then put it back down.

"Thornapple is such a weirdo. Don't you see how he tries to get everyone to like him? He pretends to have all these friends, but the truth is, nobody likes him."

Simon looked at her and said slowly, "Maybe that's a reason to be his friend."

Tonya's hair turned steel blue. She opened her mouth but said nothing. In fact, she didn't say much at all until dinner.

CHAPTER 8
MENABAWS AND DRAGUNOS

"I hope you like menabaws," Mrs. Troodle said, carrying a tray full of strange-looking appetizers to the table. "I made them myself."

"Sweetie, why don't you leave the cooking to Har?" Dr. Troodle suggested as he bit into something that resembled a squid.

"I think it's good for me to cook every once in a while," she replied. "It's kind of fun."

Simon picked up a squid and looked at it closely. Three bulbous eyes stared back at him, and a mess of long tentacles dangled from his hand. Suddenly, one of the eyes blinked.

"*Ahhh!*" Simon yelled, dropping the squid on the table. It started to squirm away.

"Must not have cooked that one long enough," Dr. Troodle said, grabbing the squid and popping it in his mouth. The tentacles thrashed about the doctor's lips as he chewed. "So," he said, devouring the appetizer, "what's for dinner?"

"Honey, don't talk with your mouth full," his wife scolded with a painted-on smile. She then yelled at the top of her lungs, "Har, get in here right now!"

A large, portly boy rushed into the room, carrying a heavy tray of food. He had a much darker complexion than the other Puds, and he towered over them as well. He was even taller than Tonya–but definitely not skinnier.

"Sorry, ma'am," the boy said in a slow sort of drawl.

"Well, hurry it up," Mrs. Troodle urged.

Har served each person at the table. Tonya was first. On her plate lay a mound of long green grass with a multitude of colorful seeds spread about a lonely acorn. Simon shook his head in surprise until he remembered that the food selection on her plate was actually normal for a citizen of Paraworld Chamel. He felt sorry for Tonya because he knew she'd rather be eating a hamburger.

The adults both had the same meal: a large, black spider with various bits of vegetables surrounding the furry body. The arachnid lay on its back with its foot-long legs sticking up.

Simon cringed when Dr. Troodle snapped off a leg. The loud crunching sound was reminiscent of a crab shell being cracked open. After savoring the scent for a moment, the doctor bit into the soft, white meat sticking out of the end. While chewing vigorously, he looked up at Simon's horrified expression and said with a grin, "I'd rather be eating them, instead of them eating me."

His wife chuckled profusely at the joke.

Simon and Thorn received their food last. On each of their plates lay what appeared to be a huge, slimy maggot. Its grayish white skin had the appearance of rubber. It had no eyes, and it was easily the length of Simon's forearm. A small snippet of parsley rested atop the worm. At that moment, Simon wished very badly that he could trade meals with Tonya.

"Well, dig in!" Mrs. Troodle said.

Simon felt relieved that she didn't suggest they pray over the food. Mrs. Trimble, back at the foster home, always insisted on saying grace over all their meals. But in this instance, Simon felt that God himself couldn't possibly bless the revolting creature before him.

Staring at the thick worm, he hoped that it too would try to crawl off the table, but luck was not on his side. He looked over at Tonya. She sat in a placid manner, eating her grass. He looked over at Thorn, who was gorging voraciously on the fat worm in front of him. As the little Pud's fork ripped open the worm's hide, clear mucus seeped from the torn flesh and ran down onto the table. Simon's stomach lurched.

"Simon, you're not eating. What's wrong?" asked Mrs. Troodle.

"I don't feel very well," he said. The woman's eyes widened, and Simon felt nervous that he might have offended her. "I-I-I think it m-m-must be the shock of leaving my w-w-world . . . and g-g-getting into an accident." Mrs. Troodle still had a look of disbelief, so Simon continued. "And . . . just waking up from a c-c-coma . . . and . . . and not being able to w-w-walk."

"Oh, you poor thing," she said, as if talking to a little puppy. She turned to her husband. "Honey, I think we should let Simon and Konya stay with us."

"*YES!*" Thorn exclaimed. His dinner slipped off his plate and slid towards Simon. "Sorry." The Pud grabbed the oversized larva with both hands and placed it back onto his plate.

"Well, Sweetie, I don't know. We only have one guest room–"

"Simon can share my room," Thorn said eagerly.

Tonya rolled her eyes. "Oh, Mrs. Troodle, you're too kind, but I wouldn't want to–what's the word?–intrude," the young girl said carefully in the Pudo language.

"Nonsense! Konya, you've been staying in the hospital ever since you got here. Besides, now that Simon's awake, I don't think Nurse Salfree is going to allow you to sleep on that cot anymore."

"Come on, Butblacruze," cried Thorn. "You'll like it here."

The girl crinkled her nose. Simon sensed her inner conflict. If she continued to stay in the hospital, she could convince herself that her visit to Pudo was only temporary. Accepting the Troodles' invitation to live in a real house meant acknowledging that she was never going to leave this parallel world. But after more prods from Thornapple, she finally gave in.

"Fine, it's settled then," Mrs. Troodle said. "Konya will stay in the guest room, and Simon will bunk with Thornapple."

Simon felt strange listening to everyone plot out his future so quickly. All of this was so new to him. He was in another world! In a way, it excited the boy. He could start all over with his life. Perhaps he wouldn't be such a nerd this time. He would be part of a family–a strange family, but a family, nonetheless. The thought intrigued him.

"Come on, Simon. I'll show you my room," Thorn said, jumping up from the table.

"Hold on there, son," Dr. Troodle said. "We haven't even finished dinner yet."

Mrs. Troodle nodded. "At least have some dessert, Simon." She called for the large boy in the kitchen. "*HAR! DESSERT! NOW!*"

Har bounded into the room again, this time with a bowl of yellow custard. At first glance, it didn't seem too bad, but when Mrs. Troodle started dishing out the dessert, Simon saw what was floating in the mixture.

"Eyeball custard?" she asked with a smile.

■ ■ ■

Later that night, Simon, Thornapple, and Tonya decided to get some fresh air before retiring to bed. The Troodles lived next door to the hospital, which was very convenient for Dr. Troodle, since he served as the head physician for the facility. Consequently, their backyard happened to be a large stretch of grass leading to the entrance of the north hospital wing.

The three children found a nice spot to lie down and gaze up at the stars. Simon lay in the middle with Tonya to his right and Thorn to his left. A cool, night breeze caressed their faces. The stars illuminated the sky to form a sea of tiny flickering dots.

"It's amazing," Tonya said in awe.

"What is?" asked Thorn.

"That no matter what paraworld you're on, there's always one constant: the stars."

"Oh, wow!" Simon said, pointing at the sky. "There's the Big Dipper! I didn't realize the stars would be the same as they are back home."

"Yep," Tonya said. "With each paraworld, the solar system changes, but everything else in the universe stays the same. That's one of the biggest indications that we're not actually traveling across the universe but into another *parallel* universe. I wish I had my paratransmitter. I'm sure it could give you a better definition than I could."

"That's all right. I think I understand," Simon said. "You know, that kinda makes sense."

"What do you mean by *Big Dipper?*" Thorn asked. "All I see is a poorly designed quadrilateral."

"Just imagine that it's a cup, and those stars over there are the handle," Simon said.

Thorn looked again in frustration. "I see an obtuse triangle."

"Look harder."

"I suppose it looks somewhat like an isosceles trapezoid." The small boy squinted for a while and then shouted with joy as if he'd just discovered the world was round and not flat. "I see it! You're right! It does look like a *big dipper!* Why didn't I ever see that before?"

Tonya answered, "Because you've been trained your whole life to think a certain way. You've been taught to not be imaginative, so it's no wonder the only thing you could see was geometric shapes."

"Oh, I can't believe it," Thorn exclaimed again. "I found another one!"

"That's the Little Dipper," Simon said. "You know, Thorn, if you want to be a painter some day, you're going to have to learn to see things in a different way."

"That'll be the day," Tonya snorted. "I haven't seen a Pud yet with one ounce of artistic creativity."

Simon swatted at a large fly buzzing around his face, but the insect kept dodging his hand. Suddenly, Tonya lashed out her long tongue and snatched the bug out of the air. She quickly brought it into her mouth.

"Tonya!" Simon cried, shocked.

"You don't get many dates, do you?" Thorn said sarcastically.

"Sorry. I'm not allowed to do that on Chamel. It was just too tempting."

"You weren't kidding when you said you had lizard DNA in you," Simon remarked. He realized there was still a lot about Tonya he didn't know about.

"What do you call that bright star over there?" Thorn asked.

"Where I'm from, we call that the North Star," Simon answered.

Tonya answered as well. "On Chamel, we call it the Fulcrum of Life."

"Why do you call it that?" Simon asked.

"Because it's one of the most prominent stars, and it points the direction we should navigate our lives towards."

"Which is?" Thorn pressed.

"Heaven. The Elders of Chamel teach that if we live our lives so that we are continually climbing upward in our personal progression, then some day we will reach the Fulcrum of Life."

"Sounds silly," Thorn said. "You do know that stars are just giant balls of burning gas, don't you?

"Of course I do," Tonya said, annoyed.

Simon noted, "On Earth, people traveling on the sea sometimes use the North Star to help them find their bearings."

"Yeah, we also use the North Star, as you call it, to help us find our way," Tonya said. "I remember one time, when my parents were still together, we were going to this big party where my dad was the guest of honor. We had to walk to the party because I was too young to use magic to travel. The street was very busy, and my parents were in a hurry, and, somehow or another, I got separated from them. I remember it was pretty dark outside, and the Fulcrum of Life was shining especially bright that night. I had this feeling inside that if I just walked in the direction of that star, I'd be okay. Well, by the time I found the party, it was over. My parents were talking to some people, and when I walked up to them . . ." Tonya paused for a moment and reflected on the memory, ". . . they didn't even realize I had been missing."

"I'm sorry," Simon said. "That's terrible."

"It's okay. I guess they had a lot on their minds, and I was so young at the time. Maybe if I wasn't such a–"

At that very moment, something large and green jumped over them and scurried away. Then, one by one, three huge men leapt over the children and chased after the giant reptile.

The body of the lizard stretched about seven feet long, and its spiny tail extended another six feet. It had a long forked tongue and a mouth full of razor-sharp teeth. The large, husky men stood at least eight feet tall, and each of them held a wooden club.

One of the giants grabbed the lizard by the tail, but the reptile snapped at him, so he quickly let go. As the men circled about, the creature opened its large mouth and hissed like a cobra. The blood-curdling noise sent shivers down everyone's spine.

Abruptly, the lizard reared on its hind legs and sprang towards one of the men. Falling back with the ferocious reptile on top of him, the man put his arms around the lizard and held on tightly. The two rolled on the ground until they stopped right in front of Tonya, who by this time was sitting up. The giant man squeezed with all his might until the lizard's body went limp.

Tonya was so petrified with fear that her hair turned completely white. The man looked up from his bear hug and said in a barbaric voice, "It OK–no be scared."

He loosened his viselike grip, and the lizard fell to the ground, lifeless. The other two giants helped the injured man stand up. Still unable to move, Tonya stared at the huge lizard. Suddenly, its small eyes opened quickly and made contact with her. Then it leapt into the air towards the helpless girl, but just before it reached her, a club crashed down upon the reptile with bone-shattering force. The horrible creature fell with a thud–this time, truly dead.

Before the children could say a word, the three men walked away into the shadows, carrying their prize on their broad shoulders.

When Simon, Thorn, and Tonya got back to the house, they told the adults about what had just happened. Furious, Thorn's father called the police and yelled at the person on the other end.

He said things like: "This is an outrage!" and "What are you idiots going to do about this epidemic?" and "This is the third time this month!"

Mrs. Troodle could see that her husband was going to be a while, so she sent the children to bed. Tonya didn't say a word as she left the room. Her hair was still white.

In Thorn's bedroom, Simon rolled out of his hover chair and landed on the soft mattress below. His feet reached the end of the makeshift bed that Thornapple had made for him. The only light in the room came from the moon, which shone brightly from the open window.

Before Thorn got too comfortable, Simon asked, "What was that monster back there?"

"That was a draguno. Every once in a while they climb up the mountain and get into the city, but lately, they've been showing up more and more."

"And who were those men that were chasing after it?"

"Those were *big* Puds. Normally, they're not allowed in the city after dark, but I bet the mayor let them in so they could track down that draguno. Personally, I don't know which one is the fouler of the two: the draguno or the big Puds."

"Is Har a big Pud?" Simon asked.

"Yeah, but he's only twelve years old. When they're young, they make good house servants, but when they get older, they're just too big to keep in the house. Usually, they're put to work outside of the city."

"Oh." Simon thought it odd that Thorn referred to the big Puds as servants.

Thornapple yawned. "Hey, do you think I could ride your hover chair tomorrow?"

"Sure."

The tiny boy smiled in response and closed his eyes. Everything remained quiet for a while, but then Thornapple broke the silence. "It's good to have you here, Simon. Good night."

"Good night."

Simon turned over in his bed and stared at the milky white moon. For a moment, he almost forgot he wasn't on Earth anymore. *Am I ever going to make it back home?* he wondered as he drifted off to sleep. *Probably not.*

CHAPTER 9
GUARDIANS OF THE CROWN

Councilor Bromwell, Lady Cassandra, and her younger brother, Lord Theobolt Vaylen, were discussing serious matters of state when Tabatha burst into the room.

"Sorry, my lady," cried a guard, attempting to restrain the catlike woman, "but this Enforcer insisted on seeing you immediately. I told her you were not to be disturbed, but–"

Cassandra raised her hand. "It's all right. Let her pass." The stately woman wore a white gown with pearls and gold trim. A white tiara graced her forehead, and colorful jewels sparkled in her hair.

"Guardians of the Crown," Tabatha addressed them, "I have grave news concerning the Raiders."

"Tabatha, my dear, we haven't heard from you in almost two months. We were beginning to worry," Lord Vaylen said in a kind voice. Tabatha scowled at the man. He had always insisted on being addressed by his last name so that whenever somebody referred to the royal family, he, Theobolt Vaylen, would be foremost in everyone's mind. She disliked his political and psychological tactics. He continued, "I see you are tired and hurt. We shall hear your report when your wounds have been attended to."

"My welfare is of no concern," she responded shortly. "I must speak now, for what I have to say concerns us all."

"Speak then, child," urged Councilor Bromwell.

The ancient man's voice was soothing yet wielded a strange power that only an ultramage could possess. Many had said that Ezra Bromwell was the greatest sorcerer of all save the king himself. His long white hair fell down from his gray, pointy hat–now drooping from age–and his thin glasses seemed poised to fall off the end of his prominent nose. To an outsider, he might have easily been mistaken as merely a feeble old man.

"The Raiders have gathered their forces and are planning an attack," Tabatha said. "I don't know where, and I don't know when–"

"What good is this information, then?" asked Lady Cassandra.

"My lady, I lived with the Raiders for over eight months, and from that dreary experience, I learned one important thing: The Raiders are willing to lay waste to the entire paraverse in order to fulfill their evil cause."

"And what exactly is their *cause?*" asked Lord Vaylen.

"Genocide," Tabatha said. A moment of silence passed, but the Guardians of the Crown remained speechless. "As you know, the Raiders feel that science should be the governing factor in the paraverse, not magic, but their twisted views have become increasingly strong. They now feel it is their destiny to kill everyone who uses the E.M. waves for magic. They want to conserve the electro-magical energy for themselves and for their scientific endeavors."

"This is grave news indeed," said Councilor Bromwell. "There is more than enough E.M. energy for both parties . . . Hmm, why do they need so much electro-magical power? I wonder . . ."

"That, I do not know," Tabatha responded. "However, we now have another foe to face. While on the space carrier, I stole a datachip from General Mayham that may have contained the answers we are looking for. I faced an ultramage whose powers rival even yours, Councilor Bromwell. He took the datachip from me and disappeared."

The old man raised his bushy eyebrows and scratched the stubble on his chin. "How do you know he was an ultramage?"

"The electro-magical waves were very thin above the planet, yet he was able to call upon them as if he were sitting inside an E.M. reactor . . . and on top of that, he cast the Valamure curse."

"He did?" cried Lord Vaylen in shock, upsetting the image of his normally strong composure. "Are you sure it was the Valamure curse and not just an illusion?"

"I saw the wraith with my own eyes. I barely made it out of there alive!"

"What did this ultramage look like?" asked Lady Cassandra.

"Well, I really didn't get to see his face because he hid under a cloak, not unlike yours, Lord Vaylen," Tabatha said, a hint of suspicion in her voice. She continued, "He was very fast and powerful, but the strangest thing of all was that he used a wand to cast his spells–two wands, in fact."

"*Ahhh,*" Lord Vaylen scoffed. "He's just an apprentice who probably got lost from his master–nothing more."

"No!" Tabatha fought back. "I tell you. He was an ultramage."

"Ms. Burke," Lord Vaylen said in a patronizing tone, "it is common knowledge that an ultramage does *not* require the aid of inanimate objects to cast spells. If your wizard friend truly was an ultramage, he would not have to depend on a little stick to channel his powers."

"Theobolt," Councilor Bromwell intervened on the woman's behalf, "may I remind you that not all ultramages are pigheaded enough to rely wholly on their own strengths. I, for one, have been known to use *sticks* to aid me from time to time." At that, he knocked on the hard floor two times with his wooden cane. A plume of pink butterflies rose from the ground like smoke and formed into a pretty flower that gently rested itself in Tabatha's white hair.

Disturbed by this, Lord Vaylen took off his black hood and revealed a deep scar that ran down the length of his face until it disappeared into his thick goatee. The man's sallow skin looked ready to fall off the bone, and his deep gray eyes recoiled as if they had never seen the light before. Rumor had it that Lord Vaylen had become terribly disfigured while defending the king's life in the Civil War against the Raiders over a decade ago. It was at that time that the Raiders split off from the kingdom and formed the Scientific Society, also known as the S.S.

Vaylen spoke with stern conviction. "All of the ultramages in the known paraverse have been accounted for. Ezra, are you telling me that you believe this feline? Do you honestly believe that a wizard could possibly become an ultramage without us knowing about it first? Why else have we created these so-called schools of magical learning, if not to discover this very thing?"

"Yes," Councilor Bromwell answered, "to all your questions."

Intercepting her brother's bubbling hostility, Lady Cassandra stepped in. "Tabatha, what evidence do you have to support these accusations?"

"None but my word."

Cassandra furrowed her brow. "I believe that you *think* you saw the Valamure curse. Many E.M. Enforcers even greater than you have been tricked by illusions of this sort before–"

"But it wasn't–"

"*And* General Mayham has proven in the past to be somewhat passionate with his views . . . but to destroy a whole race of magicians?"

"I'd say you were on that ship eight months too long," added Lord Vaylen.

"*However,*" Lady Cassandra continued, "these are strange times we live in. Since the disappearance of the king and queen, nothing has been the same. Tabatha, you've never given us reason to doubt you before. Is there anything more you can say that will help us decide on what course of action we should take?"

"I wish I would've discovered more information, but I left the carrier somewhat in a hurry–if you know what I mean. We were about to join up with another spaceship. I heard General Mayham say that the meeting would be an essential key to their success. I don't know who was in charge of the other ship, but I do know it was orbiting one of the moons of the Centarious paraworld."

"Drackus!" Councilor Bromwell blurted in disgust. He turned to the chief Guardian of the Crown and said, "Lady Cassandra, I fear that Griffen's position may be compromised. If only we could send word to him."

"Griffen Lasher?" Tabatha's pointy ears perked up.

Lady Cassandra said, "We sent Griffen to Centarious as a mediator, so he could cool things down between the Centarians and the Scientific Society. Captain Drackus is determined to conduct weapons experiments on the third moon of Centarious. Mining operations have ceased because the workers are too afraid that the Raiders will attack them while they're in the caves."

"We need to stop Griffen," Tabatha said frantically. "When General Mayham tells Captain Drackus that I stole the datachip, the S.S. will be furious with the royal family, and Griffen will be caught up in the middle!"

"It's too late," Lord Vaylen said. "He left hours ago. There's nothing really we can do now."

"Griffen Lasher is not expendable!" Tabatha said. "He's one of the greatest E.M. Enforcers we have. He's noble and brave and–"

Lord Vaylen interrupted, "Tabatha, my dear, if I didn't know better, I'd say you had feelings for this man."

Tabatha gasped, and her cheeks reddened. She closed her eyes and then opened them.

"Griffen is a great asset to the Crown," she said. "Besides, I wouldn't want him to die because of something I did. Let me warn him–please?"

Swayed by Tabatha's emotion, Lady Cassandra instructed, "You may take a small craft, *but*, know this: If what you said today is true, General Mayham will want revenge. Travel with speed, but if you find that you are too late, under no circumstances are you to pursue the Raiders . . ." Tabatha beamed with gratitude. "I don't want to lose a perfectly good spacecraft," Cassandra concluded with a smile.

"Thank you, my lady."

"Councilor Bromwell, will you escort Ms. Burke to the docking bay?"

"Of course I will," the old man said, putting his arm out for Tabatha to hold. They headed towards the exit, but before they reached the door, it swung open, and in rushed a bald man with a look of anger in his eyes. Lord Vaylen recognized Tonya's father at once.

"Sorry, my lady," came the distressed voice of the same guard as before, "but this man–"

"Mr. Doyle, how may we help you?" Lord Vaylen said.

"Lady Cassandra, Guardians of the Crown, how many months have gone by since my daughter was separated from that madman you call a teacher? I'm starting to lose track!"

"Excuse me," Councilor Bromwell said as he tried to get past the tall man, "but we have urgent business to attend to."

"That's all right," Mr. Doyle shouted. "I'm sure there's many more important things than the welfare of my daughter. Go ahead! See to your precious business."

"Thank you," Tabatha said, pushing Councilor Bromwell out the door.

Distraught, Mr. Doyle paced the room. The thin man wore an expensive business suit with a white, pinstriped shirt and black shoes to match. He didn't bother to put his leather briefcase down–an indication that he was on his way to some critical engagement. Large beads of sweat ran down his face. Although his head had been shaved, tiny stubs of vibrant red hair poked out of his scalp. It was an embarrassment for a shrewd businessman, such as himself, to allow anyone to see what he felt.

"With all the money I've thrown at this institution, you'd think people would be dying to help me find my daughter. But, alas, *NO*–All I get is excuses!" The man moved about the room furiously. "I get no respect, I get little help, and I get no results!"

"Mr. Doyle," Lord Vaylen said, trying to calm the man. "Let's take a walk in the garden. It's much cooler outside than in here."

The three adults strolled into the spacious courtyard and found themselves surrounded by lush vegetation and beautiful flowers. A small brooklet of clear water ran lazily around the perimeter, and multicolored birds sang in the distance. The school for the magically gifted could be seen over the tall trees, adjoining the huge castle. After a few moments in the tranquil environment, the little stubs of hair on Mr. Doyle's head faded into a subdued bluish hue.

"Mr. Doyle," Lord Vaylen said delicately, "we are very grateful for your generous contributions to the school and to the government. If your daughter is alive, I promise I'll personally see to it that she is brought back to the school safe and sound."

"How safe can she be with Leander Payne running the school?" The man's hair started to change colors again. "I demand that you replace that incompetent fool immediately!"

Lady Cassandra spoke up. "Mr. Doyle, we have no intention of releasing Principal Payne. He is a very competent supermage. In fact, it was he who discovered the pathway Tonya took when she split off from the class."

"Yes, but it was also *he* who was in charge of ensuring that the equipment was in good working order in the first place. My daughter is the most gifted student in her class, and I've surmised that the only plausible cause for her disappearance is that her paratransmitter must have been defective–well, I suppose it also could have been tampered with; I'm sure Tonya made a lot of students jealous." Mr. Doyle began pacing again. "Professor Gwyn is also to blame. That coward of a teacher should have gone after her. The only reason I haven't killed him myself is because of the simple fact that Tonya's still alive."

Lady Cassandra responded hesitantly, "Not to be insensitive, but how exactly do you know she's still alive?"

The man pointed to the silver band around his finger. "Life-ring," he stated. "I gave one to Tonya for her birthday. This light on the ring indicates her life force. She has an identical ring that shows her my life force."

"Amazing," Cassandra said. "I've never seen anything that traverses parallel worlds like this. I imagine it took an impressive amount of skill and magic to create these rings."

"Well, I paid an impressive amount of money for them. They're one of a kind," he boasted. "But anyway, that's beside the point. Lord Vaylen, you said that if Tonya was still alive, you'd bring her back to the school safely. Now you know she's alive, so I'm going to hold you to your promise."

"Of course, Mr. Doyle," the cloaked man said politely. "The pathway your daughter took led to an uncharted region of the parastream. If you will excuse me, I'll prepare another search party immediately."

"You're a good man, Theobolt," Mr. Doyle said. "It's a pity you're not the king."

"The Power of the Ancients has passed over me," Lord Vaylen explained, seeing the disturbed expression on his sister's face. "The magical force will bestow itself only on the rightful heir of the throne. I was late in the race–albeit by mere seconds, a minute perhaps–and the honor was given to my good brother instead."

"But you are next in line to be king."

"True," Lord Vaylen said. Cassandra became more agitated. "However, as your life-ring reassures you that your daughter is alive, my lack of receiving the Power of the Ancients reassures me that my brother and his wife are still alive. And if all goes well, I will never have the burden of carrying the Crown."

"Curse the rebellion!" Mr. Doyle spat. "Whatever happened in the Civil War to cause the king and queen to go into hiding is simply deplorable. How many more years must we wait before their return?"

"Who knows? Only time will tell," Lord Vaylen responded. "Only time will tell." The cloaked man limped to the edge of the courtyard. "Until we meet again." He disappeared down one of the garden walkways.

Mr. Doyle raised his briefcase. "Well, thank you for your time, my lady, but I really must go now." He started to leave.

"If there's anything more we can do for you–"

"No, thank you. You've been more than helpful already." Without waiting for a response from Lady Cassandra, he rushed down one of the secluded pathways.

A few moments later, he heard the voice of Lord Vaylen talking to someone in the shadows. Mr. Doyle hid behind a tall partition of shrubbery. He put his ear to the wall of foliage and listened in on their private conversation.

"We can't just let them blow up everything they fancy," the stranger whispered.

"Yes, I know that, but I now have some leverage that will keep them in check," Lord Vaylen hissed under his black hood.

"What possible leverage could you have with the Raiders?" the man asked incredulously.

"All in good time, my friend. All in good time. I will be delayed for a short while. I promised an important benefactor I'd find his daughter, and I am a man of my word."

"Yes, of course, Lord Vaylen, but until your return, how shall we deal with the Raiders?"

"Let them be."

"Begging your pardon, my lord, but is that a wise decision?"

"I have my reasons. The council will just have to be patient."

"Lord Vaylen, there are some in the Senate who believe that the Guardians of the Crown can no longer bring order to the paraverse. Many grow tired of waiting for your brother's return. Others disbelieve that the Power of the Ancients even exists. They feel it is just a story perpetuated by the Guardians for the purpose of bringing compliance to your laws."

"How dare they forget the supreme power of King Vaylen!" the cloaked man exclaimed. "Without the Power of the Ancients, the whole paraverse would crumble and fall into utter chaos. It is the very fabric that binds the parallel worlds together!"

"Yes," the man said, "but it has been over a decade since anyone has witnessed this power you speak of. With the attacks of the Raiders on the rise and the recent leak of information to our enemies, our patience has grown thin."

"One day the Senate will see the awesome Power of the Ancients, and when they do they will cower in submission. Leave the Raiders to me. I have Drackus and Mayham in the palm of my hand."

"All right then," the stranger said. "I will relay your message to the Senate. Farewell, my lord."

The two men parted ways, leaving Mr. Doyle alone in the garden to muse upon the conversation he had just overheard. He twisted a jewel on one of his rings, and a faint hologram of a man appeared in the air.

"Drackus," Mr. Doyle rasped, "I have some interesting news for you . . ."

■ ■ ■

At the docking bay, Tabatha and Councilor Bromwell were saying their goodbyes. A young couple with catlike characteristics stood a few paces off; their tails intertwined in a romantic gesture. Tabatha glanced in their direction, and they both cringed as if they'd just smelled something horrible.

The ultramage spoke. "Listen to me, Tabatha. You have sacrificed a great deal to serve the Crown, and because of this, you have been ostracized by your people. Your tail was removed in order to conceal your identity, and you have joined the Order of Gee–both of which are disgraceful in the eyes of your paraworld; nevertheless, your law expressly forbids you to become involved romantically with another race."

Tabatha stopped him right there. "I'm not involved with Griffen!"

"Hush, child," he said, quieting the woman. "I've seen the way you look at him when he enters the room. It is more than mere admiration I see in your eyes. I say this as a warning and not by command: Be careful that the passion of the moment does not dilute your vision of the future prize that awaits you in life. You are still young. Be patient."

"Thank you for your wisdom, Counselor Bromwell, but I have no intentions of getting involved with anyone, let alone a pompous outsider like Griffen."

"Very well then. I told the young man to stop at Parallel World 698 to recharge his electro-magical thrusters before heading to the next jump point. I'll set the coordinates for you." At that, the old man waved his hand, and the space shuttle lights lit up. Tabatha climbed into the tiny vessel and looked down at Councilor Bromwell.

He spoke again. "Griffen is very diligent in what we ask of him. Although he will be forced to stop several times on the way to recharge his ship, I suspect that he will neither rest nor eat until he is at Centarious. If only we knew how to communicate through the parastream, we could save ourselves a lot of grief. It may take days before you catch up with him. Good luck and godspeed."

Tabatha sealed the cockpit and maneuvered the ship towards the open bay doors. She engaged her E.M. thrusters, and the spacecraft shot out into the sky like a rocket. Councilor Bromwell watched as blue electricity wrapped itself around the shuttle, forming a magical bubble. A second later, the ship exploded against the white clouds and entered the parastream.

CHAPTER 10
FORGOTTEN LANGUAGE

Simon found himself floating in a sea of swirling mist. He felt as though his heart might burst when he saw the beautiful young woman emerge from the billowing clouds above. The majestic beast carried her gracefully down the marble staircase and brought her close enough for Simon to see the loving expression on her face. She spoke.

Great potential awaits at the door,
yet doubt consumes your soul.
Watch, therefore, for pride's deep snare.
It eats, ever hungry, consuming all
yet is never satisfied–wanting more and more,
devouring mighty kings of worlds,
as well as lowly paupers without lands or gold.
Peace, equality, and civility must subdue the beast's hunger
lest this evil destroy you all
and the enemy, long since forgotten, returns to rule once more.

Simon didn't understand her message, but he held onto each and every word as if they fell from the lips of a goddess. Oh, how her sweet voice rang forth in a harmonious string of music whose melody could outplay a whole symphony of musicians! The boy's tender heart reeled in torment as the mysterious woman turned to leave.

"Wait!" Simon pleaded. "What's your name?"

She turned her head and smiled, her countenance white and pure. Remaining silent, she blew Simon a kiss and disappeared into the clouds as she had done before.

"Simon . . . Simon . . . Simon, wake up! You'll be late for school."

"Go away, Dimitri," he moaned.

"What? Who's Dimitri?"

Simon opened his eyes to see Thornapple's smiling face, and it suddenly dawned on him that he wasn't in the orphanage anymore.

"I had that dream again," he told the midget-sized boy.

"The one about your dream girl?"

"She's not my dream girl," he said defensively. "Besides, she's probably ten years older than me."

"Then why do you keep dreaming about her?"

"I don't know. She seems familiar somehow. She keeps telling me that something bad is going to happen."

"Well, it's been almost a thousand years since we've had any wars, and the astronomers don't detect any rogue meteors headed our way . . . Oh, I know what it could be!"

"What?"

"Something bad is going to happen to you if you don't go to the dance next week."

"How can I dance when I can't even walk?" Simon asked. He crawled out of bed and flopped onto his hover chair.

"It's been two months now. You're not trying hard enough . . . or maybe you just don't want to walk so you won't have to go to the dance."

Thornapple didn't realize how close to the truth he really was; the upcoming week terrified Simon. The dance was part of a festival that commemorated the thousand-year anniversary of the Battle of Lisardious: a confrontation that almost wiped out the whole race of Puds–big and small.

"You better get ready for school," Thornapple warned. "If you're late one more time for Mrs. Larz's class, she'll have your hide for sure."

If Simon loathed going to school on Earth, it was nothing compared to what he felt now. Mrs. Larz was a plump lady about three-and-a-half feet tall. She had long tangled hair and a demeanor that made cockroaches look good. The only thing that made the class half bearable for Simon was that Tonya had to suffer through it with him.

When Simon and Tonya got to the school that morning, they waved goodbye to Thornapple as he entered a classroom full of other students his age. Simon and Tonya were deemed *intellectually challenged* by the school examiners, but because the Puds held strong beliefs that everyone should go to school (that is, if you weren't a big Pud), the two children were allowed to sit in with the kindergartners.

They sat at their tiny desks just as the school bell rang. Mrs. Larz waddled to her chair and plopped down. She brought out what looked like a red crayon and started drawing on her desk. Each mark appeared magnified in the air at the front of the classroom.

"How do you find the volume of a square pyramid?" Mrs. Larz asked. She drew a pyramid on her desk.

Everyone in the room raised their hands–except for Simon and Tonya.

"Ralfus," she said, calling on one of the students in the front.

Ralfus stood up and recited the formula from memory. "The volume of a square pyramid equals the altitude times the area of the base, divided by three."

"Very good, Ralfus. I see that *most* of you have done your homework." She glared at Simon and Tonya distastefully. "Now here's a trick question: We haven't looked at other types of pyramids yet, but who can tell me what formula I'd use to find the volume of a hexagonal pyramid?"

She drew a pyramid with a six-sided base and pushed a button for it to automatically rotate in the air. The children wrote frantically on their desks to come up with the answer.

Simon turned to Tonya and said under his breath, "When I was as young as these kids, I think I was still learning the alphabet. This is ridiculous."

Tonya smiled and tried to choke back a laugh.

"Simon," Mrs. Larz said, overhearing his comment, "do you have the answer for us?"

Simon's heart sank. Mrs. Larz seemed to always call on him, even though he never had the correct answer. This time being no exception, he stuttered, "Wh-Wh-What Ralfus said."

The four- and five-year-olds laughed, but Mrs. Larz silenced them with her raised hand. "That," she said calmly, "is correct." Her words shocked the entire class, including Simon. "The volume of *any* pyramid can be found using the same formula."

Tonya looked at Simon with newfound respect, but all he could do in response was shrug his shoulders and smile.

"All right, class," the teacher said, erasing the marks on her desk with her sleeve, "I think that's all the math for today. I just wanted to make sure you understood yesterday's lesson. Today, I would like to discuss an important subject that I'm sure you've all heard about: the Battle of Lisardious. I have with me a copy of an ancient record written by our ancestors a thousand years ago."

She brought out a thin slate with a computer screen attached to it.

"After long, strenuous research, our scientists have been able to translate the history of this great battle. The top line shows the ancient text, and the bottom line shows the translation. Let's read the translation, shall we? Please read a paragraph and then pass it along."

Mrs. Larz walked to the back of the class and handed the slate to a tiny girl wearing pigtails. The child began to read. "Only a few of our kind have survived the great Battle of Lisardious. We have been driven into the darkness of the volcano in hopes that our enemy will not follow."

The girl with pigtails passed the slate to a boy next to her, and the boy continued the history. "The larger Puds are a hindrance to our progression. We have started to fight amongst ourselves."

The boy passed the slate to Tonya. Rosy streaks appeared in her hair as she stammered over the words. "Uh, we are *jogging*–no–*running* out of food. Um, let's see. I-do-not-see-how-we-can . . ." Tonya couldn't remember how to say the last word. "I don't see how we can . . ."

"Survive!" Mrs. Larz filled in the rest of the sentence for her.

Bowing her head, Tonya handed the slate to Simon. He looked down at the Pudo language and, as usual, the strange characters morphed into English before his eyes. Simon assumed that being able to read Pudo was just part of his unique gift.

"Millions of these monstrous creatures are emerging from the sea every hour. Our crops have been consumed, and everything we have labored to build has been destroyed in less than a day. Could this be the same apocalypse our ancestors faced a thousand years ago? We have concluded that it–"

"Simon, what are you reading?" Mrs. Larz asked, trotting over to his desk. "That's not how it goes." She looked at the computer screen. "Show me where you are."

Simon pointed to where he was reading. Mrs. Larz snatched the slate from him and exclaimed, "You're not even reading from the correct line! Didn't I say the translation was *beneath* the actual text? Simon, you need to listen better."

"But all you said was to read a paragraph and pass it along."

"Don't get smart with me, young man. It took our best scholars years to decipher this ancient language. Class, this is what the actual translation reads: 'The aliens are increasing in numbers, and they ride upon the seas. The aliens are stealing our food and are trying to take possession of our cities. It will take us many years to rebuild what has been destroyed.'"

Mrs. Larz handed the slate to the next student. Simon stayed quiet for the rest of the class. Afterwards, he and Tonya met up with Thorn in the hallway.

"You should have seen the look on Mrs. Larz's face," Tonya said, laughing. "She was so furious. That was quick thinking, Simon. I don't think I could have made all that up so fast."

"But I wasn't making it up," Simon said.

"Of course you were. You can't read ancient Pu–" She stopped herself, suddenly recalling how Simon had miraculously learned the Pudo language just after waking up from his coma. "You *weren't* making it up?"

"No."

Thorn chimed in, "Wow! Do you know what this means? Simon could solve the mysteries of Pudo's history. Our scientists still don't know what the aliens looked like and how they invaded the planet so quickly without being detected."

Simon adjusted his glasses. "I don't think they were aliens."

"Really? That contradicts everything our scientists have claimed for generations! We should go to the library after school. I wonder if they'd let us into the historical section so you could read some of the ancient history books."

Tonya responded sarcastically, "That sounds *real* fun, but after school, Simon has therapy–with me."

"Oh, come on, Simon," Thorn said. "You can miss one therapy session."

"Well, I guess I could."

Tonya frowned and was about to say something, but the school bell cut her off. "Oh, darn. We're late for physics class," she said wryly.

■ ■ ■

Physics class was as boring as ever and so was computer science, microbiology, and genetics. When school ended for the day, Simon and Thornapple went to the library, but Tonya decided to go home.

The library was a magnificent building, made of thick granite walls that climbed upwards towards the sky. The courthouse, the sheriff's department, and several other prominent buildings stood within the same complex as the library.

Simon felt as if he were about to enter the cave of a huge stone mountain. Thornapple pushed the humongous library doors open, and the two children made their way through the many 3-D terminals that lined the walkway. They passed a group of three-year-olds who were sitting on the ground, listening to a hologram explain how "our bodies are made of atomic molecules." Simon used to love libraries and the way they gave him the opportunity to escape from reality; however, the Pudo library was in no way a fun place to visit.

Thornapple walked over the hard marble floor to the front desk, where a decrepit old man slept. Simon, sitting in his hover chair, rose a couple of feet to meet the librarian, but the chair wouldn't go high enough for him to see the man face-to-face.

"Excuse me, but could you let us into the sealed portion of the library?" Thorn asked politely.

The old man didn't answer. He wore a red and white outfit with little mittens over his hands and a cone-shaped cap that covered his long white hair. If gnomes existed, they'd look just like this librarian. Simon laughed out loud at the thought, causing the sleeping man to wake up with a grunt.

Startled, the librarian peered over his tall desk at the boys below and said in a thick, drawled accent, "*Shhh,* don't ya know you're in a library, boys?"

"Yes," said Thorn. "We want to see the sealed portion of the library."

"Sorry–can't help ya," the whimsical old man replied. "But I do have the newest edition of *Mathematicians Weekly.*"

"No, thank you," Simon said.

"Well, now–how 'bout the Scientific Lecture Series? I hear they're better than the four-volume set that came out last year."

"Maybe later," Thorn said. "Why can't we see the sealed portion of the library?"

"Wouldn't be sealed if I opened it!" The old man chuckled loudly.

"*Shhh!*" another old librarian scolded from across the room.

"Oh, don't let your knickers get so tight. I'm just try'n to help these two boys."

The old woman scoffed at the comment and ran over to help a group of patrons who had just entered the main door.

"Oh, hello, boys. May I help you?" the old man said, as if he had forgotten all about their previous conversation.

Simon frowned. "Uh, can you direct us to the sealed portion of the library?"

"Why, certainly!" The librarian pointed to a steel door with a digital keypad embedded in the wall directly behind his oversized desk. "Now," he said, getting ready to share his joke again, "do ya know why I can't letch-ya in?"

"Because it wouldn't be sealed if you opened it?" Simon said, grinning at the peculiar man.

"Yeah!" he roared. "You've heard that one before, haven't you?"

"Glumly*! SHHH!*" hissed the other librarian from across the room.

"*Ahh!*" The old man waved his hand to brush her off. He looked at Simon and Thorn with a puzzled expression and then said, "Oh, hello. Welcome to the library, boys. Did ya know this great building is the only thing that survived the Battle of Lisardious?"

"No," Simon said, trying to hold back his laughter. "I didn't know that."

"So, what can I do you for?"

"We were just browsing," Thorn said in a discouraged tone.

"Well, enjoy yourselves." The old librarian shuffled some papers around.

"Come on, Simon," Thorn said. "Let's go home."

They left the building and took a shortcut under the pavilion which was being set up for next week's dance. Dr. Troodle's home stood within eyesight of the library, and as they walked towards the house, something strange grabbed their attention. A large mammal with massive hind legs and a wide, muscular body grazed on the grass not too far from the Troodle's front porch.

"Oh, no," Thorn groaned.

"What is it?"

"It's a farbearus."

Thorn ignored the animal completely and rushed to the front door but hesitated to open it when he heard the loud conversation coming from inside.

"We bought him fair and square! You yourself signed the contract," Mrs. Troodle's harsh voice sounded.

"Yes, but seven years–so long," came the agonized reply.

"You should be grateful Har is in a home like ours."

"I is grateful," Har's mother said in a drawn-out voice, "but next week–little Har's birthday. Please let little Har be with family. Please."

Simon's eyes widened at hearing Har's mother describe her son as being *little*. He shuddered at Mrs. Troodle's response.

"Get out of here–now–before I call the police and have you sent to the mines. We still have six good years out of him. I don't want to see your ugly face until then!"

The front door flew open and almost knocked the boys off the porch. A large, hunched-over woman staggered out. From what Simon could see, she had looped earrings, dark, leathery skin, and a hideous face full of scars. Simon grimaced. But just as the giant strode off, he looked more closely and realized she also had big blue eyes full of tears. All the coarseness of her appearance seemed to wash away with those watery tears, and, for a brief moment, Simon glimpsed her inner beauty and the love she had for her son. His heart ached in sympathy for the pathetic creature, but there was nothing he could do to help her.

■ ■ ■

That night at dinner, the Troodles discussed the upcoming celebration and the historical significance behind the Battle of Lisardious with great enthusiasm.

". . . and if it wasn't for the genius of the small Puds, we wouldn't even be here today," said Dr. Troodle.

"Quite true," his wife said. "But sometimes I wish the aliens would have gotten rid of a *certain group* of Puds." She nodded to Har as he refilled her glass.

"But, Sweetie," Dr. Troodle countered, "if we didn't have the big Puds, who would do the menial labor?"

"You're right again." She smiled. "So, children, what did you learn in school today?"

Tonya looked up from her plate of seeds and grass and said, "I learned about the same amount of information today as I did yesterday." She finished the rest of her sentence in her mind–*which was equivalent to nothing*.

"Wonderful!" Mrs. Troodle laughed mechanically.

Thorn squirmed excitedly in his seat. "Simon discovered the true translation of the ancient writings of the Battle of Lisardious."

"Fantastic!"

"Wait a second," Dr. Troodle argued. "The history of the Battle of Lisardious has already been translated."

"Yes," Thorn said, "but our scholars messed up. Simon can read the ancient language correctly."

"That's ridiculous," his father said with a half smile. "So, Simon, what exactly did *you* see in the ancient text that our *best scholars* didn't see?"

Thorn answered on Simon's behalf. "He found out that the enemy invaders who almost destroyed the planet weren't really aliens."

"Then where did they come from?" asked Mrs. Troodle.

"From the ocean–I think," Simon said quietly.

Dr. Troodle laughed heartily. "So you think our entire civilization was almost annihilated by a bunch of fish?" He held up his plate.

Simon was sadly reminded of what they were having for dinner: some sort of blue jellyfish with three black eel heads jutting out of the top. Mrs. Troodle chortled at her husband's witty remark. Her fake laughter, mixed with occasional snorts, was starting to get on Simon's nerves.

"Simon, you have such a wild imagination," she said. "And I suppose that's acceptable behavior for someone . . . well, for someone with an inferior intellect, but people on Pudo don't waste time using their minds for frivolous activities. I'm surprised at you, Thornapple, for allowing yourself to start . . . *imagining things.*"

"Mother, we weren't just wasting our time *imagining* what happened to the ancient Puds," Thorn said. "We even tried to get more information at the library."

Dr. Troodle raised his eyebrows. "Children, if you find you don't know something, just ask us. We pretty much know everything there is to know."

"That's right," Mrs. Troodle said proudly. "Go ahead, Simon, ask us anything."

At first, Simon couldn't think of anything to ask, but then he remembered the dream he had that morning.

"What does *civility* mean?"

"Good question," the woman said, beaming. "Civility means being polite and courteous to others."

Dr. Troodle added, "It also means being a good citizen and showing respect to everyone you come in contact with."

Simon nodded and asked, "And what does *equality* mean?"

"Goodness, Simon, where did you come up with these words?" asked Mrs. Troodle.

"I heard them in a dream."

"Heard them in a dream," the woman repeated, shaking her head. "See, Simon, that's exactly what I was talking about. Even in your dreams, your mind wanders around aimlessly, thinking of unimportant things." Simon gave her an earnest look, and she sighed. "Think of equality as a math problem: 1 + 1 = 2. When both sides of an equation are equal to each other, we have equality."

Simon frowned. "I didn't think it had anything to do with math."

Dr. Troodle chuckled. "Sweetie, remember who you're talking to. You can't just throw out math problems to someone like Simon and expect him to understand them."

Simon clenched his fists under the table to control the anger that swelled inside him. He knew he wasn't that great at math, but being treated as if he were an idiot was infuriating.

"You're quite right, Honey–like always," she said. "Equality deals more with people. It means that everyone should be given the same rights and the same opportunities. So when people aren't treated as equals, you have the opposite of equality. Does that make sense?"

"Yeah," Simon said, "so it's kinda like the situation between the big Puds and the small Puds."

Dr. Troodle choked on his drink and sprayed liquid everywhere–some of it even came out his nose. Thorn's eyes expanded, and Mrs. Troodle looked like she was about to explode. But before anyone could say another word, Tonya suddenly screamed, "I can't stand it any longer!"

The red-haired girl sank her fork into one of the eels protruding from Simon's jellyfish and ripped it away from the strange organism. She gnawed at the eel like a dog attacking a bone. Ripping through the tough skin with her bare teeth, she made her way to the tender meat inside.

Everyone else just sat there with their mouths hanging open in shock. Thorn was the first to respond. "Wouldn't the Elders be a little upset with you, Butblacruze?"

Through a mouthful of meat, she muttered, "The Elders can just kiss my–"

"Tonya!" Simon stopped her. "What's wrong with you?"

The young girl looked at Simon. Tears welled up in her eyes. Without warning, she threw the eel down on the table and ran to her room.

"That girl's been acting strangely ever since she got home from school," Mrs. Troodle commented.

Simon scooted into his hover chair and followed after her.

"Tonya," he called from behind the closed door. "Tonya, can I come in?"

"*NO!*"

"Tonya, what's wrong?"

No answer.

Simon waited a while. As he turned to leave, Tonya finally said, "It's just not fair."

"What's not fair?"

"You . . . me . . . everything!"

"What do you mean?"

She ranted on and on. "I can't stand living here. I can't stand being treated like an imbecile every day. If I have to eat another seed, I'll go ballistic. I can't bear to think I've missed my first year of school. And most of all, I'm going crazy, not being able to use magic! Speaking of magic, there aren't any E.M. waves on this planet, but, somehow, you're able to do things that can only be explained by magic."

Simon realized she was referring to his newfound language abilities. "Tonya, I don't know how I'm able to speak the Pudo language," he said. "I just talk like normal, and everyone seems to understand me. To me, it sounds like everyone is speaking English."

"But that's exactly how the language spell works," she said.

Simon lowered his chair to the ground and sat with his back to the door. In the guest room, Tonya sat with her back pressed against the door as well.

The girl continued, "Do you know how long it took me to learn the language spell?"

"How long?"

"Three years."

"Wow! But you've mastered it now, haven't you?"

"Yes–well, sort of–but, Simon . . ." She paused. "When you cast the language spell, you're only supposed to be able to speak the same language as the people nearby. I don't even think the Guardians of the Crown would be able to learn a language that hasn't been used for hundreds of years–let alone learn it without E.M. waves."

Simon was dumbstruck. He thought for a moment that he should mention the woman from his dreams but decided against it. "Tonya," he said slowly. "I'm sorry you're stuck on this paraworld. Sometimes I feel a little out of place, and if it wasn't for you, I'd probably go crazy too." The girl smiled, and Simon continued, "I think you're wonderful–even without magic. You and Thornapple are the best friends I've ever had. You're the only friends I've ever had, really–at least, my age. I'm not so sure if I want to go back to Earth anymore. This is the closest thing I've ever had to a family."

The door opened suddenly, and Simon fell over backwards. Tonya knelt down and gave him a warm embrace. A sweet fragrance entered the young boy's nose as her long green hair brushed against his cheek.

Tonya, her face streaming with tears, whispered, "Thank you."

"Hey," came a squeaky voice from behind, "don't I get a hug, too?"

Simon and Tonya stretched out their arms, and Thorn joined them in a group hug.

CHAPTER 11
GRIFFEN LASHER

The man's deep-set eyes were light brown–almost a honey color–but in the darkness of space, they looked like two lone stars being swept away into a black hole. He stared out into the night with iron determination, like a hawk scanning its prey.

An explosion of red light forced its way into the dark confines of his small cockpit, revealing his face for a brief moment. Illuminated by the light, his nose appeared to be slightly broken–probably from some battle long ago.

The man's name was Griffen Lasher–a devoted servant of the Crown, skilled swordsman, and master of the healing arts. His journey had led him to the third moon of the Centarious paraworld. Unfortunately, all that remained of the moon was crumbling pieces of rock and dust; it had just been destroyed by General Mayham and Captain Drackus. In fact, the debris was now rushing toward Griffen's small shuttle craft.

Griffen veered his ship away from the river of rock flowing in his direction. Knowing that he'd never make it in time and feeling compelled to die facing his doom rather than fleeing from it, he jerked the ship around and headed towards the onslaught of boulders.

Surprisingly enough, his sharp reflexes allowed him to make it past the first two waves of debris unscathed; however, his luck appeared to be running out. As he flew past a mountainous piece of moon rock, the twin space carriers on the other side started shooting at him. In an attempt to destroy his little vessel, they cleared a path through the asteroid field with their lasers–unwittingly giving Griffen a small window to escape the rushing moon rocks. But as he zipped through the opening, a small rock tore through his outer hull, while another glided off the metal plating of his ship and collided with a boulder, splitting it in two.

Griffen flew between the pieces of fragmented boulder and headed full force towards the space carriers. He was welcomed with a shower of laser fire that rived his craft and sent him spiraling. In a desperate act of valor, he plunged his burning ship downward, as if to ram the carrier commanded by Captain Drackus.

Dodging the barrage of laser fire and rubble, Griffen flung his ship closer and closer to the enormous carrier. He was only meters away when he saw the main cannon erupt in bright color as it fired some sort of explosive in his direction. Instantly, the trained pilot yelled out a magical word and slammed his fist onto the ejection button–just in time to be jettisoned from the ship. A globe of clear liquid engulfed his body, protecting him from the cold void of space.

The shock wave of the explosion sent him hurling towards the space carrier. Griffen's lungs burned for the want of air as the long seconds ticked by. He grasped at the walls of the bubble–resembling a chicken trying to free itself from an egg–but the transparent shell did not break.

The round ball smashed into the space carrier. Similar to a drop of acid eating its way through metal, the sphere dissolved a section of the thick protective plating and created a sizable hole. Then the magical orb split open, expelling Griffen into the ship with a gush of liquid–like a baby emerging from the womb.

Gasping for air and slipping on the wet floor, the brave warrior drew his glowing sword. In the dim light, he looked to be of average height and build, yet there was something different about him . . . something mysterious and exciting. Shocked at seeing the intruder's fantastic entrance, the men and women in the room jumped from their seats and fled out the doors.

Griffen wiped the gooey residue from his arms and face and flicked the strange substance onto the ground. Bubbling and steaming, the curious liquid danced on the metallic floor and then subsided.

He turned briefly to see the thick skin of the magical sphere weld itself to the ship, sealing the breach. Peering out of the makeshift window, Griffen looked past the remnants of his spacecraft and saw the turmoil that the loss of a moon was causing on the parallel world below. The two remaining moons obviously weren't compensating enough to offset the disproportionate surge of gravity the planet was now experiencing.

Suddenly, all three doors in the room opened, and in rushed a dozen soldiers carrying guns. They surrounded Griffen completely.

With a charming smile on his face, he ran his fingers through his short black hair and said, "Gentleman, can any of you please point me to the nearest bathroom?"

Grunting incoherently, a few of the soldiers took off their helmets and stepped closer, allowing Griffen to see that they were Skydroes–hired mercenaries from an off-limit parallel world. The skilled warrior calmly lowered his sword and reached into his vest pocket with his free hand, upon which all twelve guns jerked in response. Slowly, Griffen brought out a pair of black sunglasses.

"Hold on, boys. They're just glasses," he said coolly.

Griffen put them on and looked around at the werewolf-like men.

Saliva ran down their hairy faces, and their dirty clothing smelled of urine.

"Now aren't you a sorry bunch? Looks like none of you have any idea where the bathroom is either." Griffen chuckled. "All right then–"

With lightning speed, he threw up his hand and released an explosion that blinded the Skydroes' sensitive eyes. He sliced his unusual sword through four soldiers before they even knew what had happened. A yellow light enveloped the body of each victim for a brief moment and then dissipated.

Griffen continued to mow down the soldiers, one by one. Some of them began to recover from the initial explosion, so he raised his hand again, but nothing happened. There wasn't enough E.M. energy in the area to complete the spell.

Still dazed, the Skydroes fired their weapons. Griffen jumped over a desk and crashed into one of the unsuspecting soldiers. He lost his grip as he landed, and his sword slid across the floor.

Before Griffen could react, a muscular hand tightened around his neck and lifted his whole body off the ground. The ugly Skydroe snarled ferociously and bared his sharp, yellowing teeth as he held his captive in the air. Griffen noticed the careless soldiers preparing to fire. He clutched the Skydroe's shoulders, placed his feet on the creature's knees, and kicked off into a handstand long enough for a volley of lasers to hit the soldier squarely in the chest.

They both fell. Griffen immediately rolled across the floor, using the dead Skydroe as a shield. Once he reached his sword, he tossed the scorched body to the side and slashed at the remaining soldiers. The mercenaries were crude fighters, despite their unnatural strength, and it didn't take long before Griffen was the only one standing.

"Computer!" he yelled, striding to the main console.

A chime signaled, which indicated that the computer was listening.

"Show me where the main database is located," he commanded.

"*Access denied*," came the cold reply.

"Oh, come on. Give me a hint."

"*Access denied.*"

"Computer, what room is this?"

"*Engineering.*"

"Excellent. Now show me the layout of the ship."

A layout of the ship appeared before him, but after scanning the many corridors and rooms, he couldn't make up his mind where the main computer was hiding. Just then, he noticed sparks coming from a series of wires that had been torn out of the wall during the fight.

"Where do those wires lead to?"

"*Access denied.*"

"Look! This is engineering, right? I can't fix the damage to the ship unless I know what it is I'm repairing. Now show me where those wires lead to."

Within a nanosecond, the computer system processed thousands of possible scenarios and deductive solutions. In the end, its artificial reasoning came up with the conclusion that the wires did, in fact, need to be rerouted or else the engineering department would be seriously crippled.

The naive computer announced, "*Limited access granted.*"

"Thank you."

The map of the ship expanded to show more detail. Wires and conduits ran to each room like spaghetti.

"I don't care about the power lines. Take them out."

Many of the wires disappeared.

"Get rid of communications," he added.

Wires used for communications vanished as well. One more quick glance at the map, and Griffen noticed that most of the remaining network cables could be traced back to one central location on the ship.

"What's in that room?" he asked, pointing to the map.

"*Access denied.*"

He laughed, quite amused that the computer system was so easy to fool. "Thank you, computer. You've been most helpful."

"*You're welcome.*"

A chill of uneasiness ran down his spine when he heard those words. Cracking the system was just too easy. It was as though someone *wanted* him to find the main computer room. Just then, it occurred to him that no audible alarm had gone off when he entered the space carrier. In fact, other than the first onslaught of soldiers, he couldn't hear or see anything out of the ordinary–no footsteps of additional soldiers coming to burst into the room, no sirens, no flashing lights . . . just the faint buzz of severed electrical wires giving off sporadic sparks.

Cautiously, he walked over to the transportation tube. The door was already conveniently open. He stepped inside, and the computer's soft voice asked, "*Destination?*"

"Take me to the third floor."

"*Access denied!*"

Griffen had no time to respond. The floor beneath him suddenly dropped. Everything became a blur as his body was hurled down several decks. With tremendous speed, the tube sent him racing through the space carrier until it finally spit him out into a dark and spacious room.

In the center of the room stood a white pillar with a single computer console attached to it. A short man with glasses and an ugly brown suit typed busily at the console. He turned and asked, "May I help you?"

"You sure can," Griffen said in an irritable tone.

He got to his feet and started to rush towards the man, but after a few paces, he felt his body lean so far to the right that he fell over. The warrior stood up and tried to balance himself, but he fell again. The wild tube ride had taken its toll on his body.

Standing up one more time, he brushed off the dizziness and limped over to the console. It was so dark in the room that he kept bumping into the round metallic balls that littered the floor. Without warning, he thrust his sword right into the man's stomach.

"This is just the lowest setting," Griffen informed him as he twisted the sword around. "Just imagine how painful this would be if I were to increase the density level."

The computer technician moaned, "What do you want?"

"How did you destroy that moon?"

"I can't tell you *THAT!*"

The density of the sword increased ever so slightly, causing the man to double over. Griffen held him up against the pillar and whispered in his ear, "Tell me, have you ever had the molecules in your body scream out in pain?" Steam rose from the insertion point of the transparent blade. "My patience is wearing thin. Either you tell me how you destroyed that moon or I–"

He stopped in midsentence and stared at the computer screen. A schematic of a holographic robot flashed across the monitor.

"What is that?" Griffen asked, nodding towards the console.

"That's my own creation," the man responded with a great deal of pride in his voice. "Fully functioning holodroids. You're looking at the future of modern warfare."

A startling voice came from behind. "Excuse me."

Griffen spun around, tearing the blade from the technician's body, and sliced his sword into the chest of the person who had just spoken. Without even flinching, the man stepped forward and revealed himself to be Captain Drackus–or at least, the holographic image of Captain Drackus.

"Who are you?" the captain asked calmly.

"Griffen Lasher, ambassador of the Crown. I've been sent to keep the peace–"

"An ambassador?" Captain Drackus asked skeptically. "Then tell me, sir, if you really were sent on a mission of peace, why exactly are you killing my men?"

"My blade has never taken a life. I only incapacitated your men."

"Interesting . . . a displacement sword," the captain mused while inspecting the blade that was still embedded in his chest. "I've never seen one before. Such a pity that a marvelous weapon such as this is in the hands of a coward."

Griffen tightened his face, appalled. "Coward?"

"Yes," he said. "Only a coward would refuse to use the full potential of the technology in which he possesses."

"Only a fool would use technology to destroy a helpless planet," Griffen shot back.

"Oh, you must be referring to that terrible incident that my colleagues were involved in last year." Any indication of contrition in his voice was merely a facade. "What was that drab world called, anyway? Oh, yes– *Marmasuel.*"

"That was my parallel world," Griffen said with clenched teeth. "The Raiders killed millions of people. In fact, I haven't seen a single person from my race since the *incident*."

"Oh. Well, I'm dreadfully sorry for your loss. However, when I instructed my men to destroy your planet, I told them to annihilate every man, woman, and child. I suppose they missed one."

The captain moved effortlessly away from the sword. That's when Griffen realized the holographic projection was coming from one of the silvery balls, which now floated a couple inches off the ground.

"You're the filthy swine who destroyed my planet?" Griffen yelled, his rage starting to consume him. "You sadistic animal!"

"Yes, well, your people were a threat to our advancement."

"My planet was peaceful! We never even fought amongst ourselves."

"Oh, we weren't afraid of ever fighting you–a world full of religious monks," Captain Drackus explained coldly. "No, it's *what you can do* that scared us."

"I'll show you what I can do!"

Griffen lashed out with his sword, but the hologram was left unscathed.

"Please–stop–that tickles," Drackus said in jest.

Griffen slashed at the silver ball and split it in two. As soon as the hologram disappeared, the lights in the room turned on, one section at a time. Griffen's mouth hung open as he beheld thousands of metallic orbs–all about the size of soccer balls–scattered about the room

"You're gonna get it now." The technician chuckled as he tapped furiously at the computer console.

All at the same time, a sea of identical holodroids materialized from the spheres. Griffen watched in horror as a small compartment opened up from within each metal ball, revealing a handgun. In sync, each holodroid reached down and took its weapon.

The technician laughed unpleasantly as the enormous wave of holographic images pointed their guns at Griffen.

"Oh, *shoot*!"

Griffen snatched a small device from his belt and activated it. The device expanded to form an energy shield–just in time to absorb the storm of lasers. Protected by the shield, the impact threw him across the floor. Friendly fire destroyed most of the spheres nearby.

Griffen scrambled for the transportation tube, holding his shield behind him as he ran. Suddenly, he felt a searing pain run up his body as multiple lasers pierced his legs. The warrior slid across the floor, carried by the momentum of his own weight.

Knowing that he'd never make it to the exit, he adjusted the shield so that it expanded over his entire body. Wave after wave of lasers pelted the force field–weakening it with every blow. Griffen tapped some buttons on the little device, and the lasers started to ricochet off the shield, causing dozens of spheres to explode all around him.

Despite his efforts, Griffen could see that the battle was hopeless; for every sphere he destroyed, ten more took its place. Even worse, his defenses were failing. A red light on the device flicked on and off, signifying the almost depleted energy of the force field.

He heard a rumbling sound coming from the far wall. The floor vibrated as a yellow tidal wave of lightning split the room in half, tossing the droids everywhere. Hundreds of round balls crashed against the ceiling like bowling pins, breaking most of the lights.

From within the chaos emerged a sole figure. Dark in appearance and foreboding, he walked slowly through the rubble. The whole army of holodroids turned their guns and fired at the mysterious man, but, surprisingly, the lasers dissipated in the air before reaching him.

Griffen watched in awe as the man manipulated the magical waves in the room to do his bidding. Spheres on both sides of the ultramage melted as he walked past them. Surely the entire ship did not contain this much E. M. energy–let alone the room! A seasoned magician like Griffen would have sensed it.

"Thank you," Griffen said, massaging his wounds.

It was too dark to make out the stranger's face, especially because he hid behind a black cloak.

The man stood above the fallen warrior for a moment or two, as if contemplating the situation. Then, without warning, he brought out both hands from his cloak. The last thing Griffen saw was two wands emitting a painful blast of energy that penetrated his shield and struck him in the chest.

The dark ultramage turned to see the technician peering from behind the console. Completely terrified, the short man made a run for the exit, but he didn't get very far before he was hit in the back by an evil spell. He screamed for only a second as the magic ripped the molecules from his body. Soon, he was gone entirely.

The holodroids continued to fire relentlessly at the ultramage, but none of the lasers made contact. The dark man threw something down at his feet, and a puff of smoke appeared. Just then, Captain Drackus–the real Captain Drackus–rushed into the room with a group of men.

"Stop!" he yelled at the holodroids. "I said *STOP!*"

A laser blast grazed his arm.

"*STOP FIRING, YOU IDIOTS!*"

The holodroids froze. Fuming with anger, Drackus ran to the droid that had shot him, picked up the metal orb, and smashed it against the wall. He then pulled out his gun and destroyed another sphere nearby.

"Charles!" he boomed.

A short, balding man ran to his side.

"Yes, sir?"

"I want you to recalibrate their aiming algorithms." He kicked one of the holodroids, and it went spinning down the room, bumping into its companions like a pinball. "When they fire their weapons," he growled, pointing to his bloodied shirt sleeve, "I expect them to shoot to kill!"

"Pardon me, sir," Charles said, "but I'm not the one who wrote the weapons subroutine. I'm in charge of the physical traits division. If you'll remember, it was I who discovered how to manipulate the photonic energy so the droids could carry weapons. That aspect works perfectly. In fact–"

"Then who wrote the weapons program?" Drackus interrupted.

"George," the technician said. "George wrote it . . . Where is he, anyway?"

Captain Drackus prodded a brown, smoldering suit on the ground with his foot. "It appears that your brother has been vaporized." His voice lacked any trace of sympathy.

Horrified, Charles knelt down at the pile of burnt clothing and sobbed. He picked up a pair of broken glasses from the ground and held them tightly in his hands.

"You're now in charge of the weapons division," Captain Drackus informed the technician. "I want those droids shooting straight." The captain looked across the barren room–searching intently for any sign of Griffen–and asked in a puzzled voice, "Now where did he go?"

CHAPTER 12
DISCOVERING MAGIC

Simon slowly opened his eyes and let them adjust to the darkness. Thorn snored loudly across the room, and a faint breeze rustled the drapes at the window. He rolled quietly onto his hover chair and activated the armrests as he sat down.

Trying to be as quiet as possible, Simon maneuvered his way through the bedroom and started down the dark, ominous hallway. A creaking sound from somewhere in the house caused his heart to race. Panicked, Simon froze in place and held his breath . . . Nothing. He started to breathe again, but his breaths were short and forced.

Quiet, Simon, he told himself. *You must be quiet.*

A moment later, he calmed himself–enough to make his way through the hallway once more.

He emerged into the dining room, where he had spent quite a few nights laboring to eat the strange concoctions that Little Har had created for the family. Simon shuddered involuntarily. He then turned his attention to the mantelpiece.

When he squinted his eyes, he could almost make out the smiling faces of Dr. Troodle and his wife–as well as Thornapple, Tonya, and himself. He inched his way closer to the pictures. A bright flame suddenly appeared in the fireplace. Simon jerked backwards, away from the motion sensor, and the fire died out.

Clutching his chest with one hand and the joystick of the hover chair with the other, Simon moved to the opposite wall. He slowly opened the door so it wouldn't squeak and entered the next room with caution.

There were no windows in the room, which made it difficult to see anything at all. Simon eased his way forward until he bumped into something hard.

"Is that you?" he whispered hoarsely.

There was no answer. The boy started to breathe hard. His veins flowed with adrenaline, making him jumpy and uneasy–as though he were doing something illegal.

A thick, giant hand curled itself around his shoulder from behind.

"Si-moan," came a slow, deep voice.

"Har, you almost scared me to death!"

"Sorry," the big Pud said. "Si-moan hungry?"

"I sure am! What have you got for me tonight?"

The large boy uncovered a plate and revealed what looked like a peanut butter and jelly sandwich, except the green jelly was slightly luminescent in the dark.

"Oh, you are a lifesaver!"

"Life . . . saver?" Har asked slowly.

"Yeah. Without you, I'd starve to death."

Simon grabbed the sandwich and started to devour it. Har handed him a glass of milk, and the boy guzzled it down. Just then, a light turned on in the dining room.

"Oh, no! What do we do?" Simon whispered frantically.

"Come," Har said while turning around. "Hide."

The large Pud got on his hands and knees and crawled through a plastic flap in the wall. He looked like an animal squeezing through an oversized doggy-door. Simon zoomed over to the entrance but couldn't fit through because of his hover chair. Quickly, Har pulled Simon out of the chair and carried him into the dark cubbyhole. He then pulled the hover chair in as well, just as the kitchen door opened.

Simon could see the outline of Dr. Troodle through the plastic flap. He was walking right towards them! Then, just before he reached the cubbyhole, the tiny man stopped. Simon watched nervously as Dr. Troodle pulled a bottle out of a drawer, opened it, and took a sip. He put the container back into the drawer and said, "Colder, please." The drawer closed itself and opened again immediately. "Thank you." He withdrew the bottle and drank from it once more.

Dr. Troodle leaned against the counter for a moment and then saw the half-eaten sandwich that Simon had left behind. Mildly interested but wary, he approached the sandwich as if it could be a trap. After sniffing it and prodding it with his forefinger, Dr. Troodle seemed a bit more confident. He finally picked up the sandwich and took a bite but quickly withdrew, acting as though it were laced with poison.

Dr. Troodle threw down the sandwich in disgust and marched out of the kitchen. The lights in the dining room went out, and everything became silent and dark once more.

Simon whispered to Har, afraid of what the answer might be, "What is this little room we're in?"

The cubbyhole wasn't much larger than a doghouse. It even had another plastic flap leading to the outside, and the only thing separating the boys from the cold dirt below was a small, ragged blanket.

"This Little Har's room," the large boy answered.

"You mean, you sleep here?"

"Yes."

"That's crazy! You're not a *pet*–you're a *person*."

"Har is big Pud," he explained.

"That doesn't make any difference. I can't believe this. Come on. You're sleeping in our room tonight." Simon crawled out of the hole and got onto his hover chair, but the large boy wouldn't follow. "Come on, Har."

"Har no go."

"Why not?"

"Little Har for-bidden. Har go to mines if Har break rules."

"That's not fair. I'll talk to the Troodles–"

"*No!*" the large boy exclaimed, grabbing Simon's arm suddenly. "No get Har in trouble."

Simon looked into the boy's brown eyes and saw that they were full of fear. "Okay," he said reluctantly, "I won't say anything."

"Har see Si-moan next night?"

"Yeah . . . I'll see you tomorrow night . . ." he whispered. "Goodnight, Har."

"Good-night, Si-moan."

Simon left the kitchen and went back to his bedroom. He glanced at Thornapple and wondered if his friend realized the injustice he and his family were committing. The little Pud slept soundly. For nearly two hours, Simon struggled to fall asleep. He kept thinking of Har stuck in that cramped doghouse all by himself while everyone else slept in comfortable beds. It wasn't fair.

The next morning, he woke up abruptly with the sound of yelling coming from the dining room. Thornapple sat up in his bed and said with a smile, "Har sure is in trouble now."

"If we ever catch you stealing food again, we'll send you straight to the mines," came Mrs. Troodle's scathing voice.

Simon threw the covers off and jumped into his hover chair. Still dressed in his pajamas, he left the bedroom and zoomed down the hallway. Har whimpered in the corner of the dining room, while Dr. Troodle and his wife loomed over him.

"What's going on?" asked Simon.

Dr. Troodle answered, "I discovered last night that Har has been sneaking food from us. No telling how long this has been going on."

"It's not his fault," Simon confessed. "He was just–"

"I sorry," Har interrupted quickly. "Har no steal food again."

Simon tried to speak, but the terrified look on Har's face told him to stay quiet.

"Well, you better be sorry," scolded Mrs. Troodle. "Things aren't going to be so good for you anymore. We're going to have to cut down on your privileges. First off, no more second meals for you, young man. You can survive with just one meal a day."

"Yes," Dr. Troodle said, joining in, "and I'm not so sure if I like the idea of you walking around without a security collar."

"That's right," Mrs. Troodle said. "I think he's starting to outgrow his tranquilizer injections. Honey, why don't you set up an appointment at the clinic to have Har fitted for one of those new deluxe security collars? I heard they're integrating them with more and more features every day."

"That's not a bad idea. I wouldn't mind getting one with a wireless connection to the Holonet."

"Just as long as it has a built-in filter," his wife said. "I don't want Thornapple getting to any of those *underground* sites. The last thing we need now is for him to come in contact with Puds writing fiction or painting pictures."

Har grimaced as the Troodles discussed the dreaded security collar. Simon felt sorry for the big guy, and he didn't want to get him into more trouble, so he decided to break off his nighttime meetings.

"Har, I don't think you should have any late-night snacks anymore. Do you understand me?" Simon broke up his next sentence into clear, distinct words. "No-more-food-at-night."

The large boy frowned and nodded in response. "No more food?"

"Yes, no more food."

Har exhaled loudly and furled his eyebrows in acknowledgment.

"See, Simon. That's the problem with big Puds," Dr. Troodle said. "Not only are they dumb as rocks, but they don't understand half of what you tell them. I'm not even sure they have a conscience. Sometimes it's nice to have them around, but I find that if you get too comfortable with one–just like with a wild dog–sooner or later you're going to get bit."

"Good morning," said Tonya as she walked into the room. Her green hair was tied up in a bun, and she wore an oversized shirt that went down almost to her knees.

"Honey, let's go see what else he's gotten into." Mrs. Troodle beckoned the large boy to follow them into the kitchen. "Har, come!"

"What's up?" Tonya asked Simon with a yawn.

"Har got in trouble because–"

He stopped himself.

"Because why?"

"Because he made me a sandwich last night. The Troodles think he's been sneaking food for himself, and I tried to tell the truth, but Har stopped me. He doesn't want them to know that I've been meeting with him."

"Oh," she said thoughtfully. "It's funny that such a civilized people would practice slavery. Usually, the more advanced a paraworld gets, the less likely they are to enslave their own kind."

"They're not slaves," Thorn chimed in from behind. "They're *indentured* servants. And besides, they're not really *our kind.*"

Tonya sneered as Thorn entered the dining room. "They look like slaves to me, and they are *your kind*–only bigger."

"Har is free to go when his contract is finished."

"Yes, but where will he go after that? To the dank mines or to the sun-blistered fields? He doesn't have many options, does he?"

"He has more options than that. In fact, I think his father is a fisherman."

"The point is: Your people force the big Puds to do the things that no one else wants to do. You don't let them expand. You even rip away their childhoods so they don't get an opportunity to go to school and learn."

Thornapple laughed nervously. "Can you imagine Har in school? We wouldn't even be able to put him in with the kindergartners."

"You can hardly put us in with the kindergartners," Simon muttered under his breath.

Thorn cleared his throat. "The big Puds are put to work so they don't get into trouble. It's safer that way."

"For who?" Tonya retorted. A red streak ran down her hair.

"Let's just drop it, okay?" Simon said. "There's nothing we can do about it anyway. I mean, it's not like we can change the culture of a whole civilization."

"Yeah," Thorn said. "Besides, we have more important things to talk about–like my birthday!"

"*Ahhh!*" Tonya cried. "Do you have to bring that up every single day?"

"Well, tomorrow's the big day–right before the anniversary of the Battle of Lisardious. Speaking of that, have you decided to go to the dance, Simon?"

"No, I don't think I'm going."

"*WHAT?*" Tonya blurted out. "You have to go!" Simon and Thorn looked at her in surprise, and the red in her hair turned pink. "I mean . . . well . . . I want *someone* my size to dance with."

"I don't know," Simon mumbled. "I'll think about it."

"Well, guys," Thorn said, "something tells me that Har's not going to make breakfast for us today. We might as well get ready for school."

Soon, the three children were on their way to school. All day long, the teachers felt the need to share stories about the Battle of Lisardious. Each story seemed to get wilder and wilder as the day went on. One teacher said the aliens had sent a virus to wipe out the Puds. Another teacher told his students that the aliens invaded because they wanted to take the Puds back to their homeworld to replenish their food supply. By the end of the day, the students were led to believe that not only did the small Puds destroy the enemy single-handedly, but they did so without the aid of weapons.

After school, Tonya met Simon at the hospital for his therapy session. Simon held himself between two metal bars. As Tonya walked in, he started swinging like a gymnast. Over the past two months, his arms had become very strong, but, unfortunately, his legs had not.

"Good," said Tonya. "Now that you've learned to swing like a monkey, let's see if you can walk like one."

"Very funny."

Simon put his feet down on the ground. He stood for a few seconds but soon grabbed the bars for support.

"You're not trying hard enough," she told him. "You give up too soon."

"I am trying," he said, "but my legs hurt."

Tonya knelt down and massaged his lower legs.

"Can you believe all that garbage we heard today about the Battle of Lisardious? Thornapple told me one of his teachers said the war was actually just a made-up story and that there isn't any scientific proof that a battle even took place. No debris from any spaceships was ever found." She paused and then said, "Well, I guess that does correlate with your theory of the Lisardians not being aliens."

Tonya slapped his calves, which nullified all the soothing she had just given, and stood up.

"All right, what's all this about you not wanting to go to the dance?" she probed. "You're not gonna make me go there by myself, are you?"

"Thorn will be there."

"Yeah, right! Like I'm gonna dance with that pipsqueak."

"I just don't like dances."

"Have you ever been to one?"

"No."

"Then how do you know you don't like dances?"

Simon stared at his shoes. "I don't know how to dance."

"Oh my goodness!" Tonya exclaimed. "Is this why it's taking you so long to walk–because you don't wanna go to the dance?"

"Well, maybe a little."

"I can't believe you! All this time I've been working with you–for all I know, you probably can walk."

She put her hands to her hips, and Simon cowered. An evil grin stretched across her face.

"Simon, how would you like a *big* kiss?"

"Wh-Wh-What?" he stuttered in shock.

"Yeah, I think that's just what you need."

Her hair suddenly turned neon blue. She walked towards him slowly and provocatively. Simon struggled backwards on the bars to escape.

"St-St-Stop it, T-T-Tonya!"

When he reached the end of the bars, Tonya said in a sultry voice, "What's wrong, Simon? Haven't you ever kissed a girl before?"

She opened her mouth and lashed out her long tongue. It snapped in the air next to Simon's face. Shocked and scared, he let go of the bars and jumped backwards without thinking, but to his surprise, he didn't fall.

"Hey, I'm standing!" he cried.

"No," Tonya said quietly, her expression somber. "You're floating."

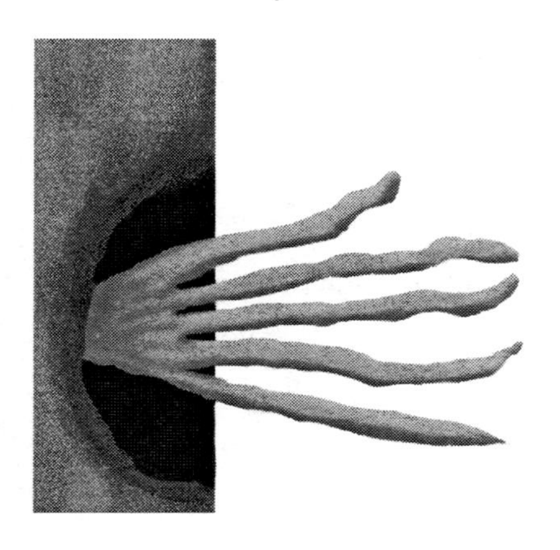

CHAPTER 13
A WALTZ IN THE FOREST

Simon's feet dangled in the air. "What?" he said, looking down incredulously.

He collapsed the second he realized his feet weren't touching the floor. Tonya rushed to his side, but Simon scooted backwards on his rear.

"Get away from me!"

"Oh, don't flatter yourself, runt." Her hair had already turned back to its normal green color. "I was only trying to get you to stand up by yourself."

"Did anybody see that?" Simon whispered.

Tonya looked around. All the nurses were helping other patients.

"I don't think so."

"Good. Well, don't ever do that again."

"Don't worry," Tonya said in a superior tone of voice. "Kissing you is the last thing on my mind." A thin, almost unnoticeable, white line ran down her hair. "That was amazing!" she remarked. "Simply amazing! You were using magic for sure. What did it feel like?"

"It just felt like I was standing."

"I didn't hear you say anything. What were you thinking?"

"I wanted to get away from you–that's all."

"Oh . . . Well, I'd say something strange is going on. You just cast the Halo-Marine spell. It's supposed to be very difficult to perform. No one in my class can do it yet. How did you cast that without E.M. waves?"

"I have no idea."

Tonya nudged him and said, "Come on, Simon. Get up. I wanna see something."

"I can't stand."

"Oh, yes you can." She grabbed his hands and pulled him up. His legs wobbled a bit, but he was standing. "See! You've been too dependent on those bars."

When she let go of him, a surge of pain ran up his legs. He put his hands out to balance himself, as if he were standing on a high wire.

Tonya skipped a few feet away and coaxed, "Come on, Simon. Let's go do some magic."

"I can't walk."

"Okay, then . . . I'll see ya later." She turned towards the door.

"Wait!"

Simon took a step forward. He took another step. The muscles in his legs ached but held him up, nonetheless. He felt like a baby walking to his mother for the first time.

One more step and then another and then another. Tonya walked backwards, which irritated him even more. He realized the pain in his legs had gone down considerably–maybe he was just getting numb. Finally, he reached Tonya. She allowed him to lean on her like a crutch.

"I need my hover chair," Simon said.

"Well, go get it then."

Simon breathed a long sigh of frustration. Tonya let go of him again, but this time the pain didn't return as strongly as before. He wobbled to the wall where his hover chair lay and threw himself down onto the mechanized contraption. It rose into the air.

"That was wonderful," Nurse Salfree said, rushing over to them. The husky woman gave Simon a hard pat on the back. "Konya, you should have told me Simon was walking."

"This is actually his first time," Tonya said with a wink.

"Good work, Simon. I'm pleased you've finally decided to walk. Your muscles have been reconditioned for some time now, but Dr. Troodle instructed me not to push you. Earthlings are slow creatures, he said." The nurse smacked him again–this time, so hard he wondered if something in his chest had become dislodged. "How do you feel?"

Other than the stinging sensation on his back and the slight numbness in his legs, he felt marvelous.

"Great," he answered. "Never better."

"Good. You're recovering just nicely. I'm so glad we were able to save your legs."

Simon nodded. "Nurse Salfree, you've done amazing work, and I never did thank you. Not only did you help restore my legs but you also cured me of being sick all the time."

The short woman frowned. "Simon, we didn't do anything to stop you from being sick. In fact, we haven't seen any signs of illness in you since you arrived."

"What about my asthma?"

"We never detected any respiratory problems."

Simon adjusted his glasses. "That's weird. I wonder what happened to me."

"Nurse Salfree," Tonya said anxiously, "Simon and I need to get back home. Is it okay if we cut today's therapy session short?"

"I suppose so, but I want you in here double time tomorrow."

"All right," Tonya said quickly. She grabbed Simon's fanny pack and urged him out the door.

"What's going on?" asked Simon.

"You'll see. Let's get out of here."

They left the hospital and traveled through the open field of grass towards home. About halfway through the field, Tonya bent down and started to hike up her dress.

"What are you doing?"

A second later, Simon spotted Tonya's small wand attached to her leg with a lacy Velcro-like strap. He laughed. "I can't believe you're still carrying that thing around."

"I always like to be prepared," Tonya replied. She removed the wand and handed it to him. "Here ya go, Simon. I wanna give you a magic lesson."

"Magic lesson?"

"Yeah, just to see if you can do it."

"I don't think I can, but I'll try." Simon nervously rubbed his mother's medallion between his fingers. The thought of performing magic was both intriguing and scary. "What do I do?"

"Okay, here's an easy one. I learned this when I was five. All you do is point the wand at your hand and snap your fingers while saying the word *Shawnee*. Oh, and make sure you keep your thumb pointed upwards and away from your face when you do it."

"Why's that?"

"You'll see. Don't worry. It's just a little trick I do at parties sometimes. It probably won't even work."

With the wand pointed towards his hand, Simon took a deep breath, snapped his fingers, and calmly said, "*Shawnee*."

A tremendous flame erupted from the top of his thumb and shot eighty feet into the air, forcing a flock of birds to scatter. Simon turned his face away because of the immense heat that emanated from his thumb. He shook his hand, and the stream of red and orange fire followed like a whip.

"*How do I turn this off?*"

Tonya screamed, "*Eenwahs!* Say *Eenwahs!*"

"*EENWAHS!*"

The hot flame recoiled and was sucked back into his thumb in an instant. Simon's jaw dropped at the sight of the scorched pathway he had just made in the luscious green grass.

"Cool!" Tonya marveled.

She grabbed her wand from his trembling hand and blew out the candle-like flame that had caught hold of the tip.

Simon yelled hysterically, "Tonya! You could've at least warned me!"

"Hey, Simon, I'm just as surprised as you are. That spell's only supposed to turn your thumb into a harmless lighter, not a flame-thrower."

"Do you think anyone saw that?"

"I'm not sticking around to find out." She rushed towards Dr. Troodle's house. Simon followed behind.

Tonya took three steps up the back porch, then turned around and asked, "Don't ya think it's a little strange that no one in your paraworld knows anything about magic, yet your planet has the most concentrated source of E.M. energy I've ever seen? I'll admit that my magical abilities are pretty weak, but in your world, they were put on overdrive. For an hour or two, I was like . . . an ultramage or something."

"Yeah, that's kinda strange."

"And now that we're on a paraworld that doesn't have *any* E.M. energy, all of a sudden you're able to perform magic that even an ultramage couldn't do."

Simon shrugged. "Don't ask me."

Tonya opened the back door, and both children went in. They saw Thorn and Har sitting on the carpet, facing each other.

"How ya doing, Har-buddy?" Tonya asked, patting his head. The large boy winced in pain. "What's wrong?"

Thorn answered, "His new security collar is still integrating itself with his neural pathways. He'll be back to normal again in a couple days. Billy next door said that when their big Pud got his collar, he moped around for a week. I guess it's like neutering a dog–they're never the same afterwards."

Tonya scowled at Thornapple. She knelt down and brushed Har's face with the back of her hand. "Are you okay, big guy?" The boy twitched his head and stared blindly at the wall.

"I hope Har goes back to normal soon. I don't know how long I can stand Mom's cooking," Thorn said callously. "But hey, look at this!" He touched a button on the collar, and a holographic screen projected in the air. No matter where they stood, the screen appeared to be facing them. "Show me area 5 dash 7 sector 8," he commanded.

The screen turned black, and tiny specks of light appeared in the darkness. "Look, it's the Big Dipper," he exclaimed, pointing to the constellation on the screen.

Tonya furrowed her eyebrows. "How demeaning; you've turned Har into a walking encyclopedia."

"Not only that," Thorn said. "He's upgradeable, too! Dad says next week we might even add the weather channel to his database."

Tonya's face and hair reddened. "That's horrible! I don't want any part of this." She marched to her bedroom, slammed the door, and didn't come out until dinner.

Dinner that night consisted of a wide assortment of food that Mrs. Troodle had found in the cupboards, none of which looked very appetizing. Even her husband had nothing good to say about the pathetic meal. Breakfast the next morning was about as enticing as dinner had been, and most of the family decided to go hungry.

Everyone sat groggily at the table, minding their own business. Thorn broke the silence. "Does anybody know what today is?"

Tonya answered smugly, "How could we not? It's the day before the thousand-year anniversary of the Battle of Lisardious."

"No, silly–it's my birthday!"

"Oh, that too," Tonya added.

"We didn't forget," said Dr. Troodle. "Your mother and I have a surprise for you, Thornapple, but you'll have to wait until tonight to find out."

Thorn beamed while Tonya rolled her eyes.

Before the children left for school, Tonya whispered to Simon, "Here, take this." She handed him some fruit. "I have plans for us today, and they don't include going to school." She gave him one of her mischievous grins.

Simon adjusted his hover chair. "Are you sure we should ditch school?"

"What sounds like more fun: learning magic or doing geometry problems with Mrs. Larz?"

He didn't have to think long for that one.

"Okay, let me go get my stuff."

Simon zoomed to his bedroom and came back a minute later with his fanny pack bursting at the seams.

Halfway to school, Tonya announced, "Ah, nuts! I forgot my homework. I guess I'll have to go back and get it."

Thorn looked at the girl suspiciously. "You did your homework?"

"Of course I did," she fibbed. "Simon, will you walk back with me? I don't wanna go home alone."

"I'll go with you," Thorn said.

"Oh, no," Simon said, playing along. "You don't want to be late for school on your birthday. I'll go with Tonya."

"Well . . . okay," the small Pud said with a slight twinge of uneasiness in his voice. "I'll see you later."

Thorn continued down the cobblestone road alone and was soon out of sight. Like a giddy schoolgirl, Tonya leapt from the pathway and ran into the forest.

"Wait for me!" Simon yelled, trying to keep up.

The two children played tag for a while. Despite the awkwardness of the hover chair, Simon sped through the forest with great agility. The quick reflexes he had gained from the countless hours of video-game playing were finally paying off.

Exhausted from both running and laughing, Tonya stopped to catch her breath. Simon looked up at the tall trees surrounding them and marveled at their size. He looked closer and realized that a family of slothlike creatures was nestled in the branches above; their hooked arms grappled the boughs of the trees as they climbed.

"Look at that." Simon pointed at the long-armed sloths as they swung from one tree to the next.

At least twenty of the playful creatures were now visible. Some were about the size of a full-grown human, while others were as small as a cat. All of them had great big eyes and furry gray coats.

Simon noticed one of the bigger animals easing itself to the opening of a rather large and strange-looking tree. Five bright-green branches jutted from a crevice in the tree like a bony hand. The sloth's three curved toes wrapped around the welcoming branches, allowing the curious animal to stand up and peer into the tree. The old sloth poked its head closer to the gaping hole in the trunk and then quickly withdrew. It did this a few more times–getting closer with each peek.

"I love being around nature." Tonya took a deep breath of fresh air. "Everything is just so peaceful out here."

She had barely finished speaking when the five green branches clenched like a fist around the unsuspecting sloth. The wooden fingers pulled the terrified animal into the yawning mouth of the tree. Loud crunching sounds echoed from within the trunk. The other sloths screamed and moved about wildly as the tree devoured the poor creature.

After the horrible noises had finally died, the five green branches slowly emerged from the hole once more. Glimmers of red blood dropped from the hungry branches as the devious hand stretched its stiff fingers. Becoming still, it patiently waiting for another tasty morsel of food to come along.

"Holy cow!" Tonya exclaimed.

"I guess things aren't always what they appear," Simon said.

"Yeah, remind me not to climb any trees while we're out here."

Although a little sick to their stomachs, they decided to move on. The forest grew thinner and thinner as they traveled.

"Are you sure you know where you're going?" Simon asked. He opened his fanny pack and pulled out an apple.

"Of course I do. It's not much farther. I used to go here all the time when you were in your coma."

Twenty minutes later, they found themselves at the edge of a small hill covered with thick green grass. Tonya crawled up the hill with great difficulty, sliding backwards a few times because of the slippery vegetation. When she got to the top, Simon extended his hand to help her up the last few feet. For a second she wondered how he had gotten to the top so fast, but then she realized he must have zoomed up the hill with his hover chair when she wasn't looking. Tonya took his hand and yanked him out of the chair. He fell onto the grass.

"You little booger!" she said, standing up. "If you don't stop using that chair, you'll be sorry."

Simon rubbed his side. "I know, I know," he said. "I guess I'm just getting lazy." He pressed the button on his glasses to release them from his face. They seemed okay.

Tonya grabbed his hand and helped him to his feet. They limped to the edge of the precipice and looked over the vast stretch of fields bearing lakes of wheat, tanned by the hot sun. Thousands of giant Puds labored with their hairy farbearuses–the same type of animal Har's mother had ridden earlier–to harvest the crop. From the high vantage point of the mountain, they looked like tiny ants.

Beyond the rich farmland lay a blue ocean, which extended as far as the eye could see. The bright sun cast its rays onto the cracked watery mirror of the placid ocean, causing the different shades of red and orange to spill like paint upon the cool waters.

"Isn't this beautiful?" Tonya sighed, her hair turning a light auburn color. The tranquility of the scene masked her fear of heights.

Simon nodded in agreement. The whole time he had been on Pudo, he had never traveled very far from the hospital. He knew the city was built upon the flattened summit of a high mountain, but he didn't realize how high they really were.

"So then," Tonya said abruptly. "You put one hand on my back, like this." She placed Simon's right hand beneath her left shoulder blade. "And then you take my right hand, like this–"

"Wh-Wh-What are you doing?"

"I'm teaching you how to dance."

"I thought we came up here to do magic."

"Oh, you have your *whole* life to do magic. But how many opportunities do you get to dance on a *mountaintop* overlooking the world?" Tonya said in a misty voice.

She batted her eyes at him and tossed her hair playfully. Simon opened his mouth to object, but he could see that it was no use arguing, so he consented . . . reluctantly. Tonya placed her left hand near his right shoulder and then raised their arms up high. Simon had to stretch because he was shorter than her.

"Okay, now step forward with your right foot." The boy stepped forward. "Your other right."

"That *is* my right!"

"Oh, sorry. Step forward with your *left* foot." Simon felt silly, but she pushed him on. "Now bring your right foot to the side, and then slide your left foot over. Good! Now bring your right foot back . . . Left foot to the side and let your right foot slide over. Good!"

She dragged him around like a rag doll. "ONE–two–three . . . ONE–two–three . . . ONE–two–three . . ." she called out the rhythm. "You're getting it."

Simon stumbled but regained his balance. Soon, he was actually leading them in the waltz. It was exhilarating. He was doing it–he was dancing!

"Are you sure you've never danced before?"

"Positive."

"You're pretty good, for a beginner. Let's quicken the pace."

The young teenagers danced merrily upon the cliff top, and after a while, it didn't even seem like their feet were touching the ground. They gracefully glided in every direction–both smiling happily. Tonya's long auburn hair swayed back and forth in the cool, fresh breeze. Simon had never seen her hair this color before. He liked it.

Finally exhausted, they stopped their waltz to take a rest. Tonya bent over to catch her breath. She brushed her hair out of her face and smiled affectionately at Simon.

"That was actually fun," the boy said, panting lightly.

"See, Simon, dancing is fun."

Tonya was still short of breath. She straightened up and said carefully, "Someday . . . when you find a girl you like . . ." She took one of his hands and placed it around her slim waist. "You'll hold her like this . . ." She brought his other hand to her waist as well. "And she'll put her hands on your shoulders . . ." She rested her hands on his collarbone and nudged him softly to move. "Then, you'll dance–slowly . . . like this." They started to rotate–ever so delicately. "This gives you a chance to relax," she said. "To forget about everything and just enjoy the company of the person you're with."

Trying to avoid eye contact, Simon looked out at the ocean. Birds dressed in colorful robes swam joyfully through the white clumps of cloud painted upon an azure sky. It seemed peaceful, in a way, to look out and see the majestic ocean waves becoming smaller and smaller, their frothy curls eventually merging with the horizon.

Simon noticed that Tonya was humming. He recognized the melody immediately; it was one of the songs they'd heard at the café back on Earth.

The boy now faced the mountain. He could see the high-rise towers of glass and metal glimmering in the distance. He'd never been in that part of the city before; Dr. Troodle's home was located in a more prestigious part of town–away from the hustle and bustle of city life.

What a contrast, he thought as he turned towards the calm ocean once more.

"The Elders would be upset with me right now," Tonya informed him. "Young girls are not allowed to be alone with boys."

"Why's that?"

Simon fixed his eyes on Tonya's beautiful hair. It was changing into an even deeper auburn color.

"Because something might happen," she said, closing her eyes.

Simon replied slowly, "I think I agree with the Elders . . . If you put two people together long enough, you never know what could happen."

They seemed to be getting closer and closer as they danced. The boy finally looked into Tonya's eyes, and everything around him seemed to disappear–everything, that is, but her lovely face. Like a magnet, he was drawn closer . . . closer. Her hands were now wrapped around the back of his neck. Was she pulling him in or was he moving closer of his own accord? Simon couldn't seem to fight it any longer. He closed his eyes.

Just then, a loud and annoying voice startled them both. "What are you guys doing?"

CHAPTER 14
MAGIC LESSONS

Tonya shoved Simon away, which made him lose his balance and fall. He looked up from the ground to see Thorn walking over to them.

"You were standing!" Thorn said. The tiny boy stood with his mouth gaped open and his eyes wide with excitement.

Tonya flung up her hands and yelled melodramatically, "It's a miracle!"

Simon crawled to his hover chair and sat down. "Wh-wh-what are you doing here?" he asked, trying to hide his embarrassment.

"I followed you," the little Pud replied. "I wanted to see what you guys were up to."

"Nothing!" Tonya blurted in her native Chamelean language. She switched to Pudo so that Thorn could understand. "Absolutely nothing." Her beautiful auburn hair turned a fiery red.

"Yeah, I could see that."

Ignoring the comment, Simon cleared his throat and said, "Tonya was just about to give me a magic lesson. Do you want to join us?"

Thorn's eyes lit up. "Sure! That would be fun."

"Just remember, Thorny," Tonya said, "this lesson is meant for Simon. He's the only one who can do magic on this planet."

Thorn raised an eyebrow. "Whatever you say, Butblacruze. But I still want to try."

"And don't call me Butblacruze!"

Tonya brought out her wand and slapped it into Thornapple's hand. He winced in pain.

"All right then," she said. "First off, you have to understand what electro-magical energy is–"

Thorn interrupted, "I thought you said there wasn't any of that on Pudo."

"There isn't."

"Then why bother teaching us about it?"

"Because, know-it-all, *you* can't do magic without it. Besides, I don't plan on being in this horrible paraworld my whole life. My father is a very rich and powerful man. If there's anyone out there who can find me and get me out of here, it's him."

She caressed the silver ring on her finger. The dim light representing her father's life force flickered on the band. Thorn opened his mouth to speak but stopped. He nodded for her to continue.

"Think of E.M. energy as waves of light," she said, trying to speak clearly. To Simon, she spoke perfect English, but to Thorn, she had an awful accent. "Except for the parastream and the lousy paraworld we're in right now, this energy fills every nook and cranny of the paraverse, but its intensity varies dramatically. You can have a bunch of electro-magical energy in one spot, while just a couple feet away, hardly any. And just like light, those waves are constantly moving around. So when you feel a pocket of E.M. energy, that's the time to cast your spell. Unfortunately, it's kinda hard to time it right. And to make things even more difficult, each spell requires a different level of electro-magical energy to perform."

"So how do you know when you're standing in a pocket of E.M. energy?" Simon asked.

"Well, it takes a lot of experience to recognize it. That's why the royal family set up the schools of magical learning. The more often you cast spells, the easier it is to recognize the energy and use it to your advantage. Other than that, I can't really explain it. You just have to feel it to know what I'm talking about."

"But you said yourself that Earth had more E.M. energy than any other paraworld you'd ever been to. How come I wasn't able to do any magic when I was there?"

"That's the same question I've been wondering," Tonya said. "I think Earthlings must be different from everyone else in the paraverse. Instead of being able to cast spells using E.M. energy, you can cast spells without it." She put her hand to her mouth and gasped. "In fact, I bet E.M. waves nullify your magical abilities! That must be it–that's the answer! It explains everything."

"I don't know," Simon said, meticulously rubbing his mother's medallion. "Maybe there's something more to it than that."

"What else could it be?" she argued, now speaking in the Chamelean language. "I heard there are some crazy people out there who put themselves in strange electro-magical devices–kind of like a tanning booth–but instead of trying to get a tan, they're trying to become more endowed with magical abilities. What ends up happening is that they usually die from overexposure. Maybe . . ." Her excitement peaked. "Just maybe, because you lived in a paraworld that had ultra-high levels of E.M. energy, your body developed an immunity!"

The theory sounded plausible. Simon felt much better physically on Pudo than he ever did on Earth, but he couldn't rule out the young woman from his dreams–or his medallion, for that matter.

"You might be right," he said, trying to pacify her. For some reason, he felt hesitant to divulge his unusual dreams to Tonya. Perhaps he fancied the idea of being special, even if he really wasn't. Tonya didn't have to know his true source of power–not yet, at least.

"Of course I'm right. Look, Simon, I'd say your homeworld has the highest levels of E.M. energy in the whole paraverse. Any normal person would die within a few hours of visiting your planet, but somehow, your people are able to withstand the prolonged exposure. I just don't see any other explanation."

"So are you saying I'm a mutant or something?"

"Maybe. Anything or anyone exposed to high levels of E.M. waves for an extended period of time becomes altered by that energy."

Thorn's squeaky voice broke into the conversation. "I'm sure whatever you're talking about is interesting and all, but when are we going to get to the actual magic?"

"Patience, young one," Tonya said in a condescending tone. "Patience."

Thorn pursed his lips together and squared his shoulders. "Who ya calling young? I just turned thirteen today!"

"Well, I'm fourteen and that makes me the oldest, so there."

The little Pud snickered. "It doesn't make you the smartest."

"Maybe not, but it does give me more experience. I've seen things your scientists can only dream of . . . and I'm the only one here who knows about magic, so be quiet and listen."

Simon grabbed an apple from his fanny pack and took a big bite while Tonya continued her lesson.

"Magic," she said, "is produced by the E.M. waves–or the lack of E.M. waves in your case, Simon–but it must be harnessed by a person. As you summon the energy, it enters your body and then is released when you cast your spell. Most people as they start learning magic use something or other to focus that energy. I like to use a wand, but you can use whatever you want: a staff, a ring, a bracelet, or anything."

"How about a rock?" asked Thorn.

"Yeah, you could use a rock."

"How about a hat?"

"You could use a hat."

"What about a book?"

"Look, you could use a handful of dog poop if you wanted to. The point is that whatever you use, it'll help you to channel that built-up energy so you can cast your spell." She glanced at Simon as he opened his mouth to take another bite. "Let me see that apple, Simon."

He handed it over reluctantly, and she placed it on a flat rock nearby.

"Okay, Thorny, flick the wand at the apple and say: *Voluminous*. When you do it, imagine in your mind that the apple is getting bigger. Can you do that, or do I need to paint a picture for you?"

"*Voluminous!*" Thorn said, ignoring her insult. He flicked the wand with every syllable, "Vo-lu-mi-nous," but the apple didn't budge.

"Voluminous–Voluminous . . . *VO-LUMINOUS!*" He looked like he was conducting an orchestra.

"All right!" snapped Tonya. She grabbed the wand from his hand. "Yelling at it isn't gonna make it grow." She flicked the wand nonchalantly at the red fruit and said calmly, "*Voluminous.* That's how you do it. Here, Simon, you try."

Tonya handed the wand to Simon. It was black with a white tip–similar to what a magician would use at a party. He inspected the smooth, waxy surface and realized that some of the paint had chipped off.

The image of the beautiful young woman from his dreams entered his mind. *Who is she?* he wondered. *She didn't start coming into my dreams until I got to this planet . . . Is she giving me these powers, or am I really special like Tonya says I am?*

Simon had never thought he could be *special.* Special was a word used for someone great–someone with fantastic skills or attributes . . . surely not someone like himself: a sickly young boy too small for his age with big ears, unruly hair, and glasses.

"We're waiting, Simon." Tonya interrupted his thoughts.

"Oh, sorry." He held the wand tightly and flicked it at the apple. "*Voluminous.*"

The apple began to tremble. Then it shook so violently, it hopped off the rock and rolled to the edge of the steep cliff. It started to grow . . . and grow . . . and grow! Soon, it grew taller than Tonya. The red skin stretched like a balloon being filled with air. Even the place where Simon had previously taken a bite expanded. When the apple stopped growing, it was easily ten feet tall.

Bewildered by the strange sight, Thorn exclaimed, "*Wow!* That was stupendous! I can't believe you did that!"

"I can't believe I did, either," Simon said, completely dumbfounded. He moved his hover chair to get a closer look. The giant fruit leaned partially over the cliff.

Thorn yanked off a small chunk of the apple and popped it in his mouth. "Tastes great," he announced. "It's nice and firm–just like a normal apple." He smacked the juicy flesh of the oversized fruit as he talked.

Just then, the crunching of rocks sounded in their ears. The apple teetered backwards.

"Stop it before it goes over," Simon yelled. He grabbed the torn skin at the edge of the huge bite mark and tried to stop the apple from falling off the cliff. "If this goes over, someone below might get killed!"

Tonya and Thorn grabbed the apple as well, which stabilized it for the moment. "We can't hold this forever!" Tonya cried.

A faint grumbling sound resonated from within the apple. Thorn pressed his ear to the side of the fruit, and a troubled look appeared on his face. "Guys, do you hear that?"

"Yeah, that's my heart racing," Tonya shouted, readjusting her grip.

"No, there's something else."

"I think I do hear something," Simon said as the grumbling became louder.

Suddenly, the side of the apple exploded outward, and the head of a giant worm emerged. The strange snakelike creature had two sharp horns on the top of its green head as well as two beady little eyes. Its massive jaws opened wide, and it gave out a loud screech that shocked Thorn so badly, he lost his grip and fell backwards. Seeing the helpless boy lying on the ground, the worm lunged towards him with its mouth gaped open. But just before it reached Thorn, the apple rolled over and fell off the cliff–taking the huge worm with it.

Simon still held a flap of red skin in his hands. He watched helplessly as the apple descended the tall mountain. Thorn scurried to the edge of the cliff and looked down.

"Well, Simon," he noted, "there goes your lunch."

SMASH! The apple splattered on the ground below, causing pieces of fruit to mushroom out into the field. Giant Puds dodged as parts of the juicy apple rocketed through the tall shocks of wheat. Although some of the workers had gotten messy, no one was seriously injured–that is, no one except the worm, which now lay dead.

"Sorry!" Simon yelled, but he was too far away for any of the Puds below to hear his apology.

"Wow, Simon, that was pretty impressive, but for the next spell maybe we should try something simpler . . . and less dangerous," Tonya said. She looked around for a tiny rock or twig they could practice on. "There we go," she said, pointing to a weed that resembled a pussy willow but had a thick, cylindrical end like a cattail. She snatched her wand from Simon and demonstrated the next spell they were to perform. "*Foonati,*" she intoned, waving the wand over the peculiar weed.

"What does it do?" asked Simon.

"Sometimes you can't quite reach something, so you cast a moving spell. *Foonati* is the most minor moving spell of all. Really, about the only thing it's good for is flipping switches. So with your hyperactive abilities, you'll probably snap that weed in half, but other than that, I can't imagine anything horrible could happen."

"Let me try first." Thorn begged like a little kid.

"Okay," Tonya said, handing him the wand with reservation. "Just wave the wand *slowly* from right to left and say the magic word."

"What's the magic word?"

"Foonati."

"Oh, of course." He waved the wand slowly from right to left with an exaggerated motion. "*Foonati.*"

Nothing happened.

"All right. Simon's turn," Tonya said bluntly.

"*FOONATI!*" Thorn yelled. He cut the air with the wand so that it made a swooshing sound as it passed over the strange weed. "*FOONATI! FOONATI!*" Finally, he got so frustrated, he sliced the weed in half with the wand. "There! That moved it."

Tonya grabbed the wand from Thorn and gave it to Simon. "All right, that does it! You've lost your wand privileges," she growled.

Thorn demonstrated his skill of annoyance by picking up the severed weed and handling it as if it were a sword. "Oh, lighten up, Butblacruze. I'm just having some fun." He pretended to fight an imaginary person. "Why don't you teach us some fighting magic?" He swung the weed so close to Tonya's face that it almost nicked her nose.

"I'll show you fighting magic!"

Streaks of red swam down her waist-length hair as she lunged after the little Pud. She chased him around the hill, but he was too quick for her.

Meanwhile, Simon gazed lazily at the long row of furry weeds in front of him. He took the black wand and brought it as far back as he could. Tonya yelled loudly as she chased after Thorn. Simon paid little attention to his friends; his focus was centered on the strange weed at his feet. He felt a cool breeze brush against his face, and for a moment everything became silent.

"*Foonati,*" he said, waving the wand through the air like a scythe.

Immediately, the weed trembled and jerked, but something stopped it from launching into the air. The dirt where it stood broke apart. A thick root suddenly burst out of the ground, allowing Simon to see that the weeds actually sprouted from the same source.

Each weed, in turn, moved out of place as the root buckled under the soil. It flailed about wildly like a power line that had just been cut. Oblivious to what was happening, Tonya and Thorn were both thrown to the ground as the grassy carpet underneath them yanked away. A large crack ran down the hill, causing an upheaval of rocks and grass to form on each side. Two more cracks ripped through the soft dirt and headed towards the base of a large tree that was covered with the same pussy-willow weeds.

Similar to giant tendrils, the roots sprang upwards and twisted around the tree furiously. A chill ran down Simon's spine when he heard the painful crack of the tree being split in half by its own roots. As if that weren't enough, the possessed roots continued to spread throughout the entire forest like a pernicious virus, attacking the rest of the pussy-willow trees.

Within moments, Simon realized that all of the willow trees were interconnected by the same root system. Perhaps the strange trees were actually one organism whose appendages expanded throughout the whole forest. Needless to say, no other type of tree was harmed, and when the scene of destruction was over, not a single pussy-willow tree remained standing.

From where Simon sat, he could see the winding pathways that had been cut throughout the forest from the carnage that had just taken place. The forest now looked like a huge maze.

"That was some spell!" Thorn gasped as he walked towards Simon. "You really gave that weed a *nudge*, didn't you? I'd hate to see what a *major* moving spell would do!"

Simon stared at the fallen trees in disbelief, his mouth hanging open. "I think that's enough magic for today," he mumbled.

"We're just getting started!" Thorn exclaimed.

"Maybe we should go home now. I've done enough damage already."

"We can't go home or we'll get in trouble for playing hooky," Tonya countered. "Besides, after what you just did, the forest will be crawling with adults. I doubt they'll find us up here."

"That's right," Thorn said. "Let's see how big you can make a banana grow." The little boy unzipped Simon's fanny pack, and out popped two peaches and a banana. He threw a peach to Tonya who, after catching it, scanned the surface closely for worm holes. "Oh! Oh! Here we go!" Thorn squealed, bringing out Simon's video game machine.

Simon frowned. "You want me to make my video games grow?"

"No, silly, I want you to make them work."

His face brightened. "Oh, I was kinda hoping Tonya would show me how to recharge the batteries. That's why I brought it with me in the first place. It was going to be a surprise for your birthday."

Tonya reacted quickly, "Oh, no-no-no-no-no! I wouldn't do that if I were you. That would be *way* too complicated. You might not use enough wattage or you might use too much voltage. Spells like that are just so intricate you'd have to be a professional to be able to do it. Besides, you'd probably fry the–"

POOF! A thin stream of white smoke came out of the colorful screen, and mechanical-sounding music filled the air.

". . . circuits," Tonya said, finishing her sentence.

"You did it!" Thorn yelled. "Now you have to show me how to get past level ten. Tell me, when you're fighting the end boss, do you use the flame-thrower or the grenade launcher?"

"Oh, no," Tonya moaned. "I wish you hadn't done that."

But it was too late; Simon and Thorn were instantly and completely enthralled with the video game. Playing it brought back many happy memories of Earth that Simon had forgotten. The boy hadn't realized until now how much he really did miss his home. He missed the food. He missed the interaction with normal children. He even missed being awakened by Dimitri every morning.

Tonya sat away from the boys and made comments such as, "Don't you think we should go now?" and "How much longer are you guys gonna be?" and "You guys are pathetic."

Annoyed and upset, Tonya rested on her back and stared at the clouds overhead. She picked out the especially long blades of grass around her and ate them one by one, imagining they were French fries.

The bright sun made it difficult for her to keep her eyes open, and after a while, she decided not to fight it any longer. Soon, the young teenager was fast asleep–away from the realities of life and especially away from that blasted video game machine.

The day passed by quickly.

■ ■ ■

Tonya stirred in her sleep. "*No . . . No! Run!*" She screamed herself awake. It was only a dream, yet it seemed so real.

"What's wrong?" asked Simon, not bothering to raise his head from the game.

"It was just a dream," Tonya said, yawning. "I dreamt we were being chased by those lizard things . . . You don't think there's any of them in the forest, do you?"

The boys nodded slightly but didn't respond.

Tonya sighed and then suddenly looked around, realizing how dark it was. The sun was starting to hide behind the mountain. A quickly-growing shadow cast itself across the forest as the sun descended from view.

"I can't believe you guys are still playing. Thornapple, didn't your dad say he had a surprise for you back at home?"

"Oh my gosh! I forgot all about my birthday."

"That's a miracle."

Simon turned off his video game and said, "We better go while the sun is still out."

They packed up their things and slid down the hill–what was left of it. The forest appeared much darker now and more ominous, but they trudged on, nonetheless. Simon started to recognize the pathway; there was the sloth-eating tree–except, its green hand was curled up inside for the night. A little ways farther, they heard voices ahead of them. Simon quickly turned off the lights on his hover chair.

"This is the strangest thing I've ever seen," a man said.

"Do you think the dragunos did this?" another replied.

"No, I don't think so. It almost looks like the trees attacked themselves, but that's impossible."

"Look at how the roots have come right out of the ground. It would have taken something pretty big to do that, but I don't see any tracks at all. Surely we would have detected if the aliens had come back, wouldn't we?"

"Lenny, the Lisardians have been gone for a thousand years now. They're not coming back."

"Yeah, but you've heard the rumor that the aliens return every millennium. Last time they sprang up out of nowhere. What if–"

"Lenny! Let's just finish surveying the area and leave the speculations to the scientists."

The three teenagers slowly made their way through the clearing, but when a stick snapped under Thorn's foot, Lenny shrieked.

"Did you hear that? They're coming for us!"

Simon cranked his hover chair into full gear and zoomed past the inspectors like a speeding ghost. Because of the darkness, the only thing the little Puds could see was that someone or something had just flown by.

Tonya and Thorn followed Simon while Lenny screamed, "They're back! The Lisardians are back! Don't let them get me!"

After reaching the main cobblestone road, all three teenagers burst into laughter. "*Don't let them get me*!" Thorn imitated. They joked all the way home; however, their faces were soon wiped clean of merriment when they reached the porch. Standing there in the doorway with hands on her hips and a scolding expression on her face was Mrs. Troodle.

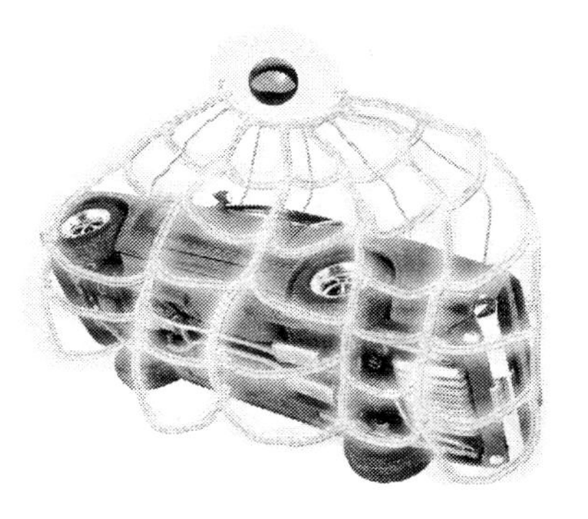

CHAPTER 15
THE BIG FIGHT

Do you know what time it is?" Thorn's mother snapped. "We've been waiting all night for you to come home, Thornapple. If we don't hurry, we'll be late."

Thorn swallowed hard and asked, "Late for what?"

Mrs. Troodle threw both hands into the air. "Your birthday surprise. We're taking you to the big fight tonight."

"You're kidding me! I thought it was sold out."

"It is sold out, but we bought our tickets early." She turned her head and yelled into the house,"Honey, they're here! Let's go!"

"One moment, Sweetie. I'm just finishing up on the news."

She twisted her lips and murmured, "Oh, you're just finishing up on the news."

Mrs. Troodle marched into the house, followed by Thorn, Tonya, and Simon. They found Dr. Troodle watching the news from a semi-holographic projection that emitted from Har's security collar. The poor kid was foaming at the mouth, and he couldn't seem to keep his eyes focused on anything. All three teenagers looked at each other nervously as the tiny reporter presented the news.

Earlier today, every single willow tree in the Zapaneen forest was mysteriously torn down. Specialists on the scene have told us that there is no scientific explanation for this phenomena, yet they are not ruling out foul play. Authorities have no comment at this time.

On another note, eleven more draguno attacks were reported today—one attack involving a daycare facility. Two big Puds were killed protecting their owners, and five more were severely injured. Scientists still haven't discovered where these reptiles are coming from, but they assured us that the situation is under control . . .

Mrs. Troodle pressed a button on Har's collar, and the 3-D projection turned off. "All right, let's go."

"Hey, I was watching that," Dr. Troodle said.

"You can watch it when we get back." She turned to Har, who was drooling profusely onto the gray carpet, and commanded, "Har, record the news."

A red light on his security collar blinked on and off, indicating that the news was being recorded from the Holonet.

■ ■ ■

"Honey, if you don't hurry it up, we'll miss the first round!"

"I'm going the speed limit, Sweetie. Just be patient. We'll be there before you know it."

Because of the awkwardly designed vehicle, Simon was forced to sit with his head between his knees, and Tonya was obliged to curl up on the seat with her legs folded over in a sort of kneeling position. And of course, there wasn't enough room to bring Simon's hover chair, so they left it at home.

"Honey, maybe I should drive," Mrs. Troodle said.

"We're almost to the highway . . . Oh, look at that line!" They slowed down to a crawl. "It looks like we're not the only ones headed for the big fight."

Mrs. Troodle pulled on a lever, and the car lurched upwards and started to fly over the long row of cars ahead of them.

"You're going to get me pulled over," the doctor said, steering the vehicle upwards.

He cut into a row of traffic that flew overhead. Simon felt his stomach drop as they sped onwards. Soon, a small flying ball zoomed up to the front window, and a mechanical voice asked, "*Destination*?"

"Hollywhip Stadium," Dr. Troodle said.

"*Destination confirmed . . . Directions are now mapped out . . . Please sit back and enjoy the trip*."

A white light shot out of the metallic ball and engulfed the car in a strange glowing web. It dragged the vehicle through the highway, hopping from lane to lane to make their journey as efficient as possible. Looking out the side window, Simon noticed similar devices leading the other cars as well.

A series of tall buildings came into view. Because Simon had never been in the inner city before, he didn't realize how grand it really was. The buildings stood so high, he could scarcely see the ground below. Holographic billboards lined the invisible highway, advertising things such as schools of higher learning, new advancements in security collars, items for conducting experiments, special seminars on science, and even informational books on how to potty train your big Pud.

Vehicles of all shapes and sizes flooded the entire sky. For a race of people who didn't seem to care much about anything other than science, the little Puds sure did have a huge variety of flying cars. And if it weren't for the aid of the floating balls, the whole network of highways would be in total chaos, but, surprisingly, every car was able to compensate for variances in the wind and openings created when cars jumped to different roadways or lanes.

As they neared the tallest building, their car started to sputter and cough. Suddenly, the tractor beam surrounding the vehicle shorted out, forcing the car to brake loose from the highway and fall.

"*Ah, great,*" Dr. Troodle mumbled under his breath. "I've been meaning to get the magnetron converter fixed. Hold on, everybody!"

They dove through several rows of cars–all of which moved out of the way in perfect unison.

The metallic ball chased after them frantically. "*Malfunction: the magnetic coupling has been disengaged . . .*" came the mechanical voice. "*There is no need to panic. Please stay calm while I attempt to regain control of the vehicle.*"

"That's easy for you to say!" Mrs. Troodle said.

She pulled down on the throttle to help bring the car out of its nosedive. Abruptly, the car shot upwards, and everyone fell back against their seats. All the while, the flying ball kept shooting its tractor beam at them, but the web of light just couldn't seem to take hold. Now the car was rising higher and higher, dispersing traffic like a speedboat cutting through water.

Dr. Troodle smashed through four floating billboards in succession and then leveled off long enough to scatter a line of cars that were waiting to get into the parking lot on the top of the largest building. Thorn screamed as they raced towards a tall partition that separated the coliseum from the parking lot. Then, just before they were pulverized against the wall, the metal orb that had been trailing behind finally grabbed hold of the vehicle.

"*Destination arrived. I hope you enjoyed the trip,*" it said as they came to an abrupt halt. The ball gently rested the car onto a convenient parking space near the entrance.

"Well," Mrs. Troodle said, brushing her hair out of her face, "that was a nice shortcut. We're not even late."

The arena sat on top of the building like a bowl. Spotlights danced around the noisy crowd, and the smell of food filled the air. Everyone around them seemed to be staring at Tonya; it wasn't every day they saw a tall, green-haired alien in their midst.

"You guys didn't get any dinner, did you?" yelled Dr. Troodle over the cheers of the crowd. "Here, take this." He gave some money to each of them.

"Thanks!" all three of them said.

Tonya and Thorn raced to the concession stands, while Simon trailed sluggishly behind. He took one look at the selection and decided to go hungry. Thorn ordered a chicken wing–feathers and all–and Tonya ordered some deep-fried rhubarb.

"Aren't you going to get anything?" Thorn asked Simon.

"I'm not too hungry."

Just then, the crowd roared. The announcer said in an exaggerated voice, "To my left, we have the challenger: Alvin Bottlebrush! He has been fighting professionally for two years now. His favorite science is chemistry, and he holds two doctorates in biology . . . And girls, I hear he's single."

The noise was deafening. Everyone but Simon turned around to get a closer look.

"Come on, kids, let's go!" Mrs. Troodle urged.

Simon exchanged his money for something sealed in a white plastic wrapper. He promptly put the item in his fanny pack before anybody could see.

The announcer spoke again. "And to my right, we have the champion: Bo-Bob Dungbeat! Mr. Dungbeat has never lost a fight yet. He enjoys chemical engineering and computer science. He is currently studying at Highland City's very own Northcliff University, where he hopes to teach someday."

Simon made it to his seat just in time to see two small Puds strutting around the stage, flexing their muscles like bodybuilders. He thought it odd that such a civilized people would endorse a violent sport such as boxing. Mrs. Troodle seemed especially interested in Alvin Bottlebrush, who was clearly the better looking of the two fighters.

"The rules are simple," the announcer continued. "Keep it clean while the blue light is on–nothing below the belt. Watch for the chaos light. When you see it, you'll have thirty seconds of no-holds-barred. Good luck, gentleman. Shake hands and let the fight begin!"

The two boxers attempted to shake hands, but their gloves proved too cumbersome. They then turned around and left the ring, which Simon found very confusing. Standing just outside the ropes, each fighter was outfitted with wires and electrodes that led to a plastic headband.

The crowd screamed wildly as two trapdoors opened up on the stage. Slowly, two giant figures emerged from the floor. They were the biggest Puds Simon and Tonya had ever seen.

Simon still didn't know what was going on until he saw the big Puds start to fight. Somehow, the large men were being remotely controlled by the little Puds. For instance, every time Alvin or Bo-Bob swung an arm, their counterpart in the ring would swing his arm as well.

The two giants exchanged blows to the face–one after the other–until Bo-Bob's Pud began to bleed from a cut under his eye.

"This is barbaric!" Tonya cried.

"Yeah, this doesn't seem very fair," Simon said.

Thorn smiled. "Don't worry, guys. The pain receptors aren't transmitted to the little Puds–just the movement. Alvin and Bo-Bob are quite all right."

Tonya rolled her eyes in response.

The blue light that surged through the top rope surrounding the ring started to flash the primary colors.

"It's berserk time!" exclaimed the announcer over the roar of the crowd.

The large Puds ran to the sideline and quickly picked out weapons. Bo-Bob selected a wooden bat, and Alvin chose two rubber batons. In a demonic fury, the giants lashed out at each other.

At first, it looked like Alvin was going to lose the fight. Bo-Bob kept hitting Alvin's fighter across the back, but then his bat suddenly shattered. With two seconds left in the round, Alvin clashed his hands together, as if he were clanging two cymbals. His Pud followed suit by smashing the rubber batons against the other Pud's sides.

A loud buzzer rang, and the round ended.

Tonya turned to Mrs. Troodle, who was clapping like crazy, and yelled over the hysteria of the crowd, "I thought little Puds didn't have time for frivolous things. This fight doesn't seem like a very productive use of your time."

"Konya, you're missing the whole point. The fight is just a demonstration of the new advancements in security collars. We're getting a peek at the future!"

"At the expense of injuring two helpless people?"

"I wouldn't really call them *people*, Konya," Dr. Troodle chimed in. "The whole purpose of this line of science is to control the animalistic nature of the big Puds. I can't even imagine what the world would become like if we didn't have security measures like this."

Tonya murmured under her breath, "I don't think it's the big Puds with the animalistic nature."

The buzzer rang, and round two began.

Sweat poured down the bodies of the large Puds, causing their muscles to glisten in the spotlight. Even their owners perspired as they threw their fists into the air. Simon thought it strange to see the dramatic expressions on Alvin Bottlebrush's face as he shadow boxed in unison with his big Pud. Bo-Bob Dungbeat, on the other hand, remained cool and collected; every movement he made was well thought-out and purposeful.

During this round, the fighters became much more rambunctious than before. They used their feet to kick, and they danced around the mat to avoid getting hit. Although Bo-Bob and Alvin were somewhat hindered in what they could do, they were still able to maneuver their fighters around with remarkable skill.

The crowd roared with excitement when the chaos light flashed again. Alvin, the challenger, made his Pud run to the sideline to get a weapon. This time the selection was more deadly than before. His fighter picked up a knife, but before the large man could turn around to use it, Bo-Bob's Pud kneed him in the back. Being a more experienced fighter, Bo-Bob had decided that, instead of getting a weapon, he would make a surprise attack instead.

After Bo-Bob completed his first assault, he compelled his fighter to pick up Alvin's Pud and throw him off the stage. Bo-Bob raised his feet as though climbing a ladder, which in turn forced his Pud to climb up the ropes and stand on the top rung. The little Pud waved to the crowd and then threw himself to the ground. His Pud did the same, but instead of hitting the mat, he smashed heavily onto the other big Pud.

"*Ooooh*, that's gotta hurt!" the announcer commented. "If Mr. Bottlebrush doesn't start doing better soon, he's gonna have to find himself a new Pud."

The crowd laughed, and the round ended.

Simon turned to Thorn and asked, "They don't kill each other, do they?"

"No, hardly anyone ever gets killed," Thorn replied. "They just beat each other up until one of them can't fight anymore."

"*Animals!*" Tonya spat.

"Yes, they are animals," Thorn said.

"I meant you–everyone here! Except for the ones in the ring, you're all animals!"

Thorn screwed up his face. "How can you say we're animals? Look at what we can accomplish! We have the power to control–"

"Your people are the real animals because you don't seem to have the power for compassion." She stood up, and everyone around them gasped at seeing her long red hair. "Civilized people don't take advantage of others. They treat each other with equality and civility." Simon perked up when she used those words. "Your technological advancements are worthless if they don't help you to become better people. Even my father wouldn't participate in something like this!"

"Sit down, young lady," Dr. Troodle said in a stern voice.

Deeply embarrassed, Mrs. Troodle hid her face so that none of her peers would recognize her.

"No! I won't sit down! I won't just sit and watch this go on any longer! Come on, Simon, let's stop this fight right now."

She grabbed the boy's arm, but he resisted. "There's nothing we can do," Simon said, staring at the floor.

"There's always something you can do," she scolded. "Simon, you need to stand up for what's right. When a problem comes up, you can't just ignore it and hope it goes away."

"But–"

"But nothing! Listen to me, runt. You and I don't really meet this paraworld's intellectual standards. You never know . . . maybe after a while, they'll turn us into slaves as well."

Her words pierced his heart like a knife, and he felt awful that he had been so passive about the whole thing. Feeling a strange courage he had never felt before, Simon leapt from his seat and followed Tonya down the steps towards the stage. He vowed never again to look the other way when someone needed him.

A million thoughts ran through his head. He wondered if there was a spell he could use to free the giants. Perhaps he could transport them out of the city. But what if he couldn't control the magic? And how would the little

Puds react to his spell? Now was not the time to doubt.

He looked up and saw that Bo-Bob's Pud held some type of revolving blade–like a chainsaw. Alvin's Pud had only a rod of iron to defend himself. The chaos light flashed wildly.

Simon and Tonya were almost to the stage when the big Pud who welded the chainsaw took a swipe at his opponent, slashing him across the abdomen–but only slightly. The injured man doubled over from the pain, and the crowd went wild. Fortunately for Alvin, the thin blade had only grazed his Pud.

Bo-Bob raised his hands up high and readied himself for the kill. The heartless crowd screamed in approval. Without warning, Alvin Bottlebrush thrust up his hands, causing his Pud to swing the rod of iron with all his might at his would-be executioner. The rod struck the other Pud across the neck so forcefully that it knocked him backwards onto the mat.

Staggering to his feet, the giant clutched his throat and broke off the shattered collar that had saved his life. He looked around the ring in a dazed stupor. Suddenly, he made eye contact with Bo-Bob, and a spark of hatred ignited within him. He charged at his master full force, but before he reached the ropes, the other big Pud, controlled by Alvin, tackled him to the ground.

Half-a-dozen little Puds jumped into the ring to help. They zapped the fallen giant with energy sticks that flared with every jab.

Determined, the large Pud grasped through the ropes at his master, but he couldn't quite reach. Bo-Bob Dungbeat just stood there with a solemn look etched across his face . . . He had just been defeated for the first time.

Simon covered his ears to drown out the screams from the hysterical crowd. He looked around at the people in dismay. Many raised their fists and jeered or called out for a rematch. Some were disappointed, while others overjoyed. Most of the Puds near the Troodles had not recovered from seeing Tonya's flaming red hair and overhearing her derogatory comments–neither had Mrs. Troodle.

The doctor stood by his wife, statue-like, except for the tightening of his clenched jaw muscles. Thornapple hung his head down. A gulf seemed to separate Simon from his tiny friend. The Earthling had turned his back to the family who had taken him in. He had trodden over their culture, embarrassed them beyond measure, and for what? Nothing had changed. Nothing he did would ever make a difference.

"Thank you," came a broken whisper from within the chaos.

Simon turned to Tonya and saw the tears streaming down her face. He reached over to pat her shoulder or to hold her hand–anything to comfort her. She threw her arms around his neck and sobbed.

"Thank you, Simon," she said again. "You stood by my side when no one else would. Thank you."

Simon held her, amidst the roaring crowd. He closed his eyes and opened them a few seconds later. Further up the coliseum, he spotted

Thornapple, standing in the aisle, alone; his parents were already marching towards the exit.

Thorapple's ashen face remained void of expression–the gleam gone from his sullen eyes, his customary smile dissolved from his face. The little Pud gazed at Simon and Tonya with big, troubled eyes. All Simon could do in response was stare back and frown. A shiver of dread ran down his spine. What was he doing on this strange planet? He didn't belong on Pudo. He wasn't sure if he belonged on Earth, either, but at least there he knew where he stood. Had his friendship with Thornapple just been severed–torn apart, along with half of his heart? Tonya held the other half. Simon embraced her more tightly and wondered what the future would bring, now that his world had just been turned upside down.

CHAPTER 16
CELEBRATION

It took over an hour for the tow truck to bring Simon, Tonya, and the Troodles home from Hollywhip Stadium. Exhausted and upset, they all went to bed without saying a word.

Simon waited for the familiar sound of Thorn's rhythmic snoring before he crept out of bed. His legs throbbed, so he decided to use his hover chair to carry himself to the kitchen.

"Har–you awake?"

He opened the plastic flap in the wall and peered at the large Pud sitting in the dark, bobbing his head uncontrollably.

"Are you okay?"

The large boy looked at Simon and blinked. "Si–Si . . ." he fumbled. "Si-moan hungry?"

"No, I'm not hungry. I just wanted to wish you a happy birthday." Simon handed him the present he had purchased at the concession stand. "Open it. It's for you."

Confused, Har broke open the white plastic wrapper and brought out a little chocolate cake. A tear dropped down his cheek.

"For Har?" he asked.

"Yes. Happy birthday, big guy."

"Thank–you, Si-moan."

The large boy stared into the darkness once more and continued to bob his head up and down.

Simon brushed a tear from his eye and whispered, "Have a good night."

He zoomed back to his room and got into bed. The soft covers were warm and inviting, but his muscles refused to relax. He sighed deeply. Tomorrow was not going to be a fun day. He rolled over, yawned, and looked across the room at Thorn. As his eyes focused in the dark, he realized Thorn was staring back at him. Simon drew in a quick breath and sat up.

"Are we still friends?" the little Pud asked.

"I . . . I don't know. I think so," Simon answered slowly.

"Do you think I'm an animal?"

"No." He paused. "But I do think you should treat Har better. He's had a rough time lately."

"So that's who you've been going to see every night."

Simon gasped in shock, but Thorn just smiled. How long had the little Pud known of his midnight excursions?

Thorn continued. "Did you know that today is also Har's birthday? We're the same age."

"Yeah, you two could be twin brothers."

They both laughed.

"Of course! We look *so* much alike," Thorn joked. "So we're friends?"

"Yeah . . . friends."

The little Pud smiled so widely that Simon could sense it across the room.

Despite the fact that his legs ached from all the strain he had put on them during the day, Simon fell asleep surprisingly fast. The beautiful young woman from his dreams appeared once more, but this time, she did not smile.

"What's wrong?" Simon asked.

"The enemy has awakened. They draw near, even as we speak. Soon, all will be destroyed."

"What can I do?"

The mist around them grew violent, and a howling wind came out of nowhere. The majestic beast the woman sat upon stood on its hind legs and panicked. Tossed back and forth like a tiny boat swallowed up in the heart of a raging storm, the young woman was almost flung from her companion's back, but she held on tightly, nonetheless, with admirable strength and perseverance. Finally, like a soothing breeze, she calmed the beast with a cool voice and then continued her warning.

Listen, dear Simon, for survival's recipe is thus:
A measure of strength from high places,
a pinch of cunning from below,
the mixture of two races becoming one,
and the language of old to open the door.

Simon struggled to remember the cryptic riddle. "I don't understand."

She opened her mouth to speak but was interrupted by the sharp voice of Mrs. Troodle. Simon opened his eyes to see Thorn's mother yelling at Tonya. The irate woman bellowed, "Don't lie to me, Konya! The forest rangers reported that one of the suspects had long green hair. *Hmm,* I wonder who that could be. There isn't anyone else on this whole planet with green hair!"

Simon sat up, and Mrs. Troodle exclaimed, "Good! You're awake.

Simon, I want you to tell me what you were doing in the forest yesterday."

Simon rubbed the sleep from his eyes. "Um," he started. "I-I-I don't know." He reached for his glasses and put them on. They stuck to his face like glue.

"Come on. Tell me the truth," she said.

"We were just practicing for the dance."

"See, that's what I told you!" Tonya shouted with glee.

Mrs. Troodle sighed heavily and said under her breath, "I don't even know why they're having this stupid dance in the first place." Tonya smiled in an *I-told-you-so* sort of way. Mrs. Troodle looked Simon squarely in the eyes and asked, "What else were you doing up there?"

Simon didn't want to lie, so he told the truth. "I was learning how to do magic, and a couple of the spells got out of control. Sorry."

Mrs. Troodle rolled her eyes in disbelief. "Thornapple, I don't know if letting Simon and Konya stay with us was such a good idea. They're obviously unstable."

"No, Mother," Thorn told her swiftly, "Simon's telling the truth. Konya was teaching us how to cast spells."

Tonya's smirk quickly disappeared. For the longest time, Mrs. Troodle just stood there with a shocked expression on her face. Then, suddenly, she screamed, "*HONEY! GET IN HERE, RIGHT NOW!*"

Dr. Troodle bounded into the bedroom. "Look what I just found in the kitchen," he said, holding a white plastic wrapper. "I think Har's been getting into our food again."

Simon blurted out, "No he hasn't. I gave him some food that I bought at the fight last night."

The Troodles gasped.

Thorn's mother closed her eyes and tried to regain her composure. She spoke quietly but sternly, "You did what?"

Simon lowered his eyes. "It was his birthday. I was just trying to make him feel better."

"That's it," Mrs. Troodle proclaimed, her voice rising again. "I want both of you out of my house, right now!"

"Sweetie?" Dr. Troodle said, surprised.

"You're a bad influence on my son."

"But, Mom–"

"Thornapple, just what am I supposed to tell the forest rangers when they come knocking on our door?"

"But it's the anniversary of the Battle of Lisardious!"

"Sweetie, he does have a point. Maybe they could stay just one more night. The whole city is closed down for the celebration. There's nowhere they can go today."

"All right, Honey," she said in a strained voice. "Whatever you say. I guess this celebration only happens every thousand years . . . but tomorrow, they're gone!" At that, she stormed out of the bedroom.

"Dad, you're not really going to let Mom kick Simon and Konya out of the house, are you?"

"She is pretty mad. We'll see. I suggest you guys don't hang around here today. Why don't you go to the fair while you still can. I have to go to the veterinarian. Har's having a bad reaction to his security collar." He headed towards the bedroom door and mumbled, "I hope I can find someone available to see him today."

"Oh, yeah! We don't have school today. This is the first time I can ever remember school being canceled. Seven days a week of school is too much, if you ask me."

"Yes, well, you better enjoy it while it lasts," his father said, just before leaving the room.

The three teenagers got ready for the day and met outside.

"You're not bringing that along, are you?" Tonya chided, referring to Simon's hover chair.

"My legs are really sore from all that walking I did yesterday."

"You're just a baby," she said. "I better not see you in that chair at the dance tonight."

Simon wondered why she was so interested in the dance. He couldn't imagine it being very fun. The dance, after all, was sponsored by a bunch of intellectual snobs.

As they neared the fairgrounds, they saw numerous little people running around to get to the next attraction. The event was exactly what Simon expected it to be: a big science fair.

One popular game allowed people to compete against each other by solving complex math problems. A problem would appear on a screen, and everyone would scribble frantically on their pads to get the correct answer.

At another location, a little Pud measured people's brain activity with a strange contraption. The machine flashed over each participant like an x-ray.

"Ever wonder what capacity your brain is at?" the man sang over the busy crowd. "Come now and find out what you're really made of! How 'bout you, young man?"

Simon glanced at the sign nearby. It mentioned something about not being held responsible for irreversible damage. "No, thank you," he said politely.

They walked to a tiny booth covered with electronic gizmos and gadgets. The salesman was showing some little kids the newest R6005-1 calculator–the most advanced model of its kind.

"Not only will it help you solve just about every equation you can think of . . ." The man looked around suspiciously. ". . . But I can give you a software patch that will enable it to snoop into your teacher's databases for possible test questions."

"That's a great idea, Salamoose. Why don't you just teach them how to pickpocket their parents while you're at it."

"Oh, Mayor Gordon! I didn't see you."

"Obviously."

The man who had just spoken wore a baseball cap with the image of an exploding spaceship embroidered on it. His tee shirt had the words "*I Survived the Battle!*" written across the front.

"Hello, Mayor," Thorn said eagerly.

"Hello to you," he responded. "You're a Troodle, aren't you?"

"Yes, I am."

"And you two must be our alien visitors. I've reviewed your biological scans. Nice to meet you, finally. I'm the mayor of Highland City."

He shook their hands vigorously.

Thorn introduced them. "This is Simon and this is Butbla–ah, I mean, Konya."

"It's Tonya. With a *T*," she said.

"Konya," the mayor repeated. Tonya closed her eyes and shook her head. The mayor continued, "Well, I assume you're not Lisardians. Here, have a souvenir. I've won so many prizes today I don't know what to do with them all."

He handed them some pillowcases with pictures of green aliens on them.

"I think they glow in the dark," he said. "Well, I have to be off. You guys should have a look at the archaeological exhibit. It's very interesting." He started to leave but then turned back and said, "Salamoose, no more software patches. Understand?"

"Yes, sir."

"Archaeological exhibit, huh?" Thorn mused. "Let's go there next."

"That sounds boring," Tonya said, wrinkling her nose. "Why don't we play some games instead?"

"All right," Thorn conceded. "I guess we do have all day to go to the exhibit."

They walked over to a table where a woman was placing large puzzle pieces in front of an old man. One after the other, she put the pieces down, but the man just couldn't seem to guess what the picture was.

He kept saying, "Just one more piece." And the woman would say in return, "That'll cost you another doongle."

"Some genius this guy is," Tonya whispered to Simon. "It's clearly a duck." Simon nodded in agreement.

Only one piece remained, but the man was still clueless. "Can you give me a hint?" he pleaded.

"Sorry," came the reply. "No more hints. You have to solve this one on your own."

He clenched his fists and bit his lip. "I give up. What is it?"

She put the last piece down, and it formed a yellow duckling. The crowd around the table roared in surprise.

"You cheated," the old man said. "You left the most important piece 'til the end."

"Sorry, sir, that's just how the game is played."

Thorn shook his head and said, "This game's too hard. Let's find something else to do."

"Are you kidding?" asked Simon. "A three-year-old could do this."

Thorn snorted. "If you think you're so smart, why don't you give it a try?"

"I would, but you'd have to lend me some money."

Overhearing his comment, the woman came to Simon's rescue. "I'll tell you what, young man. The first one's on me."

"Thank you. What are the rules?"

"You have to guess what the picture is within five puzzle pieces or else you'll have to pay one doongle for each additional piece. Your prize is dependent on how many pieces have been placed when you guess correctly. I haven't had anyone win yet without paying for extra pieces, but if you do win within the first five rounds, you can either collect a prize or go double or nothing."

"That sounds easy."

The woman smiled in response. From under the table, she pulled out a large puzzle piece and placed it on top of the red, glowing outline that appeared on the table.

"It's a chicken."

The woman opened her mouth in shock. "You won! I've never seen anyone win so fast before."

Thorn laughed. "I can't believe you did that! How did you know it was a chicken?"

Simon pointed to the puzzle piece and explained, "Those are chicken feet."

"Okay, kid, double or nothing?" said the woman impatiently.

"Sure."

She removed the piece and put another one on the table.

"It's a rattlesnake."

"Lucky guess! You did it again."

"Simon, are you using magic?" Thorn asked in disbelief.

"Of course not. What other animal has a rattle on the end of its tail?"

"Well, I know of a few."

The woman wrung her hands and shook her head. "Come on. Let's go. Double or nothing?"

"Let's do it again."

"Okay, this time, no more animals." She put another puzzle piece on the table.

"Uh, it's a piece of rubber."

"Ha! Wrong."

She put another piece down.

"Wait a second. Thorn, remember that first night I ate at your house? Your dad was eating a giant spider and you dropped that big worm on the table. What was that thing called?"

"That was a gilaworm."

"Gilaworm," Simon told the woman.

She gritted her teeth. "You're correct–again."

"Hey, I thought you said you weren't doing any more animals?" Tonya boomed.

The woman blushed. "Well, I was just trying to make the game more interesting. Double or nothing, kid?"

Simon continued to play the game while the crowd around him got larger and larger. "How does he do it?" one of the Puds asked. "He must be superintelligent," another person answered.

The puzzles went on and on.

"A house."

"The moon."

"A tree."

"A pair of socks."

Simon was growing tired of the game, but everyone around him couldn't seem to get enough of it. The woman put down the fourth piece of the current puzzle.

"Is it a castle?"

"Nope!"

The crowd moaned in disappointment as the woman placed the fifth puzzle piece on the location the table indicated it should go.

Thorn contemplated on the puzzle. "I can't quite put my finger on it," he said.

The crowd chanted, "*Si-mon–Si-mon–Si-mon.*"

It was all up to this piece now; if Simon didn't guess correctly, he would lose everything. The boy thought for a moment and then smiled. "It's the library."

Everyone looked at the woman in anticipation. She closed her eyes and took a deep breath. The crowd remained silent, but their hearts raced. Finally, the woman opened her eyes and said, "Yes."

The Puds cheered, while the woman gathered the pieces in a huff. "One more?"

Simon yawned and said, "No, I think I'm finished."

"Just one more puzzle," she urged.

"I'm tired of this game. I want to get my prize now."

"You have enough points to get anything you want," exclaimed Tonya.

"Then go ahead and pick something out for yourself," he said.

"Really?"

"Yeah, sure."

Instantly, she reached for the necklace she had been eyeing throughout the whole game. "Are these real pearls?"

"Yes, but I didn't intend to give that away," the woman answered sharply. "I only had it there for show."

"*Really?*" Tonya said, putting her hands to her hips in a threatening manner. "You know, Simon, I bet Mayor Gordon would love this game." She turned to the crowd and asked, "Does anybody know where the mayor is?"

"All right, you little brat. Take it! I don't want to see your faces here again."

"Thanks for the game," Simon said as they left.

"Wow, Simon, are you sure you weren't using magic back there?" asked Thorn.

"No, I wasn't."

"Then how did you get so smart all of a sudden?"

"It had little to do with being smart. Remember when we were explaining to you that to become an artist, you'd need to be able to look at things in a different way?"

"Yeah."

"Well, it's the same thing with the game I just played. I was just using my imagination to fill in the blanks."

"Oh . . . I don't think I could do that. I guess my parents are right. Maybe I just need to stick with the cold hard facts of science."

"Then you'll never pass level ten on my video game."

"What?"

"Yeah, in order to pass level ten, you'll have to be able to see where the end boss is hiding. He keeps merging into the background of the scenery. That's probably why you never found him."

"You'll have to show me later. You never did tell me what weapon–"

"Guys," Tonya interrupted, "I think I'd rather go to the history exhibit than listen to you two talk about stupid video games."

"All right, all right," said Thornapple. "Let's go to the exhibit."

The museum contained old fossils and relics of the once magnificent civilization that inhabited the planet before the great battle had taken place. Broken computer chips were scattered everywhere, and old books, protected by glass cases, lined the walkway. Full-sized skeletons of both small and large Puds were held suspended in the air for all to see.

Tonya and Thorn left to go to the restrooms, leaving Simon to stare in awe at the huge projection screen above. A documentary about the Battle of Lisardious played on the screen.

"Hard to believe we were almost completely wiped out."

Simon turned around to see a gray-haired man holding himself up with a cane. His deep-blue eyes were penetrating and serene, and his lower lip quivered as he spoke. "Our ancestors were much more advanced than we are today, but yet they couldn't even overcome the Lisardians."

"I was told that they won the battle."

The old man snorted and waved his hand towards the dilapidated artifacts. "Does this look like the remnants of a people that were victorious?" Simon didn't answer. "The Lisardians destroyed our world and left us for dead. To think of it! We had the power to transport ourselves to other galaxies. We were probably the most advanced planet in the entire universe, but the Lisardians still defeated us within a single day."

Simon summoned the courage to ask the stranger a question. "Why do you think your people were destroyed so fast?"

"I think their pride got the best of them." The man pulled out a small bag from his pocket and asked, "Would you like some chips? They give me gas."

Simon looked at the bag of chips in the man's shaking hand. The label on them read: LISARDIAN CRUNCHIES. "Thank you," he said, taking the bag half-heartedly.

At that moment, Tonya and Thorn showed up. "Did we miss anything exciting?" Tonya asked wryly.

The old man walked away to get a better look at one of the displays nearby.

"Who was that?" Thorn asked.

"Just some stranger I met. He told me your ancestors were more advanced than your people are today."

"Well, that's a prevalent theory, but I don't know if I agree with it. I mean, take a look at this stuff. They were still using paper books back then."

"Yes, but he also told me your ancestors were traveling to other galaxies."

"Really?" Tonya asked with strong curiosity.

Thorn nodded. "Some of the writings our scholars translated talk about people from other planets, so we can assume the ancient Puds traveled to other solar systems."

"Or other parallel worlds," Tonya said.

"Uh, well, I guess that could be the case. I never thought of it that way. But wouldn't that mean–"

"Exactly," she said, getting excited. "That would mean, at one time, this planet had electro-magical energy on it!"

"*Crazy!* Simon, why don't you see if you can read some of this stuff?"

Simon went from book to book. Because each manuscript was secured within a glass enclosure, he could only read bits and pieces. And what he could read was of little value. He skimmed through part of a romance novel and then went on to a cookbook and then to an instruction guide on origami.

Simon munched on his Lisardian Crunchies while he read. Despite the fact that they were cut into the shape of little aliens, the chips tasted quite good. After reading part of an old newspaper, he started to laugh.

"What? What is it?" Tonya asked impatiently. "Did you find something?"

"No, I was just reading this comic strip. It's actually pretty funny. I guess I can say one thing, Thorn. Your people weren't always so uptight."

"Comic strip?"

"You know–the funny papers."

Thornapple looked confused.

Tonya said, "I know what you're talking about. It's a bunch of made-up stories written with the purpose of making you laugh. We have something similar back home."

"You're kidding me," Thorn said, gasping. "My ancestors used to make up stories so that people would laugh? I didn't realize they were so . . . so . . .

creative."

"Wait a second," Simon announced, looking at another comic strip. "This one talks about a shopping center on Paraworld 687."

"Yeah, I've been there," exclaimed Tonya. "They have the best mint truffles I've ever–" She paused. "Simon, do you know what this means?"

"What?"

Her hair turned orange. "We may be able to get off this horrible planet!" She hugged Simon with so much excitement, he almost fell out of his hover chair.

"But–"

"Keep reading!"

Simon obeyed. "This one mentions a king," he noted. "Let's see . . . King Pentagola."

"Oh, he sounds familiar. Where's my paratransmitter when I need it? I vaguely remember reading about him in my history books. The empire has had so many kings–it's hard to keep track of them all. Keep reading, Simon!"

Thorn said with a laugh, "Out of all these ancient manuscripts, the only one that gives us any valuable information is the comic strips. I find that quite amusing."

"That's why they call them the funny papers," Simon said. Tonya rolled her eyes at his feeble joke.

Simon continued to scan the newspaper when a crowd of teenagers filled the room. "Come on, big guy. Let someone else have a turn," one of the young men said. Simon looked over his shoulder to see who the little Pud was talking to, but nobody was there.

"Go somewhere else," Tonya said in a rude voice.

"We have the right to be here just as much as you do."

"Yeah," said another boy, "and we want to see this stuff before the museum closes."

A surprised expression flashed across Tonya's face. "Thornapple! What time is it?"

"Relax, the dance doesn't start for four hours."

"Four hours?" she screamed. "Four hours!" Simon and Thorn exchanged confused glances as she ran towards the exit. "Oh, no! I have to get ready!"

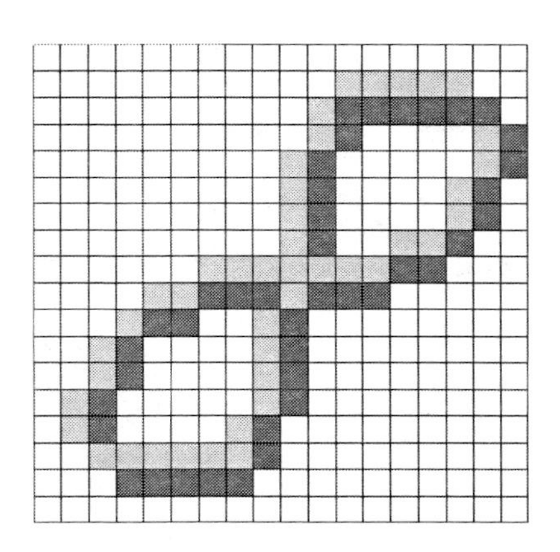

CHAPTER 17
THE DANCE

Tonya marched out of the museum with Simon and Thorn trailing behind. It wasn't long before they reached their home. As Simon walked inside, a feeling of gloom descended upon him. Was this really his last day with the Troodles?

Thorn headed for the main bathroom located in the hallway between his bedroom and the dining room, but when he reached for the door, Tonya pushed him aside and rushed into the bathroom with a bundle in her hands. After thirty minutes, Thorn knocked on the door and asked, "What are you doing in there? Hibernating? Some of us need to use the bathroom too, you know. How much longer are you going to be?"

The door opened slightly, just enough for Tonya's head to come into view. Her long green hair glistened, as if she had just come out of the shower.

"Cool it, buster! If you had three feet of hair, you'd take a long time too." She shut the door before anybody could get a closer look at her.

"Sheesh! If I had three feet of hair, I wouldn't have to bother wearing clothes."

Simon cringed at the thought.

"You can use my bathroom," Dr. Troodle said from the dining room.

"Do you think Mother would be okay with that?"

"Your mother is out with her friends tonight. I'm staying home so I can catch up on my reading."

"Where's Har?"

Dr. Troodle stared at the floor. "Well, actually, that's kind of why your mother is with her friends right now. As I was taking Har to the veterinarian, the car came off the skyway again, and I got into an accident. No one was hurt, but . . ." He hesitated a moment and then finally confessed, "Har escaped."

"*No way!*" exclaimed Thorn. "How in the world did that happen? Why didn't his security collar work?"

"It must have been damaged in the accident. Anyhow, the police are too busy to help because of all the festivities going on today. We'll have to find him tomorrow."

"Wow, Dad. It looks like we're all in the doghouse tonight."

His father smiled nervously in response.

It took Simon and Thorn only a few minutes to get ready for the dance. They both wore white button-down shirts with dark vests and black slacks.

After a long while, Tonya finally crept out of the bathroom. She walked over and stood at the entrance of Thornapple's bedroom. Thorn was watching Simon intently as he furiously pounded the buttons on his video game machine. Tonya announced in her sexiest voice, "The bathroom is available now if you still need it."

Simon looked up and stopped playing.

"Hey, why did you quit? You were almost at level nine!" Thorn said.

Simon couldn't answer; his mouth hung open in surprise. Thorn raised his head and caught his breath at the vision before them. Tonya wore a lovely white dress with clear sequins and lace trim. Her new pearl necklace rested upon her chest, accentuating her feminine attributes. The most amazing thing of all was her bright blue hair, which was curled into long ringlets that formed a stunning design upon her head. Except for their first meeting, Simon couldn't remember ever seeing Tonya with curly hair. The young woman was immaculate. Beautiful. Breathtaking . . . and she knew it.

"Hello, boys," she said with a warm smile that made her cheeks sparkle in the light. "Are you ready to go to the dance?"

"Yeah, we're r-r-ready," Simon stuttered. He put on his mother's medallion and walked over to his hover chair.

Tonya shook her finger and warned, "Don't even think about it."

The three teenagers left the house and cut across the hospital lawn to get to the pavilion where the dance was being held. Simon noticed that the streak of burnt grass he had made a couple of days earlier was already growing back.

Since Simon had never been to a dance before, he didn't know exactly what to expect, but after a few seconds of listening to the queer music, he was pretty sure the Pudo dances were far different from the ones back on Earth. For one thing, a robotic orchestra performed the strange music. Each computerized machine played its instrument superbly and in sync with the others; however, the techno rhythm of the music sounded so mechanical that it was devoid of emotion.

"Hello, everyone!" Thorn announced loudly. "I'm here . . . You can start the dance now."

Tonya scowled, embarrassed to be in his presence. "Thornapple," she said, "have you looked at yourself in the mirror lately? You're not exactly God's gift to women."

"That may be so," he retorted, "but nobody here believes in God anyway."

"It's only an expression. It means that not everyone's life revolves around you."

"Well, Butblacruze, I think–"

"Don't call me Butblacruze!"

"Look, I can't help it!" he shot back. "If there's ever a time to call you *Butblacruze*, it's right now. So, Butblacruze, if you'll excuse me, I'm going to go have some fun." He walked away without even letting Tonya respond.

She turned to Simon, who was stifling a laugh, and growled, "What are you smiling at?"

If you only knew. He straightened his face and replied, "Nothing. Nothing at all."

"Well, I didn't get all dressed up for nothing. Aren't you gonna ask me to–"

"Dance?" A young man in a turtleneck sweater interrupted her.

"What?"

"Would you like to dance?"

Caught off guard, she paused for a moment and then answered reluctantly, "I guess so."

"Have fun," Simon said with a jovial smile. "I think I'll sit this one out."

"Just remember, Simon," Tonya said as she left, "you can't stay on the sidelines forever."

The white tiles under her feet illuminated as she pranced over them. Simon searched for Thorn and found him standing alone at the punch bowl.

Simon smiled. "I see you've discovered the best part of this dance."

"It's a little watered down for my tastes," Thorn said.

Simon picked up a glass of the pink liquid and took a sip. The sour taste, similar to concentrated lemon juice, made his lips pucker and his eyes water.

"Hah! Hah! I was just joking. It's pretty potent stuff, isn't it?"

Simon's eyes were still hurting, but he managed to nod his head in agreement.

Thorn took a big gulp and said, "I can't believe this dance is taking place."

"Why's that?"

"Many officials didn't think it was appropriate. Dancing has little scientific value, but some of the city council thought we could benefit from the music."

"The music?"

"Yeah, music can be very complicated. First off, when you compose a song you have to make sure it follows all the normal rules of musical theory–like key changes, rhythm, and tempo. Then you have to find the correct instruments that will compliment each other. It's like forming one big equation. Finally, you have to program the robots to play in sync with each other, and I hear that's no easy task."

The orchestra finished playing and then started up another song with an entirely different tune from the one before. Tonya tried to walk back to her friends but was interrupted by three little Puds who wanted to dance with her.

"Looks like Konya is popular tonight," Thorn said. He leaned casually against the table.

Simon stole a furtive glance at her. "She doesn't socialize much at school. I guess there's a lot of people who've been wanting to get to know her."

"Yeah, and she is pretty hot!"

Simon raised an eyebrow but didn't respond.

The night dragged on while the two boys guarded the punch bowl and chatted about girls. Simon felt that if he took one more drink, he'd shrivel up and die from the tartness of the punch.

"So who would you like to dance with?" asked Thorn.

Simon remained silent. He fixed his eyes upon Tonya and her latest dancing partner: Alvin Bottlebrush. *What is she doing with him*?

"Simon . . . Simon?"

"Huh? Sorry, what was that?"

"I said, who do you want to dance with?"

"I don't know . . . Nobody, I guess. I wish Tonya hadn't talked me into coming."

"Come on, Simon. You just need some pointers on women. See that girl over there?" He pointed to an attractive girl across the dance floor. "That's Gwin. She's the prettiest girl in school. Now, I've had my eye on her the whole night. I've been studying her patterns and the way she reacts when someone asks her to dance. She only says yes when she's alone or when all of her friends have someone to dance with. Women are very loyal. They don't want to abandon their friends."

Thorn kept talking about how observant he was and how he knew exactly how to win Gwin's heart. Simon faded in and out of the conversation; he was too busy staring at Tonya and Alvin.

". . . So if we could just find enough boys to ask her friends to dance . . ."

Simon flinched when he saw Tonya laugh at something Alvin had said. Her hair radiated a vibrant blue color, and she seemed especially happy to be with this young, handsome man–a man whom, just last night, she had labeled an *animal*.

The song ended, and Tonya attempted to make her way to Simon and Thorn once more.

". . . So you see, Simon, if you just sit back and be more observant of things, you'll notice that there might be a girl out there who wants to dance with you."

"Okay, Thorn. Here's a question for you," Simon said. "What do you do when the girl you want to dance with is walking towards you?"

"What?"

Simon pointed to Gwin, who was headed straight for them. Upon seeing the beautiful girl, Thorn became so excited, he almost spilled his punch.

"All right, Simon, let me show you how it's done."

At that moment, Tonya finally made it to where Simon and Thorn were standing, having had to decline several dance proposals on the way. With a big smile, she said in jest, "My goodness! How much punch are you boys gonna drink?"

"It's actually pretty good," Simon lied. He took another sip and fought back the urge to spit it back up.

"Well, you're gonna have to get on the dance floor eventually . . ."

Thorn remained oblivious to Tonya's words. Beaming from head to toe, he opened his mouth to speak to Gwin as she approached, but the pretty girl walked right past him to get to Simon.

"Would you like to dance with me?" she asked with a cute smile and a wink.

Simon glared at Tonya and said curtly, "Please excuse me."

He promptly turned around and walked off with Gwin, leaving his friends behind.

"Who's that?" Tonya asked. A troubled look appeared on her face.

"That's the prettiest girl in school . . . She was supposed to dance with *me*."

Thorn hung his head in dejection.

"All right, Thorny. I can't see you like this. Come on. Let's dance."

On the dance floor, Simon asked, "Now, you're Gwin, right?"

"*Yes!*" she responded excitedly, as if he had just asked her to marry him.

"My name is–"

"Simon Kent," she finished his sentence with even more excitement. "Everyone knows who you are. You're the alien from Earth."

"Well, I never thought of myself as an alien."

"Sorry." She blushed. "I didn't mean it in a bad way. Everyone here is so serious. I think it's great to have some new people in the city."

Simon studied the lights on the floor and frowned. "Well, Gwin, I have to admit something to you. I'm not the best dancer."

"That's okay. This is the first dance I've ever been to. I didn't really catch everything myself when they were teaching us how to dance yesterday."

"Who was teaching you how to dance?"

"Weren't you at school yesterday? We all had a special class on how to dance."

"Oh, I must have missed it. Can you help me out? I'm not sure what to do with all these lights on the floor."

She instructed, "When the outline of a tile lights up, we step on it. You're supposed to step on the tiles that turn red, and I'm supposed to step on the ones that turn blue."

It seemed simple enough, so Simon took her hand, and they started to dance. When he stepped on the first red tile, a faint but pleasant sound came from the floor, and the tile lit up completely. Gwin stepped on a blue tile, and it too lit up and began to hum slightly–but in a different octave than what Simon's tile had given.

"Looks like you've got it," she said with a smile that would have rivaled even one of Thorn's famous grins.

In her enthusiasm, she stepped backwards onto an inactive tile. The tile glowed yellow and then gave off an awful sound–like a note played off key.

"Why did it do that?" asked Simon.

"I messed up, so we have to start all over."

"What do you mean, *start all over?* Isn't this just a dance?"

"Well, sort of. We're supposed to form patterns and shapes with our dance steps."

"You're kidding me."

"No, I'm not."

"That's ridiculous."

"I agree. It's pretty dumb that we can't just enjoy ourselves. Oh, it's your turn, by the way."

"Sorry."

Simon stepped on his tile, and then Gwin stepped on hers. After a few more tiles, Simon realized the strange dance wasn't as bad as he thought it would be. It was actually similar to a video game in which the player had to use his or her reflexes to step on the correct spot. The only problem with the peculiar dance was that they were concentrating so hard on stepping on the correct tiles, that it became difficult to talk.

"So tell me about your planet . . ." Gwin said, panting lightly. "I hear it's much different than our world."

They finished making a double helix up the dance floor. A chime sounded a congratulation, the red and blue lights disappeared, and they embarked on a new shape. Simon looked up to see Tonya staring at them from a distance, but she quickly turned her head.

"Well . . . everyone is taller . . ." He nearly missed his tile. "Not everyone is . . . so concerned with science . . . We have people who do sports . . . people who do musicals and plays . . . we have people who raise animals and people who race cars for a living . . . We do have scientists . . . and mathematicians . . . and biologists . . . and a lot of the same jobs that you have here . . . but it's different."

"How so?" She leaped to her tile and hit it square on.

"For one thing, most people on my world believe in some sort of supreme being . . . We even take a day off from work and school so we can spend time with our families and worship God if we want to . . ."

As they danced, the humming of the tiles harmonized with the robotic orchestra. In a sense, the floor functioned as an instrument, which allowed the dancers to participate with the orchestra in completing the melody of the song.

"We like to listen to music and play games . . ." Simon continued. "We don't live our lives so we can work . . . we work so we can live our lives . . . in a more meaningful way . . . We have families–"

"We have families, too," Gwin said defensively. She stepped on a blue tile three times in succession.

"Yeah, but our families have fun together . . . Not everything has to have a scientific purpose to it . . ." Simon and Gwin were really dancing fast now. They had already completed a rhombus and a figure eight. "Sometimes, we go to the park to feed the birds . . . or we watch a movie just for the sake of entertainment."

"That's amazing!"

They glided up the dance floor, hitting every other tile as they went.

"We don't even go to school every day like you do . . . Sometimes we'll take a whole week off or even the whole summer . . . just so we can have a break from school."

"Wow! Now, that is different."

Gwin took her eyes off the floor for the first time and looked up at Simon. Consequently, she stepped on the wrong tile again. The partially formed geometric shape on the floor disappeared.

"Oops, sorry!"

"That's all right."

Loud clapping suddenly came from every direction. Simon glanced around and discovered that nobody was dancing; they had all been watching Gwin and him successfully make the shapes on the floor. Evidently, the two must have been dancing faster than he had realized; furthermore, he and Gwin were probably the only couple who could keep up with the beat of the music.

"I suppose we're a hit," Gwin said, squeezing his arm and laughing.

Tonya dragged Thornapple across the dance floor. She pulled on Simon's other arm and asked, "May I cut in?"

Simon hesitated, so Tonya shoved Thornapple forward with a sigh and said to Gwin in an exaggerated tone, "Look, this guy won't stop talking about you." Thorn blushed. "It's driving me crazy! If you don't dance with this boy, I'm gonna have to kill him. And then the whole thing will get really messy. I mean, do you know how hard it is to get blood off a satin dress?" Tonya grabbed Gwin's shoulder. "Please," she said, her voice dripping with melodrama, "don't make me kill him. Save his life. Dance with this poor boy."

Intrigued by Tonya's high-spirited personality and feeling somewhat flattered, Gwin held out her hand, but Thorn shied away from it, as if confused by the gesture. Tonya whispered to the little Pud, "This is the part where you take her hand and dance with her."

A silly grin formed on Thorn's face. He grabbed Gwin's hand clumsily and led her to a vacant spot on the dance floor.

Proud of herself, Tonya took Simon's hand and said with a chuckle, "I think Thornapple's gonna kill me when we get back to the house."

Simon pursed his lips in disapproval.

"I think you had too much of that punch. What's wrong, Simon?"

He took a purposeful step on the wrong tile. Tonya cringed from the sour note that emitted from the floor. "I can't believe you were dancing with him!" he exploded.

"Simon, I've danced with just about every Pud in this city. Who are you talking about?"

"Alvin Bottlebrush."

"Oh, him. He just started dancing with me. The guy didn't even ask."

Simon took another step on a bad tile, and the sound that sprang forth echoed his temperament. "You looked pretty happy to be with him. I saw you laughing. Didn't you just call him an animal last night at the fight, or was all that just a show?"

"Look, Simon," she growled, slamming her foot on an inactive tile. "I was laughing because he was such a clumsy dancer." She stepped on another clear tile and said, "I have to admit, he is pretty good-looking . . . for a Pud. But I still don't approve of what he did last night."

Simon dragged Tonya with him while stepping on three more blank tiles. Yellow lights appeared with each step, accompanied by sour notes.

"*Really?*" he accused.

Tonya twirled around and stamped on several more white tiles. She even jumped over the blue tile so she could cause more havoc on the floor.

"Really!" she retorted. Her hair was now a fiery red. "What's this all about, anyway?" She looked at Simon closely to see his expression. "This doesn't have anything to do with Alvin, does it?" Simon remained silent, so she stepped on three blank tiles to emphasize each of the following words: "You–are–*jealous!*"

Simon responded by stepping on three blank tiles with each of his words as well. "No–I'm–*NOT!*"

He stomped so hard on the last word that a spark ignited from underneath his shoe. He wasn't quite sure if he had just cast a spell or if there was a malfunction with the tiles, but yellow lights spread across the floor like a nasty crack in a windshield. The floor moaned for a few seconds, and then the yellow lights died out.

"Children!" cried Mayor Gordon, running up to them. "Children, what's the problem here?"

"He's jealous," Tonya said matter-of-factly.

"Simon, are you jealous?"

"No."

"He says he's not jealous."

"He's lying."

The mayor turned to Simon again. "Are you lying?"

Simon closed his eyes and sighed.

"Look, kids, you're disrupting the whole dance. See that tile, Konya?"

"Tonya!" she corrected.

"Konya. I want you to step on that tile." She did as she was told, and the rest of the tile turned blue. A pleasant-sounding hum could be heard. "Now doesn't that feel good?" He turned to Simon. "Okay, Simon, your turn.

Step on that red tile." Reluctantly, Simon stepped on the tile with the red outline, and a faint hum sounded. "Wonderful! Now just keep that up and everything will be fine." He turned to the robotic orchestra and yelled, "Conductor, give me something slow."

"*Roger!*" came the mechanical voice of the conductor.

"And let's have some singing."

"*Right-eo, pops!*"

Mayor Gordon shook his head and gave himself a mental note to talk to the orchestra's linguistic programmer first thing in the morning.

The orchestra played a surprisingly beautiful song.

"Circles! We're all doing circles now!" Mayor Gordon yelled to the crowd on the dance floor. Ignoring the red and blue tiles, everyone began to move in circles with their partner. A gross sound spewed from the floor as several dozen tiles glowed yellow at the same time. The mayor put his hands to his ears and yelled at one of the technicians. "Turn those stupid tiles off!"

Finally, he faced Simon and Tonya and said, "I have to get ready for my speech, so you two be good. Try to stay within the lines, will you?"

They both nodded, and the mayor left. Simon glanced across the dance floor and saw Thornapple and Gwin both smiling at each other.

"So do you wanna try this over again?" Tonya said in a cool voice.

Her hair had already returned to the same sultry blue color as before. A soft breeze caressed her face. Simon stared into her yellow-green eyes and thought for a moment that she looked like an angel in the moonlight. He melted like butter in a skillet.

"Yes. I'm sorry," he said.

"I'm sorry, too. You're right–I shouldn't have danced with Alvin." She rubbed Simon's arm affectionately. "Besides," she added with a playful smile, "he's much too old for me anyway."

Simon put his arms around Tonya's thin waist, and they began to dance. At first they were rigid, but they both loosened up as the music played. One of the robots started to sing. Simon thought it was odd that such a lovely voice could come from a lifeless machine.

"So where'd you get your dress?" Simon asked, trying to make small talk.

"I made it."

"You made it! When did you do that?"

"I've been sewing it for over a month now. This is why I've been so excited for the dance. I wanted to see your reaction when I wore it."

Simon examined the workmanship of the dress more closely. It was actually much more modest than what he would have expected her to wear at a formal dance. He reflected back on the skintight outfit she had worn the first day they met. A lot of things had happened since that day. Although Simon had known about Pudo for only two months, Tonya had lived in the new parallel world the whole school year. Standing next to the young lady, Simon felt like a little kid; he couldn't believe how mature she had become over the past nine months.

"Your dress is beautiful. You did a fantastic job."

"Thank you," she said, blushing. They rotated a couple of times before Tonya spoke again. "Simon," she said in an oddly hesitant voice.

"Yes."

"You said my dress was beautiful, but . . . what about me?"

"Huh?"

"Do you . . . do you think *I'm* beautiful?"

Simon's eyes widened in shock. A flood of emotion inundated his body. Intensely hot all of a sudden, he felt the need to fidget with his top button.

"Well, I–" He fumbled for the words.

Just then, Mayor Gordon's voice boomed over the loud speakers. "May I have your attention, please? May I have your attention?" The orchestra stopped playing. "Thank you. Good evening, fellow citizens of Highland City. As your mayor, I'd like express my gratitude to everyone who made the festivities today possible."

Everyone cheered–especially Simon, who was focusing his whole attention on the mayor.

"It's been one thousand years to the day since we were victorious at the Battle of Lisardious."

The people cheered again.

"We've come a long way since that dreadful day, and I hope we never see another alien again . . . well . . . except for our Chamelean and Earthling friends, of course."

He nodded towards Simon and Tonya, and the crowd laughed in agreement.

"So that we will always remember our past," the mayor continued, "and to remind us of what we've become over the last thousand years, I present to you this statue."

Pulling away a thick, gray cloth, he revealed a life-sized bronze statue that portrayed a group of smaller Puds sitting on the shoulders of larger Puds. The smaller Puds wore expressions of celebration and triumph on their faces, while the larger Puds resembled beasts of burden–like oxen–forced into bondage by the yoke of oppression.

"This statue was found in an archeological dig beneath the city some time ago. Those little Puds have been riding on top of the big Puds for almost a thousand years, and I'm sure they're a bit saddle sore by now." Sporadic laughter rang forth from various parts of the crowd. "But our scientists refuse to let them rest. I'm sure if these ancient Puds could talk, they'd probably ask to go back into the dark catacombs where they were found just to get away from the archaeologists. Now that our scientists have translated the engravings, taken dozens of samples, and done all of their superfluous experiments–" Mayor Gordon turned to a group of men standing nearby and asked, "You are finished poking and prodding it, aren't you?"

Wringing his hands and looking quite anxious, the head archeologist, a tiny man dressed in a white overcoat, responded in earnest, "Actually, now that you mention it, we would like to take another look at the translation. There's been some debate recently regarding the interpretation of some of the ancient characters. Maybe if we could just study it for one more–"

"Oh, nonsense!" Mayor Gordon said. "The translation sounds good to me." He turned back to the audience and exclaimed, "This monument is finally ready for the public to enjoy. The engraving on the statue reads as follows:

> "'*See the brave warriors of Pudo, the small and the big, extinguishing our enemies so that our children may live to be wise and strong for thousands of years. With this memorial, let us never forget the great Battle of the Lisardians.*'"

The crowd clapped their hands and shouted with joy. Mayor Gordon, beaming with pride, said, "Now, I don't want to interrupt your dance any further, so I'll end with this reminder–"

Ignoring the mayor's speech, Simon squinted his eyes to read the inscription on the statue. The strange characters glowed and then melted into English. The first line read: "*Here lie the brave warriors of Pudo . . .*"

The mayor's words crept into Simon's ears. "Our city was forged from the blood of our ancestors. We are the superior race, and if it were not for the little Puds, we wouldn't be here–"

Mayor Gordon raised his arms towards the statue. Simon jerked his head around to see the words on the next line of the inscription. "*The big and the small–fighting as one, living as one, dying as one . . .*"

"So I encourage you all to pay your respects to those that gave their lives in the war," Mayor Gordon concluded. "Please enjoy the rest of the dance." The mayor turned to the mechanical orchestra. "Conductor! Continue where you left off."

The music started back up again, and the lead robot resumed singing from the exact syllable it had last sung before getting interrupted. Tonya put her hands around Simon's neck and pressed him to dance. Before they rotated, however, Simon read the next sentence on the statue. "*May our progenitors be wiser than us when our enemies awake from their slumber one thousand years from now . . .*"

The boy's stomach lurched in anticipation to read the next line. His back now faced the monument, so he had to wait a few more seconds.

"Well?" Tonya's clear voice broke his concentration and startled him. He had almost forgotten she was there.

Simon responded impatiently, "Well, what?" He could almost see the statue now.

"You never answered my question."

"What question?"

"Do you think I'm pretty?"

Ignoring the question completely, Simon read the next sentence. ". . .

and let this memorial serve as a commemoration of the folly of our wise yet foolish nation . . ."

He moved out of range again.

"I'm sorry, what was that?" he said, trying to look back at the monument.

"Hey, if you don't wanna answer, you don't have to," she said. Simon urged her to rotate faster. "I'm just trying to figure you out, that's all. We've spent a lot of time together lately, and . . . I don't know–I thought maybe you–"

Simon read the last line of the inscription on the statue. "*Let us always remember the great and terrible Battle of the Dragunos.*"

"Oh my gosh!" Simon interrupted.

"What is it?"

"The Lisardians . . . They weren't aliens."

"*Ahhh,* can we just spend one night without talking about Pudo history?"

Simon was frantic. He had to do something, fast. Tonya obviously didn't care about his discovery, so instead of arguing with the apathetic girl, he blurted, "I have to go, Tonya. Thanks for the dance." He left her without saying another word.

The poor girl just stood there, fuming with anger and hurt as she watched Simon rush off towards Thornapple and Gwin. Her bottom lip started to quiver, and her hair faded to a murky black.

"Thorn!" Simon cried. "They weren't aliens . . ."

"Simon, what are you talking about?" Thorn asked with a disturbed expression on his face; he had just been in the middle of telling a joke to Gwin.

"Your scientists have it all wrong . . ." Simon said, trying to catch his breath. "They were lizards, not aliens!"

"Who were?" Gwin asked.

"The Lisardians! This whole time, everyone has been calling it the *Battle of Lisardious*, but it's actually the *Battle of Lizards*–or dragunos–whatever you call them."

"Wow," Gwin marveled. "How do you know that?"

"I read it on the statue."

"If that's true," Thorn said, "then this could be pretty serious. We have been having a lot of draguno attacks lately."

"It's more serious than you realize," Simon said in haste. "I also read that the dragunos are coming back soon. Thorn, we have to get into the sealed portion of the library."

"This is awesome," Gwin exclaimed. "Let's go."

"Hold on, Gwin," Simon said; her supportive attitude shocked him. "You're not coming with us. We're going to have a hard enough time as it is sneaking into the vault. There's no reason for you to get involved."

She shook her head. "If the Lisardians–I mean dragunos–are coming back to destroy the planet, then that's a pretty good reason to get involved, don't you think?"

"I don't know, Gwin," Thorn said, siding with Simon. "We're not exactly leaving on a mission to save the world. We're just going to look at some old books."

"Okay," she conceded, "but let me know what you find."

"All right," Thorn said. "We'll see you later." They started to walk away, but then Thorn whirled around and added, "Most likely we'll be right back. Save me a dance, will you?"

"I'll be waiting for you," she said, winking. Thorn debated whether she had directed the wink towards him or not, but he blushed nonetheless. Simon's cheeks reddened as well.

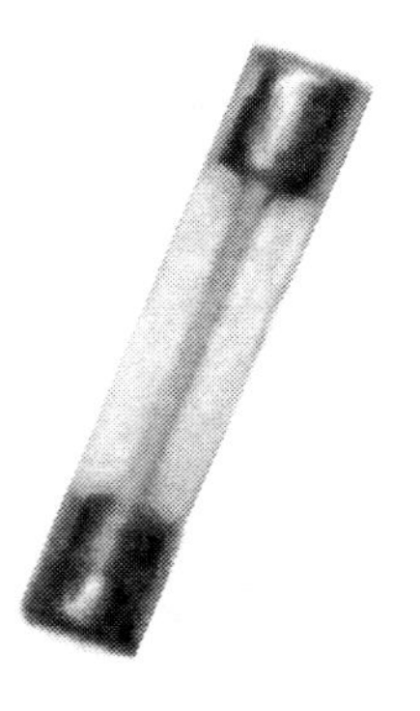

CHAPTER 18
THE LIBRARY

Except for the old librarian sleeping at the front desk, the library appeared empty. Most of the lights had been turned off to conserve energy. An eerie sensation filled the pit of Simon's stomach as he crept past the tall desk and headed for the vault.

"How are we going to get in?" Thorn asked in a half-whisper.

The librarian stirred in his seat.

"*Shhh!*" Simon scolded. "I'm going to use magic." He put his hand on the digital keypad.

Thorn raised an eyebrow. "You'll probably set the whole place on fire or something."

"*Shhh!* Let me concentrate. I got my video games working, didn't I?"

"Something tells me this security system is a bit more complex than your video game machine."

The old man at the desk snorted loudly, and both boys froze. A few moments later, the librarian readjusted himself in his chair and fell back asleep. His deep breathing echoed across the marble floors and pierced the silence of the library like a dragon struggling to sleep.

"Keep your voice down," Simon said. Overwhelmed, the inexperienced magician glided his hand along the seam of the metallic door. The hinges that held the massive door in place were wider than his fist.

Simon put his hand on the digital keypad again and closed his eyes. In his mind, he visualized the circuits and conduits of the security system. He traveled along a blue wire and then a red one. A series of white beams of light reflected off a diamond prism and ran down various tunnels. Feeling euphoric, Simon chased after one beam and soon found himself deep into the circuitry of the electronic system.

Tiny nanoprobes zoomed around in the air to defend the microchips from foreign objects. Simon visualized a speck of dust shooting out of an opening in the floor. Like mosquitoes attacking a helpless child, the nanoprobes pounced on the dust particle and broke it up into tinier fragments with their minute lasers.

Simon's consciousness moved down another tunnel and into a huge opening. He saw a gigantic globe with blue electricity surging up the sides to reach the top. It was the kind of glass ball that made your hair stand up when you touched it. He had seen one at a school field trip to the planetarium last year. The only difference was that, somehow or another, he was inside of it.

A colorful arrangement of diodes and capacitors lined the floor, and a huge tower of microchips sprang upwards in the center of the room–attracting the energy like a lightning rod. Simon became discouraged at seeing the millions of electronic components.

Which one is it? he thought.

Then, out of obscurity, he saw something almost hidden within a bed of strange-looking electrodes. It was a tiny, insignificant thing–too small for anyone to notice–but it seemed important for some reason. As Simon's consciousness drew closer, he realized it was just an ordinary fuse–the type one might find in a strand of Christmas lights.

No, he argued. *This little thing? How could this tiny fuse bring down the entire security system? How could something so small make a difference?*

He wanted to give up and go back into reality, but his inner self forced him to stay. The little glass cylinder came more and more closely into view. Soon, his vantage point was such that the fuse was all he could see. He concentrated all his energy on the tiny thread contained within the glass tube.

Outside this strange mechanical world, Thornapple watched patiently as Simon manipulated the security system. From the little Pud's viewpoint, it looked like Simon was merely stalling. He was about to comment on this but stopped himself when he saw a bead of sweat run down his friend's face.

Simon's jaw muscles tightened. His cheeks turned red, and he began to tremble from the terrible strain he was under.

"Are you okay?" Thorn grabbed his arm, but Simon wouldn't let go of the digital keypad. "Simon!"

Inside the security system, Simon watched as the tiny thread in the fuse snapped in two. Instantly, the entire system turned off, and everything went black.

"Simon, are you okay?"

Disorientated, Simon realized he was back in the library. "*Shhh!* You'll wake up the librarian," he warned.

"It looks like it didn't work," Thorn said.

"Well, you interrupted me! I think I almost had it–"

A loud *pop* sounded, and the thick door creaked open a quarter of an inch. The librarian jumped in his seat.

"Is someone there?" the old man asked while fumbling for his cone-shaped cap.

Simon and Thorn held their breath. They watched the librarian stand up and rotate towards them. Just then, a clap of noise echoed throughout the library.

"Sorry about that," someone said.

A feeling of relief swept over the two boys as the old librarian sat back down.

"May I help you?" he asked in his deep-drawled voice. The man peered over his desk to see Gwin picking up a holographic pad from off the floor.

"Yes, you can." She winked at the two boys behind the desk. Simon could have sworn her wink was directed towards him, but Thorn would beg to differ. "I hear you have the newest edition of the Scientific Lecture Series," she said with a perky grin.

"Why, yes, we do," the man squealed. "Let m'see, here." He looked down at the monitor on his desk and tapped some keys. "Lecture Series . . . Lecture Series . . ." he mumbled to himself.

Gwin signaled for the boys to go into the vault.

As they left, Simon mouthed the words, "*Thank you.*"

Gwin smiled and winked again. This time Simon felt positive she was winking at him.

Not waiting another second, the two boys slid into the vault and shut the door behind them. They began to choke on the noxious fumes that billowed from the vents. Simon dropped to his knees and tried to feel his way through the dense clouds of neon-blue smoke, but he kept bumping into things.

"Take this," came a strange, mechanical-sounding voice.

Simon turned around and saw the silhouette of a small Pud behind the veil of thick smoke. The strange figure stepped forward, breaking through the blue fog like a knife cutting through butter. Unprepared at seeing the futuristic-looking mask the person was wearing, Simon took a gasp of the vile air and started to cough.

"It's me–Thorn!" the little Pud said from behind the frightening disguise. He handed Simon a gas mask.

Feeling slightly foolish, Simon took the mask and put it over his head. The black rubber suctioned itself to his chest and drowned out the external noise completely. His glasses pressed into his face, but he ignored the discomfort.

Simon looked through the telescopic eyepieces of the mask and realized he could now see through the blue fumes. In fact, he soon discovered he could manipulate his perception at will. When he looked at Thorn, he noticed that descriptive readings such as body temperature and weight appeared at the borders of his peripheral vision.

He concentrated on the label engraved on Thorn's mask, and his vision magnified so that the label came right up to his face. He stared at the words, and they too became magnified. The label read: PRESERVATION GAS MASK.

Like a two-way radio, Thorn's mechanical voice broke the silence. "The mist preserves the books. That's how they've lasted all these years."

"That's cool," Simon responded, shocked to hear that his own voice sounded a bit synthesized as well. He looked around and saw rows and rows of bookcases spanning the length of the vault. In the middle of the room sat a very large book upon a white pedestal.

"Let's start with that one." Simon motioned towards the pedestal.

"Wow, that's huge," cried Thorn. "What does the title say?"

Simon walked over to the oversized book and inspected the cover. The strange characters danced around and then turned into English.

"*The History of Pudo*," Simon read. "*By John Willmaker*."

Thorn jumped with glee. "What luck. Open it up."

Simon turned over the heavy cover and read the first page. "*Volume 13. Dedicated to my lovely wife . . . My strength . . . My beacon . . . My everlasting joy . . . My–*"

"My goodness! At this rate, we'll be here forever. Let's just skip to the end."

Simon could tell that Thorn obviously wanted to get back to the dance. He, on the other hand, was happy to be away from the noisy crowd. However, Thorn did have a point: The book was enormous, and the time they had was limited.

Simon moved to turn the page when something odd caught his eye. "Wait a second, Thorn. Take a look at this." He pointed to the bottom of the page where a picture of a large woman was printed.

"*Ewww*–I can't believe that!" Thorn crinkled his nose. The gas mask filtered his voice, making it sound two octaves lower. "This guy was married to a *big* Pud?"

"I think he *was* a big Pud," Simon noted.

"Oh, come on! They can't even read, let alone write."

"Why do you think this book is so big then? I don't think even Alvin Bottlebrush could bench-press this thing."

"History books are always big. Anyway, we're never going to get back to the dance if we keep looking at ugly women."

"All right." Simon flipped to the last page of the book. "*The year is now 1999 AD*." He stopped reading and mumbled, "Huh? That's weird. My language spell must be messing up. This couldn't have been written in 1999–that wasn't too long ago."

"Maybe they had a different reckoning of time."

"Yeah, you're probably right." Simon read again, *"The year is now 1999 AD, almost two thousand years since the first draguno attack."*

"There you go," Thorn interrupted. "AD most likely stands for *After Dragunos*. So that means the draguno attacks have been going on for three thousand years. Now we're getting somewhere."

Simon read the last paragraph of the book. *"Although our ancestors were unsuccessful at defeating the lizards the last time they emerged, we are confident we will be victorious. We will not allow these demons to destroy our world for a third time. With the help of the High King and with the blessings of God above, we will prevail!"*

Simon closed the book.

Thorn wrung his hands. "So we really are in trouble, aren't we?" The impending doom was finally starting to sink in.

"Yes, and the worst thing of all is that no one is going to believe us."

"Maybe they will," Thorn cried, his voice sounding a little muffled from his gas mask. "We just need to find some evidence that the ancient Puds were fighting lizards and not aliens. Let's keep looking."

"What about the dance?"

"I guess this is more important." The little Pud sighed. "And to think . . . It took the near destruction of the entire planet to finally convince the city council to sponsor a dance . . . and I'm going to miss it."

"Cheer up," Simon encouraged. "I'm sure there'll be other dances."

"Yeah, like in another thousand years." The little Pud's voice became even more depressed. "That is, if anyone survives . . . How could we be so dumb?"

Never did Simon think he would ever hear a smaller Pud call his own race *dumb*, but before he could answer, Thorn spoke again.

"Simon, there's a beautiful girl just outside of this building who is waiting to dance with me, and even though I'd really like to be with her right now, I can't help thinking that a bunch of lizards are on their way to kill everyone. My ancestors said they were confident they'd defeat the dragunos, but even though they were prepared, they still lost. So how can we possibly protect ourselves when our scientists are looking up in the sky for aliens while right under their noses the real enemy is preparing to destroy us?"

"That's what we have to find out," Simon exclaimed. "We have to find out what happened a thousand years ago. Why did your ancestors lose the battle?"

"You're right," Thorn said, taking courage. "Let's find the next volume of this history book."

"Good idea. You start on that side of the vault, and I'll start on this side. Just look for these words."

Thorn memorized a few of the strange words on the cover of the history book and then vanished through the blue mist to the other side of the room.

Simon proceeded to rummage through his portion of the vault. As he searched through the old books, his mask did strange things. It was clearly evident that the functions of the mask included more than the ability to filter out the blue preservation fumes.

Simon soon discovered he could pinpoint a book high on a shelf and signal his mask to shoot out rays of light that would scan the book and pull out a holographic representation of it. Because no one actually had to physically handle the books, this was another way the Puds were able to preserve them for so long while still being able to study and translate them.

With the twitch of his eyes, he could move the hologram around and even flip through the pages. Simon wished he had a mask like this back on Earth; because of his short stature, there were many times he couldn't reach the higher bookshelves at the school library.

After a while, Simon got a kink in his neck. He sat on a stone bench that was carved right into the wall and relaxed. He tried to look through the dense fog, but the mask couldn't penetrate far enough to allow him to see the other side of the room.

"Any luck, Thorn?" he called out into the blue air.

"Not yet. But I do have to say that these masks are pretty cool."

"Yeah, I agree."

"I wonder if you could see through clothing with these."

"Don't get any ideas."

"Oh, I know. I was just wondering."

Simon couldn't help but smile because of the obvious embarrassment in Thorn's voice. He sat, musing on the idea of being able to see through clothing, when, all of a sudden, something caught his eye: a tiny red book lodged between two enormous ones. It just seemed out of place–like a hummingbird trying to make its home in an eagle's nest.

He attempted to scan the cover with his mask, but the rays of light couldn't seem to reproduce the tiny book. Maybe it wasn't really a book at all. Simon extended his hand and manually pried the book out of the bookcase.

An insignia protruded from the front cover. Simon tried to open the little red book, but it was sealed tight. He flipped it over and read the back cover. "*The key to the machine that will save us all.*"

Deep in thought, Simon tapped the armrest of the bench, contemplating the strange insignia on the cover. *What machine?* he thought.

Simon stared blindly into space. He played with the engravings in the armrest. Using his forefinger, he followed the strange grooves until they were swallowed up into a shallow hole. He was just about to put the book back when he looked down at the cavity in the armrest. At first, he thought the round hole was some sort of cup holder, but then he realized it looked exactly like the emblem on the little red book, only concave.

A surge of excitement ran through his body. Had he just discovered a clue to the mystery of the ancient Puds? He pressed the book onto the armrest until he heard a click. The insignia snapped into place perfectly. Looking around and feeling anxious, he turned the book until he heard another click, but nothing else happened.

Suddenly, the seat he was sitting on–as well as a section of the wall–fell backwards, throwing Simon onto the ground in the process. Shocked at what had just happened, the boy picked himself off the cold earthen floor and tried to regain his composure.

It didn't take long for Simon to realize he was no longer in the library. A shroud of darkness prevented him from seeing anything at all. The settings of the mask must have been adjusted when he fell.

Simon blinked, and his vision changed. Everything remained black as night, but now he could see the outlines of blue formations floating in the dark, musty air. As he moved towards the faint images, he walked into something cold and hard. He put his hands up to feel the invisible wall but then got the shock of his life. Instead of seeing his hands, Simon saw the faint blue outline of his bones! The mask had given him x-ray vision, and the blue images he had seen floating in the air must have been the skeletal remains of something embedded in the wall.

Simon stared at his arms and marveled at the many bones in his wrists. He looked down at his legs and spotted the place where they had been torn off from his car accident. He couldn't believe what he was seeing.

"Well, Thorn," he said aloud, "I guess these masks *can* see through clothing."

Simon blinked, and his eyesight changed again. Although his x-ray vision was gone, he could now see shimmers of pastel light reflecting off of everything. As he moved his hands, they left a trail of yellow behind–like what a sparkler does when someone waves it in the air.

Simon looked closer at his surroundings and realized for the first time that he was in a cave. Overwhelmed, he took a step forward and tripped on something: the little red book.

When he picked it up, the walls came alive with a greenish-gold color. Simon moved the book closer to the cave wall, and, like magic, strange writing appeared on the rocky surface. The ancient characters morphed into English for the boy to read. "*Inside the heart of the volcano, we will purge this world of the dragunos.*"

Simon moved his head, and the optical settings of the mask changed the way he viewed his surroundings once more. As he made his way down the tunnel, he saw the heat signatures of the cave–mostly blue and white images with small trickles of red and yellow.

Simon blinked, and his infrared vision changed to some sort of sound wave vision. The ceiling reverberated slightly, and as he walked through some puddles, his footsteps became whirlwinds of inaudible sound that bounced off the walls and collided into each other. Simon began to feel nauseous as he watched the sound waves–or at least, the visible representation of the sound waves–move about the cave.

Frustrated with the malfunctioning mask, Simon closed his eyes, but when he opened them again, he saw absolutely nothing. Even the ancient words which had illuminated from the walls had vanished. Darkness–complete and utter darkness: It was something Simon did not like one bit, especially because he had no idea where he was.

He blinked one last time.

A pounding *flash* shocked his nervous system as the darkness transposed itself into a radiant white light–a contrast so drastic and sudden that it blinded him. He covered the telescopic eyepieces with his hands, but it did not help. Even when he closed his eyes, he could still see the pure-white images of stalagmites and stalactites growing from the floor and ceiling of the cave.

Dazed, the boy stumbled forward and smashed his head into a jagged rock formation. He crumpled to the ground. The white images–now burned into his retina–faded into black as Simon drifted out of consciousness and into a deep sleep.

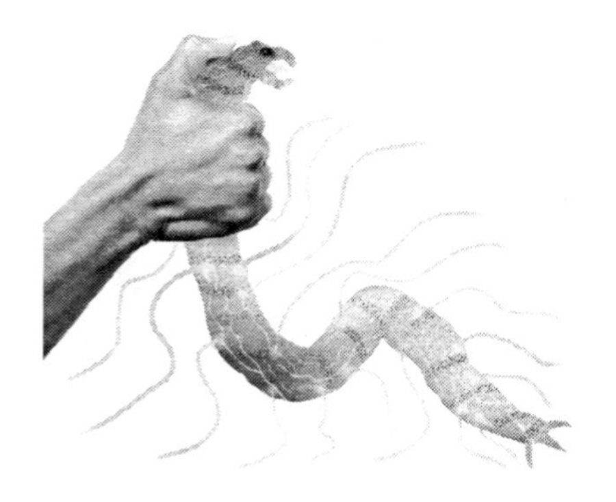

CHAPTER 19
UNVEILING THE DARK FORCES

The snow-encrusted planet could hardly sustain life. A blanket of stormy weather stretched its cold fingers into every crevice of the barren land. Emerging from the harsh elements, a towering castle broke through the thick ice and held strong against the raging wind that bit the sky. A white and lonely speck in the paraverse, this parallel world was home to Lord Theobolt Vaylen, Guardian of the Crown.

"Shut it down!"

"But the master said–"

"Do you want the master to die, Merworth?"

"But, Commander Wright–"

"I'm in charge here, and I say shut it down!"

Cowering in obedience, Merworth pulled a lever, which caused the E.M. machine to shake violently in response. The deafening noise gradually decreased as the power to the machine slowly drained away. Everyone stared in anticipation as the display lights died out one by one. Like a wounded beast giving in to submission, the machine finally relaxed and then turned off completely.

The room became deathly silent.

"Master Vaylen?" Merworth called out, cautiously approaching the large machine.

There was no response.

"Master?"

The room remained quiet. Merworth tried to peer through the murky round window on the front of the machine, but the white steam from within clouded his vision. The tension in the room became even more profound as the long moments passed. None of the other physicians dared to move or make a sound.

Merworth turned to look at his colleagues. Suddenly, a gruesome face pressed itself against the glass. The doctors shuddered as Lord Vaylen slid down the window. Part of his skin remained behind.

"Get him out of there!" the man in charge screamed. Two guards pried open the door, and Lord Vaylen fell out onto the floor. "Are you all right, Master?" the commander asked, rushing to his side.

Lord Vaylen looked up from the billowing steam and rasped, "Didn't I say that under no circumstances should you stop the procedure?"

"Yes, but you've never been in the machine for that long."

"I require strict obedience, Commander."

"Yes, of course, Master," the commander stammered while stretching out his hand to Lord Vaylen. "I was only concerned for your welfare."

Lord Vaylen took the commander's hand and pulled himself to his feet. "Well, my old friend," the dark lord said calmly, "allow me to relieve you of your concern."

Still clutching his master's hand, the commander felt an overwhelming surge of energy flow through his body. In an instant, the helpless man crumbled to ashes before the ultramage's feet.

Turning to the group of doctors, Lord Vaylen announced with a cruel smile, "It appears as though the treatment was a success."

The horrified doctors nodded in agreement but were too scared to say anything. Merworth grabbed Lord Vaylen's black cloak from the wall and brought it to his master.

"Thank you, Merworth," the wizard said kindly as he hid himself behind the dark cloak. He moved his hand to grasp the physician's shoulder, but Merworth flinched instinctively. "Oh, come now, Doctor," Lord Vaylen chided. "Do you really think I would kill my best friend?"

"But you already–"

"*Shhh!*"

Lord Vaylen raised his hand to silence the doctor. He stooped down and fixed his eyes upon the pile of ashes smoldering at his feet. Quick as a snake, the ultramage plunged his hand into the hot ashes and pulled out a writhing creature.

Merworth gasped. "A sneaker worm!"

"I'm afraid Commander Wright has been dead for some time now," Lord Vaylen explained sympathetically. "Replaced by this *spy*." He squeezed the worm in his hand.

"But how did you know?" Merworth asked.

"The E.M. machine. It opened my eyes like never before. Thanks to our special guest, I feel I can withstand anything."

"*Excuse me, Lord Vaylen,*" a voice from the intercom chimed. "*The Raiders have just entered our paraworld. General Mayham and Captain Drackus would like to speak with you.*"

The Guardian of the Crown bit his lip and snapped, "I'll talk to them in my office. Follow me, Merworth."

After a brisk walk through the tall and spacious corridors, the two men entered Lord Vaylen's office. Holographic images of both General Mayham and Captain Drackus stood in an alcove in the wall.

General Mayham spoke immediately. "Lord Vaylen, we demand that you release Griffen Lasher into our custody at once. We know you have him, and we're not–"

Lord Vaylen raised the sneaker worm in anger and spat, "Gentleman, I believe I *do* have something of yours . . . but it is *not* this man you are seeking." With a sharp twist of his wrist, he cracked the worm's spine and threw it down. The worm convulsed sporadically about the floor and made a shrill clicking noise as it died. "I do not appreciate being spied on."

"And we don't appreciate being lied to," Captain Drackus responded coolly. "My security cameras filmed you destroying my holodroids."

"I assure you, gentleman, that I have never set foot on either of your space carriers."

"But my cameras–"

"Are inaccurate," Lord Vaylen finished his sentence. "Check your security system again, and you will find that it was not I who invaded your ship."

"But the intruder was wearing your black cloak," Captain Drackus argued.

"Did he walk with a limp?"

Drackus thought for a moment. "No."

"Then it couldn't have been me. Now gentleman, I do not wish to discuss this any further. I have pressing business to attend to. Good day."

Before the captain or the general could say another word, the transmission cut out and the holograms vanished. Lord Vaylen pushed a button on his bracelet and said, "Please inform me when the Raiders have entered the parastream."

"Yes, sir," came the reply.

The sly wizard walked to his desk and sat down. He pulled out a thin cylinder of blue liquid from a drawer and poured himself a drink. That was when Merworth realized his master's limp had disappeared.

"Your limp is gone, Master!"

"Yes, but for how long? That is the question, Merworth. That is the question." He took a sip of the blue liquid. "But for now, I feel twenty years younger. Tell me, doctor, what progress have you made with our patient?"

"He recovers from every experiment remarkably fast. I can't explain why. His race is truly unique."

"*Ahh!* Yes, they are . . ." Contemplating what he had just said, Vaylen added quietly, "Yes, they *were* . . . If only the Raiders hadn't destroyed them all. Imagine the power we could have obtained."

"Do understand, Master, that the antibodies we extracted have a limiting time factor. The side effects you're experiencing will eventually wear off, and everything will be back to normal . . . even your limp will come back."

"Yes, that is why you must discover his secret."

Lord Vaylen waved his hand, and an image appeared in the air. Several doctors were busy running tests on a man strapped to a table. A sheet covered most of his body, but his upper chest and neck were bare. The viewpoint of the image zoomed in and magnified the man's face, revealing him to be Griffen Lasher.

"We haven't much time, Merworth," Lord Vaylen said calmly. He took another sip of his drink. "Not much time at all."

■ ■ ■

Councilor Bromwell and Lady Cassandra walked through the lush, beautiful garden just outside the castle walls. A flock of strange-looking birds blotted out the sunlight for a moment as they flew by.

"You don't think the Raiders would dare to attack Imperial City, do you?" Cassandra asked.

"The heart of General Mayham's hatred stems from the very ground we walk on," Councilor Bromwell answered. "I feel that he is taunting us . . . trying to make us lose our focus. Now that we know the diabolical reason for his harboring of the electro-magical energy, it is only a matter of time before the Raiders attack our paraworld."

"Can we defend ourselves from such a weapon?" Lady Cassandra asked with a hint of desperation in her voice.

The old man's response was both blunt and dreadful. "No . . . In time, I'm sure we could devise a countermeasure . . . but I fear that time is not on our side. Even now the Raiders are powering up their weapon."

Lady Cassandra drew a deep breath. "And what do we know of this weapon?"

"Our E.M. Enforcers have just reported that Captain Drackus and General Mayham have discovered how to unleash a deadly strain of electro-magical energy that is capable of destroying an entire planet. That's why they met at Centarious."

Lady Cassandra's eyes widened. "But Drackus was born on Centarious."

Bromwell nodded. "If Drackus is willing to harm his own homeworld, there's no telling what he's capable of doing. With such awesome power, I assume the Raiders would be forced to charge their E.M. reactors to maximum capacity before they could fire. This being the case, I would further postulate that they would hide themselves at a nearby paraworld to charge their ships. This, my lady, would be our only window of opportunity to stop them."

"There are thousands of paraworlds just minutes from here," Lady Cassandra said despairingly. "They could be hiding in any one of them."

"That is why we must act now . . . before our paraworld suffers the same fate as Centarious."

"Agreed," Cassandra declared. "We shall disperse our fleet among the parallel worlds until we find the twin space carriers. Meanwhile, we can send messenger probes to warn the neighboring worlds of the danger and command them to cease all paratravel for the time being. If only we had put more stock in Tabatha's warning. Alas, she has fallen to the Raiders as well."

"I hope you are wrong," Counselor Bromwell said. "Tabatha has a fire within her that breeds hope and determination. I pray we will have that same conviction in the next few days to come."

"As do I," the woman said, looking at the beautiful buildings that housed the governing body of the known paraverse. "For all our sakes."

■ ■ ■

Enveloped in a blue energy field, a tiny spacecraft, bearing the royal insignia, raced down the parastream at full speed. Except for the quiet sound of a woman crying, the inside of the cockpit remained silent. Tabatha Burke sat alone in the dark, mourning the loss of her friend.

The woman had not eaten or slept for two days, but she didn't care; she had a lot on her mind . . .

■ ■ ■

"Scan for life signs," Tabatha had said just two days previously.

Her ship floated above the remains of the destroyed Centarious moon. Minor fragments of Griffen's ship drifted aimlessly in space.

The computer's response echoed in her ears. *"Zero life signs,"* it had said.

"Can you find any trace of him–any trace at all?" she begged.

"Zero life signs," came the cold reply.

"How about on the planet?"

"Zero life signs."

Tabatha gasped in dismay. "What?"

"There are zero life signs on the planet," the computer expounded.

"How did this happen?" she cried.

As if quoting from a science lecture, the heartless computer said, *"Because of the deteriorating orbit of the moon fragments, the tidal force of the oceans has eroded the continents, thus fracturing the outer crust of the planet and allowing volcanic eruptions to melt the polar caps. Sensors indicate that, with the moon's current rate of descent, the estimated time of impact will be–"*

■ ■ ■

"Enough!" Tabatha yelled herself awake.

She looked at the thousands of portals whizzing by. Her ship was still cruising through the parastream. Reprimanding herself for falling asleep, she vowed not to rest until she reached her destination.

Her destination, however, was still undetermined. Her ship headed in the direction of home–as she was instructed to do by Lady Cassandra–but it also followed the trail of the twin space carriers. Tabatha figured she could catch up with the Raiders in a day or two.

The white-haired woman urged her ship to go faster. She couldn't decide what her final destination would be. Where did her loyalties lie? The crown or a friend? She continued to stare at the mystical walls of the parastream. The hypnotic waves of orange and red seemed to force her eyes shut. Sleep took her within moments.

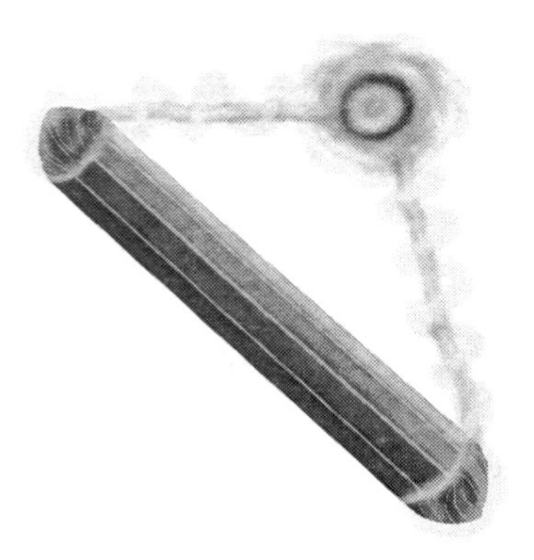

CHAPTER 20
THE SECRETS OF PUDO

Simon opened his eyes. A soft white light penetrated everything around him. He felt extremely disorientated, even dizzy, to the point of not knowing whether he was lying down or standing up. As his eyes focused, the boy noticed that a thick blanket of mist encompassed his entire body.

His gas mask was gone and so was the throbbing pain in his head; however, his dizziness remained. A warm breeze gently touched his face, amplifying his lethargic state, and a peaceful feeling swept throughout his body, giving him the strong desire to go back to sleep . . . Sleep? Maybe he was already asleep.

Feeling the presence of someone familiar close by, Simon focused his eyes more deeply into the white mist and realized the woman from his dreams was desperately trying to speak with him. Although the thick vapor swallowed up most of her form, he could still see the concerned look upon her delicate face.

Riding atop her majestic beast, the young woman quickly drew near–so near, in fact, that Simon could see the urgency in her eyes. She was trying to tell him something, but the boy couldn't make out her words; he saw her lips move, but no sound came from her mouth.

"What?" Simon whispered hoarsely.

She spoke again, but he heard no sound.

"I can't hear you," Simon said with a yawn.

He felt so sleepy, his eyes began to close involuntarily. The young woman hopped off the animal and glided across the floor to where Simon lay. As she knelt down, the steam curled around her long hair and engulfed her face.

She brought her soft lips to the boy's ear and, with a sense of urgency in her voice, whispered, "*Simon, wake up!*"

Simon opened his eyes but wasn't quite sure if he was still dreaming or not. The white mist had vanished, but what he saw in its place was strangely familiar. Two little knives vibrated above his glasses–just like in his daydream back in Mr. Bartholomew's English class. However, this time Simon saw tiny words floating in his peripheral vision.

Weight: 591.32 lbs . . . Height: 7.69 feet . . . Species: Arachnid.

Simon suddenly realized he wasn't dreaming anymore. The two daggers removed themselves from the telescopic eyepieces of his mask, allowing him to see the faint outline of a giant spider above him. Its sharp fangs came crashing down again but stopped abruptly when they entered the mask. The tips of the fangs scratched against Simon's glasses, trying to penetrate his head.

Shocked and horrified, he cast the first spell that came into his mind: "*Voluminous!*"

Simon brought his hand to his mouth, as if to erase the spell from being cast. "Oh, no! What have I done?" he cried aloud.

The gigantic spider trembled. Black hair sprouted from its soft abdomen and grew like a terrible weed. Its legs became the size of tree trunks. Shaking and convulsing, the spider repeatedly hit its head on the cave ceiling as it underwent a grotesque metamorphosis.

Simon grabbed the little red book next to him and rolled out from underneath the creature's legs. Quickly, he ripped the shattered gas mask from his face and sprinted down the dark tunnel.

Illuminating gold and green as he ran past them, the ancient runes gave Simon just enough light to maneuver through the cave. He glanced back and wished he hadn't. The ever-growing spider dragged its swollen abdomen across the floor as it charged. Fortunately for Simon, the narrow passageway hindered his assailant from moving its expanding legs. In fact, the spider had grown so large that its tough exoskeleton ground against the ceiling and walls.

Just as the spider became lodged in place, it shot its silky web at Simon, striking him so hard across the back that he almost fell. At the same time, Simon heard the gruesome sound of the arachnid crunching against the walls of the cave. The spider's hard shell finally cracked open, releasing a gush of light blue blood that spilled out onto the floor.

Simon peered into the darkness, towards the dead spider. "Oh, boy," he said, panting. "That was a close one."

Out of breath, he turned around and took a step forward, but the next thing he knew, he was plummeting downward off the edge of a steep cliff.

Simon yelled at the top of his lungs while the hot air whisked through his clothing and hair. A fiery lake of molten lava came into view. He screamed even louder. Suddenly, he felt himself come to a full stop and spring upwards a few feet. The spider's web! It had saved him.

Now he dangled helplessly in the air–literally by a thread. He looked around and beheld a massive spider web woven to form a bridge across the pit. The web was immaculate, yet deadly. It stretched out in all directions, filling the entire cave above him.

Simon could see dozens of large cocoons held securely in the air. He also noticed the many skeletons strewn about the web. It was a catacomb of the dead! This alone discouraged him from going near it. Besides, the makeshift bridge lay far beyond his reach.

Several passageways were cut into the other cliff wall, but Simon's side of the pit contained no such passageways.

The boy looked upward. He had fallen quite a long distance, and although his arms had become very strong over the past few weeks, he wasn't sure if he had enough strength to climb all the way back up.

Burning magma bubbled just thirty feet below him. Simon felt grateful for the newfound light the magma emitted, but he could hardly bear the hot steam that saturated his clothing. He crammed the little red book into his deep pocket, wiped the sweat from his forehead, and contemplated his next move.

Out of the small handful of spells he knew of, none seemed very suitable for his current predicament. Just then, Simon noticed tiny specks of light glowing above him. He squinted to see through the darkness and observed that the tiny lights were getting closer . . . and closer.

Then he saw them. Spiders! Hundreds of them–all descending the chasm. Frantically, he grabbed the silky cord attached to the back of his vest and soon discovered that, although the spider's web had a tremendous hold on his clothing, it reacted in just the opposite way to his skin. Furthermore, the chemical reaction to the oils in his hands caused the acidic thread to burn his fingers. But Simon had no choice. Ignoring the searing pain, he held onto the strong web and attempted to swing to safety.

The glowing eyes got closer with every swing . . . *Whoosh!* Simon cut through the air like a pendulum . . . *Whoosh!* Another swing and his fingertips brushed the intricate latticework the spiders had created . . . *Whoosh!* Only seconds were left before the spiders would be upon him . . .

This would be his final swing. Simon headed towards the wall and kicked off, just as a handful of smaller spiders–each about two to three feet tall–jumped towards him. All but one of the furry creatures fell to a fiery grave; however, the remaining spider sank its fangs deep into Simon's left shoulder blade. The boy yelped in pain as he swung towards the main web.

Summoning a fierceness he didn't realize he possessed, Simon struck the spider with his free hand, causing the vehement creature to tumble off his back. But this particular spider had an unnatural determination; as it fell to the fire below, the demonic creature spurted out its web, which wrapped tightly around Simon's ankle.

Making things even worse, when Simon finally made contact with the bridge, the strand on his vest snapped him back so that he almost lost his grip. He pulled and tugged, but the elasticity of the thread had reached its utter limit. Simon was trapped, and a horde of black spiders was about to pounce on him.

He had to act quickly. "*Shawnee!*" the young wizard shouted in desperation.

A bright flame sprang from his fist and ate its way through the entire web–including the strand on his back–until it smacked against the domed ceiling above. Hundreds of scorched bodies fell to the lava below. Bubbling and spewing, the lake reacted adversely to the chemical composition of their bodies and began to rise. Molten rock spilled into the lower tunnels.

"*Eenwahs,*" Simon said, canceling the spell.

The glowing red fire magnified the deadly beauty of the artwork that spanned the diameter of the dome. For a second or two, the fledgling wizard felt sorry that he had destroyed the poor creatures and their home; however, the realization that he was lugging around one of these giant spiders–from a web attached to his leg, no less–made him come to his senses . . . Make that a giant *climbing* spider!

Although the tips of its legs had been singed off from touching the lava below, the spider continued to limp up the silky strand, relentlessly pursuing its prey. Simon heard the crackle of fire devouring the web right above him, so, hand-over-hand, he carried his body across the deteriorating bridge. The acidic thread steamed every time he clenched his fist, but he continued on, nonetheless.

Like a chain reaction, the flame ran along the spider web, consuming everything in its path. When Simon had cast the Shawnee spell, he had tried to avoid the web in his general vicinity, but it didn't matter; the fire had now found its way to him. He looked down at his unwanted passenger and saw that the injured spider was only a few feet away. His situation could not get any worse.

Suddenly, he heard a snap from behind.

"*Noooo!*" Simon screamed, falling towards the menacing lava.

Still holding the thin cord, he swung over the lake of fire–just barely missing the deadly flames. His pesky companion, on the other hand, plunged right into the hot lava, releasing its web from Simon's foot in the process.

Simon's heart sank when he saw the sheer cliff wall ahead of him. In that instant, he realized what his fate would be. He would crash into the rock and slide into the boiling magma below. His life, his friends . . . everything would be gone. He'd never experience his first real kiss. Tonya and Thorn would continue their lives without him, and he'd never discover where his powers truly came from or the identity of his parents. There was nothing he could do to prevent his untimely demise. He was going to die. Closing his eyes, he waited for the inevitable . . . but it never came.

Simon opened his eyes warily. The cave wall stood just inches from his face. Dumbfounded, he looked down and realized he was floating. Somehow, he had cast the Halo-Marine spell.

A horrible thought entered his mind: The last time he cast the levitation spell, it wore off the second he looked down. Panic-stricken, he jerked his head up to keep himself from thinking of the bubbling lava below. But this was a poor alternative. Instead of peering down at a fiery doom, he looked up at hundreds of baby spiders racing down the cliff wall for their dinner.

Simon stretched out his arms and caught hold of a tunnel entrance. He started to pull himself up, but as his muscles flexed, a hot surge of pain ran down his left shoulder. The spider venom began to attack his nervous system.

Blood trickled from the spider bite as he pulled himself into the dark tunnel. Moaning from the pain, he grasped his shoulder and flailed about the hard floor, as if to massage the wound. The spiders would be upon him at any moment.

Without warning, he felt himself slide down the tunnel uncontrollably. Deeper and deeper into the mountain he slid, until, finally, the tunnel ended, and he shot out into the air. Fortunately, he landed onto something soft and rubbery.

The boy felt so exhausted that he just lay there in the dark. He closed his eyes and, for the first time in weeks, wished he were back home on Earth. The toxins in his bloodstream made him feel very sleepy, and for a few minutes, he experienced a floating sensation.

Fighting against the lethargy, he forced his eyes open and shuddered to see the ground rippling beneath him. The ancient words on the cave walls glowed brightly–so brightly, in fact, Simon saw that he had landed on a gigantic worm. The grayish-white skin reminded him of a maggot. Was this the same type of worm–a gilaworm, as Thorn had called it–that Mrs. Troodle had served him the first night after he had woken up from his coma? How did it get so big?

Simon lay flat on his back and tried to forget the pain in his shoulder. He took out his mother's medallion and played with it in his hand. The glowing runes on the cave walls reflected upon its shiny surface. He noticed the similarities of the medallion and the emblem on the red book. How strange.

"I wouldn't be alive if it wasn't for you," Simon said to the medallion. His voice possessed a distinct twinge of pain. "What other tricks do you have for me?" He clenched the medallion tightly as the poison traveled down his arm. "Can you stop this poison?"

As if his own body mocked his request, Simon sneezed. It was the first sneeze he could remember since . . . since living on Earth. He wasn't sure if it was the poison or not, but he felt a sudden urge to take a puff from his inhaler. He sneezed again.

"*Ahhh!*" Simon yelled in disgust. He had forgotten how sickly he used to be in his own paraworld, and it made him angry to remember.

Abruptly, the gilaworm stopped moving. It reared its head upwards and then doubled back towards Simon. Terrified and in pain, the boy tried to stay calm. Although the huge worm didn't have any eyes, it obviously could hear and smell. The massive creature opened its giant mouth and sucked in deeply as it probed the intruder on its back. Simon held his breath and gazed into the toothless mouth above him. He felt another sneeze coming on but forced it to go away.

The gilaworm must not have sensed any immediate danger, because it brought its head back to the front and started moving again. Simon exhaled quietly.

After a couple of minutes, he glanced around and realized the worm was moving on top of an old monorail built inside a deep trench. Dim artificial lighting replaced the glowing runes in this part of the cave. Curious, Simon sat up and discovered that the tunnel had opened up into a large and spacious cavern. High above him, he saw a giant machine that filled half of the room. The tremendous height of the machine took his breath away, but the fact that it appeared to be turned on astounded him even more.

Simon couldn't believe that after hundreds of years the colossal machine, built by an ancient civilization, still hummed with power. He wanted to get closer to it, but there was no way; the narrow channel he and the gilaworm traveled along sunk into the floor like a moat around a castle and prevented him from getting to the machine. Even when standing on the worm, Simon couldn't quite reach the top of the ditch. The ancient Puds must have used the track to haul out the rubble when they dug the tunnels. And the ditches, he realized, correlated with the height of the big Puds.

Even the ancient Puds practiced slavery, he thought to himself.

While pondering this topic, Simon spotted a glint of metal shining near the track below. An insatiable urge came over him to pick it up, but he didn't know why. The artifact might help him convince the little Puds of his journey under the city, but it could also be a trap. He felt like a moth drawn to a flame. Should he risk losing his ride for the chance at getting a piece of worthless metal? The shard seemed to beckon him closer. He felt himself lean towards it.

Before the boy realized what he was doing, he slid off the worm and picked up the strange object. He promptly thrust it into his pocket and ran back to his ride, but when he tried to jump on, he slipped off the worm's rubbery exterior. After a few more attempts, Simon finally clambered onto the giant creature.

Terribly exhausted, he lay on his back and rested. The effects of the poison crept into the joints of his left hand. He flexed his fingers to keep the numbness at bay and wondered how long the poison would taunt him like this. Did he have minutes to live, or would the spider venom string him along for days before it finally snuffed out his life?

Simon closed his eyes and then remembered the artifact in his pocket. He pulled it out and ran his fingers along the smooth surface. Paper-thin grooves decorated the silver device. He wondered how it had kept its shine after all these years. Upon close examination, Simon could find no discernable buttons to activate it. The internal batteries were most likely dead anyway. It was probably just a child's toy or trinket–hardly worth keeping. Then, near the top of the object, Simon saw ancient words engraved in the metal, so he read them aloud. "Holo-649."

"*Voice activation enabled.*" An elderly woman's voice sounded. A needle shot out of the device and pricked Simon on the wrist.

"*Ouch!*" he yelled.

The boy quickly sat up and looked over at the worm's head, but the docile creature didn't seem to care that he had just raised his voice.

"*DNA confirmed.*" A pleasant chime welcomed the image of a tiny hologram that fit in the palm of Simon's hand. "What is your request, Master Pentagola?" the old woman asked pleasantly.

"Um," Simon stammered, "I think–I think you made a mistake."

The miniature woman looked up in shock at the boy before her. "Oh, dear me." The image stuttered for a few seconds. "Re-sequencing for new owner . . ." she announced. "Complete." She smiled. "What is your request, young master?"

"Call me Simon," he responded.

"What a lovely name," she said. "What is your request, Master Simon?"

"Well, I was kinda wondering what your name was?"

The old woman raised her little hand and cried, "How rude of me! My designation is Holo-649. How may I be of service?"

Simon pointed to the monstrous machine. "What can you tell me about that big machine over there?"

The old woman laughed. "Very funny, Master Simon. I'm glad to see that you have a sense of humor. King Pentagola was always so drab."

"No, really. I don't have a clue what that machine does."

"You don't know what it does!" she declared, aghast at his ignorance. "The very key to this planet's survival and you have no idea what it does?"

"Key," Simon repeated. He brought out the little red book excitedly and read the inscription. "'*The key to the machine that will save us all.*' Does this have something to do with it?"

"Well, my stars! Of course it does, Master Simon. That key you're holding turns on the machine."

"I read that the ancient Puds were going to get rid of all the dragunos. What does the machine do, exactly?"

"Ancient?" the hologram asked with a frown. "How long have I been deactivated?"

"Um . . . maybe a thousand years," Simon broke the news to her.

"A thousand years!"

"*Shhh!*" Simon tried to hush her.

The gilaworm startled slightly but kept moving. They had just left the huge room and were now winding down another dark passageway.

"So you're telling me, young man, that the machine was *never turned on?*"

Simon shrugged. "It looks like it's on."

"That's just the generator sucking up all the electro-magical energy to give power to the machine."

"So there *is*–" Simon started. "I mean, there *was* electro-magical energy on this planet at one time?"

"Oh, dear me." The old woman paced around Simon's hand. "If the generator has been charging this whole time, then I suppose the magical energy from this parallel world has been utterly drained. That would also mean this world has been completely cut off from the outside. Oh, dear, dear me. And Pudo has probably been designated a dead planet." She put her hand to her face. "Please wait a moment, and I'll process the final datastream I received from Master Pentagola."

The hologram faded in and out for a moment and then came back to normal. "Horrible!" she exclaimed. "Simply horrible!"

"What is?"

"The final battle of the dragunos."

"Holo-6-4, uh–" He forgot her designation. "Holo, I have to know what happened. Tell me everything you know, starting from the first."

"Do you want the long version or the short version?"

"Long version, I guess."

A second projection sprang from the shard of metal and showed an image of a little baby eating. A deep, melancholy voice spoke from within the device. "*Here we observe as the infant takes his first few bites of solid food. Notice how he enjoys the savory carrots. Soon, he will dine on other delectable vegetables such as peas, green beans, butternut squash, sweet potatoes, bananas, pears, apples . . .*"

"Okay, okay! Give me the short version," Simon belted out impatiently.

The image fast-forwarded to show a large egg resting on the bottom of the ocean. As the camera panned out, it revealed hundreds of thousands of similar eggs lining the ocean floor.

"*Dragunos,*" the deep voice sounded. "*The word is synonymous with terror. Here we observe one of the many reptilian nests, but, unfortunately, for every one nest we find and destroy, ten more lie hidden.*"

The image changed to show three scientists cutting open an egg with a laser.

"*The tough shells are lined with a unique chemical that preserves the embryo from calcification. Scientists have discovered that the creatures have a thousand-year gestation period. This allows the lizards to ravish the planet for food and then lay their eggs so the cycle can continue again. The draguno life expectancy is not known, but experts suggest that these deadly reptiles live for only a few weeks.*"

"What about the machine?" Simon asked.

"Don't worry," Holo-649 assured him. "We're getting there."

The little projection zoomed out to show the mountain where Highland City lay.

The deep voice of the narrator continued. "*Project Purity: the combination of both the big and the small citizens of the capital city joining forces to rid the planet of the dragunos.*"

The next scene showed a big Pud speaking before a grand audience.

"As your president, I promise I am doing everything possible to ensure the safety of the planet." A roar of clapping ensued. "This is a momentous occasion. For the first time in my life, our two races have become one in purpose." More clapping followed his words. "Magic alone cannot save us from this impending disaster. As you know, our smaller brothers are more adept at harnessing the powers of science, so under the direction of General Banton, they have written up the plans to build a great machine that will save us all."

The crowd yelled with ecstatic fervor, but the big Pud raised his hands to calm them down. He needed their full attention before he could introduce the controversial conditions of the plan.

"However," he began carefully, "sacrifices must be made." The crowd grew silent. "In order to generate enough power to protect the entire planet, the machine must collect an enormous amount of electro-magical energy. This being the case, we'll have to put our magical abilities on hold for a time."

The big Puds protested loudly.

"Furthermore," the president spoke over their incessant moaning. "Paratravel will be discontinued until the threat is over."

The people were now in an uproar. The president tried to continue, but the crowd was too loud. Suddenly, amidst the chaos, a blue bubble of electricity appeared in the air, and out walked a man who looked more like a human than a Pud. The enormous crowd bowed in unison as the High King floated to the ground.

"Citizens of Highland City. I ask you to listen to reason. Your lives are more important than magic," he said. "The smaller Puds do not even care for magic, yet they live happy lives. Do not give up the *needs* of tomorrow for the *wants* of today. You *must* carry on with this wise and prudent plan."

The king looked out at the people, both big and small, and saw that he had pacified them–at least for the moment. "General Banton," he called. The leader of the tiny Puds bounded up the stage. "If I may?" King Pentagola said as he picked the tiny man up and placed him on the shoulders of the president.

"Here stands the brave warriors of Pudo . . ." he spoke methodically. "The big and the small–fighting as one, living as one, dying as one. May we always look back to the day we overcame our pride, stood up for what is right, and defended our planet from the evil forces within."

The galvanized crowd roared with approval. Soon, all of the little Puds were sitting on the shoulders of the larger Puds, and everyone was cheering with excitement. The years of segregation and turmoil had finally ended.

"That was a happy day," the old holographic woman noted somberly as the projection faded away into the darkness. "My master was very fond of this planet," she continued, still deep in thought. "He met his wife on this planet . . . His first son was born on this planet . . . Even his life was taken . . . on this planet . . ."

"What happened?" Simon asked.

The woman wiped a holographic tear from her eye. She looked up slowly and then snapped to attention. "*Duck!*" she screamed.

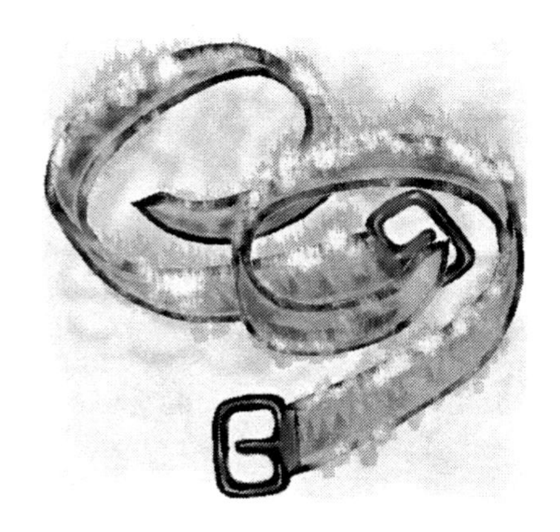

CHAPTER 21
THE CREATURES OF PUDO

Simon looked up quickly to see the gilaworm's head enter a burrow. The sharp overhang of the entrance came at him in a rush, but he lay flat on his back just in time.

He stuffed the hologram and the little red book into his pocket and then rolled over and gripped the rippling body of the gilaworm as it plunged into the dark abyss. Deeper and deeper into the mountain they slid.

Just as Simon felt he couldn't possibly hold on any longer, the bumpy ride came to an abrupt halt. They appeared to be in some sort of resting chamber. Dozens of giant worms lay dormant on the warm floor, and a faint rumbling sound echoed throughout the cavern. A crack in the ceiling allowed the beginnings of morning to slip in. Had he really been in the cave that long?

The tired gilaworm's huge body sagged to the ground, and the creature quickly fell into a deep sleep. Gusts of sweltering air made Simon want to sleep as well. Tingling sensations spread throughout his body as the spider venom slowly attacked his nervous system.

Forcing himself to stay awake, the boy stood up and reached for the crack in the ceiling but couldn't quite get to it. If only he weren't so short. He then tried jumping, but when he landed, he slid off the worm's rubbery hide and smashed onto the hard floor.

Sprawled in the hot dirt and too tired to move, the young wizard contemplated for a moment whether or not he should cast the growing spell on the gilaworm. The gruesome image of the giant spider crunching against the walls of the cave entered his mind. He quickly decided against it.

Simon pressed his ear to the ground. The rumbling seemed to be getting louder every second. Previously, he had assumed the sleeping worms were just snoring, but now he realized the noise must be coming from somewhere else. He decided to investigate.

The morning light crept up the rock wall, which made the mineral deposits sparkle. Simon followed the grumbling sounds all the way to the other side of the chamber. Now it sounded like a thousand wheels grinding all at once. He stretched his hand to touch the vibrating wall but withdrew it immediately and thrust his burnt fingers into his mouth. The boiling magma must be right on the other side!

Simon started to run when, suddenly, the wall gave way, and a pool of deadly fire began to flood the room. He jumped on the first worm he could see and ran down its rubbery body. When the burning lava touched the unsuspecting creature, the gilaworm immediately reared its head high into the air.

Simon jumped to the next worm nearby and ran down the length of its body as well. It also jerked as the hot lava pierced its thick skin. One by one, the helpless gilaworms awoke from the scorching river–each worm standing up on its tail before collapsing.

Simon frantically hopped from worm to worm, desperate to stay alive, but the fiery demon remained close behind. The silent screams of the poor creatures were heart wrenching, and the young wizard wished he knew of a spell that could stop the senseless carnage, but he didn't.

Wrought with despair, he looked longingly at the wide crack in the ceiling and felt that, soon, he too would feel the wrath of the volcano. He threw himself over to the last gilaworm–the same one that had carried him so far, and at that very moment, the cruel lava awakened the creature from its slumber.

As the worm sprang upwards from the pain, Simon landed on its head and, as a result, catapulted high into the air. The boy grasped for the opening in the ceiling and made contact. He readjusted his grip and looked down to see his traveling companion being devoured by the flames below.

Tears filled his eyes, but the heat reminded him of the immediate danger. He continued to pull himself to safety, despite his left arm threatening to dislocate itself. Simon wished his arm would simply fall off. Then perhaps the pain would subside.

Fresh air filled his nostrils as he finally emerged from the cave. The bright sun blinded him temporarily. He tried to stand, but his legs gave out, and he tumbled down the grassy slope of the volcano. He had exited near the bottom, so he didn't have far to roll.

The boy rested on a patch of grass at the base of the mountain. He was too tired to even rub his freshly bruised body nor dwell on the excruciating pain in his shoulder.

Lying flat on his back, Simon gazed past the blemished lumps of mountains that pierced through the hard, earthen floor and saw the yellow disk of sun bleach the sky with its magnificent glory. He felt so small and so alone. How could he possibly save the planet from the dragunos?

Just then, a large tongue came out of nowhere and licked his face. Startled, the boy realized that something big stood above him: a farbearus. Simon had first seen one when Har's mother had come to plead for her son's freedom. He also remembered seeing the big Puds use the docile creatures to haul the wheat in the fields. This one must have gotten left behind by accident.

A broken strap, attached to a leather harness, dangled freely in the air, but upon closer observation, Simon noticed the end of the strap had been gnawed through. The animal hadn't been left behind; it had escaped.

Fighting back the pain in his shoulder, he grabbed the harness with his good hand and sluggishly pulled himself onto the hairy beast. Delirious, Simon dropped the reins, allowing the large creature to roam as it pleased. With his strength depleted, all he could do was hug the animal's back and pray that it would take him to someone who could help.

They trod through the barren wasteland where, just a few days earlier, golden rows of wheat had stood. The big Puds had stripped the entire field clean.

An hour sped by quickly while Simon went in and out of consciousness. When he awoke, he realized his companion was drinking from a small pond. Simon threw himself to the moss-covered bank, blazing with thirst, and stuck his head into the clear water. The cool, refreshing liquid revived his spirits a little.

He cupped his hand and was about to drink when something in the water startled him. At the bottom of the innocent-looking pond lay thousands of bones.

Simon jumped to his feet and staggered back a few paces. He noticed a small ripple in the center of the pond that grew bigger and bigger. Black oil bubbled to the surface. Slowly, the dark liquid collected into one body until it coagulated into the consistency of tar. Without warning, the dark mass raced towards the shore.

"Come on, big guy," Simon yelled, tugging on the leather strap to get the farbearus to move, but the stubborn creature refused to budge.

The hairy beast looked up from drinking just in time to see a huge mound of black jelly leap from the water. Thick goo engulfed the entire mammal, as well as Simon's forearm. The black jelly gave a tremendous yank, which pulled them both towards the pond.

The farbearus didn't have a chance, but Simon was more fortunate. As he fell to the ground, the black goo ripped off him like putty and removed his shirtsleeve in the process. Simon looked at his bare arm and realized that the burning sensation he felt was due to the fact that most of the hair on his tender skin had just been pulled out.

Lying flat on his belly, he watched the pond as it erupted into a commotion of thrashing waves. Somewhere in the turmoil, an item ejected from the water and landed next to him. The scared boy looked over to see a leather harness, mutilated and foaming with acid.

At that moment, Simon found his second wind. He sprinted away from the pond, screaming in terror, not daring to look back.

He slipped on the moist grass a couple of times but kept running. After reaching a small hill, he spun around to check on the creature, but to his horror, he found it standing right behind him.

Simon darted up the steep hill just as a couple of oily tendrils shot out of the black jelly. He thought that surely the monster wouldn't be able to follow him up the hill, but it proved him wrong.

The grass turned brown as the strange creature pulled itself up the hill with its two wiry arms. Simon fervently wished he had his hover chair. His body protested with every movement.

When he finally reached the top, a sickening feeling spread throughout his entire frame. He stood at the edge of a steep ravine, and down at the bottom of the gorge lay a rushing river.

Without hesitation, Simon jumped. Unfortunately, the dark blob spilled over the edge as well. But as it fell, a strong updraft thrust into the monster's formless body, causing it to balloon like a parachute.

A moment later, Simon plunged into the river below . . . *SPLAT*–and so did the blob of jelly. But as it splattered against the water, its liquidlike body broke up into a million droplets of black oil that soon vanished within the harsh current.

Simon felt the hammer of a thousand little bubbles attempting to smother him. His lungs were about to explode, and he feared his handicapped arm would prevent him from reaching the surface. But just then, he touched the hard bottom of the riverbed, so he kicked himself upward with all his might. A rush of air filled his lungs as he burst through the surface of the river.

Trying to stay afloat, Simon grasped at nearby debris, but after a short while, he found himself still struggling to stay above the cold water.

If I could just find a branch big enough to hold onto . . .

Something large brushed against him. Petrified, Simon gasped but then saw, to his relief, that it was just an old log. A log! He seized the long piece of timber with his good arm and held on tight. Now that he was relatively safe, Simon glanced around at the sheer walls of rock that enclosed both sides of the river. Gray birds with long beaks and sharp talons watched him closely as he floated by. One after the other, they thrust off the wall and plunged into the water for hard-shelled crustaceans. Two of the birds never emerged from the river.

The frothy water chilled Simon to the bone but also soothed the pain in his shoulder. In fact, he hardly noticed the tingling sensations of the poison anymore.

After a few minutes, the cliff walls finally disappeared and were replaced by fertile banks filled with lush vegetation. Sago palms and leafy ferns lined the river, and tall prehistoric-looking trees jutted everywhere.

Despite the picturesque scenery, Simon's eyes widened at what else he saw. Ferocious creatures, full of menacing teeth and claws, bathed at the river's edge. The boy doubted he'd be able to swim to the embankment anyway, especially because of the swift current. He ducked as a bear-like animal with extraordinarily long arms raised its head to stare at him. It took a step forward, but a reptile nearby gave a warning hiss. The water was no place for mammals. Simon hugged the log and held his breath. The bear-like animal growled and then backed away.

Simon found it difficult to exhale. How much longer would he have to endure these trials? He hungered for food and water. He yearned for a warm bed. And most of all, he wished for the pain in his shoulder and arm to go away. But none of those things really mattered. If he didn't get back to the city soon, everything and everyone might be lost. He thought of his friends and gained an added measure of hope and determination. He had to try.

The width and depth of the river increased rapidly. Every once in a while, the boy thought he saw the end of a jagged tail or the tip of a sharp fin. He wondered how much safer he really was in the river. For all he knew, there could be piranhas–or even worse, dragunos–in the water.

While contemplating this very thought, the long timber he held onto suddenly bobbed up and down. Choking on a mouthful of icy water, Simon turned to see a twenty-five-foot crocodile chewing on the far end of the log. Even more shocking, the strange reptile had several rows of tall, colorful spikes running down its back and two thrashing tails.

The monster spun the large piece of wood around like a toy, causing Simon to lose his grip and float off in another direction. Attracted by the boy's movement, the scaly reptile abandoned the log and headed towards him. It opened its hideous mouth and let out a deep, gargled roar.

Just then, a giant fin glided past Simon's small frame. The boy looked down to see something dark and massive swimming directly underneath him. In a sudden fury, a gigantic yet agile shark sprang upwards and clenched its jaws around the two-tailed crocodile.

Like a crippled frog, Simon floundered through the bloody water for the safety of the log. Although he no longer had any feeling in his left arm, he still reached the floating piece of driftwood. By this time, the giant shark was dining on its fallen prey at the bottom of the deep channel.

Simon began to shiver uncontrollably. He wasn't sure if the trembling came because of the cold water, the frightening experience he'd just had, or the spider venom, but what he did know was that he couldn't stay in the river much longer and expect to live.

Almost as if in answer to a prayer, the boy glimpsed a school of small boats just up ahead. The river spilled into the ocean, and there, the fishermen waited to catch the fish that swam out to sea. Simon's heart jumped for joy as he got closer to the skiffs.

He felt a dull numbness enshroud his body, and when he breathed, he couldn't seem to get any air into his lungs. Hypothermia was setting in–either that, or the spider's poison had finally chosen to kill him.

The boy tried to scream, but his chest hurt so badly that he was forced to stop. He looked up at the closest boat and saw the big Puds pointing in his direction. He was saved!

Simon watched in earnest as the fishermen rowed their boat frantically towards him. Some of the men continued to wave their hands and point. After seeing the strange looks on their faces, Simon realized that maybe they weren't pointing at him. Confused, the boy looked behind and saw a twenty-foot-long shark jumping out of the water–just like a swordfish would do. In fact, it even had a tiny sword-like beak attached to its upper jaw. The white, slender shark glided across the water in his direction.

"It's not fair," Simon moaned. "Just leave me alone."

He watched sorrowfully as the shark's mouth drew open in what looked like a menacing grin. Simon was too sleepy and exhausted to care anymore. Not wanting to give the shark the satisfaction of a stationary kill, he released his grip on the log and descended into the ocean. But before his head was even completely submerged, he felt a large hand clutch his shoulder and pull him out of the water.

A second later, the shark struck the log with its sharp beak, splitting the wood in two. Angry, the aggressive creature circled around and leapt right onto the small wooden skiff. It slid across the bow towards Simon.

Delirium swept the boy to his knees. His eyes fluttered. The shark opened its jaws for the kill. Suddenly, a spear pierced through the shark's head from behind, bit into its brain, and came out of the creature's gaping mouth. At that same moment, Simon fainted.

The large fishermen attacked the shark with their clubs, and the giant who had slain the creature approached Simon. He reached down with his mighty hand and picked up the black medallion that had fallen from the boy's neck. A look of understanding came into the big Pud's eyes as he stared in awe at the young wizard before him.

CHAPTER 22
MORBRAS WILL SAVE US

"Simon . . . Simon . . ." came the cool, delicate voice from the woman in his dream. The words left her lips like notes from a song.

You have proven strong and overcome
The tribulations thus far.
From a boy to a man you have grown,
Yet many trials you still must face.
From fiery demons to icy snow,
You shall triumph over all.
Yet to conquer all, you must be humbled,
Or pride will conquer you.
Your second gift, I now bestow:
Poison begone!
To harm you nevermore.

The beautiful young woman began to disappear into the mist once more. "Please don't go," Simon begged. "You still haven't told me who you are."

As she faded away, her final words echoed in his mind. "My dearest Simon. The answer is found within."

Perplexed by her response, Simon opened his eyes. His vision slowly came into focus. He saw a large face staring down at him.

"Si-moan almost fish bait."

"Har?" Simon said, astonished. The roaring fire nearby illuminated the grassy interior of the hut. Evening shadows danced upon the walls and played with the light from the crackling flames. "How did I get here?"

"Father find Si-moan. Father save Si-moan."

A giant man approached the bed. His clothing consisted of animal skins, musty and worn. A long rope wrapped around his shoulder and chest, as if it were part of his natural attire.

"Simon," he said. "I is Harr." He extended his huge hand. "Nice . . . to . . . meet . . . you."

"Nice to meet you," Simon said, shaking the large paw. "Thank you for saving me. I thought I was a goner."

"Simon almost die," the man explained, trying to piece the words together into an intelligent sentence. "Cold water slow down poison. Simon smart to go in river."

"I didn't realize," he said, sitting up. "I just kinda fell into the situation." He stretched out his tired arms. "Wow! I feel great now."

With a look of surprise, Harr reached over and removed the bandages on the boy's shoulder. He then dug his big thumb into the spider bite.

"This no hurt?"

"Ouch, ouch!" Simon yelped. "Yeah, that's pretty tender. What I meant to say was that I can move my arm again. The poison must have worn off."

"Poison no . . . no . . . no wear off. Poison kill," said Little Har.

"Poison no kill!" his father exclaimed. The large man opened the front door and yelled out to his tribe, "Morbras! Morbras! Morbras comes!"

A group of giants entered the hut with looks of amazement on their faces. One by one, they approached Simon's bed and touched his shoulder while chanting, "Morbras comes."

Simon whispered to Little Har, "Who's this *Morbras* they're talking about?"

"Si-moan . . . is Morbras," he said slowly. The big Puds bowed down in reverence. Har concluded, "Si-moan our king."

"*WHAT?*" His response was so abrasive that everyone stopped chanting at once. "I'm not your king!"

Big Harr stood. "Legend say . . . Morbras will come . . . and protect us . . . Poison cannot hurt Morbras . . . Morbras our king." As the big Pud spoke, two giants placed a wicker basket at the bedside.

"Look, guys, I know you might believe in some old fable, but I have a perfectly good explanation for this."

The big Puds backed away from the bed while an old man opened the basket with a long stick. Before Simon could continue, a pit viper emerged. In an instant, the venomous snake rose high enough to become eye level with the boy. Simon froze.

He stuttered under his breath, "Wh-Wh-Wh-hat are you d-d-doing? I'm not Morbras."

The snake swayed back and forth, staring at the frightened boy. Then, without warning, it struck and bit Simon on the arm with its two-inch fangs. Har's father grabbed the serpent's head and pried it from Simon's flesh.

Still holding the squirming snake in his hand, Harr said, "Now we show you . . . that you *are* Morbras."

Simon felt the neurotoxins race through his bloodstream. The room started to spin, and intense pains jabbed at his stomach. Falling back onto the bed, he moaned, "I'm not Morbras. I'm not Morbras. I'm not . . ." Suddenly, the pain disappeared, and the room stopped spinning.

"Simon . . ." came the deep voice of Har's father from above, ". . . *is* Morbras."

The boy sat up and looked at his arm in dismay. The nasty-looking fang marks were still there, but the poison in his body seemed to be gone.

The big Puds continued their quiet chanting. "Morbras comes . . . Morbras comes . . ." They all bowed down again; some even prostrated themselves upon the ground.

"Please," Simon cried. "Don't."

Har's father put the viper back into the wicker basket and said, "Morbras needs rest." He shooed the crowd from the hut, but Little Har remained at Simon's bedside.

"I don't understand," Simon groaned, trying to nurse his wounded arm.

Harr pulled out some herbs from a pouch on his belt and ground them with a stone. "I is sorry," the giant said as he worked. "So sorry."

He spit in the mixture twice to give it a pasty consistency. "I plucked you from river," the man boasted. He rubbed the herbs onto the puncture wounds. Simon winced. "Sent from God . . . you are."

The man took some bandages from his bag and wrapped them around Simon's arm to stop the bleeding. "Morbras . . ." he mumbled softly. "Morbras will free us all."

"Please don't call me that. My name is Simon."

"Si-moan?" said Little Har.

"Yes, just Simon."

"Simon must rest," Harr said calmly. "Come, Little Har . . . Let us go."

"Wait," Simon called out. "I'm starving."

"Si-moan hungry?" said Little Har.

"Yes, big guy . . . and thirsty."

Har's father consented. "I go . . . get food for king." The giant left the hut to gather some food.

Simon opened his mouth to speak when he noticed two identical twins sneaking into the room. They eased their way closer and closer, as if frightened to approach the young wizard.

"Come. No be afraid," Har said to the young men. "Si-Moan, here my brothers. This Harrr and this Har-rr."

"You're kidding me." Simon laughed; the pain in his arm had subsided. "You all have the same name?"

"No," Har said, scratching his ear. He pointed a finger at each brother and then crossed his arms and pointed at them with the opposite hand. "This Harrr and this Har-rr."

"No, Har. I Harrr," the first Pud said, drawing near.

"And I Har-rr," the other one chided.

Just then, three more Puds bounded into the room. "This Har-r-r," Har introduced. "This Harrr-r . . . and this Har-rr-r."

Simon could hardly tell a difference in the way Little Har pronounced their names. "Man, I bet your family reunions are just a blast to go to," he joked. They all looked puzzled. "I mean," Simon tried to explain further, "everyone probably has a hard time remembering your names." Still, none of the large boys seemed to understand what he was referring to. "I bet your mom and dad mix up your names all the time," he added with an uncomfortable laugh.

This time, the big Puds all looked down at the ground in sorrow.

"Did I say something wrong?"

"Momma no come back," Little Har said. "Momma get water at river . . . and no come back."

"Dra-goon-nos eat her," Harrr blurted.

His twin brother punched him in the arm and cried, "No say that! Momma no get eaten!"

Harrr-r joined the fight. "Har-r-r find dra-goon-no tracks! Huh, Har-r-r?"

"Yes," Har-r-r answered.

"No mean Momma get eaten," Har-rr-r said, including himself in the argument. He slugged Harrr-r in the arm as he spoke.

"Guys!" Simon intervened. "Guys! You don't have to fight about this. You lost your mother, and that's a terrible thing. I should know. I lost my mother as well, but you can't just argue about it. You have to stick together."

"Si-moan bring Momma back?" asked Har with an innocence so sweet, he seemed like a child fully expecting his father to find a lost pet.

Simon's heart swelled within him. Oh how he wished he could bring his own mother back. But despite his newfound powers, not even he could bring someone back from the dead.

"I'm sorry, Har," Simon choked, "I can't."

Their father entered the room. "Children. Simon needs rest. Go!"

The big Puds scurried out of the room, but again, Little Har stayed behind. His father didn't seem to mind, though. "Little Har," he said, "stay with Simon . . . I go sleep . . . Must fish in morning."

"Actually, Harr," Simon said, "I really need to get to Highland City as soon as possible."

He looked around for his clothing and was about to stand when Harr stopped him. "Too dangerous at night . . . Simon must sleep . . . Tomorrow . . . Tomorrow we go to city." At that, he placed some food and a glass of water in the boy's lap. "Good-night, Morbras," he said, winking.

Simon yawned deeply and admitted to himself that he probably should get some rest. From a window above his bed, he saw the stars shining in the black sky. It had been a very long day, and he welcomed all the sleep he could get.

"Si-moan eat?" Har asked.

Simon took a long drink of the cool water and noted that it tasted exceptionally good. He looked down at his food: various roots of some sort–not really a fitting meal for a king. After building up the courage, he bit into a yellow root and gagged from the bitter flavor.

"Si-moan no like?" asked Har.

"Big surprise, huh?" Simon said with a smile. "I guess I'm just too finicky."

The large boy opened a cedar chest and withdrew from it a tiny chocolate cake. He stretched his arm out to Simon and presented the gift.

"Si-moan like?"

Simon stared in confusion at the bruised but mostly intact cake and suddenly realized it was the same chocolate treat he had given to Har two days earlier.

"Oh, no," he protested. "I couldn't possibly. That was your birthday present."

The large boy beamed from head to toe. "Har save present . . . Si-moan friend." He offered the cake to Simon again and urged, "Please, eat."

Not wanting to be rude, Simon took the chocolate cake and devoured it in less than a minute. It was the tastiest thing he had ever eaten–not because of the actual cake, but because the present had come full circle.

"Tell me, Har," he asked, licking his lips, "what else do you know about this Morbras fellow?"

"Morbras will save us all."

"Save you from what?"

The large boy thought for a while.

"Har not know," he finally confessed.

"I figured as much," Simon said, chuckling.

He lay back down and tried to rest, but the faint pain in his shoulder reminded him of the impending doom that awaited the planet. What could he do? He looked over at the little red book lying on the table. Somehow, he had to get back into the volcano and turn on the machine.

Tomorrow, his body groaned. *Tomorrow*.

Sleep pulled on his eyelids so that he could barely keep them open. "You have a nice family," he said. "So how many brothers and sisters do you have?"

"Har has . . . this many brothers." The large boy brought up six fingers.

"Your parents had seven boys?" Simon said. "Wow, that's amazing."

"And one girl," Har added.

"You're very lucky that your family is still together. Back where I'm from, no one seems to care–"

"No," Har interrupted. "Not together . . . brother work in mines . . . and little sister . . . still servant."

"Oh, I'm sorry to hear that. I want you to know, Har, that I don't agree with the way your people are treated. I think it's awful that your family was split apart."

"Si-moan have family?" Har asked.

"I don't know, really. My mom is gone, and I've never met my dad, so I don't know if he's even alive. As for brothers and sisters . . . I have no idea. I've just always been alone."

"Not alone," Har said, pointing to Simon's chest. "Family always in here."

"Yeah, I guess you're right." Simon rubbed his mother's medallion to bring him comfort. He turned towards the wall and looked out the window again. "The stars sure are bright tonight," he said, yawning.

"Har travel to stars . . . someday."

"Well, actually, Har," Simon began, "if you ever got near a star, you'd probably burn up–" He stopped himself immediately. "Oh, great! Now I'm starting to sound like Thornapple."

The large boy laughed deeply.

"Har, I'll tell you what," Simon said. "If I ever get off this planet, I'll take you with me, okay? That way, you won't be sent to the mines when the little Puds find you."

"Si-moan leave?"

"Someday . . . maybe." He looked at the starry sky and yawned again. "But I won't be traveling through outer space. I guess I'll be traveling to a different planet parallel with this one. At least, that's what Tonya says."

"Par–Parr–Pa–ra–Par–"

"Parallel worlds," Simon said. "And don't ask me what it means." He closed his eyes and mumbled, "I'm still not sure myself . . ."

"Har travel to par-par-par-world with Si-moan," the large boy said, beaming. He looked over at Simon and realized the young wizard was already asleep.

"Good-night . . . Si-moan."

■ ■ ■

"Morbras, wake up," Har's father yelled. Simon didn't even have time to open his eyes before the man dragged his body out of bed. "Danger! We go now!"

"Wait! Wait!" cried Simon. "Let me get my clothes."

"Hurry! They come!"

"Who comes?" Simon yelled back. He looked out the window and saw that it was barely morning.

"Dra-goon-nos."

The word made his blood run cold. Simon grabbed his shirt and vest from the table and threw them on. Just then, Little Har rushed into the hut with a panicked look on his face.

"Hurry," Harr prodded.

"My pants! Where's my pants?" Simon yelled.

"There," Little Har said, pointing to the far wall.

Simon dashed over to get them.

"Strange under-wear," Little Har commented after seeing Simon's colorful Batman boxers.

"Yeah." Simon chuckled nervously and pulled up his black slacks. "They give me special powers."

"Really?" Har asked.

Simon zipped his pants. "No, I'm just kidding."

Suddenly, the wall burst open and knocked Simon to the ground. Surprised, he looked up to see a giant lizard scurrying towards him.

CRACK! Harr smacked the creature so hard with his club that he knocked it into the roaring fireplace. The flame-covered draguno set fire to the grass hut as it writhed on the ground.

"Come," Harr growled, pushing Simon towards the door.

"Wait! I need my book."

"No time!"

"If I don't get that book, we're all dead."

Simon ran for the table and dodged the hot embers that fell from the roof. Right there on the table lay his possessions. He grabbed the little red book and the shard of metal and stuffed them in his pocket. But as he reached for his glasses, the dying draguno swiped his legs from underneath him with its strong tail.

Flat on his back, Simon watched the lizard spring into the air. Jaws open and clawed fingers extended, the reptile descended upon the boy. Simon raised his hands and yelled, "*FLY!*"

The draguno glided right over his body and smashed against the wall. Like a rubber ball, the lizard ricocheted around the room until, finally, it launched itself through the window. Outside, the flaming draguno left a trail of fire as it bounced off trees and huts.

Simon snatched his glasses and ran out of the crumbling building. He soon found, to his horror, that the whole village was on fire. Several big Puds were fighting a draguno as it rampaged through a flock of woolly animals. Terrifying shrieks could be heard from somewhere in the distance.

"Come," Harr shouted. "We ride!"

Har and his father climbed onto some hairy beasts that stood lazily nearby. Simon recognized the stubborn creatures immediately: farbearuses. Reluctantly, he climbed onto one of the muscular animals.

"Don't you have anything faster?" he complained.

Harr whistled loudly, and the docile creatures sprang into flight. Little Har inserted his hands into a pair of gauntlets attached to the sides of the hairy beast he rode. Wondering what the strange gloves were for, Simon followed suit and discovered that inside each glove was a bar of metal for him to hold. Just then, the farbearuses stood up on their massive hind legs.

Simon struggled to keep his feet in the stirrups and his hands in the gauntlets at the same time, but he was too short, despite his animal being smaller than the others.

The group sped on a little ways when, suddenly, an enormous draguno leaped out of a thicket and rammed into Harr's farbearus. The hairy mammal tumbled to the ground, taking its rider with it.

Harr staggered to his feet just as the lizard pounced on him. The two giants rolled on the forest floor until Harr finally threw the reptile off. Frantically, he scrambled for his club, but it was nowhere to be found.

The reptile lunged for him once more, but Harr quickly picked up a rock and shattered it against the draguno's skull. The giant lizard shook its head angrily and reared back in preparation to jump. Just then, Simon noticed the strange tree right behind Little Har's father.

"Harr," Simon yelled. "Throw it into those green branches!"

As the lizard jumped, Harr fell on his back and used his legs to catapult the reptile into the branches behind him. Like a Venus flytrap, the malevolent tree closed its fingers around the lizard and pulled it inward. Loud crunching sounds echoed from within the tree trunk. The lizard's tail flailed about wildly, until, finally, it dropped to the ground. Simon recalled the death of the tree sloth a few days earlier; it too had come to a grisly end. He watched in disgust as the severed tail continued to thrash about. When the crunching sounds ceased, the five bloodstained fingers slowly emerged from the tree to await its next meal.

Harr limped over to his ride and clambered onto its back. He pointed away from the mountain and yelled, "This way."

"Wait a second," Simon said. "I need to get to Highland City."

"No," Harr countered. "Morbras stay . . . Fight dragunos . . . Morbras will save us."

"I don't think so!" Simon shouted. "Listen to me, Harr. Pretty soon now there's going to be thousands of dragunos flooding the land, and the only way your people will have a chance is if you take me to Highland City. You see, there's a machine–"

At that moment, a herd of big Puds–each riding upon a hairy farbearus–rushed past them and quickly disappeared from sight. The forest remained silent for a few seconds, but then an awful hissing sound found its way to their ears. Simon's skin began to crawl with uneasiness. The thick foliage started to rustle, and soon they witnessed the shocking danger that was upon them. Row after row of hungry dragunos came into view, causing the anxiety level in Simon to grow exponentially.

"Trust me, Harr," Simon yelled. "You *don't* want to go that way!"

Without arguing, the giant turned his farbearus around and whistled loudly. Simon didn't have to do anything at all; his ride turned automatically and sprinted towards the mountain at full speed. The dragunos pursued them, but after a while, the cold-blooded reptiles could no longer keep up with the fast pace. It wasn't long before Simon and his companions left the forest and entered a large clearing where the rest of the tribe had gathered. Their steeds went down on all fours again and munched heartily on the green grass.

"Harr!" a large man who appeared to be the tribal leader called out. "Will Morbras save us?"

"Yes, Grog . . . Morbras will save us," Harr reassured him while holding onto the man's shoulder.

"Then we go . . . to ocean . . . Ocean safe."

"*NO!*" Simon burst out. "No, no, no! Don't go to the ocean. Whatever you do, don't go to the ocean! That's where all the dragunos are coming from."

"Si-moan say," Little Har informed Grog, "we go to High-land City."

"We no go to city!" the tribal leader said, aghast at the very thought of disobeying the law. "Not allowed."

Simon stood up on his farbearus's wide back so that everyone could see him clearly.

"If you truly believe I'm Morbras," he said, "then that means I'm your king. And as your king, I *ask* you to go to Highland City. There's a huge library at the edge of town. You have to take me there. That's the only way we can stop the dragunos."

Worried looks spread over the faces of the giants. They stroked their security collars nervously. Simon was asking them to disobey the laws of the land; big Puds were not allowed in the city until daytime, under penalty of imprisonment in the mines.

"Listen to me," Simon said. "Your lives are more important than an immoral law. You can't always follow every rule with blind obedience. Laws are made for people, not the other way around."

The tribal leader raised his hand and yelled ecstatically, "Grog follow Morbras! Morbras will save us!"

The rest of the crowd cheered in agreement. "Morbras will save us!" they exclaimed.

Simon looked at the giants in amazement as they praised and idolized him. For the first time in his life, he didn't feel quite so small anymore. The excitement came to a halt, however, as a pack of deadly dragunos spewed from the forest. Immediately, Grog led his tribe towards the mountain.

The reptiles could run very fast for short distances, but when it came to long sprints, the hairy mammals were far superior runners. The group arrived at the base of the tall mountain after a short while. Without even resting, they proceeded to climb the windy pathway that led to the city. The large muscular legs of the farbearuses gave them a particular advantage over the short legs of the dragunos.

About halfway up the mountain, Grog stopped for a moment to scan for any pursuers. "What is . . . *that?*" he asked with a horrified expression.

Far out in the distance, a sea of strange darkness spread across the surface of the ocean. The morning sun was just beginning to uncover the valley, which in turn revealed a tremendous horde of dragunos racing towards the mountain.

"Ocean . . ." Harr said slowly. "Alive!"

"Oh my gosh." Simon gasped, seeing the millions of giant lizards swimming towards the beach. The dragunos infested the entire ocean.

Harr whistled loudly, and the hairy creatures bounded up the mountain once more. At times, the narrow pass became so thin that Simon's body hung over the steep ledge. He held on tightly to the gauntlets but continued to struggle with the stirrups.

A few minutes later, they came to the edge of Highland City. Sirens were blaring and little Puds were running in every direction.

"What are you doing here?" barked a tiny police officer. Two other officers stood beside him. "We don't have time for this," he spat.

The officers pointed their weapons, which looked more like TV remote controls than guns, at the group of big Puds. Suddenly, the large men and women grasped their throats as electricity surged through their security collars.

"Stop that!" Simon shouted, jumping down from his farbearus.

Everyone in the tribe fell to the ground in agony . . . That is, everyone but Little Har. The boy remained unaffected by the remote controls because most of the security features in his collar had been disabled during Dr. Troodle's car accident.

Har leapt from his farbearus and rushed towards the three police officers. With surprisingly quick reflexes, he disarmed each officer and crushed their weapons with his bare hands. He snarled at the little Puds–as if taunting them–but instead of fighting back, all three men screamed and ran away.

Smiling, Little Har turned around just in time to see the hairy beasts darting off. He then realized why the officers had been so terrified: The first wave of dragunos had just reached the top of the mountain.

"Come on!" Simon yelled, helping Har's father to his feet.

Still recovering from the jolt they had just received, the big Puds stood up and brushed themselves off. The library wasn't too far away, but neither were the dragunos. Desperately, Simon and Har pushed the weary group in the right direction.

They were almost there now . . . Just a little farther. Then Simon saw something at the edge of the forest that made his heart sink: a swarm of dragunos shredding the home of Dr. Troodle.

Tormenting anguish overwhelmed Simon's entire frame and dropped him to his knees. "*No,*" he sobbed. "*I'm too late!*"

The young man had never felt such strong feelings of both anger and sorrow before. Tonya! Thornapple! Had they escaped, or were the dragunos tearing them to pieces at this very moment?

Then, in answer to his fears, Simon heard someone call his name from a distance. He turned around to see a young woman with long, green-white hair rushing towards him. It was Tonya. She was alive, and Thornapple was running alongside her.

"Tonya!" Simon yelled with profound joy.

He stood up and was about to run to his friends when Har's father threw him back to the ground–just as a draguno sprang at him. The giant lizard collided with Harr and knocked him down. Before Simon could even register what was happening, the reptile raised its head high into the air and slammed it right into Harr's chest.

Simon watched helplessly as the draguno clenched its jaws around the body of the poor man–the man who had saved Simon's life twice . . . the man who, in their brief time together, had shown the young wizard that he had a far greater potential than he had ever realized . . . the man who was now dying–in essence, sacrificing himself to save Simon's life a third time.

In his weakened condition, Harr looked over at Simon and said something that broke the young wizard's heart: "Morbras will save us."

The ferocious draguno raised its head one last time and was about to finish the man off when Simon yelled, "*NOOOOOO!*"

Surprisingly, the heartless creature hesitated. It looked at Simon and turned its head to the side, scanning him. Then it released its sharp claws from Harr's broken body and slowly crawled towards the young man. Simon tried to scurry to safety, but he saw another lizard in his pathway. And then another. And then another . . .

Soon, at least fifty dragunos surrounded him. For some reason, the lizards seemed to be drawn to his presence. The devilish creatures inched their way closer and closer, savoring the moment before they attacked. Simon clutched his medallion and closed his eyes just as the pack of lizards pounced on him.

CHAPTER 23
GENERAL BANTON'S LEGACY

"No!" Tonya screamed. Tears streamed down her face, and the green in her hair changed to a murky-blue color. Little Har held her back from running to Simon's aid.

While the lizards were occupied, Grog picked up Harr and carried him to safety. He looked back to see all fifty lizards dog piling on top of Simon in what appeared to be an unrestrained feeding frenzy.

Everyone raced across the lawn to the entrance of the towering library. Just as the massive doors began to shut behind them, Tonya cried out, "*Wait!*"

A blue light emanated from the pile of lizards. Although a few of the reptiles limped around on burnt stubs, most of them lay dead. From within the smoldering heap of carcasses appeared Simon . . . floating in the air. He was curled up in the fetal position with his eyes still closed and his fist still grasping his mother's medallion. Pastel light filled the general area around him, and plumes of thick smoke billowed from below.

Tonya felt Little Har's warm hand on her shoulder. "Si-moan will save us," the large boy reassured her.

The smoke parted on both sides of the young wizard as his frail body drifted from the pile of dead lizards. Simon opened his eyes as his feet gently touched the ground. He was alive!

The aura around him faded away, revealing his unscathed condition to everyone. Shocked at what had just happened, Simon looked around at the lifeless dragunos. He then noticed the second wave of lizards racing towards him.

Not wanting to tempt fate, Simon turned and ran as fast as he could. He soon heard the cackling of the dragunos behind him, but he didn't bother to look back. As he neared the library, he could see Thornapple and Tonya cheering him on.

Simon leapt through the open doors just before Grog slammed them shut. *THUD! THUD!* The dragunos crashed against the heavy doors in pursuit of their prey. Simon bent over, out of breath. Adrenaline pumped through his veins. He sat down and tried to rest.

"Simon!" Tonya cried, hugging him. "That was so close. I thought I lost you."

Simon looked up to see streaks of white running through Tonya's beautiful hair. He held onto one lock of white hair and delicately ran it through his fingers. The long strands turned auburn.

"I don't know what happened back there," he said, still trying to catch his breath, "but it wasn't me." He looked over at Thorn's smiling face and continued, "I thought the dragunos got you guys for sure. You mean so much to me. I can't imagine losing you."

Just then, the lock of hair in his hand turned bright red.

"Simon, where have you been!" Tonya reacted abruptly. She stood up as though the tender moment they were sharing had never happened. "You left me alone at the dance."

"Yeah, Simon," Thornapple chimed in, "where'd you go? One second we were looking at books and the next second you were gone."

The young man stood up and realized that everyone in the dimly lit room was staring at him. "Yeah, my boy," Mayor Gordon said, walking up to join the conversation. "We were going to give you first prize for the dance contest, but we couldn't find you. We had to give it to Dr. Troodle's son instead."

Thornapple blushed as Gwin winked at him from across the room . . . At least, Thorn was pretty sure it was him she was winking at.

The nonstop pounding on the doors made Simon uneasy. He looked over at Harr, who was resting against a wall. Grog attended to the man's wounds with some herbs, while Little Har offered him comfort. The remaining tribe members stood apart from the crowd.

"I found out how to destroy the dragunos," Simon said, trying to sound confident and authoritative.

"I think we have a nastier problem on our hands than a bunch of overgrown lizards," announced Dr. Troodle. "What are we going to do with these big Puds?"

"I'm feeling nauseous just looking at them," his wife added.

Several other women agreed. Soon, just about every little Pud was complaining about the presence of the larger Puds.

"Maybe we should send them out to the dragunos as a peace offering," a man joked.

"Or better yet," said another, "let them fight the dragunos for us. Fifty doongles say that the big one will be the last giant standing."

Grog grunted at the remark.

Tonya opened her mouth to defend the big Puds when Simon intervened. "Stop it! Don't you know your two races were equals at one time?"

The small Puds gasped as if they had just heard something utterly profane. Shaking her head, Mrs. Troodle put her hand to her mouth and closed her eyes.

Simon continued. "If it weren't for Har and his family, I wouldn't even be alive. The least you could do is let them stay."

"Har!" Dr. Troodle exclaimed. "I didn't even recognize you." The doctor strutted over to the larger Puds. "You people all look the same to me." He took a quick glance at Har's father and said apathetically, "Doesn't look life threatening." He pressed on Harr's chest, which caused the giant to wince in pain, and gave a quick prognosis. "Broken rib . . . a few cuts . . . You'll be strong enough to work in the mines in no time."

The small Puds laughed at his pathetic joke. Dr. Troodle smirked at the injured man and turned to walk away. Without warning, Little Har grabbed the doctor and raised him off the ground. A vengeful expression appeared on the young Pud's face as he squeezed the air out of his master. This was his opportunity to make up for all the times he ever wanted to lash out at the Troodles for mistreating him.

At that moment, Nurse Salfree smashed a chair against Little Har's back, causing the enraged boy to drop his captive. A horrendous brawl ensued among the Puds, while at the same time, the dragunos continued to batter the outside doors.

"Stop it!" yelled Simon and Tonya.

But the fighting continued–the smaller Puds trying to trample down the larger Puds and the larger Puds retaliating against the smaller Puds. Even Mrs. Troodle got into the action.

Although outnumbered, the big Puds tossed the little people off themselves like rag dolls, but the tiny people just kept coming.

Suddenly, a bolt of fire sprang upwards. Everyone stopped. Light inundated the multi-tiered building as the flames brushed against the vaulted ceiling dozens of stories up.

"*Eenwahs,*" Simon whispered. The fire vanished immediately.

Everyone froze with gaping mouths and open eyes directed towards the young wizard who stood before them.

"Listen to me," Simon growled. "You're just like a bunch of ants fighting over a lousy leaf. While all the while you don't even see the car about to run you over. Do you not understand that there are *millions* of dragunos ready to wipe out all civilization on this planet?"

Many of the small Puds rolled their eyes, but they didn't dare to argue.

"The Lisardians were not aliens. They were giant lizards–the same kind that are trying to get in here. Your ancestors built a great machine to destroy them, but something went wrong."

Simon put his hand in his pocket and pulled out the shard of metal. Holo-649 appeared in his palm.

"Has it begun, Master Simon?" she asked.

"Yes."

"Then you must turn on the machine or else all is lost."

"First I need to know what happened a thousand years ago. I need to know why the machine never got turned on in the first place." Simon faced the crowd. "I want everyone to hear the true story of how the Battle of Lisardious was lost."

Holo noticed the crowd around her. "Oh, hello!" she said with a smile. "Let me see . . . where to begin?"

"Si-moan," Little Har said hesitantly, "Har no understand."

"Well, at least we agree on something," Dr. Troodle said. "Simon, your friend's not even speaking Pudo."

"Master Simon, I'm afraid I didn't understand what that man just said," Holo informed him. "It appears as though the Pudo language has become corrupted over the centuries."

"Then I'll interpret for them," Simon said. "Show us what you were going to show me in the cave before we got interrupted."

The shard of metal projected a scene high enough for everyone to see. This time, the hologram was much larger than before. The three-dimensional representation showed millions of dragunos emerging from the ocean.

"The Battle of the Dragunos," Simon translated for them.

The scene then showed the magnificent city, which was even grander and larger than the current Highland City. Simon repeated the words from Holo's lively narration.

"At one time, the larger Puds were the dominant force on the planet because they were well endowed with magic and physically stronger than the smaller Puds."

"That's ludicrous!" Dr. Troodle said.

Mayor Gordon broke in, "*Shhh!* I want to hear this."

Simon continued as the scene changed to show the inside of the mountain. "But on the eve of battle, the two races joined forces to build a magnificent weapon that would save the planet and stop the vicious cycle of draguno destruction. Project Purification was envisioned by General Banton, set in motion by the president, and even endorsed by the High King himself. Its purpose was to eradicate the planet of all dragunos."

The projection showed the gigantic machine from different angles and then zoomed in to eavesdrop on an intense conversation taking place at the base of the machine.

Simon listened in on their conversation but didn't translate because they were talking too fast.

"We have to turn it on immediately," the president said quickly.

"No," General Banton argued. The small Pud held the little red book in his hand as though it were a delicate baby. "The generator doesn't have enough power yet. Your people have been too greedy. If you would have enforced the restrictions on magical uses more severely, we wouldn't be in this predicament."

"General, our people are being slaughtered as we speak!"

"We have to think about our posterity," the little man shot back. "If we don't purify this entire planet, then generations from now our progenitors will face this same problem."

Mayor Gordon interrupted, "Simon, what are they saying!"

Simon quickly explained, "They're fighting over whether or not they should turn on the machine. The little Pud is General Banton. He says they have to wait until the machine has enough power."

The projection showed the king walking up to them. "That's King Pentagola," Simon noted.

"The same king from the comic strip?" asked Thorn.

"Yep."

"But he looks more like you and Tonya than a Pud."

"He's not from Pudo. He's from another–" Simon stopped himself because he didn't want to miss what was being said. "I'll explain later."

"What is the meaning of this?" the king roared. "Why haven't you turned on the machine?"

"General Banton says the generator hasn't stored up enough power yet."

"What?" The king closed his eyes and raised his hand as if he were touching something invisible. "I sense deception in the room. General Banton, as High King of the known paraverse, I evoke my general authority and release you of your command."

"But, my king!" the little man sputtered.

"Your military responsibilities have clouded your judgment. I'm not willing to sacrifice millions of lives just so we can make sure every single draguno is destroyed."

Simon translated briefly, "The general just got fired."

King Pentagola grabbed the little red book from the general's hands and ran to the machine. The camera zoomed in to show the king sticking the key into a spot on the main control panel. It looked like he was about to turn the book, but, instead, the most peculiar expression appeared on his face. The viewpoint of the camera then panned out to show that General Banton had just stabbed the king in the back with a knife.

"Looks like you're the one with the clouded judgment," the general snickered. "You don't realize how serious the situation really is."

"You fool," the king gasped as he stumbled away from the control panel and fell to the ground.

He left a trail of blood on the marble floor as he attempted to crawl away. Suddenly, a group of tiny soldiers rushed into the room with their weapons pointed towards the larger Puds.

The president uttered a spell but nothing happened because of the lack of E.M. waves in the cavern. "How could you do this?" he exclaimed. "What about our people?"

"Mr. President . . ." the general said coldly. A tiny soldier slapped the large Pud on the back of his legs, causing him to kneel down. General Banton walked up close to the president, stared him in the face, and said quietly, "Project Purification was not meant to purify the world of lizards . . . It was meant to purify the world of you and your kind."

Before the president could respond, two small Puds snapped a security collar around his neck.

"You can't . . ." The president's speech became slow and awkward. "You . . . Um . . . You can't . . ." He couldn't seem to finish the sentence.

"I already have," the general said, laughing.

In the background, the king was still inching his way towards the trench where the monorail lay, and several soldiers were walking towards him. The final scene showed the king drop a little shard of metal over the ledge just before the soldiers pointed their weapons at him. The 3-D projection then faded to black so that only Holo remained.

Simon looked at the somber crowd and said in a stern voice, "The real enemy during that great battle wasn't the dragunos."

"That's preposterous," Dr. Troodle said.

"Is it?" Simon questioned. "Just a few minutes ago, you were ready to feed the big Puds to the dragunos. Your people found an opportunity to become the dominant race on this planet at the expense of millions of lives."

The young man spoke with such power that the small Puds cowered at his words. He seemed a little taller, in a way. In fact, he even felt taller.

"General Banton let the dragunos destroy this planet so you could rise from the ashes and start a new civilization with the big Puds as your slaves . . . and the general's legacy has been passed down ever since."

"How dare you talk to us like that," Mrs. Troodle huffed. "After all we've done for you!"

"I think you're missing the point," Tonya countered. "What Simon's trying to say is that if you don't let go of your pride, this war's gonna end up just like the last one."

Mrs. Troodle started to argue again, but Mayor Gordon interrupted her. "He's right." The little Puds stared in shock at hearing the mayor take the alien boy's side. "We've suppressed their brain activity for so long, we've fooled ourselves into thinking that we are the superior race. What Simon has done is shown us that they are real people . . . just like you and me."

"I can't accept that," Mrs. Troodle's said. "Just look at them! How can you possibly expect me to believe–"

"*Shhh*, Mom," cried Thornapple.

"Don't you *shhh* me!"

"No, listen!"

The room was completely quiet.

Tonya broke the silence. "The dragunos have stopped."

"Maybe they've gone home," Dr. Troodle said.

Simon looked around warily. "Or maybe they're trying to find another way in. We probably shouldn't stand out here in the open."

"Nonsense!" Dr. Troodle said. "This library is built like a fortress. Those walls over there are three feet thick of solid granite. Nothing's going to get in here."

CRASH!

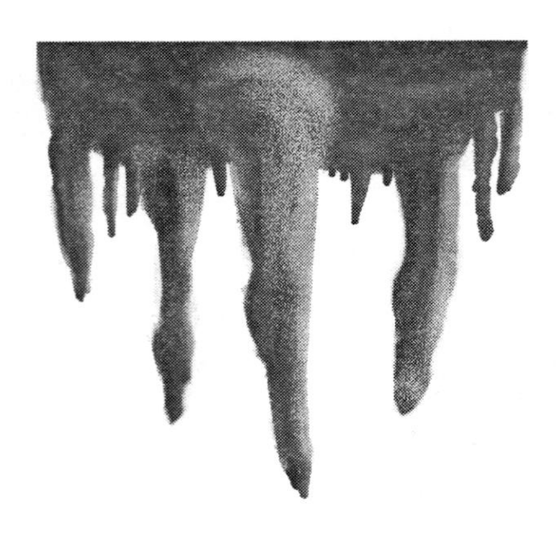

CHAPTER 24
PRELUDE TO BATTLE

High above, the skylights shattered, causing an avalanche of broken glass–as well as several dragunos–to fall from the ceiling. Down–down–down the lizards descended, until *THUD*–their bodies were crushed against the marble floor.

"Oh, dear," said Holo, who was still resting on Simon's hand.

The determined reptiles spilled out of the gaping hole and climbed across the ceiling until they reached the top balcony. In their frenzy to get to the wall, a few of the dragunos lost their grip and fell to their deaths below. The Puds scurried around frantically, dodging the bodies that dropped from above.

"Grog!" Simon yelled over the commotion. "It won't take long for those lizards to get down here."

"Approximately 3 minutes and 11.52 seconds at their current speed," chimed Holo.

Simon continued, "Grog, I know how to stop them, but I need your help."

"Harr help, too," Little Har's father said, standing up.

"No, you're injured. You need to find shelter."

"Harr *will* help Morbras," he said with unbent determination.

Some of the dragunos were now climbing to the lower balconies while most were racing down the winding stairs. Dr. Troodle and the mayor sprinted from door to door, but none of them budged; the entire building was locked down. With the doors sealed on every floor, the hungry lizards had no choice but to funnel through the corridors–which, unfortunately, led to only one destination: down.

"We're going to die! We're going to die!" screamed Mrs. Troodle.

Simon ran to the vault that he had broken into earlier and, to his amazement, found that it was still unlocked. As the heavy door creaked open, a gush of neon-blue smoke escaped. Mrs. Troodle shrieked as a gnomelike figure wearing a gas mask stepped out of the room.

"What in tarnation ya try'n to do, woman? Gimme a heart attack?" the old librarian said, taking off his mask and clutching his chest.

The mayor rushed over. "Glumly! Glumly!"

"Ah, Mayor. Do you know what I just heard on the news? Millions–I'm talk'n millions–of them draguno things have been spotted come'n out of the ocean! Can you believe that?"

"Yes, I can," Mayor Gordon said quickly. "Glumly, listen to me. I need you to unlock the doors."

"Well, I don't know 'bout that," the old man drawled lazily. "It's not even 8 o'clock yet. You shouldn't even be here."

"Tell that to them!" Dr. Troodle yelled hysterically as a draguno smashed onto the floor nearby.

"What's going on here?" exclaimed the librarian.

"Glumly, *NOW!*" cried the mayor.

"Alright, alright. Keep your trousers on!"

The old man ran to his desk and slid open a compartment which revealed a touchpad.

"Let's see here," he mumbled while taking off his mittens. "Thumb . . . Pinky . . . Thumb . . . Pinky . . ." He touched his fingers one by one onto the pad to initiate the open sequence. "Forefinger . . . Thumb . . . uh . . ." He thought for a moment and then finally said, "Pinky" as he touched the pad one last time with his smallest finger.

Just about every door in the library opened at the same time. Now that the dragunos could pillage the building freely, most of them got sidetracked into various parts of the library.

"This won't do." The librarian shook his head at the hundreds of dragunos running along the balconies. "Come on, everyone. This way!" He beckoned the Puds to come over to his desk.

After touching the pad a few more times, a secret door built into the tall desk opened.

"What's down there?" asked Dr. Troodle as he peered at the steps that led into a wall of darkness.

"That's the bank vault. No draguno will be able to follow us down there. Hurry. Get a move on!"

Like a stampede, the Puds rushed down the stairs into the vault until only Simon and his companions were left.

"Aren't you coming?" asked Mayor Gordon.

"No," Simon said in a somber tone, "I'm the only one who knows how to stop the dragunos."

The mayor sighed deeply. "I feel an obligation to right the wrong that my people caused a thousand years ago. I'm going with you."

"So am I," Tonya declared.

"And me, too," Thornapple chimed in.

"No, it's too dangerous," Simon said.

"Ah, let'm go," the old librarian coaxed. "There ain't much air down in the vault. In an hour or so, we'll all be dead anyway." His words gave little comfort. "You're a very brave boy," he continued, "but I just have one question for ya . . ." He put his gas mask on and asked, "Where in Sam Hill did you get them crazy-looking underwear?"

"I knew it!" shouted Thornapple. "I just knew you could see through clothes with those masks."

Simon blushed while Tonya smiled.

Dr. Troodle bounded up the steps. "Thornapple, what do you think you're doing? Get down here before you become a snack for those lizards."

"I'm going with Simon," the boy said.

Dr. Troodle stepped out of the doorway in a huff. "Now's not the time to play heroics, son. Any moment now, those dragunos are going to jump on us, and when they do–"

A giant lizard landed on top of the tall desk and hissed loudly at the people below. Its deep breathing sounded like a congested dragon trying to cough up a fur ball.

"Master Simon," Holo advised, "I suggest we leave immediately."

"Good idea!"

Little Har jabbed at the lizard with his spear while Grog swung his club menacingly above his head. At the far end of the library, a herd of dragunos emerged from the stairs and slid across the slick marble floor. Simon darted for the sealed portion of the library while Tonya, Harr, Thornapple, and the mayor followed behind.

"Get back here," Dr. Troodle yelled.

He was about to chase after his son but stopped when he saw Grog swinging his club towards him. The club swished over the little man's head and struck the draguno that had jumped down from the tall desk. Upon impact, the reptile hurled towards the secret passageway but fell short–just a few feet away from Glumly.

"Well, I think that's my cue," the old librarian said just before shutting the door. "Good luck."

"No, wait," Dr. Troodle screamed.

The draguno raised its bruised head, which made the doctor think twice about approaching the doorway.

"Come!" Grog commanded.

Dr. Troodle turned around to see a swarm of giant lizards scrambling towards him. Terrified, he raced into the sealed portion of the library to join the others. Harr pulled the massive door shut just as the dragunos flooded the area. The hungry reptiles pounded relentlessly on the thick metal door, causing the latch to open by itself.

"Won't lock!" Harr shouted while struggling to breathe through his gas mask.

"Yeah, Simon broke the lock last time we were here," Thornapple's mechanical voice sounded from within the blue haze.

Grog tried to put on a gas mask, but it wouldn't fit over his large head. The noxious fumes burned his lungs as he pressed the mask to his face.

Thorn stared intently at Tonya's lovely figure but stopped when she noticed him scanning her. “You look good in that mask,” he said nervously. “It does something for you.”

“Don’t get any ideas, pervert!”

“Oh, I wouldn’t dream of it, Butblacruze.”

She grabbed him by the collar and threatened, “If you call me that one more time, I’m gonna personally feed you to the dragunos.”

Just then, the door popped open a few inches, allowing several lizards to wedge their narrow heads through the crack. Harr immediately pulled on the handle to keep the door from opening all the way.

“Help!” the big Pud yelled as the dragunos frantically clawed at him.

Grog and Little Har pushed the lizards back and held the door in place while Harr tied a piece of rope around the latch and fastened the other end to a bench embedded in the wall. With the door now secure, the three big Puds attempted to blockade the entrance with a large bookcase.

“That’s not going to do any good,” Dr. Troodle scoffed. “The door opens the other way, you dummies!”

“It’s broken!” Simon cried from across the room.

The young man was trying to fit the little red book into the armrest of the bench, but the insignia wouldn’t snap in place like it had before.

“It appears that the engravings have deteriorated over the years,” Holo informed him. “The primitive fumes in this room are not sufficient to preserve metallic alloys.”

“Any suggestions?”

“Try harder.”

“Simon, I don’t know what you’re doing, but whatever it is, you better hurry it up,” Dr. Troodle shouted from across the room.

Simon yelled back, “I can’t get the key to work! If I can just get it to snap on, this wall will open up and we’ll be able to get out of here.”

He twisted and grinded until, suddenly, a large piece of the armrest chipped off and fell. Simon’s heart sank as the metal piece rattled against the hard marble floor.

“Oh, dear,” Holo said. “That wasn’t good.”

In despair, Simon hit his forehead with the book and gave out a moan that reverberated from within his gas mask. A loud yell pierced the room. Simon looked up to see Grog rushing towards them with his club.

The giant lashed out with such great force that when he struck the granite, a long crack ran down the face of the wall, revealing the stonework to actually be a thin veneer put there to conceal the whereabouts of the secret passageways below the city. Simon dropped to the ground as the wild man above him smashed away with his club. Fragments of masonry and dust sprang from the wall as the secret door shattered. Soon, a gaping hole appeared before them.

“Wow!” Dr. Troodle exclaimed as the mouth of the cave sucked away the blue fumes. “If we would have fed your people to the dragunos, I bet you really would be the last one standing! Tell me, are you familiar with the boxing tournaments?”

"*Father!*" Thornapple scolded.

"Just wondering."

After entering the damp cave, Simon removed his gas mask and took a deep breath of the foul air. Everyone else removed their masks and followed the young wizard down the dark tunnel. The ancient runes on the walls, as well as the holographic light from Holo-649, gave them just enough light to see.

"Watch out for spiders," Simon warned.

"Oh, spiders don't bother me," Dr. Troodle boasted. "In fact, I love spiders, especially with a nice vinaigrette sauce–*mmm*, and garlic! Of course, you can't ever have enough–"

He stopped in midsentence. They had come upon the giant spider that had attacked Simon earlier. The enormous creature's back was cracked open, and its tissues were already starting to decay.

"What in the world is this?" Mayor Gordon gasped. "I've never seen anything like it."

"Well, I accidentally cast a growing spell on it," Simon admitted. "But I think it was around seven feet tall before the spell."

"*Crazy!*" Thornapple said. "What could have caused it to grow seven feet in the first place?"

"Some sort of mutation, I bet," Mayor Gordon said, examining one of the legs. "Or maybe it's a new species we've never discovered before."

"Let's not just stand around speculating," Dr. Troodle said. "May I remind you that we have a pack of dragunos on our tail?"

The spider blocked most of the tunnel, so the party was forced to crawl over it . . . or, more specifically, *through* it. Simon climbed up the hairy body and crawled over the muscular tissue of the spider's broken back. The ceiling pressed closely against him as he made his way through the crack in the hard shell. Part of the exoskeleton peeled away in his hand, revealing hundreds of maggots feasting on the spider's tender insides.

Tonya was next. She almost turned back when she got to the top of the spider and saw the bloody carcass she was supposed to crawl through. Her hair changed to a muddy brown color as her foot sank into the decaying flesh.

"*Eewww!*" she cried. "This better not leave a stain."

With one hand holding up her hair and the other pulling herself forward, she crawled over the sticky flesh. One by one, the rest of the party followed suit, until they were all on the other side.

"That was the most disgusting thing I've ever done," Thorn declared. "I can't wait to go back!"

Tonya rolled her eyes in response.

Simon walked up to the ledge and looked down. A gust of hot wind filled his nostrils and stung his eyes. He could see the faint glow of the hot lava below.

"How are we going to get to the other side?" Thornapple moaned.

"With this," Simon answered, picking up the spider web that dangled over the ledge–the same web that had saved his life earlier. The acidic thread reacted to the moisture in his hand as he touched it; however, it had also been badly scorched, and most of the stickiness was gone. "Come on, guys, help me pull it up."

Simon found that if he didn't touch the web in one place too long, the pain became more manageable. Soon, the thin strand lay in a bundle at his feet.

"Harr, please tell me you have something in your pouch we could use to grapple the other end of the pit?"

The giant opened his leather sack and pulled out some fishing sinkers and a very large hook.

"My goodness," Dr. Troodle exclaimed. "What type of fish do you normally try to catch?"

"Big fish."

"Very big," Grog added with a smile.

"That's excellent," Simon cheered. "Now tie it to the end of this thread."

Harr quickly threaded the hook with the end of the singed spider web. After completing the knot, he licked his burning fingers–then yelped because his tongue now stung from the acid.

"Dumb ox," mumbled Dr. Troodle.

"Holo, could we have a little more light?" asked Simon.

"Certainly, Master Simon." The little hologram flickered for a second and then cast a holographic light across the chasm. "How's that?"

"Perfect! Now, Harr, do you think you could throw that hook to the other side of the pit?"

"Harr will try."

The skilled fisherman cast out the line with all his strength. Surprisingly, on his first try, it sailed across the chasm and landed securely between two rocks that jutted up next to each other.

"Fantastic throw!" Mayor Gordon said.

Harr rubbed his broken rib and smiled.

"Ah, you were just lucky," said Dr. Troodle. "So, Simon, you don't really expect us to burn our hands off climbing that spider web, do you? I don't think I'm . . . I mean, I don't know if my son is strong enough to make it across."

Thornapple shot him a dirty look.

"Well, since you're the lightest adult here, I was hoping you could carry Harr's rope across."

"Me?" he stammered. "I don't know about that. My hands are very sensitive. I'm a surgeon, you know, not an acrobat."

"Here," Harr said, pulling out some plastic gloves from his leather pouch. The gloves were several sizes too big, but the little man tried them on anyway.

"Thanks . . . Thanks a lot."

Harr fastened a loop around the spider web with his rope so that the doctor wouldn't have to carry all of his weight as he crossed.

"Watch where you're touching me, you big oaf," Dr. Troodle whined as Harr tied the rope around the little man's waist and legs.

"Don't worry," Simon said. "If the spider web breaks, we can still pull you back up with the rope."

"Oh, that's comforting."

"We're going to give you a little push, okay?"

The doctor started to protest, but Grog picked him up anyway and gave him a gigantic shove. Harr held the line high above his head to make the little Pud slide even farther.

Yelling at the top of his lungs, Dr. Troodle slid all the way to the edge of the opposite precipice. Harr promptly tied the spider web around a stalagmite jutting from the floor.

The doctor climbed onto the ledge. "Grog, you idiot" he yelled. "I could've been killed!" He attempted to get out of the makeshift harness but had trouble untying the knots.

"Please hurry, Dr. Troodle," Tonya urged nervously.

Hissing sounds came from within the tunnel.

"I'm going as fast as I can. If that stupid Pud wouldn't have tied this so tight, I'd be finished by now," he yelled in frustration. "Harr, when we get out of here, I'm going to send your whole family to the mines!"

The doctor looked across the chasm just in time to see Harr snatch his son's spear and launch it across the pit. The tiny man screamed as the projectile whistled through the air with tremendous force. Then, with happy relief, he watched as the spear passed over his head.

"Hah! You missed!"

He turned around to see a huge black spider pinned to the wall behind him. Its legs were still twitching.

"You . . . you just saved my life."

"Tie rope," was the giant's stern response.

Dr. Troodle wrapped the rope around a large rock and tied it with a surgical knot. Then Harr pulled the rope tight and secured it to an icicle-shaped stalactite hanging from the limestone ceiling.

Fighting back her fear of heights, Tonya grabbed the rope above her waist and stepped onto the thin web, but after only a few steps, she lost her footing and slipped. Like a guitar string being plucked, the silky thread sprang up and down wildly. Still clinging to Harr's rope, she reached for the spider web with her foot.

"Slide your feet, Butblacruze!"

Tonya turned her head and scowled at the small boy. The elastic strand stopped vibrating when she stepped back onto it. This time she turned to the side and slid her feet.

A great commotion sounded from behind. The dragunos had gotten past the vault door! Simon looked back into the tunnel to see the dead spider rocking back and forth as the giant lizards gorged on the rancid meat.

"We have to go across," Mayor Gordon yelled.

"Will the rope hold?" Tonya yelled back.

"We don't have a choice!"

Grog grabbed the rope and began to cross the chasm with surprisingly great speed. Simon quickly put Holo-649 into his shirt pocket and followed the mayor. Thorn was next, and then Little Har and his father.

"Hurry," Dr. Troodle shouted.

Simon was about three-fourths of the way across when he felt something wet and sticky fall on his cheek. He looked up to see a group of giant spiders dangling about twenty feet above him. Saliva dropped from their vicious mouths.

"Spiders!" he shouted.

At that same moment, a throng of dragunos rushed into the cavern, but in their haste, several ran off the edge of the cliff. Like a herd of lemmings, the dragunos continued to push each other forward, forcing a dozen more lizards to fall down the pit and into the hot lava.

Suddenly, the spider web snapped and fell away. This time, Tonya screamed when the thread disappeared beneath her feet, but, fortunately, neither she nor anyone else lost his or her grip on the rope.

"I can't hold on!" Thornapple shrieked.

The giant spiders were starting to descend.

Without warning, the rope slid a few inches down the stalactite. Tonya screamed even more loudly. Then the rope slipped again until it was dangerously close to coming off entirely.

"This just can't get any worse," yelled Mayor Gordon in despair.

Just then, a group of savage-looking red dragunos appeared at the ledge.

"Master Simon," Holo said quickly from within Simon's pocket, "did I fail to mention about the red dragunos?"

"Yes, what about them?"

The red dragunos opened their mouths and took a deep breath.

"They breathe fire."

CHAPTER 25
THE FINAL BATTLE OF THE DRAGUNOS

"A*hhhh!*" screamed Thornapple as the red lizards sprayed a barrage of fire from their mouths.

The first stream hit the spiders above, but the second one headed right towards the party. Before the flame made contact, the rope slipped off the stalactite, and the group swung towards the other side of the cliff. Just as they struck the wall, Harr extended his legs and absorbed most of the blow, but upon impact, Thornapple lost his grip and fell. With quick reflexes, Little Har shot out his hand and grabbed the small boy in midair.

"Hold on," Har said slowly as he pulled Thornapple onto his back.

"That was a close one. You saved me!"

"Go!" Grog urged Tonya to climb.

She peered down at the hot lava and clung desperately to the rope. "I can't," she cried. "I'm not strong enough."

"It okay," Grog said, pulling himself up the rope. He climbed past Tonya without even using his legs and got onto the ledge above. "I help."

The giant man grabbed the rope and started to pull the entire party upwards. His enormous muscles flexed as he heaved, and beads of sweat ran down his face. Dr. Troodle just stood there and watched the amazing feat in awe.

Suddenly, a spider web wrapped around the giant's bare arm. He looked up just in time to see another thread strike his shoulder. The acidic web steamed as it burned into his flesh.

Grog grabbed the thin strand on his shoulder and gave it a good snap, which in turn threw the web's owner into the neighboring spiders. He continued to make the spiders collide into each other by whipping the thread around and around.

"Little man," he barked at Dr. Troodle, "get knife!"

Dr. Troodle grabbed the dagger from Grog's belt and jumped on the man's back. "I promise I'll never eat another one of you again," he vowed while cutting vigorously at the white thread attached to the giant's shoulder.

When the doctor had finally severed the web, Grog gave the remaining strand a huge tug, which caused the silky thread to release itself from the ceiling. The unsuspecting arachnid fell down the cliff but stopped before hitting the lake, while the rest of the spiders scattered.

Now Grog held the party with one hand and a giant spider with the other. The spider began to climb, so Grog jerked the acidic thread up and down, forcing the eight-legged creature to slide down its own web.

Dr. Troodle leaned over Grog's shoulder and sliced the thread with the knife. He sighed in relief as the huge spider fell into the molten lava below.

On the other side of the chasm, the red dragunos were mowing down the remaining spiders with their fiery breath. This gave Grog some free time to help his companions.

The big Pud pulled Tonya to safety. Mayor Gordon and Simon came next, followed by Little Har–with Thornapple still clinging to his back.

Harr climbed onto the ledge last. For a few seconds, he just lay there, wheezing and holding his side. He forced himself to stand, but after taking one step, he collapsed.

"Are you all right?" Dr. Troodle asked. He grabbed the giant's wrist and felt for a pulse. "You saved my life, you big oaf. You can't quit now."

"Legs," Harr groaned.

The doctor quickly inspected Harr's legs and said, "Looks like you fractured them. Well, there's only one thing to do now . . . I'll have to put you out of your misery."

Harr's eyes grew big.

"I'm just joking!" Dr. Troodle said, laughing. "Look, about what I said earlier. I get a little cranky when I'm nervous. Can we just . . . can we just forget about our past and be friends?"

The small Pud reached out his hand. Harr stared for a long and awkward moment at the tiny hand extended to him, the hand that represented years of oppression and cruelty, the hand that, as fate would have it, now pleaded for reconciliation. How could a hand such as this ever change? He looked up to see Little Har beaming with pride; Thornapple was thanking him profusely for saving his life. The innocence and selflessness of his son brought a tear to his eye. With forgiveness in his heart, he clasped Dr. Troodle's hand and said in a slow, deep voice, "Friends."

"We've got company," Tonya shouted.

Simon glanced up to see scores of smaller spiders clambering down the wall. Grog picked up Harr and followed the party into the tunnel. An iron grate obstructed the pathway.

"Oh, no," Thornapple said.

"Stand back," Simon yelled. "Tonya, give me your wand."

The young woman pulled up her baby doll dress and brought out her wand.

"Wow! You bring that thing everywhere," Thornapple said.

Simon grabbed the wand, tapped the iron bars, and yelled, "*Open!*"

The huge grate split open from the middle and rolled to each side like flimsy chicken wire. At that same moment, the army of baby spiders came racing into the tunnel. Just beyond the grate stood an open doorway leading to a brightly lit chamber. As they entered the strange room, the party soon discovered that it had no exit. They were trapped.

"How do you shut this?" Thorn cried.

He pressed a button nearby, and the doorway vanished into the wall–not a second too soon.

"What is this place?" Tonya mumbled in her native tongue.

The spacious room was in the shape of a cylinder with round walls and a circular top and bottom. Artificial light emanated from behind the paneling, and hundreds of colorful buttons adorned the white walls.

Holo poked her head out of Simon's pocket and responded, "I really couldn't tell you, young lady. This wasn't here before."

Tonya jumped in surprise. "Simon, your little friend's speaking to me."

"Well, if you would have told me you speak Chamelean, I would have spoken to you earlier. By the way, my designation is Holo-649."

"Nice to meet you. I'm Tonya."

"Tonya–what a lovely name. And I assume you're from Chamel? I once suggested to my previous master that he marry a woman from Chamel, but he insisted on marrying someone from Pudo instead. Tonya, I just love your hair."

"Thank you," she said with a smile. "I've been growing it out since birth–or at least, it seems like it."

Tonya's hair turned to its natural green color.

"That's what I like about Chameleans: You wear your feelings on your sleeve."

"Will you two stop chattering?" Dr. Troodle broke in. "I'm trying to concentrate here."

"I think it's some sort of puzzle," Mayor Gordon said. "Our ancestors probably used this room as a filtering process to keep unwanted guests out. I bet that–" He stopped in midsentence when he noticed Little Har reaching for one of the buttons. "Uh, son–Har, isn't it?–please don't touch that."

It was too late. The floor began to spin around.

"Get to the center of the room," the mayor yelled. "Don't touch anything!"

The room spun so fast that they struggled to stay on their feet. After losing his balance, Thornapple rolled across the floor and crashed into the wall. Unfortunately, when he hit the wall, he accidentally pressed some more buttons. Laser bolts ricocheted in every direction.

Dr. Troodle ran for his life as a row of lasers chased him down. When he reached the outer edge of the room, he tried to turn, but his momentum carried him into the wall–just as his son had done a moment earlier.

The floor slowed down, and the lasers stopped firing. Dr. Troodle cautiously moved his hand away from the button he had inadvertently pressed. Overcome with dizziness, he fell to the ground and rested. Everyone else appeared to be suffering from vertigo as well.

About the time the room finally stopped rotating, a compartment opened, and two flying disks emerged. At first they seemed harmless, but then a row of sharp blades extended out of the spinning saucers, revealing to everyone how dangerous they really were.

"Oh, boy," Simon moaned as the spinning blades grew even longer.

Little Har started to run, and the disks followed close behind.

"*Duck!*" Simon shouted.

He did as he was told, and the disks whizzed over him, scraped against the wall, and then headed towards Dr. Troodle, who was also trying to get away. Tonya and Thornapple split up and ran to the opposite sides of the room, which caused the disks to veer away from the doctor and chase after the two teenagers. Before Thornapple reached the wall, he fell to the ground, and as a result, the spinning saucer immediately turned around and zoomed towards Tonya.

"No move," said Harr, who had been lying on the floor, watching the whole thing.

"He's right," exclaimed the mayor. "They're motion sensitive."

Upon reaching the side wall, Tonya turned and froze. Spinning like saw blades, the disks whizzed through the air and stopped right in front of her face. The terrified girl whimpered as the sharp blades moved dangerously close to her forehead.

"Tonya, listen to me," Simon said in a soothing voice. "Just relax. Everything is going to be okay."

A white streak ran down her hair, and in response, one of the saucers cut off several of her beautiful, long ringlets. As the green and white locks fell to the ground, the disks reacted to the movement by dicing the strands into tiny pieces.

"Tonya, close your eyes," Simon instructed. "Listen to my voice. Don't think about anything else."

Two more streaks of white appeared in her hair. The deadly saucers jumped from the floor, but by the time they reached her shoulders, the movement was gone. Like insects studying an object, the spinning disks observed her hair closely for any sign of further movement.

Tonya could hear terrible humming noises as the sharp blades spun ever-so-close to her bare neck. One false move and she would be dead. Although her eyes were closed, she could feel the tears start to well up.

"Tonya!" Simon called out in panic, fearing that he was about to lose his best friend. His voice sounded a bit shaky, but he tried to console her anyway. "Remember the time, back on Earth, when I grabbed your wand and tried to stop that sports car? You told me later that I was holding it backwards."

A troubled yet faint smile appeared on the young girl's face. The saucers were too busy examining her damaged hair to notice the subtle movement.

"Remember the time when you were teaching me how to dance? We were all alone, and you started to hum . . . How did that song go?"

The helpless girl began to hum nervously.

"Yeah, that's it." Simon hummed along.

"I remember how beautiful the sky was that day. The ocean seemed to go on forever, and I never wanted the moment to stop . . . I remember how beautiful you were . . ." Simon paused in deep reflection and then, without even thinking, spoke his inner thoughts aloud. "I almost kissed you."

Tonya opened her eyes and stopped humming. At that same moment, the spinning disks slowly moved away and returned to the compartment where they had come from. Everyone in the room exhaled at the same time.

"Whew! That was too close for comfort," Mayor Gordon said. "All right, everyone, get into the center of the room while I try to solve this puzzle."

"While *we* solve this puzzle," Dr. Troodle contended.

Tonya moved from the wall and sat next to Simon. Neither of them said a word, but they seemed to understand one another, nonetheless. Simon reached over and gently held her trembling hand.

"I've got it," declared the mayor. "Look! There's twenty-nine green buttons, eleven red ones, and thirty-one yellow ones. Each set is a prime number. When you add them all together, what do you get?"

"Seventy-one!" Dr. Troodle exclaimed. "Another prime number!"

"Precisely. Now none of the other colors seem to follow that same pattern. Furthermore, if we take into consideration that red and yellow are also primary colors, we can now delve further into the equation by examining the distinctiveness of the green buttons . . ."

"So you almost kissed me," Tonya said without looking at Simon. "What stopped you?"

"Well, you know." Simon squirmed. "I didn't know if you wanted me to, and then Thorn showed up, and we started doing magic, and I just kinda never thought about it again."

"Oh."

"Did you want me to kiss you?"

Tonya rolled her eyes.

"So there we have it!" Mayor Gordon exclaimed.

"Excellent work," Dr. Troodle said.

"So which one is it?" asked Simon.

"This one." The mayor pointed to a purple button.

"Are you sure?"

"Well, 99.3 percent sure."

"Close enough," Dr. Troodle added. "Everyone ready?"

Tonya squeezed Simon's hand as the doctor pressed the purple button. In a flash, several dozen shafts of metal–each with sharp, pointed ends–sprang from the ceiling. Some of them pierced the floor, but most of them stopped a few feet short of the ground.

"How perplexing," Mayor Gordon said. "Is everyone all right?"

No one was hurt, but Grog had gotten scared when one of the spikes thrust into the ground between his legs.

"All right," the mayor said, getting everyone's attention. "Sorry about that. Now I'm almost certain the correct button is actually this one."

"I was going to suggest that button, too," Dr. Troodle noted.

"Okay, one more time. Everybody get ready." Mayor Gordon pushed the button, and the long shafts of metal started to slowly retract back into the ceiling. "See! What did I tell you?"

Suddenly, a grinding noise screeched throughout the room. The spikes halted and then began to tremble.

"Looks like they're stuck," Dr. Troodle said.

"Frankly, I'm surprised these traps are still functioning in the first place," the mayor said. "After all these years–"

"Watch out!" yelled Thorn.

Several of the spikes fell from the ceiling and struck the floor, shattering the hard surface. As the grinding noise got louder, smoke began to collect at the borders of the ceiling.

"I have a bad feeling about this," Tonya said, standing up.

"Tonya!" Simon yelled in shock.

Her long, greenish white hair–at least, what was left of it–was slowly rising up into the air.

"What's going on?" Thorn cried as his feet left the floor. Soon, the entire party was floating in the air.

"Amazing!" Mayor Gordon exclaimed. "Our ancestors discovered how to manipulate gravity."

Just then, the ceiling began to descend upon them. Everyone grabbed the spikes to hold themselves in place, but every time a spike touched the floor, the metal would buckle and then break loose from the ceiling. It was all they could do to hang on.

"Don't anybody panic," the mayor said. "We just need to readjust our equation a little."

Simon felt as though he were falling, but he didn't know which direction: up or down. Tonya hugged a spike with all her might, while Dr. Troodle spun out of control, banging into the metal spears as he went. The altered gravity didn't have as much effect on the larger Puds, who were bouncing off the floor like floundering fish, but everyone else continued to struggle with the zero gravity.

Thorn climbed upside down to reach the floor again, but the shaft he held broke free from the ceiling. Like a monkey jumping in slow motion, the little Pud leapt from the spike and maneuvered himself between two other shafts. With his body parallel to the ground, he felt like he was flying.

Panic-stricken, Thorn looked up to see the round ceiling still closing in on them. He glanced at the curved wall, and for a second, the colorful buttons reminded him of stars in the sky. The awkward viewpoint afforded him the ability to look at the puzzle with a brand-new perspective and, literally, from a new angle. Just as the two spikes he held were about to touch the ground, Thornapple finally exclaimed, "I see it! It was right there all the time!"

"What do you see, son?" asked Mayor Gordon from behind.

"Look at the white buttons. They form an arrow."

"I don't see it," the mayor said in a discouraged voice.

Simon looked across the room and laughed when he saw the outline of a white arrow pointing to a solitary button. Using the zero gravity to his advantage, Thornapple swung himself to the wall–almost sliding across the floor as he did so–and confidently pressed the button.

The ceiling immediately stopped moving, and an opening appeared in the wall. The gravity in the room returned back to normal, and everyone slid down the spikes.

"I don't see it either," Dr. Troodle said, brushing himself off and gazing intently at the colorful buttons.

Tonya picked herself up and laughed. "I guess I was wrong about you, Thorn. Maybe you do have some creative abilities after all. Miracles never cease."

Dr. Troodle and the mayor continued to stare at the wall while the rest of the party exited the room. Little Har stood next to them for a moment and then declared before leaving, "Har see arrow!"

"What arrow?" the doctor growled.

"This is the most frustrating puzzle I've ever come across," Mayor Gordon mumbled.

"Dad, are you coming?"

"In a minute, Thorn."

"Dr. Troodle, we really need to go," Simon said.

Reluctantly, the two small Puds left the room and followed the rest of the party. The group walked down a dim corridor and found themselves facing yet another door.

"Simon, will you do the honors?" Mayor Gordon asked after struggling with the doorhandle.

"Of course."

The young wizard pulled out Tonya's wand from his pocket, tapped the door, and was about to cast the Open spell when he sneezed. Simon regained his composure and then tapped the door again and said loudly, "*Open!*"

Nothing happened.

"*Open!*"

Still nothing.

"Try the Foonati spell," Thornapple suggested.

"All right. Stand back."

Thorn looked at the adults and boasted, "Last time he cast the moving spell, he almost destroyed the entire forest."

"That was you?" the mayor said in surprise.

"Well, uh." Simon fidgeted with the wand. "It was an accident."

"Then what's to stop you from bringing down the entire mountain on top of us?" Dr. Troodle said.

"I don't think we have a choice," Tonya said curtly.

"Okay, but be careful."

"I'll try," Simon said with a hint of nervousness in his voice. He took a deep breath and tried to concentrate. Then he waved the wand from one side to the other and said, "*Foonati.*"

To everyone's great surprise, nothing happened.

"I don't know what's wrong," Simon said, looking at the wand to see if he was holding it backwards. His eyes started to water, and he felt flushed.

"Are you okay, son?" asked the mayor.

"Yeah, I'm fine. It's just my allergies acting up."

"Grog try," the huge man grunted.

After several minutes of banging and kicking on the door, the giant finally gave up and sat down in despair with the others.

"I can't believe we've gotten this far, and now we're stuck," Thorn said. "It won't be long before everyone in the bank vault is dead." He shuddered at the thought and said, "*Oooh,* I'd hate to suffocate."

Simon held his mother's medallion in his hand and thought intently about what he should do. A peaceful feeling came over his entire body, and the memory of the woman from his dreams came into his mind.

"*. . . strength from high places . . . cunning from below . . . and the language of old to open the door . . .*"

"That's it!" Simon shouted. It had been the strength of the big Puds that helped them overcome the spider pit. And it had been the ingenuity of little Thornapple that saved them in the white room. Now it was Simon's turn to open the door using his special gift of language.

The young man stood up and pulled the little red book out of his pocket. As he did so, ancient runes appeared on the door, just like on the walls in the cave.

"Yes!" Holo said excitedly. "King Pentagola spoke these very words before he died."

Simon read aloud the writing on the door.

"It eats, ever hungry, consuming all
yet is never satisfied–wanting more and more,
devouring mighty kings of worlds,
as well as lowly paupers without lands or gold.
Peace, equality, and civility must subdue the beast's hunger
lest this evil destroy you all
and the enemy, long since forgotten, returns to rule once more."

"It sounds like a riddle," Tonya observed.

"It's got to be the dragunos," Thornapple said. "They're the ones eating everything in sight."

"No, the dragunos are the *enemy* that everyone has forgotten about," she replied.

"Surely the riddle's not talking about the little Puds?" Mayor Gordon asked incredulously.

"I know what it is," Simon said, recalling the words from his dream. Everyone stared at him with anticipated expressions. He adjusted his glasses and cleared his throat. "It's . . . It's pride."

When he finished speaking, the door opened, and in rushed a huge gush of air from the massive cavern that awaited them.

"Very good, Master Simon," Holo said. "Pride is the most devastating force in the paraverse. You would be wise to guard yourself from it."

As they approached the cavern, a ghostly voice sounded in their ears. "*Before obtaining true greatness, one must first obtain humility. You have been tried in the fires of affliction, tested by the wisdom of man, and unified by the enemy of old. Enter now, my friends, and begin anew with clean hands and a pure heart.*"

"What was that?" Dr. Troodle asked.

"Spirit," responded Harr. "From beyond."

"Nonsense! There's no such thing as life after death."

"Holo, was that King Pentagola?" Tonya asked in her own language.

"Yes, it was."

"How can that be possible?"

"The bearer of the crown is merely a steward over the entire paraverse, and as such, is entrusted with an ancient power that has been passed down from generation to generation. A remnant of King Pentagola must have been left behind to protect this world. It has been known to happen from time to time."

"Look at the size of that thing!" Mayor Gordon exclaimed, gazing up at the giant machine.

"Big," Grog stated.

A thick blanket of dust covered the floor, and Simon sneezed as they stirred it up with their feet.

"Are those what I think they are?" asked Thorn.

Huge white worms crawled along the monorail below. "Yep," Simon answered. "Don't worry–they're friendly."

"This is simply amazing," Mayor Gordon shouted. His voice echoed throughout the cave.

"*Shhh!*" Dr. Troodle scolded. "If the spiders and worms are gigantic, I'd hate to see what a bat would look like."

"Oh, you're right," the mayor whispered, cautiously peering up at the ceiling for bloodthirsty bats. "Keep it down, everyone."

Simon walked along the ledge overlooking the monorail and then stopped. The sad image of King Pentagola appeared in his mind.

"This is where it happened," Holo commented somberly. "Such a pity."

Simon wiped a tear from his eye and started to sniff. He looked over at Tonya and saw that she was watching him.

"Allergies," he said.

"Right."

"Well, let's get this over with," Dr. Troodle said. "My wife would kill me if I let her suffocate."

Simon walked up to the machine and found the spot where King Pentagola had placed the little red book. The insignia snapped on perfectly.

"One moment, Simon," Tonya said. She looked at Holo and asked with great hesitation in her voice, "Holo, how exactly does this machine kill the dragunos?"

"The machine was engineered to target lizard DNA, but more specifically, the biological make-up of the dragunos. Everything and everyone else should be safe. However, it wasn't meant to be powered with this much E.M. energy. There could be some adverse side effects, but that's doubtful."

Tonya's hair started to turn gray.

"What's wrong?" asked Dr. Troodle.

"I have lizard DNA in me. If we turn the machine on, I'll die."

Simon's heart sank at hearing those words.

"There's no way to know that for sure," Dr. Troodle said slowly. "It's possible that the machine won't affect you at all . . . Of course, our scientists are usually pretty thorough–overkill, if you ask me."

"I don't know if I can d-d-do this," Simon stuttered.

"You have to," Tonya cried. "Think of all the people that would die if you didn't."

Simon furrowed his eyebrows and pursed his lips.

"I suppose this is my chance to see if the Fulcrum of Life is real or not. Besides," she continued with a halfhearted grin, "I'm tired of this paraworld, anyway."

Simon stared at the red book. He held Tonya's life in his hands, but on the flip side, he also held the life of every Pud on the planet. He knew what he should do, but he fought it. He looked up at Thorn, at Har, at Grog and the others. They would all die if he didn't turn the key. This world and all its people would perish. He looked into Tonya's gleaming eyes. She was so strong–so full of life. But the strongest part of her was that she was willing to give up her life for him. Could he do the same for her? He gazed at her for a moment longer, then nodded his consent and bowed his head to hide the tears that trickled down his cheeks.

"I'll miss you," Thorn said, trying to hide his emotions. The little boy gave Tonya a hug.

"Miss you," Little Har said. He gave her a strong embrace.

"You're a brave young woman," Mayor Gordon said. "Your parents would be proud of you."

Now her hair had turned from gray to a gray-blue color. She smiled at Simon, but he had a hard time smiling in return.

"Goodbye," he said, wiping his face. He didn't make eye contact.

"Goodbye, runt."

Simon turned his attention to the red book. Taking a deep breath, he closed his eyes and put his hands in position. He was about to turn the key when Tonya suddenly grabbed his face and kissed him. Simon noticed the softness of her lips and the sweet aroma of her hair. Trembling, he kissed her in return and felt her tears mix with his as they embraced–perhaps for the final time.

"I just wanted to be the first one to give you a real kiss," she said, backing away slowly–her hair color even murkier than before. Simon felt as though his heart was about to burst.

"Simon," Holo said in a motherly tone of voice, "sometimes sacrifices must be made for the good of others. I know this is a hard decision for you, but it is the right thing to do."

The young wizard took another deep breath and then moved his hands to turn the little red book, but the key wouldn't budge. He put his whole weight into it, but it still wouldn't turn.

"Don't break it," Dr. Troodle warned. "Here, let me try."

As the little man fidgeted with the key, a terrifying hiss echoed throughout the cavern. Everyone turned around to see three dragunos climbing up from the monorail.

"How did they get in here?" cried Dr. Troodle.

"They must have come in through the tunnels," Simon answered hurriedly.

The dragunos slid across the dusty floor as they moved. Dr. Troodle and Thornapple stayed at the machine, but the rest of the party ran in different directions to escape.

Dust filled the air, making it hard to see anything. On one side of the platform, Grog fought to keep a rather fat draguno away from Harr, while on the other side, Little Har and Tonya tried to evade the remaining two reptiles.

Simon and the mayor ran towards the ledge but stopped in their tracks when they saw a pack of dragunos feasting on a giant gilaworm below. The lizards looked up and bared their sharp teeth.

"This is not good!" Mayor Gordon yelled.

Simon pulled out Tonya's wand and tried to cast the flame spell, but he stuttered so badly that it didn't work. One of the dragunos jumped up from the monorail and snapped its jaws near Simon's hand. The young man fell backwards in shock. As he hit the marble floor, the wand slipped out of his fingers and slid towards the machine.

Clutching his broken glasses, Simon glanced around to see Grog rolling on the ground with the overweight lizard. Tonya and Har were still defending themselves from the other two reptiles. Then Simon realized he and the mayor were being surrounded. The vicious creatures took their sweet time as they circled about–just like the lizards outside the library had previously done.

Simon looked over at Thornapple and got an idea. "Thorn, get the wand!"

The little Pud picked up the wand and yelled, "Do you want me to throw it to you?"

"No! I want you to cast the Foonati spell on the key!"

"*What?*"

A draguno swiped the mayor's legs with its powerful tail, and the man fell to the ground.

"You heard me! Cast it now!"

A million thoughts raced through the little Pud's mind. If he turned on the machine, would that mean the planet would have electro-magical energy once more, and if so, would the big Puds become the dominant race again?

He looked at Little Har bravely defending Tonya. *How could such a dumb creature have such a good heart?* After all the times Thornapple had mistreated him, Har had saved the boy's life anyway. *But we are the superior race!* Thornapple fought within himself. *Just think of our advancements . . .*

The biting words Tonya had once said echoed in his mind. "*Technological advancements are worthless if they don't help you to become better people . . . Your people are the real animals because you don't seem to have the power for compassion.*"

Thornapple looked again at Har. The large boy had never been able to live with his family. He had never been able to go to school or make friends or even think for himself . . . he was a *slave*. Thorn realized he had played a part in that servitude . . . that injustice . . . that *inequality*.

Finally overcoming his pride, the young man raised the wand with determination in his eyes and resolution in his heart.

"*FOONATI*!" he yelled, waving the wand from one side to the other.

The book turned, and the great machine was at last powered by the E.M. generator. At that same moment, the dragunos leapt towards Simon and the mayor. A tremendous burst of energy erupted from the machine and swept through the cavern like a camera flash.

Simon saw the lizards above him get pulverized in midair. In an instant, the wave passed through Simon, leaving him unharmed, and penetrated the mountain. Like a massive tsunami, the magical energy spread over the land, destroying every lizard in its path.

At the same time, bright artificial light flooded the cave–as if someone had turned on a light switch. A bridge extended across the chasm where the spiders had dwelt, and a group of doors opened up near the machine.

Within a minute, every draguno on the entire planet was destroyed. After the huge tidal wave had vanished, a clear bubble surrounded Highland City. As a secondary precaution, the ancient scientists had decided to include a force field around the city–just in case the machine wasn't as effective as they had hoped.

Inside the mountain, everyone cheered and hugged each other in joyful celebration. Then a dark silence fell over the party when they noticed the motionless body lying on the ground.

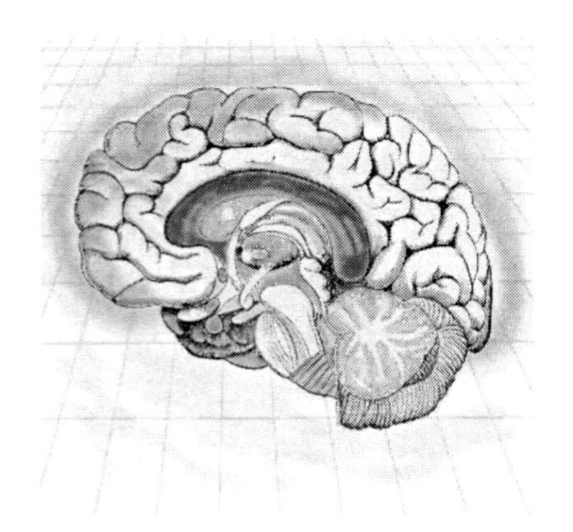

CHAPTER 26
GOODBYES

"What's the prognosis?" Dr. Troodle asked the specialist.

"It appears the patient is undergoing some sort of biological change. Her DNA is out of alignment. Many of her nucleotides have been associated with the wrong corresponding base pair. I've been able to reverse most of the mutation using the biological scan you took of her when she first came to our world. However . . ."

"Go on," Dr. Troodle urged.

"However, I've discovered an anomaly that I can't explain. She received extensive damage to the frontal lobe, and as I was repairing the tissue, I realized she was exhibiting signs of brain activity in areas that normally lie dormant. It's as if the machine jump-started a part of her brain that has never been active before. It's really quite fascinating."

Simon broke into the conversation. "Well, don't say anything to her. She'll probably think she's turning into a reptile or something."

"On the contrary," the specialist said. "Her brain is extremely complex and resilient." The man moved his hands around the holographic brain floating in the air. "Unfortunately, if she stays here much longer, I won't be able to save her."

Thornapple looked up briefly from the video game he was playing and said, "But I thought she was getting better."

"Pudo has been contaminated with a radiation that only she is affected by. The longer she stays here, the more her body will mutate. Soon, nothing will be able to reverse the damage."

Simon stood by Tonya's side and stroked her dark brown hair. The last time he saw her hair this color, she was suffering from the E.M. waves on Earth.

"I also found something peculiar with you, Simon," the specialist said.

"Really?"

"You have enough poison in your body to kill a full-grown ryophant."

"How embarrassing," Thorn joked, still glued to the video game.

Simon had no idea what a ryophant was, but he imagined something big.

"You appear to have some sort of antibody in your bloodstream with remarkable properties. Do you mind if I take another sample of your blood for further study?"

"Sure, I guess."

The doctor brought out a medical gun and placed it two inches from Simon's arm. With the push of a button, a microscopic laser shot into the boy's flesh. Drops of blood crawled up the beam and filled up a clear vial attached to the gun.

Suddenly, Thornapple gave out a scream that made Dr. Troodle jump out of his seat. "*I did it!*" the little boy squealed. "*I passed level ten!*"

"Will you keep it down a little? Some of us are trying to sleep," came a voice.

Simon turned to the bed and smiled anxiously. Tonya was sitting up.

"Butblacruze," Thorn yelled. "I passed level ten!"

"I'm so happy for you," she said sarcastically.

"Welcome back," Simon cried. He grabbed her hand. "How are you feeling?"

The specialist turned off the image of Tonya's brain and smiled at the young woman.

"I'm okay, but I was wondering, Simon. How did you know that Thorny over there would be able to cast the Foonati spell?"

Simon grinned. "Well, if you remember, my allergies were acting up in the cave."

"Yes."

"And for some reason, the closer I got to the machine, the less powerful my magic became."

"I noticed that."

"And that's when I realized the generator must have been leaking. You said yourself that anything or anyone that gets exposed for a long time to high concentrations of electro-magical waves becomes altered. That's how the spiders and gilaworms got so huge."

Tonya's eyes widened. "So is the E.M. energy back on the planet?"

"I think so."

She felt her thigh and asked, "Simon, where's my wand?"

Thorn pulled it out and tapped the little handheld video game machine, but nothing happened. "Simon, you need to teach me how to recharge these batteries."

"Good gravy!" Tonya shook her head in disgust. "Give me that!"

She waved the wand around and said, "*Aiyee, Aiyee, Aiyee bookata.*" A stream of light engulfed her for a second and then vanished.

"So what was that all about, Beauty?" Thornapple asked.

"'*Beauty?*'" She gasped. "You've been calling me 'Beauty' this whole time? You jerk!"

Thornapple blushed. "Hey, it's better than 'Spastic.' That's what I was going to call you at first."

She threw her pillow at him. "Beauty! Sounds like the name you'd give a dog. Hey, Beauty, fetch the stick. Good dog."

"Take it easy, Konya," Dr. Troodle warned. "You need to save your strength."

"*AAAH!*" she yelled. "My name is TONYA! T-T-T-Tonya! With a T!"

"Tonya," he repeated clearly. "Well, why didn't you say that in the first place?"

Tonya rolled her eyes and fell back into bed. She looked up and saw Simon smiling down upon her. He still wore his glasses, although cracks ran down both lenses.

"Simon, why are you still wearing those silly glasses?"

He took them off and inspected them.

Thornapple said excitedly, "You know, Simon, I think I can fix those glasses. I bet if I experimented a little I could even make some shatterproof lenses for you."

"No," Simon said, gazing at the broken glasses in his hand. "I don't think I need them anymore."

Tonya sat up against the headboard of the bed and looked at him. "You've really grown up, haven't you?" The specialist scanned her with a handheld device, but she ignored him. "My little Simon," she said with a smile. "Can you believe all that we've gone through together? I'd never believe . . . I'd never . . . believe . . ." She closed her eyes and mumbled, "Oh, I feel faint."

The young woman collapsed back into bed.

"I'm going to give you a mild sedative," Dr. Troodle said while reaching for his equipment.

In a flash, the image of her body appeared in the air. Quickly, the specialist peeled away the layers from the three-dimensional image until he reached the cellular level. He then brought up the previously scanned image of Tonya and merged the two holograms.

"Please stand back," he said sternly. Everyone did as they were told.

"What's going on?" Tonya groaned.

"The E.M. waves, as you call them, have been tainted with pathogens," Dr. Troodle said in a troubled voice. "I'm afraid your body is still being attacked."

"I'm resequencing your DNA," the specialist said. "This should only take a moment, but you may feel a little pain."

Tonya squirmed in the bed as a flood of light passed through her hospital gown and bombarded her delicate body. A moment later, the procedure was complete.

"We need to get you out of this parallel world," Thornapple said.

"But that's impossible. I lost my paratransmitter."

Simon replied with a sly grin, "Tonya, I think we found something better . . ."

■ ■ ■

"I can't believe it!" Tonya said as she entered the brightly lit cave. "It's only been a few hours since we turned this thing on and you guys have already decorated the place."

A group of men were polishing the statue that the mayor had presented to the city at the anniversary celebration. Simon looked at the small Puds riding on top of the larger ones and then realized the big Puds were not wearing security collars. The scene was not one of oppression but one of unity! It portrayed the reaction the Puds displayed after King Pentagola convinced them to build the machine.

Mayor Gordon walked up and announced with a big smile, "I thought this statue might be better suited in here."

"You might wanna change the inscription," Tonya suggested.

"Holo?" Simon called. The old holographic woman appeared in his hand. "What was it that King Pentagola said during that speech you showed me?"

The woman quoted: "Here stands the brave warriors of Pudo . . . The big and the small–fighting as one, living as one, dying as one. May we always look back to the day we overcame our pride, stood up for what is right, and defended our planet from the evil forces within."

"That's really good," the mayor exclaimed. He turned to his robotic assistant and asked, "Nox, did you get that?"

"Yes, sir."

"Excellent! Wait a second, Simon–I thought your hologram couldn't speak Pudo?"

"My goodness. Do you take me to be a second-rate hologram?" the old woman huffed. "I am capable of learning, you know." She paced around Simon's hand as she talked. "If you will excuse me, Master Simon, I have a thousand years to catch up on, and I want to gather as much information as I can while we're still here." At that, the old woman disappeared into the shard of metal.

"Testy little thing, isn't she?" the mayor said.

"I heard that," came Holo's muffled voice.

The mayor led the group into a side room filled with desks and machinery. At the far end of the room, cut into the wall, was an opening that looked like the entrance to an elevator.

"Oh my gosh," Tonya squealed. "It's a paratransceiver!"

"I thought it was something like that," Simon said, beaming. "What's the difference between a paratransmitter and a paratransceiver?"

"A paratransmitter only goes one way, but a paratransceiver goes both ways."

Mayor Gordon looked curiously at the control panel and asked, "So is it true this thing will take you to another dimension?"

"It sure will," Tonya said. "Where do you think I came from?"

"And it runs on magic?"

"Electro-magical energy–the same stuff the machine is powered by."

"Fascinating. So how does it work?"

Using the hover chair the specialist had given to her, Tonya zoomed over to the computer monitor and fidgeted with the keyboard. "Everything is in ancient Pudo. Simon, get over here."

Simon walked casually towards her.

"Hurry up before I turn into a lizard or something," she chided.

They scrolled through several hundred images of paraworlds, but Tonya didn't recognize any of them. All of the paraworlds she knew by heart were missing from the database.

"This is getting really frustrating," she growled. "These coordinates are all messed up."

"How's that?" asked Thorn.

"A couple hundred years ago, the High King standardized all of the coordinates so that this very thing wouldn't happen anymore. This machine uses a different set of coordinates that I'm not familiar with."

"So do we just need to pick one, then?" Simon asked.

"I hope not," Tonya moaned. "Knowing my luck, we'll probably find our way to another dead planet."

"What's a dead planet?" Thorn asked.

"Well, Pudo was a dead planet until today. A dead planet is a paraworld that doesn't have any E.M. waves. Of course, no one has actually proven the existence of dead planets. Any guesses why?"

"Because if you did find a dead planet, you wouldn't be able to report it to anyone. Without E.M. waves, you'd be stuck," Mayor Gordon answered her question.

"See, you're catching on. I'll tell you one thing . . . General Banton was a clever guy. He left the generator running so that all of the E.M. energy on the planet would be sucked up. When he killed the king and exterminated his own people, no one could call for help and no one could leave. And because they were cut off from the kingdom, even the Guardians of the Crown couldn't save them."

Dr. Troodle shook his head. "I can't believe someone could do such a thing."

"You'd be surprised what a little power can do to someone," Tonya responded.

"No," Thornapple said, contemplating the inner battle he had struggled with when the fate of the planet was in his hands. "I don't think I would be surprised."

"Bingo!" Tonya exclaimed as a white planet appeared on the view screen. "I recognize this one. I've seen my dad go there on business trips before."

"So are you sure you'll be safe there?" asked Dr. Troodle.

Tonya laughed and said, "My dad is one of the wealthiest men in the paraverse. He practically invented the mobile paratransmitter. Anyone who's anyone would jump at the chance to help me get home."

"So this is it," Thorn said. "I can't believe this is really happening."

Dr. Troodle frowned and said, "I just don't know how we're going to tell your mother."

"Tell me what?" Mrs. Troodle said from behind.

Everyone turned to see the doctor's wife enter the room–followed by Grog, Little Har, and his father, who now sported a pair of crutches.

"Mom!" Thorn said in shock. "You sure got here fast. I didn't think–"

The young Pud stopped in midsentence when he saw the beautiful girl who had just entered the room. His mouth hung open upon seeing Gwin's lovely face.

"Tell me what, *Honey?*" Mrs. Troodle prodded again sternly.

"Well, uh," Dr. Troodle stammered for the words. "We were thinking . . . it's going to take years to rebuild the city . . . and, uh . . . the schools will most likely be shut down for months . . . and . . . well, you know how important it is that Thornapple continue with his education . . . and–"

"I'm going with Simon and Tonya," Thorn blurted out.

"*What?*"

"Tonya's school is one of the best in the paraverse–"

"The what?"

"Mom, it's just a really good school. I might not even get accepted, but if I do, I think I'd really excel. And it's not like it's on the other side of the world or anything. Tonya says it's not far from here."

"Not far from here?"

"Well, it's in a different parallel world. But once you got there, the school wouldn't be very far from here."

"Absolutely not! I won't have you trolloping around with these aliens." She turned to her husband. "Honey, help me out with this."

"No," Dr. Troodle replied with conviction in his voice. He wasn't accustomed to standing up to his wife. "Recently, I've learned to see things in a different way. Though they may be strange at times, I think Simon and Tonya are the best friends Thornapple could have. Besides, I want our son to be able to magnify his talents. He can't do that here."

Mrs. Troodle's eyes grew big, and she puffed up her chest. "So, you want to send our son away to some strange land we know nothing about?"

Thorn chimed in, "Mom, I'm not leaving for good. I can come back to visit at any time."

"Really, Mrs. Troodle," Tonya explained, "parallel travel is pretty safe and fast. It would only take a few minutes for Thorn to come back to Pudo."

Dr. Troodle asked, "Are you sure he'd be able to find his way back? You did say this world has been forgotten for a thousand years."

"Oh, believe me," Tonya said, laughing. "One of the High Kings was murdered on this planet–the Imperial Council will definitely have the coordinates to this paraworld."

"And . . . who's going to pay for all this?" Mrs. Troodle demanded. She was desperately trying to find a reason for her son to stay.

Tonya answered immediately, "Your family has been so good to me. I'm sure my father would be happy to pay for Thorn's schooling."

"Well," Mrs. Troodle said quietly. Her eyes became watery, and she started to sniff. "I guess the decision has already been made." She walked up to Thorn and gave him a hug. "You're just growing up so fast. I'm having a hard time letting go."

"Har come, too?" Little Har asked in his slow, drawn-out voice.

"Now that's where I draw the line," Mrs. Troodle declared. "If Har was gone, who would take care of the house? And who would do the cooking?"

"You know, Sweetie," Dr. Troodle said, putting his arm around his wife, "your menabaws actually aren't that bad. I'm sure we'd be okay . . . And about cleaning the house–we don't really have a house anymore." He then said under his breath, "Besides, wouldn't it be nice to have someone to protect Thornapple?"

Simon cringed as the memory of Mrs. Troodle's appetizers flashed through his mind. After all this time, he could still see the three-eyed squid blinking at him.

Dr. Troodle continued in a loud voice, "Of course we'd have to ask Har's father first."

Harr smiled and said, "Little Har go. Travel to stars."

"Actually," Thornapple said, "if you were to visit a star, you'd burn up. Stars are made of burning gasses and–"

Both Simon and Little Har burst into laughter.

"What?" Thornapple asked. "Is it something I said?"

During the discussion, Gwin had slowly made her way to Thornapple's side. She looked at him with her large, beautiful eyes and said in a sweet voice, "Well, I guess this is goodbye."

"Yeah, but I'll still see you again."

"I hope so. You know, Thorn, we never did have that last dance together."

Smiling, Mayor Gordon turned to his assistant and commanded, "Nox, play something slow for us."

The robot did as it was told.

Thorn offered his hand to Gwin sheepishly. She took it, and they started to dance.

"Circles!" Gwin laughed, trying to imitate the mayor. "Circles! We're doing circles, everyone."

Dr. Troodle extended his hand to his wife. She wanted to stay mad at him but couldn't. Shaking her head, she took his hand and danced with him.

"Well, Tonya," Simon said, "care to dance?"

"I thought you'd never ask."

The young woman got off the hover chair and held onto Simon. A worried look appeared on the specialist's face as he played with his portable keypad, but he said nothing.

Tonya kept tugging on her green tunic as they moved. It was the same outfit she had worn when Simon had first met her. Except for some missing hair, she looked exactly as he remembered her that day she appeared out of nowhere and saved him from Buz and Spike.

"What's wrong?" Simon asked.

"I think this outfit has shrunk."

Simon chuckled. "No, I think you've grown."

"It just feels a little too tight, that's all."

"Well, why did you wear it then?"

"One, it's fire retardant and the rest of my clothes burned with the house, and two, I'm not about to be seen in public wearing those baby doll dresses."

They both laughed, but then Tonya suddenly winced in pain. She clutched her stomach and doubled over.

"Doctor!" Simon called.

The specialist rushed over and ran some quick scans. "It's getting worse," he said. "Stand back, Simon."

Simon rested Tonya on the ground, and the specialist swept her body with a device. When he finished, Tonya sat up and moaned, "It still hurts a little."

"You're nearing the threshold of our medical expertise. I don't think I'll be able to stop the next mutation. You should leave now while you still can."

Simon helped Tonya to her feet and led her to the paratransceiver, where Thornapple and Har were already standing. He typed in the coordinates of the white planet, and a confirmation message appeared on the screen.

"Just press that green button," Simon said, squeezing in with the other teenagers.

"Goodbye," Mrs. Troodle cried.

"We love you, son," said Dr. Troodle.

Thorn tried in vain to hide his sniffling. "I love you, too."

Harr and Grog waved their goodbyes while Mayor Gordon pressed the green button. The last thing the teenagers saw before they were engulfed in blue energy was Gwin . . . winking.

Surrounded by an electrical force field, the group was catapulted through several tunnels of the vast parastream and then pushed into their destined portal. Before they knew it, they were standing in total darkness.

"Uh, Tonya," Thorn asked nervously, "where are we?"

A faint glow appeared at the tips of Tonya's fingers, giving just enough light for them to see.

"Holy cow," she whispered as she looked around the dark chamber. "This isn't good."

CHAPTER 27
THE WHITE PLANET

Sparkling gems and gold trinkets filled the narrow room. Ancient artifacts and statues lined the walls, and a great number of old books lay on the dusty floor.

"Hello?" Thorn said loudly.

"*Shhh!*" Tonya hissed. "What do you think you're doing?"

"Trying to see if anyone's home."

"Oh, that's *great* thinking from our genius Pud. Yeah, let's just call attention to ourselves so we can thank whoever owns this place for letting us use their secret paratransceiver. Maybe they'll let us take some of this gold as well."

"I see your point," the little Pud said, looking down at his shoes.

"Why did we end up in this treasure room in the first place?" Simon asked.

Tonya stepped off the round platform and answered, "My guess is that whoever owns this place doesn't realize someone else has the coordinates for their paratransceiver."

"Or maybe they don't even know about this room," Simon suggested, after wiping away the dust on the control panel with his finger.

"I guess that's possible." Tonya messed with the control panel, but it wouldn't turn on. "Looks like it's out of juice. Let's get out of here."

She led her friends through a dark passageway until they came to a dead end.

"I think I hear voices coming from the other side," Simon whispered.

The young man put his ear to the wall, but the second he touched the cold surface, he suddenly found himself on the other side. He looked around and realized he was in a closet. The voices were much louder now.

"I never intended for you to attack Imperial City," a man with a raspy voice said from the other side of the closet door.

"Things have changed, Lord Vaylen," came the cold reply. "The weapon was a greater success than we had ever hoped for."

Just then, Tonya appeared out of thin air with her light-emitting fingers pressed hard against the wall. Surprised, she turned around and was about to speak but stopped when Simon put his hand over her mouth. She closed her fist instinctively to douse the light spell.

They moved away from the wall just before Har and Thornapple appeared.

"Don't speak," Simon whispered.

He inched his way to the closet door and peered through the narrow slats. Two holograms stood at the far wall. Their names and vital statistics hovered in the air above them.

"We don't take orders from you," spat the hologram of Captain Drackus.

Lord Vaylen turned his back to the holograms and faced the closet door. A cruel smile crept across his face. "*Oh, but you do.*"

The soft whisper had come from Lord Vaylen, although his lips had not moved. Perhaps Simon had imagined it. He caught a glimpse of the man's gnarled face and shivered impulsively.

Lord Vaylen responded in a loud voice so the holograms could hear, "I'm sorry, but I just can't allow it."

"May I remind you," Captain Drackus threatened, "that we have in our possession the most devastating weapon in the paraverse? I'd hate for an *accident* to happen to your planet."

"Yes," General Mayham added. "The weapon may not be fully charged yet, but I'd dare say that even your icy fortress wouldn't withstand an attack."

"Then my hands are tied," Lord Vaylen responded apathetically.

"Just give us another hour. Then we'll be on our way," the general said.

Captain Drackus concluded, "And if our sensors detect any sign of interpara communication or travel, then we'll be forced to change our target."

"As I said, my hands are tied."

At that, the holograms disappeared, and Lord Vaylen's countenance dropped.

"Merworth!" he shrieked.

The doctor, who had been waiting at the door, came running into the room.

"Something's not right," Lord Vaylen said nervously, "and I'm not sure what. We may have another mole in our midst. Get the armaments ready, and tell the soldiers to stand by for possible attack. They'll be monitoring communications, so everything needs to be done by word of mouth." Noticing the doctor's troubled look, he put his bony hand on the man's shoulder and said, "Congratulations, *Commander* Merworth–you've been promoted."

"But why me?" the man protested.

"I need someone I can trust," Lord Vaylen said with a scowl. He moved his hand over the commander's stomach and revealed his skeletal structure like an x-ray. "Unless there's something I should know," Lord Vaylen hissed. ". . . A sneaker worm, perhaps?"

"No," Merworth said, flinching. "You can depend on me."

"Then hurry. We haven't much time."

The two men rushed out of the room.

Simon turned to the others. "What was all that about?"

Thornapple shrugged. "Don't ask me. I didn't understand a word they said."

"No understand," Har said.

Tonya opened the closet door and said, "I think we better get out of here."

"Father?" came a voice from the office doorway. "Father, are you in here?"

Tonya looked up to see a young man about her age entering the room.

"What are you guys doing in here?" he asked abruptly.

"I can explain," Tonya began.

"Guards! Guards!" he yelled, not giving her a chance to speak. Tonya made a sudden movement, and the young man whipped out his wand in response. "*Rowque!*" he shouted.

An invisible force knocked Tonya to the floor. Just then, a group of armed men rushed into the room.

Lord Vaylen spoke from the hallway. "What's going on here?"

"I found these kids going through your closet," his son explained.

When Lord Vaylen entered the room, a look of shock appeared on his face. Tonya was lying face down on the floor with her friends huddled around her.

"Looks like your dueling lessons have paid off," he said calmly.

Tonya stood up and brushed the red hair from her face. Lord Vaylen's eyes grew wide at seeing the young girl before him.

"Rupert, go to your room."

"But, Father–"

"Go to your room–now!"

The young man frowned and walked away.

"What do we have here?" the dark man asked. "Spies?'

"No, we're just lost," Simon answered.

"And you just happen to find your way into my private office?"

"Look," Tonya said, her hands planted firmly on her hips, "you may not know who I am, but I'm sure you know who my father is–"

"Silence!" he interrupted. Turning to the guards, he instructed, "Take them to the dungeon for questioning."

"You don't understand," Simon said, taking a step forward. The soldiers aimed their rifles at him.

"I'll deal with you later," Lord Vaylen said briskly. He tore his eyes away from Tonya and left.

■ ■ ■

As the soldiers led the teenagers to the dungeon, the office became cold and silent. The only sound remaining in the room came from a mechanical clock.

Tick. Tick. Tick.

Suddenly, a camouflaged figure jumped from the wall and spun around–all the while, keeping his face concealed by the black cloak he wore. He brought out two wands–the same pair he had used to defeat Tabatha and Griffen–and waved them at the closet doors, but nothing happened. Puzzled, he looked at the closet for a moment longer, then turned and exited the room.

■ ■ ■

"You're making a mistake," Tonya yelled as the guards walked away. She rattled the bars. "*AAARG!*"

"Will someone please tell me what's going on?" Thornapple pleaded.

"They think we're spies," Simon told him.

"Spies?"

"Yes," Tonya growled. She looked over at the next cell and realized that an ugly man with a flat nose was staring at her. "What are you looking at?"

"A spy." The man laughed in a creepy way.

"We're not spies," Simon shot back.

"Oh, yes," the man responded. "We're all spies." He laughed hysterically. "And murderers . . . and thieves–"

"Not all of us," came a soft voice from the cell to their left. "Some of us are innocent." Several of the ruffians laughed at the old man's words, but he continued anyway. "I'm Thomas McCray. What are your names, young ones?"

"I'm Simon Kent," the young wizard answered. "This is Har, and this is Thornapple Troodle, and this is–"

"Tonya," she said sharply. "Let's just cut the chit-chat and get down to business. My father is Mr. Doyle . . . from *Doyle* Enterprises. Maybe you've heard of him–he probably owns some of your homeworlds."

"Right," said the nasty-looking man in the cell next to them. "And my father's the High King."

Everyone in the dungeon laughed.

"Listen to me, you idiots," Tonya rasped. Her hair turned red again. "I don't care what you did to be locked away." She looked in disgust as the ugly man next to them licked his lips. He was missing several teeth. "I don't want to know what you did," she continued. "But I do want to know if you're willing to help us escape. My father will pay you handsomely."

"Look, missy," their crude neighbor said with an unpleasant smile, "if we knew how to escape, do you think we'd still be in here?"

Tonya pulled up her tunic and unlatched the lacy strap that held her wand to her thigh.

"*Mmm,*" the ugly man said, eyeing her white leg. "I'll take a piece of that."

Tonya withdrew the wand and walked up to the bars separating the cells. "Excuse me?" she said, tapping the bars menacingly with the wand.

"Be careful," the old man warned. "Flimdore is a cannibal. His last cell mate didn't realize that, and he woke up one day without an ear."

Tonya backed away from the bars in horror while Flimdore smiled at her and licked his lips.

"I can't believe the guards missed your wand," Thornapple said.

"There certainly are benefits of being a girl," Tonya replied, tugging on her short tunic.

She touched the bars and said the word, "*Anmasee,*" but nothing happened.

"There's some sort of E.M. absorption device in place," Thomas McCray informed them.

Tonya grumbled, "It figures."

"Hello, Master Rupert," the old man announced in a loud voice to warn the others. "And Lady Margo. So good to see you on this fine day."

Tonya slipped the wand to Simon, who then stuffed it in his shirt. Rupert and Margo shared a lot of the same physical characteristics. Simon could see that they were obviously related.

"So you're the intruders?" Margo asked. "You don't look so tough."

"That's easy to say when you're on the other side of the bars," Tonya spat.

"Feisty," the girl responded. "My brother tells me he single-handedly captured you all."

"Well, I detained them," Rupert admitted. He got close to the bars and asked, "What's your name, *red hair*?"

"My name is Tonya," she said coldly. "And after my father finds out about this, you'll wish you never met me."

"*Oooh,*" the boy said sarcastically. "Big words."

"Leave her alone," Simon warned.

"And what's your name?" Margo asked. She brushed her short, blonde hair out of her face and smiled.

"I'm Simon Kent," he said quietly.

"Well, Simon Kent," Margo probed, "what brought you here to our paraworld?"

"The parastream."

She sighed. "Of course, but *why* are you here?"

"Look, we're just trying to get home," Tonya interrupted.

"And where's that?" Rupert asked carefully.

"Chamel."

"Lovely place," Margo said in a cool voice. Although the girl appeared to be genuine, Tonya saw right through her facade. "And where do you two live?" Margo asked, pointing to Thornapple and Har.

"They don't speak other languages," Tonya said.

"How odd."

Thornapple just smiled and nodded his head. Har wore an expressionless look on his face, as always. The Puds understood Simon and Tonya, but they had no clue as to what everyone else was saying.

Margo inquired further. "So if you're headed to Chamel, why were you in my father's office?"

Simon and Tonya looked down and said nothing.

"Look, I want to help you," Margo said calmly. "Was this some sort of initiation into a club?" The teenagers remained silent. "Do you guys go to a school nearby?" They still said nothing.

"Are you spies?" Rupert asked.

"No!" Tonya shouted in exasperation. "We were just going to Chamel and we got lost. And yes, I do go to school nearby."

"Which one?" Rupert queried.

"Imperial School of Magical Learning."

Rupert started to chuckle. "Imperial is so behind the times–all they teach is defensive magic. But I guess that's okay if you're afraid to fight."

Margo said with considerable pride, "We've already been accepted to Hayden's."

"Our school has won the dueling championship seven years in a row now," Rupert boasted.

"Yeah, only by cheating," Tonya muttered.

"*What?*" Rupert said. "How dare you–"

He stopped in midsentence when a guard at the door cleared his throat to get their attention. The soldier beckoned them with a nod of his head.

"Well, guys," Margo said abruptly, "it's been nice talking to you. I hope you like your stay . . . It's probably going to be a long one."

Just before leaving, Rupert grinned and said, "See ya around, *red hair*."

Tonya shouted, "The next time we meet, you'll be begging for my forgiveness!"

The two kids rushed to the exit of the dungeon. As they opened the door to leave, a part of Lord Vaylen's dark cloak could be seen in the hallway.

"Leave it to the master to have his own children do his dirty work," Thomas commented. "Those two would do anything to please their father."

"You seem to know a lot about them," Simon noted.

"I was their butler. That is, until Rupert got angry and had his father throw me in here."

"That's awful," Tonya said. "How long have you been here?"

"Going on four months now."

"We're never getting out of here," Simon moaned.

"It could be worse," Thomas McCray said. "At least you're not in that man's shoes."

Two guards were pushing a gurney across the room towards an empty cell. Bandages and bloodstained gauze covered the man's body, and a breathing apparatus partially masked his unkempt face. Something about his glazed-over eyes entranced Simon.

"What's his story?" Simon asked.

"Don't know, really. They've been working on him every day since he got here. Cutting him open . . . doing experiments, I think. Master Vaylen is extremely interested in him for some reason."

Several streaks of white suddenly ran through Tonya's hair. "Lord Theobolt Vaylen?" she asked in fear. "We're not in his castle, are we?"

"Of course. Where did you think you were?"

"I knew my father came here from time to time to do business, but I didn't realize he was working with the royal family." She hunched her shoulders in disgrace. "And that was Prince Rupert and Lady Margo! How could I have been so stupid? I didn't even put two and two together."

"Who's Lord Vaylen?" asked Simon.

"He could very well be the next High King," she moaned. "And I just made enemies with his children. My father's gonna kill me!"

"It might not be that bad," Thomas McCray said reassuringly. "The twins are inseparable–hooked at the hip since birth–but I think Lady Margo fancied Simon. She is the stronger of the two. Perhaps she'll put in a good word for you."

"I think I'm gonna be sick," Tonya said. She eased herself into a sitting position, put her head in her lap, and sobbed.

"Tonya," Thornapple said in a panicked voice, "what's going on?"

"I just ruined our chances of getting out of here," she cried.

"No, that's not what I meant," Thornapple said with a horrified expression. "What's happening to *you*?"

Simon looked down and saw what Thornapple was referring to. The veins in Tonya's arms and legs bulged from her skin. She brought up her head and revealed strange green patterns forming on her face. A grotesque design spidered out across her cheek and then ran down her throat, disappearing into the neckline of her tunic.

"I'm mutating!" Tonya screamed, looking down at her trembling hands. Har knelt beside her and tried to offer comfort, but she shook so badly that nothing he did helped.

"Guards!" Thornapple yelled in his own tongue. "Guards!"

"Oh, no," Flimdore said, laughing. "Spoiled meat."

"Shut up!" Simon barked.

Two guards entered the room with Lord Vaylen limping close behind. He shielded his face with the hood of his dark cloak as he approached. "*Aiyee bookata*," the ultramage said, snapping his fingers. The spell penetrated the anti-magic dampening field and engulfed the Puds for a brief moment.

"What seems to be the problem?" Lord Vaylen rasped.

"Tonya, sick." Har answered first.

"How dreadful," he said nonchalantly. "I'll have my physician take a look at her first thing tomorrow morning."

"But she's dying–*now!*" Simon said with obvious defiance in his voice.

"That's not my concern," he said sharply. "But the welfare of this planet is. Tell me how you got to this paraworld undetected."

"We came from Pudo," Simon said. "We didn't even know for sure what world this was."

"You lie! Pudo's been a dead planet for over a thousand years."

"Not anymore, *pigface!*" Thornapple roared.

"Insolence!" Theobolt growled between gritted teeth. A ball of electricity formed in the palm of the ultramage's hand, but before he could release it, the sirens on the walls began to scream.

"Lord Vaylen," came a panicked voice from the intercom. "Someone has just entered our paraworld, and the Raiders are attacking in response."

The dark wizard bared his teeth. "Fools!"

He rushed to the exit, along with the guards, but Simon yelled after him, "Hey, we need a doctor!"

"Now's not the time, boy." Not even bothering to look back as he sealed the door, the dark mage rasped, "She'll just have to wait."

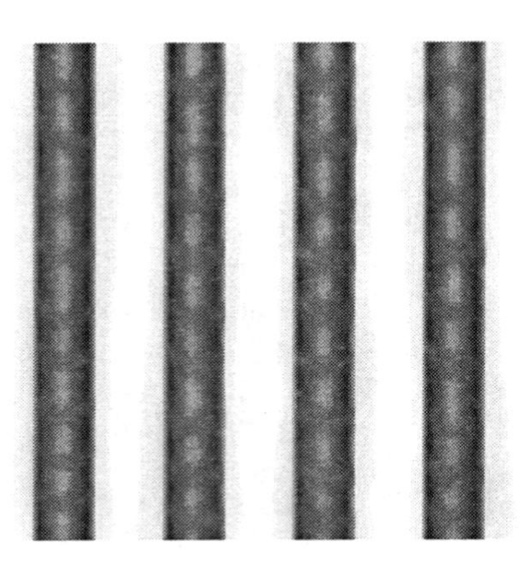

CHAPTER 28
THE POWER WITHIN

The alarms blared, and red lights flashed from above. Shivering uncontrollably, Tonya crossed her arms to stay warm.

"Simon, get us out of here," Thornapple yelled.

Simon looked across the room at the cupboard protected by metal bars. He could distinctly see his mother's medallion hanging on a hook next to the rest of their possessions.

"I don't know if I can," he said.

"Of course you can," Thornapple cried.

"I don't know . . ."

Tonya looked up in pain. Her yellow-green eyes cried out for help, and Simon's heart ached at seeing her frail body being tormented like this. What could he do? Nothing. He wasn't special. He didn't have any powers. It all came from the medallion. Without it, he was just a pathetic little boy pretending to be a man.

Little Har stood up, placed his hand on Simon's shoulder, and said with conviction, "Si-moan can . . . Simon will."

For a moment, the boy panicked. The expectations placed upon him were too great, and without the aid of his mother's medallion . . . Suddenly, a strange vigor coursed through his veins, giving him a measure of peace. The memory of his first encounter with the strange woman from his dreams flashed in his mind.

'Tis a musical prayer.
Words unsaid, unbinding, unknown.
'Tis the foundation of life, truth,
and thy inner-self entwined.
Within your destiny, it lies.
Inside your heart, it confides.

Maybe the source of his unique abilities didn't come from the pendant, after all. Perhaps his magical powers actually did come from deep within himself.

Nervous, Simon pulled the wand out of his shirt and tapped the bars–just like Tonya had done before.

"*Amnasee!*"

"Not *Amnasee,*" Tonya mumbled. "*Annn-masee.*"

Simon was about to cast the spell again when he realized the bars were starting to glow red. One by one, the bars melted into molten pools of liquid metal. Unfortunately, the spell continued to spread across the room until all the criminals were freed.

"*Oops,*" Simon said. He watched the prisoners run around the dungeon in chaos. The flashing red lights heightened the anxiety in the room.

"Thomas," Tonya called out weakly, "how do we get out of here?"

"If you can get past the door, make an immediate right. Go down the hallway until it ends. Then turn left. On the third door to the right, you'll find the hangar bay."

"Isn't there one of those paratransceiver things we could use?" asked Thornapple.

"You'd never make it," the butler responded. "It's heavily guarded and can only be activated by an authorized voice imprint."

"Thanks for your help," Tonya said, faltering.

"Why don't you come with us?" Simon asked.

"No," the old man replied, sitting down on his bed. "This is my home. Perhaps the master will see my loyalty and reinstate me to my old position."

"Well, good luck," Simon said. "And thanks."

The teenagers rushed to the melted cupboard and gathered their possessions. Simon put Holo in his pocket and his mother's medallion around his neck. He eyed the still figure wrapped in bandages a few yards away. The poor man on the gurney was staring right at him. With compassion in his heart, mixed with a bit of curiosity, Simon approached the stranger.

"What are you doing?" asked Thorn. "We've got to get out of here!"

"We need to help him," Simon replied.

Har pulled Tonya to her feet while Simon removed the cords and electrodes from the stranger's bare chest.

"He's being drugged," Thorn said, examining the breathing apparatus. Simon removed the equipment from the man's face so he could breathe some clean air. Within seconds, a spark of life ignited in the stranger's honey-brown eyes.

Tonya limped towards her friends but was suddenly grabbed from behind.

The cold voice of Flimdore ran down her spine as he cackled in her ear, "You have such pretty hair, missy. I bet it's *very* sweet."

Simon looked up in horror to see the ugly man holding Tonya's head back in an awkward position. He clutched her throat with one hand and caressed her pale, mutating face with the other.

A rush of fierce anger swept through the young wizard like a firecracker. He brought up the wand but paused as Flimdore crouched behind Tonya's thin body.

"I just want a taste," he said, laughing insanely.

Just then, the man lying on the gurney raised his hand like a whip. Flimdore screamed in pain and fell to the floor. He squirmed around in circles, clenching his fists and closing his eyes as he moved.

With his hand still outstretched, the strange wizard got off the gurney and walked towards the man thrashing on the floor. His victim screamed even more loudly. Then, when it looked like the attack would never cease, Tonya put her hand on the wizard's arm and lowered it. The screaming turned into a muffled whimper as her assailant slithered away to a dark corner of the dungeon.

Simon rushed to Tonya's side. She embraced him. With tears trickling down his leathery cheeks, Little Har put his arms around them both.

"Who are you?" Thornapple asked, dumbfounded at the man's quick recovery.

The stranger's eyes wandered around as he thought about the question. He studied his callused hands. They were the hands of a warrior. "I–I don't know."

"Thanks," Simon said, wiping a tear from Tonya's face. "I'm Simon Kent."

The stranger didn't respond. Instead, he became curious with a group of men and women huddled around a glowing sword that had fallen out of the cupboard. Every time one of the criminals touched the hilt, he or she would get shocked.

"That's mine," the warrior announced, stooping down and picking up the displacement sword. His memories were slowly coming back.

Simon tried to cast the Open spell on the exit, but it didn't work.

"You must have knocked out the E.M. absorption device," Tonya whispered. "Here, let me try."

"You can't open it with magic," Thomas informed them. "Lord Vaylen has cursed the door."

"We don't need magic to get out of here," the warrior said as he thrust his displacement sword into the thick hinges of the door. With a quick adjustment to the settings, the mass index of the blade increased to the point where the hinges finally snapped off the frame.

"Cool!" Thornapple exclaimed.

As the massive door fell over, the ceiling shook–not because of the fallen door but because of the weapons fire outside.

"We're under attack," Thomas cried. "Hurry! Get to the hangar bay."

The party took an immediate right and sprinted down the empty corridor. The rest of the prisoners–Thomas included–rushed through the broken doorway and ran in various directions.

■ ■ ■

When the dungeon was finally empty, a mysterious figure appeared out of nowhere. With strange curiosity, the dark wizard admired the puddles of liquefied metal Simon had created. After satisfying his interest in the destruction, he walked down the corridor where Simon's party had fled. The tapping of soldiers' boots echoed from the adjoining hallway, but when the soldiers rounded the corner, the mysterious figure was gone.

■ ■ ■

Har now carried Tonya in his arms because of her depleted energy. The party had been fortunate, thus far, not to come across any soldiers as they ran. Of course, the criminals were a huge distraction: flooding the corridors, attacking everyone they encountered. The rumbling outside continued, but the loud sirens inside tapered off, leaving the flashing lights as a reminder that the castle was still under attack.

As if coming to the realization for the first time, the swordsman suddenly announced, "My name is Griffin Lasher . . . I'm an ambassador of the Crown."

"Well, Mr. Lasher, you sure do recover quickly," Thornapple said.

"I'm a fast healer," Griffin responded. As the small group turned left, their newfound friend slashed his peculiar sword through two unsuspecting guards.

Simon couldn't stop gazing at the huge pictures that lined the hallway. He gradually fell behind. A quick glance at the first open door showed him an expansive dining room filled with fancy tables and plush-covered chairs. He couldn't help but imagine the fantastic parties that must have taken place in that room–parties that, perhaps, took place at a happier time.

Everyone had already entered the third door by the time Simon had reached the second one. He looked inside the second room and immediately stopped in his tracks. Strange emotions tugged at his heartstrings. He debated whether he should laugh or cry.

As if bewitched by the melody of a mystical song, the large and spacious ballroom drew him in. Huge chandeliers dangled from the high ceilings, and intricate paintings adorned the stone walls, but none were as entrancing as the largest picture hanging by itself above the enormous fireplace.

Simon pulled out his mother's medallion from beneath his shirt and looked at the strange design in wonder. The portrait on the wall was of a beautiful young woman–the woman from his dreams. She rode on a large, majestic beast and wore white robes that reached the floor. But the most shocking thing of all was that around her neck rested the very same medallion Simon held in his hand.

"A masterpiece," came a familiar voice from behind. "Isn't she?"

Surprised, Simon turned around to see Lord Vaylen gazing up at the beautiful woman.

"Who is she?" Simon asked. A tear ran down his face.

"Someone I loved . . . a long time ago."

"I have to know who she is!" Simon begged.

Lord Vaylen shook his head, freeing himself from the memories of days gone by, and said angrily, "It's none of your concern." Then he saw the medallion in Simon's hand. A spark of wrath ignited in his cold eyes. "Where did you get that, boy?"

"I–I found it," Simon lied.

"Impossible!"

The dark lord lunged for the medallion but was met with a magical blast from across the room.

"Leave the boy alone," Griffen said.

"Stay out of this," he rasped.

The ultramage lunged at Simon again but this time was struck by a glowing strand of energy. He grabbed the electric rope with his bare hand and attempted to throw it off, but the swordsman held tight to his end.

Griffen quickly shot out another glowing strand, which pounded the dark wizard in the chest. Lord Vaylen's black hood fell off as he struggled with the two bolts of energy, and for the first time, Simon saw the grotesque deformation of the man's face in its entirety.

Lord Vaylen grabbed the second rope with his other hand. Then, with great magical power, he reversed the spell and raised Griffen Lasher off the ground.

Like a puppeteer, the ultramage tossed the warrior in the air. Griffen smashed into the lower-hanging chandeliers, sending shards of glass to the marble floor below. Finally, with gritted teeth, Lord Vaylen whipped the electric strands and sent the man upwards towards the largest chandelier in the center of the room.

Simon covered his eyes just as Griffen was impaled upon the sharp bottom of the crystal chandelier. The brave warrior held onto the massive light structure as it jolted from the impact. A glass spike jutted from his back. Simon heard crunching sounds. The plaster from the ceiling started to crumble away. Then, with shocking finality, the chandelier fell.

The heart-wrenching sound of a thousand pieces of broken glass filled the room. Simon dropped to the ground and covered his head as specks of crystal pelted his body.

Lord Vaylen limped towards Simon with crazed determination. The short boy looked up at the looming figure above him.

"Now," Lord Vaylen said, panting, "give me that medallion."

The dark lord stretched out his hand, and the medallion leapt from Simon's fist and floated upwards. The ultramage's eyes widened with anticipation as the prized pendant drew near. But just as the necklace touched Lord Vaylen's grasping fingers, Simon leapt from the floor and grabbed his sacred possession.

A burst of blue light sprang from the black metal as both wizards held onto the medallion. Instantly, the Power of the Ancients filled the entire room. Simon thought the blinding light would consume him. Then, as quickly as it came, the blaze went out, and both wizards fell.

Simon discovered to his amazement that he still clutched his mother's medallion in his sweaty hand. He stood up and saw the ultramage lying unconscious on the floor. A grunt sounded from behind. He whirled around to see Griffen Lasher brushing himself off.

"*You're alive?*" Simon exclaimed.

"Like I said," the warrior replied calmly, "I'm a fast healer." Griffen looked in disbelief at the fallen ultramage. "Let's get out of here, kid."

Simon took one more glance at the beautiful woman from his dreams and then followed Griffen out the door.

■ ■ ■

Simon and Griffen had not left the room for more than five seconds before the mysterious dark figure appeared out of nowhere. Curious but puzzled, he turned his head and tried to see the significance of the large painting on the wall.

Suddenly, the building shook from a bombardment of weapons fire. Soldiers could be heard rushing down the hallway.

The mysterious man walked over the broken glass, reached into Lord Vaylen's black cloak, and pulled out a round datachip–the same chip Tabatha Burke had stolen from General Mayham.

■ ■ ■

The air became cooler as Simon and Griffen traveled down a stone tunnel. Griffen swung open a door, and they both entered the icy hangar bay.

A gust of chilly wind wrapped itself around Griffen's naked torso, making him shiver. Except for a few damaged shuttles, the hangar bay appeared empty; all of the functional vessels were out fighting the Raiders.

"Are you just gonna stand there in the freezing cold, or are you gonna get on board?" came a woman's playful voice.

Griffen smiled to see Tabatha's long white hair flowing in the crisp breeze. The top part of her slender body protruded from the cockpit of a ship that bore the insignia of the royal family.

"Nice to see you're alive," Tabatha purred affectionately as Griffen and Simon climbed aboard to join the others. "Just don't get any blood on my seats, okay?" Although Griffen's wounds were completely healed, blood soiled his stomach and pants.

Tabatha launched the tiny craft into the sky, away from the castle.

"Sorry it's so crowded back there," she said, looking back. "I wasn't expecting this many people."

"That's all right, Tabby," Griffen said. "I just hope you have enough juice to transfer us out of here."

The cat woman steered the ship away from the fighting. "I just got here," she declared. "My engines are almost drained."

"Get above the stratosphere," Tonya instructed with obvious pain in her voice. Her skin crawled with colorful movement as the rabid mutation swept over her body.

"But there's hardly any E.M. waves up there," Tabatha argued.

"Exactly."

Simon knew instantly of her intentions. Anxiety grabbed hold of his emotions and squeezed. Indicating that he understood as well, Thornapple added, "Yeah, go as high as you can."

As they sliced through the thick blanket of snowy clouds, the twin space carriers finally came into view, just a mile or so above them. Dozens of ships were retreating into the carriers.

"What's going on?" Tabatha asked. "What are they doing?"

Griffen looked up through the cockpit and said, "I have an awful feeling about this."

A blue aura began to encompass the two enormous spaceships above. The light grew brighter and brighter.

"They're going to fire!" Tabatha screamed, lurching the ship to the side.

BOOM! Both carriers were gone.

"No, they went into the parastream," Griffen exclaimed. "They could be anywhere now."

Simon whispered in horror. "They're going to attack Imperial City."

"What!" Griffen said.

"I overheard them talking. They have some sort of weapon–"

"Yes, I know–I've seen what it can do."

"Then we have to stop them," Thornapple said.

"We're too late," Tabatha cried. "It'll be hours before the E.M. thrusters are charged up again."

Tonya shook violently, but she managed to whisper, "Go into outer space."

Tabatha opened her mouth to protest.

"Just do it!" Thornapple yelled.

Har looked up with his big brown eyes and said in a slow voice, "Trust Simon."

The woman stared at the children with a bewildered expression but finally consented. "All right," she said, "but I don't know what good it'll do. If we lose power up there, we won't be able to get back down to the planet."

Tonya winced as the pain shot through her spinal column. "We're not going back down." She felt a numb, tingling sensation spread out to every limb. The coldness of space beckoned her as she looked at the heavens above, and the North Star seemed to shine more brightly than it had ever shone before. She signaled with a faint nod of her head. "Go ahead, Simon."

The young wizard put his hand on the wall of the ship and closed his eyes. How many times had he charged the batteries of his video game machine? This wasn't quite the same thing, but he had to try.

What am I doing? he thought to himself. *This doesn't run off electricity!*

He felt Har's oversized hand rest on his left shoulder; the large Pud was so trusting. Then he felt Thorn's little hand rest on his right shoulder.

Simon concentrated harder. Something deep within him stirred: a reservoir of power that had been waiting to come out. A blue light emanated from his body and filled the ship.

Griffen and Tabatha looked at each other in shock as the craft vanished from Lord Vaylen's dimension and entered the parastream. With his eyes still closed, Simon continued to hold onto the wall of the ship.

"This is impossible," Tabatha cried as she looked at the readouts on her control panel. "We're at full power."

"Then go!" Griffen shouted.

"I doubt we could catch up with them," Tabatha yelled back. She frantically ran her hands over the control panel and exclaimed, "We don't have any coordinates set, and I don't have control of the ship!"

Simon's body still glowed. A strange feeling of euphoria came over him–the same feeling he felt when the woman from his dreams spoke to him. Oddly enough, he had the distinct impression of going home.

"We're moving too fast!" Tabatha screamed as the ship turned sharply into another large tunnel.

The space carriers were just up ahead. Simon let go of the wall and took a deep breath. He felt weak for a second or two but was soon rejuvenated.

"I have control of the ship again," Tabatha announced. "Hold on!"

She dodged past a barrage of lasers. Peppered with red smears, the orange walls of the parastream absorbed the brunt of the attack. Unfortunately, several of the lasers seared through the tiny ship and tore into the hull like a can opener. Then, as if the shower of lasers were not enough, deadly rockets flooded the parastream–each one headed towards the craft.

"We're going to die!" Thornapple cried.

"I'm sorry!" Tabatha screamed as the lasers ripped open the ship.

"*PROTECTION!*" Simon yelled at the top of his lungs.

A golden sphere of translucent light instantly surrounded the ship. Simon floated in the air with one hand grasping his mother's medallion and the other raised high above his head.

"This can't be happening," Tabatha exclaimed. "There's no magic in the parastream."

"You haven't met Simon before," Thornapple said, beaming from ear to ear.

The rockets melted away as two enormous tendrils shot from the gelatin mass protecting the ship. One of the giant arms drove deep into the closest space carrier. A moment later, the electric arm burst out the other side, essentially gutting the entire ship.

Escape pods sprang from the carrier as the massive vessel crumbled in on itself. The other space carrier was now fleeing towards one of the gateways, but just before it entered the portal, the yellow tendrils wrapped themselves around the ship and crushed it into pieces.

The debris vaporized upon contact with the yellow force field surrounding Tabatha's ship. With the danger now gone, the tendrils shrank back to nothing.

Simon opened his eyes. The force field exploded all around him–just as it had done previously when Tonya had cast the Protection spell back on Earth; only this time, the shock waves rippled throughout the parastream, causing the orange walls to change colors as it passed.

"That was a rush," Simon said, holding his chest and getting up from the floor. He felt very weak yet excited.

"You're telling me," Thornapple said, laughing.

"Did you see that, Tonya?" Simon boasted.

A look of terror swept over his face. Tonya, his beloved friend, lay motionless.

Griffen rushed to the girl's side and put his cheek next to hers. "She's alive," he said quickly. "Barely."

"Is there still time?" Tabatha asked.

"Maybe."

The man put his hands to her forehead and chanted softly to himself.

"I thought you said there aren't any E.M. waves in the parastream," Thornapple said.

"*Shhh*," Tabatha replied softly.

"I don't require magic to heal . . ." Griffen said, trying to concentrate on the task at hand.

A light from his body entered into Tonya, and she suddenly gasped for air. Griffen lifted his hands and smiled at the young girl. Her skin was fair and white once more.

"You're a Marmasuelian," she whispered with a smile. "I thought your paraworld was destroyed."

"I'm the last of my kind," he said, stroking her cheek with the back of his hand. "You're going to be just fine. Rest now and dream of happier things."

She closed her eyes and slept.

"God has smiled upon us today," Griffen said to the others. "The kingdom owes you all a debt of gratitude. In fact, I'm sure the Guardians of the Crown would like to thank you in person."

"That sounds good to me," Thornapple said with a grin.

"Sounds good," Har repeated.

Simon looked at his friend sleeping peacefully at their feet. "Thanks for saving her," he said. "I don't know if I could have–" He stopped in midsentence and gasped in shock as a green swirl appeared on Griffen's face.

Sensing their alarm, Griffen spoke with gritted teeth. "Don't worry. This will soon pass. I just need to rest."

Tabatha explained further, "When he takes upon himself the afflictions of other people, a part of their suffering stays with him for a little while–just until his body can fight it off."

"Wow," Thornapple said in amazement, "my dad would love to meet you."

"Perhaps . . . someday."

A sudden burst of blue light flashed around them as the ship entered a large portal.

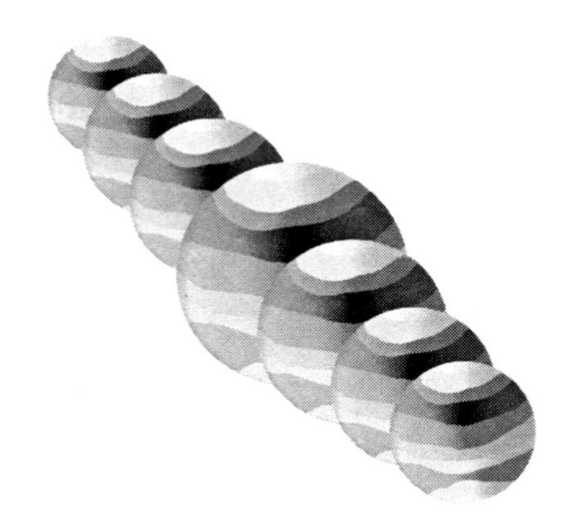

CHAPTER 29
ANSWERS

Imperial City, located on Paraworld Seven, was breathtakingly huge. Nestled within the network of tall buildings stood the royal palace, looking far different–ancient, even–from the futuristic buildings that surrounded the tranquil spot of land. Simon, Thornapple, and Har sat nervously on a bench. They were all dressed in fresh clothing and were feeling extremely out of place–especially Har, who wore a white shirt and a tie for the first time in his life. Har couldn't stop rustling in his seat as dignitaries and politicians passed by. Paratravelers from all over were discussing the recent events, and more than once, someone recognized Simon from his picture on the front-page news.

Then, from at the end of the long hallway, came a vision of loveliness, walking with a bald man at her side. The teenagers became speechless as Tonya and her father approached.

"This makes me so mad," they heard her father say. His stubs of hair turned red.

"It's okay, Daddy," Tonya responded. "I'm not ready to advance to the next level anyway."

"But a whole year–wasted!" he said. "You'll be older than everyone else."

She smiled as all three boys stood up with gaping mouths. "I don't think that'll be a problem."

"What happened to your hair?" Thornapple managed to ask.

Tonya played with her shoulder-length hair and said, "Oh, I decided I needed a change. Besides, those stupid disks in the cave hacked it all up anyway."

"It looks nice."

"Looks nice," Har repeated.

Thorn nudged Simon in the shoulder, which brought him out of his daze. "Beautiful," Simon blurted. Tonya blushed, as did her hair.

"So is this your father?" Thornapple asked.

"Yes," Mr. Doyle answered, shaking their hands briskly. "It looks like my daughter has grown attached to you three . . . even to the point where she's willing to be held back in school because of you."

"*Daddy,*" Tonya scolded.

"Well, at least she's safe. Shall we?" he said, opening the door for them.

The darkness in the spacious room gave Simon an eerie feeling. He looked up and saw thousands of empty seats. They were in some sort of coliseum.

Mr. Doyle left the teenagers in the center of the room and joined the adults, who sat behind tables. Simon could make out Tabatha's long white hair in the dim light. She was sitting next to Griffen.

An older woman arose. "My name is Cassandra Vaylen. On behalf of the royal family, I would like to express our gratitude to you for helping to save our city." The teenagers beamed. "Please accept these medals in your honor."

She snapped her fingers, and four decorative awards materialized in the air in front of them. The teenagers took the medals and placed them around their necks.

"Simon, Thornapple, and Har," she said, her voice turning somber. "We'd like to now discuss your requests to attend Imperial School of Magical Learning. Though it is irregular for us to accept new applications after the deadline–"

"Highly irregular," one of the prominent-looking men spoke up.

"Leander," Lady Cassandra said sternly. "Please."

"Sorry, my lady."

"As I was saying," she continued. "I think we can make an exception in your case."

"Quite right," an elderly man said, standing up. "Let me introduce myself. My name is–"

"Ezra Bromwell!" came Holo's excited voice from within Simon's shirt pocket. The old woman appeared in the air without any coaxing from Simon.

"Holo-649," he said in astonishment.

"I can't believe it's really you," she cried. "You were just a baby, last I saw you."

"I was 241 years old."

"Amazing. Simply amazing! And you're still kicking after all these years? I didn't expect you to live past five hundred–with your wild ways and all."

A surprised look appeared on Tabatha's face. Griffen raised an eyebrow.

The old man blushed. "Well, I have matured a bit since those days. Tell me, what are you doing with these children?"

"Simon's my new master. I've been locked to his DNA."

"Interesting," he said. "Very interesting indeed."

Leander Payne scowled. "I hate to interrupt your little reunion, but I have a school to run. May we continue with the proceedings?"

"Yes, of course," Councilor Bromwell said.

"I'll talk to you later," the old holographic woman said with a wink. "We'll do lunch sometime." At that, she disappeared.

"Children," Ezra Bromwell said, "I am the committee chairman for the school." He looked over at Principal Payne and added, "Which means, I have the final say regarding who is admitted and who is not." He turned back to the teenagers. "That being said, you must still convince us that you are worthy to attend."

"Oh, they're worthy," Tonya said.

"Thornapple Troodle," one of the committee members called, looking over a piece of paper. "I see here that you have no magical background . . . at all. In fact, no one on your planet has performed magic for over a thousand years. What do you possibly have to offer the school?"

Thornapple stood as tall as he could and said, "Well, I may not be very good with magic, but I bet I'm smarter than any of the students attending your school."

"Really?" asked an old woman in disbelief. "Tell me," she said, "are you familiar with story problems?"

A flat screen appeared in the air, showing a long page of text.

"I'll get you some paper and a pencil," she said.

The old woman reached for her handbag but stopped when Thorn announced, "3.14 hours."

"What?"

"It'll take Mrs. Redlock 3.14 hours to reach her grandmother–assuming she doesn't stop for a snack or a bathroom break."

Leander Payne whipped his head around to examine the story problem. Simon hadn't even read through the first sentence before Thornapple had answered it.

"Well, Mr. Troodle," the old woman cooed, "very impressive. Maybe you do have a place at our school. Our academic scores are not exactly up to par with the other schools."

"But this is a school of *magical* learning," Principal Payne argued. "Academics are secondary. If he's not magically inclined, then I don't think we can accept him."

"Wait," Tonya exclaimed. "I've seen Thorn perform magic. He saved his entire paraworld by casting a spell."

"And what spell was that?" Leander asked with an unpleasant smirk.

"The Foonati spell," Thornapple answered uncertainly.

Several of the council members laughed, but Councilor Bromwell intervened with a bit of wisdom. "Even the greatest event is preceded by a series of smaller steps." He cleared his throat and continued, "Though, I must admit, the Foonati spell is one of the most basic of spells."

"What is your relationship with Har?" one of the committee members probed. "I see you've submitted an application for him, but it doesn't appear that he has anything to contribute to the school."

"Well, he's my . . . uh . . . he's my–"

"Body-guard," Har said slowly.

"Yeah, he's my bodyguard."

"You have need of a bodyguard?" Leander Payne asked suspiciously.

"I am pretty small."

"Hmm." Councilor Bromwell pondered. "Tell me, son, what is the nature of the collar around your *bodyguard's* neck?"

"It's a . . . well . . . it's a security collar."

"For what purpose?"

Thornapple looked at the ground and mumbled, "To enforce obedience upon the wearer."

Several members of the council gasped at his response.

"Slavery is strictly forbidden," Lady Cassandra said. "Not just here but in all the paraworlds under our command."

"Har's not a slave anymore. He's my friend."

"Then you wouldn't mind if we removed that collar?" asked Lady Cassandra.

"*NO!* I mean, yes–I would mind. He'll die if you remove that collar. It's specifically engineered to secrete a synthetic enzyme that inhibits his brain capacity. A side effect is that his body now craves that enzyme. His brain would literally shut down without it."

"Very disturbing," Leander Payne noted. "And this is the paraworld you represent?"

"My world is changing. That's why I'm here: to help my people get a different perspective on life."

"If that's so, then why did you bring your servant with you?" asked Principal Payne bluntly.

"To protect him," Thornapple admitted. "My people have been forced to readjust their thinking. It'll take time before they learn to treat everyone as equals. If you sent Har back to Pudo, he'd probably get exiled to the mines." The little boy looked up at Ezra Bromwell and begged, "You have to believe me, sir. Most of the security features on his collar have been disabled anyway. I can't even control him anymore . . . I mean, not that I want to." Thornapple tried to take his foot out of his mouth. "I don't want to control him . . . and I can't . . . even if I wanted to."

"How compassionate of you," Principal Payne said mockingly, "but our school is not a refuge."

"I beg to differ," Councilor Bromwell countered. "The paraverse is in conflict, and the Raiders instill fear in the hearts of many, but our students take comfort in the knowledge that, here, they can leave the troubles of the paraverse behind. Is this not then a refuge?"

"You're mincing words."

Lady Cassandra raised her hand. "Gentleman, we will discuss these matters later. For now, let us continue with the interview."

"I, for one," said another man, "would like more information about Simon Kent. I've never heard of this *Earth* you come from. What is its numerical designation?"

Simon frowned and said, "We're not aware of magic on my planet, let alone the paraverse. Until Tonya came, I'd never even seen magic before."

"So there are E.M. waves on your paraworld, but nobody has ever discovered how to use them?"

"Oh, yeah–there's lots of E.M. waves on his planet," Tonya answered in Simon's behalf. "More than anywhere else, I'd say. For an hour, I felt like the most powerful sorcerer in the paraverse."

Some of the committee members chuckled, but Councilor Bromwell froze like a statue. Griffen turned his head and whispered something to Ezra that made the old man's expression grow even more solemn.

The ultramage spoke. "In a normal entrance exam, the applicant would be asked to perform certain magical spells to demonstrate his or her skills. Simon, I have been told that you have a unique talent with magic. I would like to see what you can do."

Councilor Bromwell pushed a button on the table, and the air around the teenagers ignited with wisps of green. He then turned a dial a few notches to the right and said, "I've adjusted the electro-magical waves in the arena, and I've lit them up so you can see them. Go ahead, Simon, and show us something you can do."

Tonya handed Simon her wand and stepped back. The young man pondered for a moment on what spell he should cast. Then, with a smile, he looked up to see how high the ceiling was.

"Oh, you're just gonna love this!" Tonya said, realizing which spell Simon had chosen.

The young wizard pointed the wand at his hand, snapped his fingers, and said the word, "*Shawnee.*"

He immediately turned his head, so as to not burn his face, but soon realized the normal burst of fire he had come to expect was not there. Instead, a tiny flame flickered at the end of his thumb.

"Very impressive," Principal Payne said with deep sarcasm in his voice.

The committee roared with laughter, which made Simon flush with embarrassment. A gust of green vapor swooshed through the young wizard's body, causing him to extinguish the little flame with a violent sneeze.

Suddenly, the committee members stopped laughing. Simon turned to Tonya, who was staring at him with a shocked expression on her face. He then looked down and realized that a faint blue aura surrounded his body. Every time he came in contact with the green vapor, his aura would turn red, as if fighting with the E.M. waves.

"Is this some kind of joke?" Principal Payne asked irritably.

Councilor Bromwell turned the dial to its highest setting, which flooded the arena with a green fog. Within the thick haze shone the red silhouette of Simon, pacing around, rubbing his nose.

"Very interesting," the old wizard mumbled.

Tabatha leaned over Griffen's shoulder and whispered something to

Councilor Bromwell. When she was finished, the old man put his hand over the button on the table to make everyone think he was masking the E.M. energy. But at the same time, he cast a spell, which subtly rotated the dial until the green waves disappeared from the arena entirely.

"Mr. Kent," Councilor Bromwell said, looking up, "there's just one more thing I would like you to do." The ultramage pulled a wand out of a drawer and flung it. Animated, the wand flew towards Simon–twirling as it went–until he caught it in midair. "Point the wands in the same direction, if you will." Simon obeyed. "Now cross them and say the word . . ." The old man paused for a second and then said, "*Valamure.*"

The committee members stirred in their seats after hearing that deadly word, but Simon, being innocent, knew nothing of the spell.

The fledgling wizard crossed the wands and said gently, "*Valamure.*"

Nothing happened.

Leander Payne started to chuckle but stopped when a thin stream of gray mist shot out of the wands. Within seconds, a large wraith was floating in the air above them. Tonya screamed, and the committee members jumped out of their seats.

Bromwell turned the dial to its highest setting. Surprisingly agile for one so ancient, he jumped over the table and ran into the arena. The teenagers cowered as the gruesome wraith descended rapidly through the green fog–its mouth opening large enough to swallow them whole.

"*Actcheem Surapido!*" the ultramage yelled with both hands outstretched.

The menacing phantom vaporized just inches from the group of teenagers.

"What is the meaning of this?" Mr. Doyle roared, while running to his daughter's side. He turned to Simon and snapped, "You could have killed us all!"

"I d-d-didn't mean to," the boy stammered.

Lady Cassandra pressed the button on the table to make the E.M. waves invisible again. "Everyone, please! Just calm down!"

"Ladies and gentlemen," Councilor Bromwell said in a loud, austere voice, "I think this interview is finished. Please proceed to the conference room so we can make our decision. I will join you shortly. Children, you may wait in the courtyard."

Dejected, Simon trailed after the others, but Councilor Bromwell stopped him. "Please stay," the wizard said quietly.

Simon looked into his weathered face. The old man seemed frail and worn, but a twinkle shone in his eyes–those eyes that seemed to peer into the eternities and into his very soul. Simon felt naked before those eyes. They exuded magnificent power and something else . . . love.

"Sit down," the ultramage said.

Simon sat on the floor. He looked around the dark coliseum and saw that they were alone.

Councilor Bromwell raised his hand, and thousands of tiny lights appeared in the air above them. "For eons of time, sentient beings have looked up into the heavens and asked themselves, '*Where do I come from?*'" The tiny lights above began to rotate slowly. "God created man in his own image–both male and female. That is a universal constant in all the paraverse." The old man looked down at the boy and asked, "Simon, do you believe in God?"

"Yes. I think so."

He nodded. "God has given us a minute taste of his immense power. We can create life . . . and we can crush it. We can teach our children the ways of righteousness and the pathway to Heaven. We have the power to build and to organize wonderful things out of raw materials. We are truly *godlike*."

The lights in the darkness moved together until only one sparkling light shone.

"In the beginning, there was but one world." Several more lights grew out of the main one like appendages. "Then, others were patterned after the first. Now there are numerous worlds–countless, like the sands of the sea. But each new planet is still linked to the first–receiving power and energy from a central location." The lights lined up in a row, with the original light shining brightly in the center. "All exist in tandem with each other–parallel, if you will." The long strand of lights rotated on a central axis until it finally appeared as one tiny light just like before. "Coexisting at the same time and in the same place but in different dimensions."

Mesmerized by the scene, Simon looked into the man's ancient eyes and felt a strange peace come over him.

"For countless years, men and women have searched the parastream for that original world that spawned all the others. Some have even gone mad in their pursuit. In the end, Paraworld Zero continues to eluded us . . . that is, until now."

"*What?*" Simon asked in surprise. "You don't mean–"

"Yes," he said calmly. "Earth."

Councilor Bromwell remained silent for a few seconds to allow Simon to register what he had just said. He sat down on the floor, across from the young man, and said, "Many, many years ago, there was another Earthling who left Paraworld Zero."

"Who was that?"

"The first High King. Since then, the firstborn son of the royal family has always been given the same power that you possess: the power to store electro-magical energy within himself."

"So that's why I'm able to use magic when no one else can?"

"Yes. But your gift is a two-edged sword. Outside energy prevents you from releasing your own inner power. On Earth, your body was saturated with electro-magical energy, and that is why you could not perform magic."

"So is that also why I get sick when I come in contact with E.M. waves?"

The old man looked puzzled. "Is that normal on Earth?"

"No, not really."

"Hmm, very interesting," he said, rubbing his chin with his fingers. "I can't answer that."

"Well, this is a lot to take in," Simon said. "So you don't have the coordinates to get me back to Earth, do you?"

"I'm afraid not. But do not fret. I have a feeling that your place is here, among us. I will see to it that your schooling is paid for and that you have a place to live."

"So I've been accepted?" Simon asked excitedly.

Councilor Bromwell chuckled. "Of course," he said. "You're the most gifted child in the known paraverse. The committee will have no choice but to accept you."

"And my friends?"

"That is yet to be determined."

Simon sighed.

"Is there anything else I should know about you?" the old man asked. "Anything at all?"

Simon thought for a moment and struggled within himself. He gazed into the man's kind eyes one more time, and a warm comfort, even greater than before, filled his soul.

"I have dreams," he began.

"Yes, I would assume you do."

"No–I mean, my dreams aren't normal. Ever since I received this medallion from my mother." Simon pulled out the strange medallion and continued, "I've been dreaming about this young woman. She tells me things, and they happen."

"What happens?"

"Well, I can understand other languages without even using magic. Oh, and poison doesn't seem to hurt me!"

"Very interesting," the old man responded. "Anything else?"

"Yes," Simon began slowly. "I just saw a painting of the woman in my dreams." He started to get teary eyed. "And she was wearing this medallion."

"Interesting."

"I think . . ." he said slowly. "I think that she was my . . . my . . ."

"Mother?"

"Yes." Simon wiped a tear from his cheek and said, "She died giving birth to me. This medallion is all I have left of her."

Councilor Bromwell put his arm around the boy and said, "God works in mysterious ways, and so does Lord Theobolt. I can't tell you why he has a painting of your mother on his walls, but I can say this: Sometimes a remnant of those who have passed on remains to comfort those in need. Now that you are in an environment where you can be influenced by magic, your mother has finally found a way to comfort you. I suggest you keep that medallion safe. Keep it under your shirt, and wear it at all times. Don't let anyone know about it."

"Why?"

"Let's just say, it's important to keep sacred things sacred. For now, I'm going to insist that you speak none of this to anyone. Not about Earth, not about your mother, and especially not about your special powers. There are those who would try to exploit your gifts for their evil purposes, so it is important that we be careful."

"Okay," Simon agreed.

"Now you'd better get back to your friends," Ezra said, standing up.

"Thanks," Simon said. "Thanks for believing me."

"You're welcome. Now run along."

Simon was almost to the door when Councilor Bromwell called out, "Oh, and take good care of Holo-649 for me. She can be a pain in the neck sometimes, but she will always be loyal to you."

"I heard that," Holo said from within Simon's pocket.

"I will," Simon said as he exited the arena.

Lady Cassandra appeared out of nowhere and walked up to Councilor Bromwell's side. "Does he suspect anything?" she asked.

"No."

"Should we tell him?"

"No–not yet. Let us wait and measure the boy's character. We must keep a watchful eye on him–for the time being."

At that, both ultramages began to walk out of the arena. One after the other, they disappeared in mid-step.

■ ■ ■

The dark, mysterious figure tossed the stolen datachip in the air like a coin. He looked intently at a computer screen, which showed the image of thousands of round metallic balls.

Suddenly, the datachip was ripped away from his hand.

"Give me that," Lord Vaylen rasped. The chip floated across the room. Vaylen opened his bony hand, which revealed part of the inscription from Simon's medallion; the markings had been seared into the flesh of his palm. He clenched his fingers around the datachip and hissed, "You have a lot to learn, young one."

"Of course, Master," he responded coolly. The cloaked figure removed his hood, allowing his face to touch the light. He was Francis Eugene Oswald: otherwise known as Butch.

"But you've done well so far," Lord Vaylen continued. "I think you've finally earned the right to call me Father."

"Thank you . . . *Father*."

Lord Vaylen turned to the computer screen and punched in some keys to bring up an image of a wiggling sneaker worm.

"The mole among us still needs to be found," he rasped. "But I think it's safe to continue our plans."

"What about Simon and the others?"

"They've shown that they can be a hindrance to the work, but I think we can deal with them."

"I have a feeling we'll see them again soon."

"As do I," the dark lord said, softly caressing the worm on the computer screen. "As do I."

About the Author

Matthew Peterson graduated from Brigham Young University in Business Management. He now spends much of his time writing, programming, and maintaining his website, www.ParaWorlds.com (an online community where aspiring authors can critique each other's work and discuss the business of writing).

He served a two-year mission in Alabama for the LDS church, received the Eagle Scout award, and earned a second degree black belt in karate. He currently lives in Arizona with his wife, five boys, and a giant African tortoise.

Matthew began writing the *Parallel Worlds* series in 1990 at the age of fourteen, but a computer failure put the project on hold. Over a decade later, Matthew caught the vision again and completed *Paraworld Zero*.